Travails of
LOVE

Travails of LOVE

'A different LOVE story'

Bimal Prasad Mohapatra

PARTRIDGE
A Penguin Random House Company

To order additional copies of this book, contact
Partridge India
000 800 10062 62
www.partridgepublishing.com/india
orders.india@partridgepublishing.com

DEDICATED

"This book is dedicated to all the under-privileges who are cleverly denied the fruits of India's freedom, democratic governance and quality education."

Acknowledgements

Without acknowledging the contributions of my honest benefactors, who include my friends Mr. Sudhir Tripathy, his wife Mrs. Rashmita M. Tripathy and Mr. Debasis Satapathy, my colleagues at Hi-Tech Institute of Technology Mr. Kumar S. Choudhury, Mr. Lalmohan Patnaik, Mrs. Rebecca Bhattacharya, Ms. Archana Rath, Ms. Suhasini Choudhury and Mr. Saroj Mohankudo in addition to my ex-colleagues Mr. Sumanta Sahoo at Trident Group of Institutions, Mr. Sasanka S. Pati and Mr. Birasen Dalai, I am unable to think my work of writing this book is complete.

Their contributions range from moral support at personal level to literary support in getting right and appropriate words, sentences and thoughts to keeping my lap-top user-ready.

Thanks a lot my very dear and honest benefactors! Frankly, I owe a lot to you.

Besides, I would like to thank Partridge India's Publishing Consultant, Publication Service Associate and Marketing Service Representative Mr. Earl Tristan, Ms. Gemma Ramos and Ms. Nancy Acevedo respectively for their guidance at every stage of publication, printing, book release and book marketing.

Lastly, Depu and Deepa, my children for helping to select the cover design.

Author

CONTENTS

DARK HORSE

There was unbearable sweating, the after-effect of preceding evening's drizzling and inching day temperature since morning. Of course, nothing new to peasants during the summer months in the tropical coastal region. Harvesting of traditional rabi crops and thatching of houses, the major works to be done before advent of monsoon, were almost over. And the annual village fair, which provides the peasants once-in-a-year an opportunity to invite their nears and dears for a routine yearly get-together and hosting of cultural programmes such as melody competitions among the invited neighbouring villages, local folk dances, and the plays in which the village youths and children used to participate playing the roles assigned fitting to their personalities and body features, and purchase of essential household goods, seeds and farming equipments for the year, had gone week's back. The peasants were fully geared up to go all out for kharif crop sowing. But, as the pre-monsoon thunderous rain facilitating ploughing prior to sowing of seeds with advent of monsoon hadn't yet been so kind, there was hardly any engagement for the predominantly agrarian peasants in the relatively languid Pandupur hamlet. The peasants were thus caved-in in their houses in afternoon siesta with belly full of watery rice, a great recipe during this period of the year, saved for a few while-awayers including slackers, branded 'shameless lewd . . . . loafers', loitering in the village alleyway sparingly sneaking their looks into the rooms of the houses through the open windows with suspicious intent along with contemptuous sneezing and coughing—'welcomed and rebuked, sparingly.' This had necessitated Preeti and her likes in the village to keep their bed-room street window closed, which were despite not spared of occasional irritating stealthy knocks and pebble slaps, blocking the gentle blow of north-bound miserly cool wind filtered all the way the thick green orchards of coconut, mango, jackfruit, deodar, banyan, peepal, neem, banana, pineapple, screw pine, bamboo, ... trees, shrubs and bushes surrounding the village that would to some extent have helped reduce the skin tearing sweating, they were cursed to put up with.

"Hey Bhagaban, what a painful life these loafers have forced us to live in!" Preeti cried with pain and disgust, exhausted of furling palm-leave hand fans in the season of indiscriminate power-cuts. "Boys are really blessed, not required the clothing of we girls, and are allowed free walking in open air, free from oppressive restriction imposed on we hapless girls; they are relaxing on village alleyway, at temple platform, under big banyan tree and in the mango orchards; besides, playing cards, chess and dice in open places. Alas! What a God's design? This is too favoritism!"

"But, Didi, Rabibhai isn't like these shameless lewd loafers," told her younger sister Priya bringing some kind of reprieve to her burdensome mind, and also, some mental satisfaction. However, her mischievous smile that followed was telling something else. 'These days Priya is found wanna tell something whenever anything concerning Rabi is being discussed. She is concealing,' Preeti told self.

"He is one in lakh, a rare breed. But, see his fate!" Preeti told with heavy breath and added, "These loafers call him: urchin, guttersnipe and whatnots, literally abusing him, instead of . . . . ," exhibiting all sympathy to the poor boy, and at the same time, checking if mama or anybody was in hearing distance in inner house veranda, she was afraid of. "These days mama has all ears to whatever I speak," she cried. "Eek, she is so harsh!"

"I think mama disapprove your friendship with Rabibhai and our visit to his house," buzzed Priya, checking. "You know she has told me to inform her instantly whenever you're going to Rabibhai's house and also advised to overhear when you two are talking together and inform her what is heard. Not good . . . . immoral, I've told on her face."

Preeti looked at her younger, shocked.

"Aunty and Rabibhai are so nice. And, so also our papa, very understanding! So long as papa hasn't told anything, no problem!" Priya confirmed afterward.

"But didi, without aunty's tuition, I can't clear my matriculation. You know I'm not that good a student like you and not that lucky to get a friend like Rabibhai with his mother so brilliant to guide me in my study. I want to be at least a matriculate," Priya cried and joked, "otherwise, you know, my dear brother-in-law will humiliate me calling 'under-matric!' Won't it be shame to you?"

"Stupid! What non-sense you're talking? These days you've started joking with me," Preeti told poking Priya's thigh. "Mind, I am your elder sister."

But, Priya was overflowing. "This climate is very unbearable on the day of fast. I won't fast. Again, who is there 'of my own, so loving' to fast for?" Priya shrieked with display of deprivation with an intriguing intent staring at her sister. And, later inquired guardedly as Preeti focused at her almost melting from top to toe 'seemed frightened', "Didi, if you don't mind, may I ask you something that I've been thinking long since?" And without waiting to Preeti's consent and checking street veranda peeping through the window just opening and in-house one through revolving door for anybody overhearing, told cautiously, "You are observing fast, I'm deed sure, not for your better result, but for Rabibhai's." As Preeti closed to Priya swiftly fearful, the revealer told, "Weeks back at night, I heard you praying to Maa Santoshi in your sleep for his outstanding result."

Preeti tugged.

"You're in love with him. Do you know once Bulinani and Lillididi were also talking among them at the hearing distance of mama at the bathing ghat. Since then, I believe, mama has . . . ."

Preeti turned red and choked and crying, wanted to stop Priya.

"I'm sure, luckily not a single sole other than me has heard your prayer as you weren't so loud. Grandma had just turned her side and that's all. I pinched you hard with no loss of time. Thank God, you stopped! I had checked, papa and mama were in their room—asleep."

"Thank you, thank you, Priya! You saved me!" And, she told embracing, cajoling and kissing the younger, "That's a great sister! I'm so lucky, I'm proud of you. I'm indebted."

"I assure, I won't repeat this in future. But, Priya, you must cooperate or else you know mama won't allow me to . . . . I'll die . . . . , I'll di . . e . . . . ," cried the elder resting her head on her supportive younger sister.

"This is there! Don't worry!" Priya told assuring and jocularly added, "You too . . . . in case of me . . . . no . . . . still . . . . if so required!"

"Pri . . . y . . a . . . . you," screamed Preeti.

Priya laughed and embracing her sister told, "No didi! I am not going to take advantage of this; honestly speaking. Remain assured!"

"Result should have been published by this time. Very late this year, isn't it, Priya?"

"Alas, not supportive! Shit!" Priya mocked poking and winking at her didi. "Mind, this is testing time, testing the commitment and dedication. And I believe and I can say with full conviction, my dear sister will certainly pass the test."

" . . . . "

"Tik . . . . tik . . . . tik . . . . ," chipkali chirped on the wall of Rath abode. "Surprise! Chipkali rarely chirp at this hour of the day. So, didi, what for this?" Priya asked. 'Chipkali chirps to ascertain the fact that has already happened and true,' they had heard village busybody Bulinani used to say collaborating with different issues while gossiping and chit-chatting 'she is fond of and famous for in the entire village' with the village ladies at temple platforms during evening aarti time, at bathing ghat, while husking rice, grinding cake paste, ...

"I think, result has certainly published. Possibly for this," Preeti shouted and jumped up her bed with excitement. As she walked out in hurry, she heard Priya shouting, "Didi, another chipkali chirped on the kitchen wall. Did you hear?" She felt the chipkalis were overwhelmingly unanimous today in confirming their presumption unlike on the other days during the last two weeks, the scheduled period of result publication. She rushed to her cousins' house next door, which had the only other radio set keeping the peasants connected with outside world other than the out of bounds majestic Choudhury abode in the entire village. Although she used to dislike her cousin sister Lilli for her at time irritating and envious talks and airing of foul comments along with Bulinani, which had been found progressively unbearable these days—seemed to her mostly due to the affability of Rabi and affection of his mother towards her—to check whether there was any news in the mid-day news broadcasting regarding the publication of result of matriculation examination that she, her class-mate and heart-throb Rabi besides her cousin brother Ramesh, a repeater, had appeared.

As expected Lilli was found evading on seeing her but not her elder brother Ramesh—he, however, was sulking—who had been struggling hard during the last three years to clear the matriculation for which Preeti had all sympathy to him and once suggested to take the help of Bhagyabati aunty, Rabi's mother like her which he refused on the ground that his father, an ardent camp followers of Choudhury elder, considered the lady a curse of the village. Sulking Ramesh was indeed forthcoming to share Preeti the information but he was reluctant to go to school to check his performance, it seemed to her—'might be, he was afraid of finding his name missing in the result chart like the previous years.' Preeti understood the constraint, and so, she didn't insisted and told, "Rameshbhai, if you do not like, do not go. Since I am going and so also Rabi, we'll check your result."

"So showy! Let's see!" Preeti heard Lilli jeering with grouse at her back.

'Poor girl!'

She jogged back to the Rath abode and checked the parents were still in their siesta. She thought, 'My Rabi will certainly emerge true to the Prakashsir's forecasting—a Dark Horse.' But got disappointed, not being confirmed by the chipkali, she had impatiently all ears for. She checked with her dear sister too.

'Anyway, doesn't matter!' she consoled her. She felt somebody was asking within her, "What about your result? You aren't serious that for?"

'What for? My Rabi's result is everything for me.'

Now, she along with Rabi had to rush to Chabishpur. She checked all around running all the way to aunty's cottage at village edge, and those places where the boy she knew used to visit, despite the loafers' irritating coughing and sneezing and leech following of Bulinani's itching remark—"Hey puffed, what happened? Look breaking! Has anybody stolen your chikini?"—asking everybody including irritators on the way, who were in fact very cooperative for any help on other occasions but reluctant at the moment.

'Smart boy! Want to know the result first. Must have gone to school, uninformed. Let's see who is the first to get the news,' she told self. 'About the result publication, somebody must have told him.'

She quietly changed her wears and picked up her papa's cycle, and started despite the sincere warning from her affectionate aunty about the sporadic Kalla Baisakhi thunderstorm and lewd boys' chase of her on her way to school.

"Wait for sometimes! I'm checking, Rabi would be somewhere around. You both should go together."

"No, aunty. He must have gone to Chabishpur. I've checked all the places. You want to prevent me to go to school on the day of fast. You mother-son duo are very clever! Sorry, I'm going."

"Hey Bhagaban, hey Maa Garachandi, please guard my little girl! My laadlee, my chul-bulli," her aunty prayed while placing sacred temple vermilion on the girl's forehead. "Where Rabi has gone? What I'll do?"

She ignored her physical weakness and the most frightening leech attack in the knee-deep water channel, she had to cross on the way—usually shipped to other side on the hands of Rabi, such was the enthusiasm. She was praying, 'Maa Santoshi, please listen to my prayer—award to my Rabi . . . . my lovely aunty's chand-ke-tukkuda what Prakashsir has predicted. I have observed yours Friday Fast with all holiness.'

She had a strong intuition that Rabi's better result would indeed help elevate his and aunty's status in the village community.

"Fifty one percent out of near about one lakh students appeared in the entire state have passed the matriculation examination," she heard, while passing on the passageway of Chabishpur village on her way to Chabishpur High School, the peasants was analyzing among them. "Overall percentage of result is better than the preceding years."

"Let's check our children's performance. They must have done extremely well. So also our Lalu, he had been at the top of all the class tests during last four years," predicted one elderly Chabishpuria with self-assurance.

For the peasants, this was considered as the first stepping stone of their village lads' future career—both in academy and in profession. Besides, the matriculation result carried special significance for Chabishpuria and for its surrounding villagers in view of the fact that this had the potential to show villages' their educational pre-eminence over their neighbours—"the better performance of our village kids is a prestige issue." In no time, the elder peasants along with examinees— some were on their foot and some riding their bicycles on typical dusty potholed road—rushed to the school campus. A huge gathering, mostly seen on the day of school annual function or in the village fairs or in the political meetings on the eve of elections. There was an all-round excitement.

Since the establishment of Chabishpur High School decades back, either the children from Chabishpur or neighbouring Palang village had been cornering the top positions in addition the maximum numbers of students' names in the result chart even though the students from near about three and half dozen villages of the locality study in the school.

However, for the non-Chabishpuria, the most concerned was during the last five years the maximum pass result including top position had exclusively gone in favour of Chabishpur villages, the proud promoter of the school. Many privately attributed this to Bishu Sarangi's impact. "So long as Bishu is there, our children will remain invincible," opined an elderly Chabispuria confidently.

Bishu Sarangi of Chabishpur had been at the helm of the affair in the school as President of school Governing Body during this period.

"Bishu Sarangi is a capable person, has good contact at top level in the government offices," the peasants used to discuss among them, and some, mostly his camp followers and alleged sycophants in deeply party-politics contaminated village community, were proud of him. Some also utilized his contacts for getting their work held up in bureaucratic red-tapes in government offices, a characteristic of nation's governance that the Independent India inherited from her colonial past. "As if an un-detachable umbilical cord," occasionally Social Science teacher found commenting while explaining lessons in the classes even though this had no mention in the text book, the school students checked. "This has been an accepted part and parcel by default in the nation's administration. What do we do? Sorry!"

What is more: the bulky Bishu Sarangi true to his appearance was very rough while dealing with the peasants. The peasants of Chabishpur and its neighbourhood didn't like him for his unrefined personality and high-handedness, yet a very few had dared to challenge him precisely in view of his contacts in various political outfits, packed with rugged elements; and in local Police Station, in Block and Tahasil Office, in Collector Office, etc. peopled with characteristics who allegedly un-tag the red-tape on the files only after their hands were handsomely greased or they were spoken to by the like of Bishu Sarangi.

He was the only person in the radius of about five kilometers who owned a telephone connection and could pull to his doorsill fearsome red cock-hooded police personnel within a few minutes from the distance Pipili Police station as and when he needed their service. He had on several occasions demonstrated his such an ability whenever any peasant or a group of them from Chabishpur or its neighbourhood had dared to challenge his hegemony over issues concerning village affairs or local politics or of his personal interest. In fact, he was regarded for all intents and purposes, the unchallenged ruler of Chabishpur. And, it seemed to the villagers he had got the authorities' endorsement.

This year a non-Chabishpuria, and that too, a Khandi Pandua has topped the list of matriculation result. So also, the Second is a Khandi Pandua. "This is as if a Dark Horse, the Indian Cricket Team snatching cricket World Cup from invincible West Indies lead by legendary Clive Lloyd," opined the ardent cricket lover and school teacher Prakashsir, comparing.

"A Khandi Pandua is Topper," the teasing commentary reverberated in the crowd gathered in the school campus under the big banyan tree. Many couldn't believe.

As a natural sequence of the event, the peasants gathered in the campus searched to have a darshan of the Dark Horse. And, the questions such as: "Who's this golden boy? Whose grandson? Whose son? Whose nephew? Whose brother?.....................," started doing the round in the campus.

But, it seemed, none had the answer. 'Or, it might be those who know don't have the nerve to say out of fear of apple polishing followers of bull-headed bloody Bishu Sarangi present in good number,' thought Preeti, the number two in the result chart.

"Nobody knows who his father is? He is such a boy . . . . a sonofabitch, a guttersnipe, an urchin," shrieked Lalu Sarangi, crest fallen.

"Lalu appears highly frustrated being relegated to Third position," Sankara, a class-mate, told in the crowd.

"Why he shouldn't be? He had been the topper in school level tests in our batch. The result is snatched from him," yelled another batch-mate from Chabishpur in the crowd.

Outside the campus, a handful of peasants from Chabishpur and its neighbourhood inimical to Bishu Sarangi's hegemony found blissful with the result and were celebrating; however, cagily. For them, this was a God-sent opportunity to corner the monster, and stealthily propagating, "Bishu's day of dominance started waning . . . . this is the prelude."

"The result won't be acceptable to the President," Headmaster Sarat Kar cried in the staff meeting recalling the spine shivering declaration of Bishu Sarangi waxing his standing moustache in the last staff meeting. "The result is a prestige issue for me. Again, the result must go in favour of our village or else it might give an upper hand to Sada Dash in the up-coming Panchayat Election."

"How could the result go this way, and that too when, he is the President of school Governing Body," harmonized with reasons the sport teacher, an alleged mole of President in the school campus. Excepting a few teachers hostile to Sarat Kar, who were euphoric but not displaying, all others were busy in ferreting out a means to get rid of a certain unpleasant confrontation with bull-headed President who might drop-in in the campus amidst heart piercing roar of his giant black Enfield Bullet at any moment.

"Blood curdling situation!" Abhaya peon murmured in the crowd.

"The school is in our village. Our ancestors set up this with initial monetary contribution and land donation. Topper is our village's privilege," Bishu Sarangi used to propagate whenever he was challenged by neighbouring villagers in so far as the results in school level tests were concerned.

"The results in school level examinations have tremendous impact on the overall moral of students preparing for matriculation examination that the clever Bishu Sarangi knew, and he exploits," the unfortunate peasants from the neighbouring villages had been ruing among them but in vain. Many of them out of frustration had tried to set up high school in their villages but so far hadn't been successful because in many cases the village leadership and well-off, and known for their contact in government offices, weren't co-operating with the excuses of this would promote easy inter-mingling of grown up boys and girls from lower and upper classes and castes, and there were possibility of they were going to love-marriage spoiling the age-old social and cultural fabric of villages and might cause social strife. "Up to M. E. School, this is all right!"

In Pandupur, this view was challenged. "If this has negative impact on social and cultural fabric of society, then why are the children of Choudhury elder doing their higher studies in schools and colleges in cities? And why then Chabispuria got a High School in their village and now working for a college," asked Karan Mishra. But, his lone voice was silenced with reprimand of repercussion of the fate of Biswanath Mohapatra.

Bishu was in his afternoon siesta. His agitated nephew, Lalu Sarangi, who ran to his all powerful uncle, woke him up to inform him the sky-falling news.

"Wh.a..t???" The monster exploded, and with his heaven-height ego, tearing anger and firing ferocity, Bishu Sarangi kicked his Royal Enfield Bullet hopping straight from his bed with a few steps and rushed to school campus, even without washing his on-sleep monstrous face—as if he wanted to retain his in-built human gear to scar his subjects—despite his better half's attentive provisioning of water. The bulky Royal Enfield Bullet's—only of its kind in the area—screening horn invaded the eardrums of Sarat Kar earlier than Bishu Sarangi's physical arrival in school campus. The headmaster got himself ready with his battery of obedient subordinates in no time, and reached His Highness, the President of school Governing Body, even before his omni-present sycophants—a common feature around the Indian politicians—small or big—encircled him as he landed in the campus.

"Whoop, this is a life-time view one should not miss!" Preeti heard Prafullasir, a sharp critic of headmaster, whispering to his camp followers, and concluded, "Sorry, I can't do the flattering of these elements, spit to the headmaster chair."

"What's this non-sense, I heard? Sasura, how could this happen? And what you peoples were doing all these days here? And, that too when Pandua Rabi had never been topper in the class tests? Were you bloody faking me all these days? Have you joined hands with that sasura Sada Dash? I'll finish you." And went on roaring whatnots that came to his reddish flapping tongue with fire in his burning eyes and furious body posturing, forgetting all civility in the presence of people from all age brackets, intents and substances.

Pandua little girl heard the monster roaring on the literally shivering headmaster with his tone and fire replicating Ramgarh's Gabber Singh in the supper-hit Bollywood melodrama—Sholey.

'What's wrong with this demon Gabbar? The examining board had conducted the examination and checked the papers, and found my Rabi . . . . my Rabi, the best. So, he is the Topper,' Preeti talked self. She wanted to face the monster, head-on with words, 'You bloody, Gabbar Singh, you so far have cheated us threatening the teachers for good results in favour of your nephew—stupid Lalu-valu in the school tests. But, in board examination, he is shown his real worth!'

'My Rabi is so good, I'm proud of him!'

A thought also cropped up in her heavily disturbed mind, 'These are the people whom we've been literally worshipping as demi-God on Teacher's Day.' More to the point, she recalled the lavish praise of Bishu Sarangi to teachers including headmaster. She compared in her little mind, 'What are these people saying and what they're practicing in real life situation? These people in the last school annual function made speeches blaming the GenNext for irresponsible behavior and indiscipline . . . . how they can say like this when they themselves never looked back while indulging in activities, critical to the very existence of a healthy and cultured society?' And, in despair, she thought—'Indeed, what a travesty of fact?'—looking up to the talisman, dewy-eyed.

A threatened headmaster was in search of words. He was literally shivering, and crying for the sympathy and consideration of His Highness, the President of CHS. He prayed to the monster with folded hand, "Bishubabu, please be considerate! I believe, there may be some wrong printing in the result sheet. This had happened last year in the case of Jagannath Vedyapeetha, we all know this. Let's wait to the arrival of mark-sheet; matter of three to four days only. Lalu is a scholarly student. His third position isn't acceptable to any of us in the entire school."

Many present including school teachers closed to headmaster, reconciled with the home works done by the ill-fated. But, Bishu appeared reluctant. "How could he when Sada Dash, his dreaded rival in village politics, was celebrating the result distributing sweets to his camp followers," viewed Prakashsir.

In the meanwhile, the clever office peon, Abhaya, a master flatterer and the headmaster's man Friday, as it was widely believed he could correctly measure the pulse of President and could provision the needed stuff that could cool down the monster to a great extent—served the monster his favorite cold-drink Thumps UP along with a pan pack.

"Is it cold drink?" Gabbar fired at the headmaster raising the Thumps Up bottle. He was about to punch on the bald head of dumpy headmaster the bottle, had the ever alert Abhaya, not intervened promptly pushing disturbed and guilty-stricken headmaster in search of excuses, little away.

"What the unfortunate but indebted bichara Sarat would do with rampant power-cut during this summer month of Baisakha? God knows whose face he had seen today morning, every effort he employed boomeranged at him," whispered the openly professed for self-respect, Prafullasir, who was the senior most teachers and was an aspirant for the headmaster post but didn't pursue as he wasn't ready to stomach the hegemony of unrefined and bull-headed Bishu in the school affairs.

"Sarat may be afraid of his transfer. This may be upper most in his mind. What will happen to his tuitions job for which he had already taken advances from students for the next session and invested the money in construction of his new house, if he is transferred?" jeered Prafullasir. "A splendid house he is building. One has to see it! Although small in size, yet a carbon copy of Dash House on Puri Grand Road. This time he has to give a bigger share of his loot to save him from transfer," he was found telling to Prakashsir.

"Give and take! This is nothing but business yaar. Stop teaching in the class, the students will run for tuition, unseen during our school-days. A recent phenomena, shameless . . . . corrupt!"

With the help of Bishu, Sarat could manage to dethrone the school founder headmaster, very popular among the students, and against the wishes of fellow teachers and local populace. He thwarted the scope of all other eligible senior aspirants' among his colleagues, and occupied the headmaster's post. Besides, in the last academic session, he had got his own long overdue transfer, a new policy of state government to discipline teachers—found indulging in local politics and tuitions—in semi-government rural school, canceled.

Preeti heard Prafullasir, not being part of the entourage of headmaster, making fun of him, "Bichara Sarat, you're caught and will be finished this time. Sorry, the cold-drink won't work!"

Still, Sarat Kar continued to employ his bravado and in his last bid effort to douse the fire of his God-father, appealed, "Tomorrow, I'm sending Trinathsir to Board Office to apply for re-evaluation of answer scripts of our golden boy—Lalu."

Preeti was ecstatic. She was in the peak of her delight. She was overflowing and paid homage to revered Santoshimaa for her generosity. And, her eyes were surveying all around inch by inch in the crowd, even searching over each face for the Dark Horse, again and again. 'Buddu wasn't in village. He hadn't come to here so far. Where he would probably have gone? Only friend, friend, friend . . . . moving hither and thither with them and playing, forgetting everything and anything important. Even life-time one! Ooh my God, what a boy? Aunty too . . . . not saying anything! Only laadla! He needs to be disciplined. This is too much! I'll complain to aunty.'

In between, she wished, 'I should go to Prafullasir and thank him for his audacity and Prakashsir for his forecasting of Rabi's result.' But, she was distracted by a sweet wrapped but heavy roared tone from a little distance, "Preeti, hey little girl, congratulation!"

The voice seemed familiar to the happy girl. She but felt that was certainly from Bishu Sarangi. Yet, she couldn't immediately accept the thought that the monster— bloody Bishu Sarangi could call her and congratulate. 'Why should he call me? I'm from Pandupur . . . . his today's eye-sore . . . . Nope, he would not.' Preeti concluded and got herself distracted from such a possibility.

'Nevertheless, who is calling?' She went on searching.

Voice—'Preeti, ooh little girl!'—again got aired. The class-mates and teachers found focused at her. She went on searching turning her side from right to left, left to right, front and back, and was astonished seeing the man, she unloved the most, calling her repeating— raising and shaking his hand.

'None other than Bishu Sarangi,' she got confirmed shaking her head—astonished as well as frightened. 'Shall I go?' A reluctant Preeti however couldn't refuse as her memory reminded, "Bishu is a true disciple and camp follower of Raghu Rath." This she had overheard on several occasions that her villagers gossiping among them in her village and 'Rabi is also once saying, confirming. Here, he is calling the shot and persona no. 1—everybody is running after him excepting a handful of harassed few.'

Little girl's little pair of legs with sweet jingling song from pure white silver nupurs sparking with afternoon stealthy sunray—enticing an envious environment—started carrying her to the furious Chabishpur Gabbar apathetically. Everybody's attention zeroed in on the little girl. However, she was looking around for her friend, her guide, her guru, her class-mate, and above all, her LOVE—praising as well as admonishing on the peak of her joy: 'Where are you—my heart-beat, my heart-throb, my Hero No. 1, our school Topper and Pandupur's future hope? You're always late! Buddu, don't understand significance of time. I wanna be first to congratulate you and to accompany you to this ugly demon to tell him on his very face—my Rabi is the best and he is awarded and certified with what he deserves—against all those bloody abuses and non-sense hullabaloo spoiling a very memorable moment in our life.'

"Congratulation, congratulation, little girl!" Bishu Sarangi again acclaimed, pushing another wad of pan in his big hollow mouth and spitting indiscriminately red pan juice intoxicating the surrounding around him with nose-biting hard Gopal Zarda tobacco smell. He extended his hand to her, stepping down from the giant bullet—to the surprise of all present—and continued, "You're awarded what you deserve. But, how could that urchin—'whatishisname?'—Rabi, made it to the top?"

This kind of special treatment that Bishu Sarangi laid to the little girl was a surprise to the bystanders. They had seen Bishu used to bestow such treatment to Block

Chairman, local MLA and the government official such as Police Inspector, BDO and Tahasildar—his maximum upper limit of VIPs whom he could approach in public and mingle with. This naturally provoked eyes-blinking of bystanders in the venue. "Is it because the girl is his guru's daughter?" murmured a few in the crowd. This scintillated a rather pensive surroundings with little handsome girl at the centre.

"Did Rabi copy in the examination? Not impossible in his case! A guttersnipe!" Bishu inquired with contemptuous and suspense-piercing tone, almost questioning Rabi's integrity 'which in fact,' Preeti strongly acknowledged, 'has been part and parcel of any under-privileges' social life, no matter how much honesty they're wedded to.'

Later, he forecasted looking at his flatterers, "Preeti could be a good companion to Lalu," and asked the girl, "What's Rabi? What's his social existence? No one knows who is his father? You, born to a respected family . . . . better avoid him," and wondered, "I don't understand why Raghubhai allow you to hang around with such an unrecognized urchin, shaming his family credential?"

Drop of tears refused to hide in those deer blue eyes, burst out in no time. She cried confining within her, 'What I'm hearing? All these rubbishes . . . . hey my heart-throb, hey my dear aunty—please forgive me and my ears. I know: how intelligent, how talented and how sharp a student Rabi is? What a nice boy Rabi in person is? And my aunty . . . . about her I can only say. A living Goddess! I'm proud of her.' She dropped her head down in anger and despair.

'Hey Maa Santoshi, hey Maa Garachandi, please give me your strength and the sword, and all those weapons you have, to slain this demon Bishu Sarangi standing in front of me—shamelessly—with all these filthy non-senses stuff in his mouth,' she prayed.

And, in unison, the sulking girl was thinking of the way out from the sight of this ugly demon and that filthy smell of red pan juice which might contaminate the sweet laddus, Rabi's favourite, that she had just purchased to offer him for his outstanding achievement, and Bhagyabati aunty for her all efforts in guiding them in their study. 'I'll break today's fast taking sweet from Rabi's hand.'

Her long disgusting wait ended when she noticed, the Dark Horse—'the unwelcomed!'—arrived running and breathing hard from nowhere, and pushed through the crowd towards the notice board.

"Here is Rabi," someone in the crowd murmured which echoed instantly in the crowd. Everybody present turned to him. But to the surprise of Preeti, no one went forward to congratulate him. Not even the teachers—Prafullasir and Prakashsir—that surprised Preeti and later she conceded, 'Might be they're afraid of bloody Bishu Sarangi.'

The suffocated girl regained her life. Warm happy tear flushed out of her blue deer little eyes. She cleaned her eyes with her thin dupatta, covering her on the up and burdensome embarrassing boobs stealing the looks of many walking vultures—she had already noticed—and stealthily rushed to the golden boy before he reached the notice board; and patting his back, whispered, "Congratulation, Congratulation . . . . hey my Dark Horse!"

"Dark Horse! Kalla Ghoda! Where is that?" Rabi asked looking all around.

"Arre buddu, don't you remember, what Prakashsir had forecasted after the class test? You buddu, you forget everything important," screamed the golden girl at his ear.

"For what, Preeti?" the surprised humble boy asked turning his back.

"Yaar, you're 'The Topper' and I . . . . ," replied the little mouth but abruptly stopped with jumping eyebrows and stealing smile, envious to the beholders.

Curious and impatient Rabi still trying to push him towards the notice board, asked shaking his head, "Is it? . . . . What about yours?"

"Just guess!" the sparking bud replied as her thin and clean petal hand went on pushing a sweet laddu into the excited little mouth, with her crying desire to be lovely caught by the topper's rat-teeth repeating what he did on his last birth day—in the midst of envious crowd, zeroed in on them with their preying eyes.

"Where are our laddus?" someone in the crowd growled.

"Are you Topper? She has ess . . . specially brought it for her heart-throb, the Topper," jeered Sankara.

After a little pause pulling the topper towards her, the little girl whispered at his ear, "I'm Second. Second to you . . . . my Kalla Ghoda."

"Congratulation, congratulation! But, Preeti, don't flatter me. I'm not gonna carry you," jeered the topper clapping his hands with the little girl's.

Further, he asked in disbelieve, "How could all these happen? Wow! What a miracle?"

"Credit goes to aunty! All due to her guidance and labour. And you, too! You and aunty worked so hard for my success," Preeti applauded resting her exhausted head—tired of hearing all the stinking and envious talks from the foul-mouthed Bishu Sarangi—on the topper's shoulder. The happy warm tears went rolling out from the blue deer eyes on the high cheeks, dazzling under the retreating sunray.

"Aah! What a sight?" shouted Sankara fisting on the back of green with envy, Lalu Sarangi.

Preeti strongly felt, the longer stay of the cursed golden boy in this callous, envious and hostile crowd, she herself couldn't even endure, might be harassing and heart-biting. Pulling the topper out of the crowd towards the parked cycle away from the banyan tree, the little girl pleaded, "Rabi, it is suffocating here. Let's go! Aunty must be waiting."

"I'm not going to ride on you but certainly on the cycle carrier that you, my dear Kalla Ghoda has to pull. It's getting late. How otherwise this grown up and your mama's little girl will go? Rabi, please! You know, today is Friday. I've fasted for you, for your this outstanding result. I'm tired."

"Ooh my God! You were fasting for me?" Rabi yelled and thought, "Where are you mad girl heading? But, Preeti, I've at present nothing to offer to break your fast. Very very sorry! I'll tell mama to prepare your favourite coconut cake," Rabi told apologizing as Preeti offered him another laddu which he instead fed the golden girl collecting from her hand—quite envious to beholders.

"I want this," Preeti buzzed.

'Preeti is right, mama must be waiting,' Rabi concurred. He felt in him some urgency. And, together, he wished to play with the pretty girl. 'What could be a blissful occasion than this?'

The eye-sore of envious, thrilled with the result, celebrated pedaling the cycle leaving behind the 'stealer-at-the-moment'—to run to catch. The golden girl shouted, "Rabi, I haven't seated . . . . hay Rabi . . . . stop! Rabi, stop . . . . please!"

The little girl along with sweet jingling song of nupurs ran for few steps, speeded up with renewed vigor for another few steps but failed to catch as the topper riding Michauxs' invented machine pedaled with matching breath. The little girl stopped, exhausted, ... and kneed down, cried . . . . shrieked. Rabi looked back, stopped the cycle at a little distance, cheered—"Run, run!"—at the little girl, scripting an envious scene as the losers looked at the playing buds in desperation.

"Be seated on the bar with all sympathy to bichara Lalu-Kaaliram," Sankara jeered impacting the play. In no time, the little beauty decked on the cycle carrier, and got them absorbed on the serpentine rural road passing through screw pine bushes, Chabishpur village alleyway, barren rice field, water channel and mango orchard.

She patted Rabi on his back and enticed, "You're really The Great! But, you lack—'Please don't mind!"—the presence of mind. You should have watched that idiot Lalu-valu—'What that Sankara rightly told—Kaaliram!' and bulky Bishu Sarangi's face. Poor fellows! They were almost crying. I've all pity to them!"

"Thank you, thank you very much my dear Preeti Madam for all these kind but certainly useless and non-sense information. I least bother about them," rejected the topper while negotiating for the way in the cloud of dust left behind by returning cow-herd on the rural clay bumpy road spotted with fresh cow-dung under the fast fading setting sun—seemed exhausted of its' day duty occasionally peeping amongst the scattered pre-monsoon clouds.

Enthusiast to inform his mother and the mentor about the hard found success the mother-son had struggled for, Rabi was in his unusual fast despite the pulling load from behind. The cargo was indeed sympathetic to struggling Kalla Ghoda by her words.

"I'm getting ugly-fat these days . . . . isn't it, my Dark Horse?" jeered Preeti patting the boy on his back like bullock cart driver does to the poor bullocks struggling to pull the loaded cart in the muddy field. But, there was no response.

She decided in her, 'Now, this is my turn to pay back the topper for his teasing play in the school campus.' She murmured after a while, blaming, "Aunty is responsible for this. She didn't allow me to play during the last one year whereas she allowed her chand-ke-tukkuda that helped him to retain his cute health. Very selfish . . . . favouritism! All teachers are like this, favouring their children. This is a great injustice she has done to me and her son must pay off."

"She didn't allow you to play because you're a stupid and mad girl, never read when I was in front of you, looking at me all the time. And, when she allowed you to go for play you ran after me that everybody was criticizing and taunting. Don't you know Bulinani's blabber mouthing whatnots linking you with me. This will affect your future life. You dim-wit don't understand this," Rabi shouted.

"I'm a stupid . . . . I'm mad . . . . I'm dim-wit. Okay . . . . thank you! I won't go," punching Rabi at his hip with a hair pin, the girl jumped from the running cycle. In-balanced on the narrow bullock cart road full of potholes the pedaled two-wheeler tripped to side gorge and the golden boy was in no time in knee deep water.

The girl screamed with all sympathy, "Leech, leeches are there . . . . Ooh my God! What I did? They'll suck your blood." As soon as she pulled the boy out of the gorge, she went on checking his legs for leech and cleaned the legs with her dupatta pulling that from her chest, taunting, "Hello, you stupid and mad boy, close your eyes. Don't look at my body. You opportunist boys are always searching for opportunities to look at young and grown up girls," and requested, "Please don't tell aunty . . . . I pushed you to gorge. She'll feel bad about me."

"I'm not such a fool to be trapped by you. I know this very well, your aunty will instead blame me and question me for what happened. These days she hardly finds any fault in you. You've almost stolen her," told Rabi rejecting, and later shouted, "By the way, what you told? I'm 'opportunist' and 'searching for opportunities' to look at young and grown up girls. Mind, I may be you-recognised-people's unrecognized child—a guttersnipe, an urchin; but, I'm certainly not like that lecherous and so-called recognized Kaaliram and Sankara, and their likes in our village."

"Mind, my mama will disown me if she finds this immoral fiber in her offspring."

Tear flushed out in no time. "Sorry Rabi," cried the little girl breaking down and begged, "please don't mind. I'm just joking. Please forgive me!" And holding in her hands her ears stood blocking the snot-nosed till he cooled down and opened his eyes . . . . and smiled notwithstanding miserly.

"You can look at me as much you like; you must read my eyes—my mind—my talks—my plays—I'm crying for," shouted the obsessed girl. "You're my obsession. Please don't ever deny me this. I beg to play with you."

"And, never utter for God-sake in front of me what those idiots are saying about you. I can't hear and tolerate those stinking and killing words," cried the girl, begging.

"Rabi, why there's no High School in our village whereas Chabishpur has? Has this been there, we needn't be forced to hear all these humiliating non-senses talks from that demon Bishu Sarangi and his idiot nephew Lalu," asked the girl and lamented regretfully, "and, you wouldn't have fallen in the gorge so badly. Cha . . . . cha . . . . !"

She asked a la a child asks to his grandpa searchingly for answer—seriously. Rabi smiled and softly cleaning beauty's paled and dusty face, answered, "This is a question which had been hunting me for long. As I went on searching I had ferreted out that our village indeed was blessed with a High School when the entire Delang Block didn't have any even before our nation's independence. But, the elements from our own village burnt the schools at the dead of the night in the very year the first admitted batch was about to write their matriculation examination and our High School was supposed to be recognized by the government, and the services of teachers were about to be regularized, thus completing the process of setting up the school. They did that as they were tutored by Choudhury family that this would promote co-education and vulgarity destroying age-old village culture. There's a history of it. We better avoid the issue or else we'll have the fate of visionary Biswanathdada."

As the little girl was unstoppable in her eagerness to know, Rabi illustrated, "Biswanath Mohapatra, the man who was behind the setting up of ill-fated High School in our village, was beaten after the school was burnt in a mid-night bonfire by the Choudhury family's henchmen. The real reason is: the Choudhury family is afraid of modern education in our village because they feel threatened to their family's supremacy in an enlightened environment. Humble Biswanathdada left the village forever. And, with his evacuation the hope of village salvation from Khandi Pandupur to Pandupur has been throttled till date. However, with much difficulty though illiterate but headstrong Karankaka's father rescued Primary and M. E. Schools which were by that time had got the government recognitions."

Preeti was found awkward and thinking, and after a while of curling her hair, vowed, "Rabi, however, we must work for the revival of our High School. Is not it a shame to go to other village to study?"

"Ooh, yes! This is there in our agenda. Karankaka is waiting for the right moment. But, you know, the road is very thorny," Rabi soothsaid with fear and suspense. "This is indeed a very difficult task in an environment of notion to fly abroad for world class study rather than developing world-class study facilities in our own backyard," Rabi rued and went on saying, "See, Choudhury elder who opposes modern co-education in our village is himself sending his children to city schools."

"Again, please don't mind, I would rather like to ask you, how does it matter to you . . . . a girl? You're just a WHP—Waiting Hall Passenger," Rabi asked blinking his eyes and later went on blowing a melancholic song on the ears of the golden girl, "moment the train will arrive, you'll board that forgetting everything and everybody like any typical bride. Dropping a few drops of pretending tear and hugging with pretending wail on the shoulders of near and dear, you'll leave for your prince abode in a decorated palanquin escorted by your great brother. Don't worry if you so desire, I'll be at your services shouldering the load of palanquin up to your groom's palace. I am your friend yaar! I can't do this much for the girl who fasted a day per week for last two-three month during this oppressive summer for my good result?"

He teased poking the apsaraa's cheek turning red, fast. "Now, I'm thinking to observe 'fast' for the hand of a beautiful prince for my so beautiful and lovely friend. I must payback."

"Again, you're such an intelligent, educated, and now a First Class matriculate. And, you are a beautiful Jophiel angel—one in lakhs! Princes will henceforth hang around Rath address appealing for your golden slim palm with fabulous marriage proposals."

"Let's see, who is such a bhagyaban?"

Rabi further tapping burning beauty at her ear, and flashing a funny but lavish smile in his clean cheek-chin still virgin of beard, asked, "Am I right, Preeti Madam?"

The little beauty wasn't ready to hear all these verbatim—hurt and wounded. She banged at Rabi's butterfly chest and shouted, "What did you say— WHP?" She almost cried at the boy with pain and disfigured. She couldn't hold her calm, and unhesitantly appealed, "What . . . . what do you mean to say this?" As Rabi was found evading, she blasted him in despair, "I can't bear all these words thrown at me by you so easily and comfortably, and that too, after so many years of our togetherness. Can you imagine that I can leave without you? I don't know what's there in my fate, and what you and aunty have in yours mind? But still I beg, 'For God's sake, don't hurt me again with all these stupid talks.' I'm no more a mere child. Mind it, I'm not leaving this Pandupur any way. You are . . . . my . . . ."

Rabi murmured as both ride the cycle, "You're a mad girl! You'll be another spicy Bulinani. Ha . . . ha . . . a!"

"What? Again, you told? . . . . I won't go. I'll tell aunty," Preeti dropped down, and later, sat on the carrier only after hearing, "Sorry, you're a good girl! Is it okay? Happy? Satisfied?"

After a while of musing on the bumpy road, Preeti suggested consoling, "We can together work to Karankaka for setting of a High School in our village.

And I believe, there lays our village salvation. I'll teach there."

Rabi kept quiet as if he understood what he was hearing, and had doubt of its success. 'How could I, an outcast, a pariah, a son-of-a-widow and a branded guttersnipe gets with this girl, an archangel and a socially recognized child. After all, would Raghu uncle and Prema aunty accept me as their son-in-law in a tradition bound village society? What is there with me? Even, we don't have a house on our own land and a family title for social recognition.'

Rabi was very practical. He wanted to speak to the girl, and let her realize this hard fact but hold back leaving the issue to have its own natural course as per the destiny with passing of time. He didn't like to spoil the moment of joy of the pretty girl.

'After all, I LOVE her,' Rabi confined. 'She is such a nice girl. Of course, little crazy!'

Monotonous Pandupur village erupted in joy with the news. The sky was relatively clean and the village was washed with evening cool wind. The peasants were on peak of their satisfaction and in mode of celebration. The village was lighted with Buddha Purnima's rising full moon as if uncle moon was in league with jubilant Pandupurias to celebrate the big day. The village elders, youths and children, barring a handful few, were united to give a rousing welcome to the topper and his running mate, the most important persona of the village at the moment.

"Why shouldn't? They're the first in the history of Pandupur, the village grown tots, to top the Chabishpur High School matriculation examination and the first First Class Matriculates. They'd given Pandupur an identity and to its new generation a new lease of life," Karan Mishra told befittingly.

It appeared that Pandupurias had forgotten, 'Rabi is a son-of-a-widow, a branded guttersnipe, an urchin.'

"He is the proud possession of our village and an inspiration of our crippled GenNext."

There at the doorsill of Choudhury abode was raining a gloomy silence as if the entire family was scared of Bhagyabati's determination, Rabi's success and the mother-son duo's growing acceptance in the village. 'None from their family is out in village alleyway and their house street veranda is deserted of his camp followers.' The light was off.

'Is the Choudhury family scheming against? Not impossible,' thought Karan Mishra, the inspiration and mentor of the golden tots.

Tear burst out from the happy eyes of golden boy. He raised his head and looked at the Buddha Purnima's rising uncle-moon thinking that that was none other than his papa's face, whose warmth he was unfortunate to experience. He felt his deceased father, Dibakar Choudhury was all out to congratulate him defying his father—Choudhury elder—extending his two hands vide ray of moonlight stealthily passing through the banyan tree hanging trunks. He wanted to thank him but stopped short of doing that as he had a grievance against him. Rabi felt, 'Papa is begging to forgive him for leaving them at the mercy of his father, a man, so cruel.'

The highly contented mother Bhagyabati went to village deities—'Who,' she thought, 'has listened to her prayers,'—to offer evening 'Special Aarti' with pure ghee—befitting the occasion—while the children were celebrating. Bhagyabati while offering prayers was thinking about the buddhic silence at the specious portico of Choudhury abode, the determined tormentor of her and her laadla's very existence.

'Whatever, I'm determined, but certainly not revenging. I believe, the truth is like fire. And, the fire can't be hidden. Ultimately, the truth will come out victorious, erupting like volcano.'

"Tik . . . . tik . . . . tik . . . . ," confirmed the chipkali on the temple wall.

"Hey Rabi! Come on, come on . . . . hey maa, you're weeping. This is our moment of joy. Let's celebrate," screamed the girl supplementing the appeal of mentor mildly pulling and pushing the golden boy, not understanding what was milling in his mind. She swept the drops of tear of joy from the boy's cheeks and virgin chin with her soft cotton dupatta and heard Bulinani taunting at a distance, "Kiss, kiss him! Nobody watching! What a beautiful sight?"

Preeti felt tempted to place a lovely kiss on cleaned lovely bright cheeks of Rabi to express her LOVE as she was doing as a small child years' back while playing 'child marriage game' copying the scene from plays hosted in the annual village fair but couldn't proceed as she recalled Rabi's just recited history of ill-fated Pandupur High School and Choudhury elder's propaganda. And, as she thought of public display of such spontaneity wasn't in our culture.

'We're grown up now!'

Karan Mishra, who was witnessing this lovely scene, the reflection of basic instinct, concluded in self, 'They are born for each other. Hey Pravu, I beg, please help the beautiful pair.'

And, the loafers Gandua (basket) dropped down at the temple steps, Dukhi (unhappy) crest fallen, Galu (itcher) itched, Valu (bear) growled, Sarua (narrowest) steepened and Hadu (bony) broken. They were envious. And they were murmuring, "A sonofabitch, guttersnipe, urchin . . . . has such a good fortune."

'Such is the scene, who can resist?' accepted the mentor.

Mother India

Rabi wasn't borne lucky as his mother Bhagyabati was widowed and she was thrown out from her in-law's house by the time he was born. Bhagyabati was a social outcast, not because she was born to such a social stratum but for the reason that she'd lost her husband on the fifth day of her marriage, and her parents-in-law had branded her the killer of their son, and brought bad luck to their family. Her pregnancy furthered her grief. And her in-laws and the villagers closed to her in-laws' dismissed her claim that she was carrying the gene of in-laws' family.

The mother-son had been living on the edge of the Pandupur village in a mud raised and hay-thatched 'one room for all purpose cottage' on a desolate land that Bhagyabati built with her old parents' meager financial support. She raised her fatherless son all-of-alone with little earning working as a house-maid in Pandupur houses, and later on, tutoring school students, a skill that got recognized with academic excellence of her son in Pandupur Primary and M. E. Schools.

There were knocks at the door even before cocks in their den crowed in the distanced drummers and washer men houses and the winged scavengers had cawed in the backyard mango trees before leaving their nests for cleaning dirties in the Pandupur households. And she-jackals hadn't yet delivered their last hourly yelp before they left to their holes in the screw pine bushes at the cremation and big tank mounds with their rarely yelping consorts.

The newly married couple heard the jeering at their room threshold. Bhagyabati, still in the mood of coupling, recalled poking her head with her forefinger what she was told before she was thrust physically to her husbandGod last night by her juvenile sister-in-laws.

She had to get up early in the morning on the fifth day of her marriage after the pious Fourth Night, the first night of sharing bed with her husbandGod, as strictly instructed by her sister-in-laws and the village girls for . . . . she laughed confidently.

She was proud of her husbandGod, princely Dibakar Choudhury and his family for their generosity of picking up a bride from a commoner family—for the first time in the living memory of the villagers in the locality.

"You're lucky," claimed her village mates. 'And it seems from their talk and dealing they are envious,' felt Bhagyabati. Even a few had gone to the extent of asking her, "How could you entice a bridegroom from Zamindar Choudhury family?" And, some pleaded her to teach them the modus operandi which she humble rebuffed saying, "There's nothing as such!" As a last-ditch, she was requested, "If possible please try to place our candidatures with your would-be younger brother-in-law or any other bachelor relations after your marriage." And, there was an all out competition among her village-mates to entice her.

In one such conversation, which her mother overheard, she intervened and proudly claimed, "Bhagyabati is a bhagya-bati! She is beautiful, she is humble, educated, talented, ... And she deserves what she gets!"

Also, the bad-mouthing had their inimical round. One village lad, who had vainly tried before to stealthily entice the lucky girl and was thrashed by her elder brother, had sprinkled the rumour 'out of frustration' that he'd seen her together with Dibakar Choudhury in the deep mango orchard on the way to school. "You know these days she is wearing tempting dresses."

"Must be given by Choudhury!"

"Ooh . . . . ho, this is why she prefers to go to school alone," harmonized some of her mates and rumours had their round which hadn't gone down well with her elder brother who threatened the rumour-monger—however, he wasn't that harsh this time being persuaded by the parents not to divert the concentration in preparing for the big event in the family—saying, "Let the marriage be over; Zamindar Choudhury will take care of these—envious and frustrated elements. After all, now Bhagyabati is their family image!"

But, many elders in the village and family relations were apprehensive of a known wily Choudhury elder's intention. "How could Choudhury family come down to so low level? So far, they've got matrimonial relations with their level of Zamindars and they're mostly located in cities with skeletal presence in the village, mostly during crop harvest time," told the family well-wishers.

"The matrimonial relation should be made with the family of equal social and economic status. This isn't just marriage of two individuals but two families who are supposed to seat together, eat together, talk together, share each other's happiness and sorrow . . . . respecting each other's sentiment for generations." Even many including school teachers pleaded the girl's parents not to be hurry and suggested to defer the marriage by some months or till the girl appeared her matriculation examination, she was expected to do extremely well as she was topper in all class tests.

But, the gullible parents were so enthusiast, they weren't ready to listen. Even they ignored the gossip among peasants, "The bridegroom is so-aged, more than double the age of the girl and there must have some reason for deferring his marriage so long." They went on preparing for the big event with the big family—they never dreamed about—as the proposal had come on its own. They hadn't spared anything that could be at best taken care of by them with their little resources. The mother had handed over all her ornaments she had brought with her marriage despite grudging mumbling of her daughter-in-law, the mother of two daughters; even not saving a tola for the yet to come youngest daughter-in-law, she was supposed to offer like she did in case of her elder daughter-in-law, saying, "We'll see then. Let's take care of the blessed opportunity first." The parents were so moved with the 'generosity!' of Choudhury family of Khandi Pandupur that they were thinking every suggestions from their family's well-wishers, nothing but spit out of jealousy.

———◦◦◦———

As per the tradition, Bhagyabati was supposed to take care of the in-law family's entire kitchen works on the day as tutored by her custom conscious old mother. And, also this was what she had seen her sister-in-law had done in the similar situation—starting from preparing breakfast for the family, and had to get the blessing from her in-law family elders' while serving them the breakfast prepared by her with rations she had brought from her parents' house.

She had a known task ahead to do all these ignoring body strain caused in the first encounter she'd gone through with her bull-strong husbandGod in the just passing night. Nevertheless, she was enthusiast, without any tress of irritation.

She was enjoying. 'Why not?' She was happy with her husbandGod. She was blessed with a husbandGod, whom she within one night of togetherness could understand, was very caring and sharing and open to her views. 'What more a wife can at most expect?' she concluded.

Besides, Bhagyabati had to prove to her sister-in-laws and Pandua girls what she'd already proved to her husbandGod in the past night with blood stain in her petticoat. 'This is something every virgin bride is proud of.'

Even though Dibakar wasn't ready to release Bhagyabati from his embracing grip to the call of his sisters and village girls and she wasn't keen to go too, yet she got her relieved from the mannish seize of her husbandGod pushing him back with sweet smile and a bold wink under the dim she-devil light fitted above the hand-reached height on the spotless freshly white washed wall.

'There is the call of the duty, an age-old practice; and this is the time to show her in-laws her family up-bringing.' She quickly adjusted her hair and tied her petticoat, covered her exhausted soft genteel boobs with bra and blouse picking them forcefully from under the pillow of her husbandGod and wrapped her just explored body with the sari, accompanied by mild jingling noise of her brand new bridal bangles and nupurs under the full gaze of infatuated husbandGod amid unrelenting invasion of jeering and cheering from the doorsill and irritating door chain jingling.

Dibakar was appeared not so happy. He turned his side on the Bombay-pattern bedstead, reluctant, and gave the impression to Bhagyabati, he was disgusted. But, not for a long. His princely body again twisted his side, looked at her lewdly, jumped up from the bed and embraced her with tempted body warmth. He placed the huge kiss on her forehead, high cheeks, round chins, throat, ... and where not's. And pulling out her soft boobs out of the bra under the blouse, he started chewing them like a hungry infant. Bhagyabati scared of spots with saliva, quickly cleaned them with her sari veil smiling at Dibakar and banging his chest mildly, shyly. She reacted, more of a spur-of-the-moment, "I'm afraid, how did you manage so long?"

"What? Is it required to prove the satitwa on the part of a husband?"

The blessed lady bit her tongue. 'Ooh, the fair sex's forbidden topic,' she quickly reconciled. 'Who am I to poke my nose in . . . . ?'

42

"Sorry!" murmured bichara proud virgin.

Dibakar wasn't ready to allow Bhagyabati to attend the progressively hardening knocks at the door. "Just wait! We're little busy," he smiled, murmured and wanted to say to the intruder of their life time privacy. He wanted to continue with their heavenly play of LOVE so long as they could . . . . non-stopped . . . . undisturbed. Short Bhagyabati returned the kiss at her husband's bushy chest, and looking at his eyes assuring—"I was only yours, is only yours now and will remain only yours unquestioning forever."

She pushed her praised-catch's mighty structure with her all valour to the bed and went on assuring, "Wait for the next night! Not much far! I'm sorry, I'm exhausted now."

"Aah . . . . a . . . . a . . . . !" she heard an aching cry and saw flinging of legs of her husbandGod and sudden sweating on his forehead, as she was adjusting her attire. She rushed to the door worried of being trapped again by her husbandGod assuming, 'The action and cry were nothing but some more ploys to detain her . . . . but the sweating!' Still she ignored . . . . dismissing.

She pulled down the door chain and opened the door pairs. And, she left the room to be grilled by frenzied sister-in-laws and the village damsels keenly waiting outside the room threshold, keeping their ears on the door, overhearing.

Shied but bold Bhagyabati proved to the satisfaction of her in-laws with little light of receding moon in western sky like she proved to her husbandGod last night and felt overjoyed by over pouring praise. This followed the talk among the village girls, the act of recently married Santanubhi's wife who drenched her petticoat and sari hurriedly, wasn't found co-operative.

"She was certainly not a virgin. She might have physical relation with somebody else before her marriage. She is a shame to her in-laws' family. So also, she is to Pandupur village. Alas! How can Santanubhi tolerate this?" screamed a girl.

"Is Santanu aware of all these things?" jeered Bulinani who joined from nowhere as soon as the chattering flock descended from Choudhury abode's high steps and lamented, "Alas, so simple, a man he is!"

The talks went on and on that the proud virgin heard closely along the marching of the flock towards village edge pond beyond the Maa Garachandi temple for pious cleaning of virgin's body before paying obeisance to village tutelary god and goddesses as per the decree of family priest.

"Your bhabi is a pure virgin!" cheered Bulinani poking proud virgin's sister-in-law at the full view of her.

"Bhabi, you know, she'll spread this news all over the village in no-time. Is it not our very dear loudspeaker?" told another girl frowning. "Bulinani mightn't have slept last night to collect this information."

Bhagyabati was thrilled with the raining praise from Pandupur damsels and her sister-in-laws.

"She is a proud honour of Choudhury family. And, Choudhury family is proud of her. She not only makes her in-laws proud of their choice before the community of Panduas but also her family of birth and their up-bringing of her," praised another elderly girl. Bulinani seconded and left the flock.

"Bhabi, do you have any sister?" asked a village girl. "I've a brother. But, after your marriage in Choudhury family . . . . ," she stopped abruptly as Bhagyabati's sister-in-law turned to her.

"Sorry!"

Bhagyabati was in hurry. She had many works to perform before the sun rose in the eastern sky. She pushed her for bath in the oppressive cold water of the village pond with patches of weeds amidst cracking of joke from village damsels concerning her just passing night.

"How is our brother? Bold . . . . strong . . . . pushing! A bull . . . . solid materials, isn't it?" The newly-wed heard someone jeering when she was cleaning her overflowed chest with the veil of her sari.

"Is it burning?" yet another taunted.

"Just wait! Your turn isn't much far. It won't only burn but also bleed," shied Bhagyabati, for the first time, opened her mouth, though wasn't irritated with the firing of comments. She fired back along with throwing of the cold water on the horde.

"Wow! What a realization?" the buzzing crowd jeered back with equal vigor.

While still in the bathing ghat, they heard the rare yelping of he-jackal on the screw pine mound at the village cremation ground by the side of bended Ratnachira river.

'This forecasts bad fortune and landing of bad omen and the possible death of person, an age-old belief in the village social milieu.'

Girls were frightened. They wondered looking at each others, buzzing, "What for this could be?"

"Is there anybody lying in the death bed in our village?" they inquired among themselves. Their quick survey of near about three dozens of households in Pandupur led them to no finding. They dismissed the issue saying some body in the neighbouring village might be on the death bed. But, one among them told, "The yelping was in our village cremation mound." While yet another girl recalling observed, "It seemed from beyond Ratnachira, outside our village limit."

From wherever, they didn't like to waste their moment of joy. They preferred to bury the issue and went ahead with their, at time, scandalous gossiping, they had left behind.

As they started returning, they found themselves again disturbed . . . . disturbed by the persistent wailing bark of stray dogs. The dogs were in melancholic chorus—occasionally seen in early morning hour—that followed them from bathing ghat to Maa Garachandi temple. Gals tried to silence them chasing with coconut and bamboo lath picking up from way side but to no avail as the dogs were so unanimous in their forecasting of bad times ahead.

"Certainly, there's something seriously wrong! You can't just dismiss the yelping and barking," Bulinani soothsaid again joining the flock running breathless.

A pale of gloom descended in the herd of chirping damsels. Later, they calmed down looking at each other with suspense with spicy Bulinani among them. 'It might be,' Bhagyabati thought, 'they think that I have brought them and their village bad luck.' Murmuring among the girls went on, distancing from her. She felt uncomfortable, yet she was triumphantic brushing aside all these presumed 'bullshit' murmurs.

'I'm born on the day of Ganesh Chaturthi, one of the most auspicious day in the Hindu almanac,' she told her and recalled—what her father used to say to his friends that with her birth he won a long court battle settling the long fought land dispute against his cousin brother, and had harvested good crops in that year. 'This is the reason why my father had named me Bhagyabati—the lucky girl—ignoring the horoscope prescribed name— Rebati, the unlucky girl. More to the point, the fortune teller, who had checked my horoscope for matching before the marriage, predicted that with my leaving of parental family after my marriage the good fortune may desert them.'

'I'm a harbinger of good fortune. And I'm confidence—wherever I will go, the good fortune will march with me.'

She was dismissal of her accompanied troop's apprehensive tittle-tattle. She walked to the temple of village presiding deity to pay her homage and thank the deity for her kind to get her in her blessed village despite the sudden non-cooperation from her accompanied entourage, all-of-alone. The chipkali chirped on the temple wall, "Tik . . . . tik . . . . tik . . . . ," in tandem, confirming Bhagyabati and her late distancing entourage that they were 'right' about what they were thinking respectively.

On her return to majestic Choudhury abode, Bhagyabati first walked to family's tutelary deities to pay her dutiful obeisance kneeing before them even before changing her wet cloth biting her bare soft body in the morning Magha cold, confident and dismissive of her now distancing in-laws' uneasiness.

Later, she moved to her bed room, however pausing, as she was apprehending of her affectionate husband's further time expensive lovely indulgence that might obstruct her on her path of conducting morning ritual as designed in tradition bound society. Besides, she had to change the cloth and to collect the feet dust of her husbandGod; she moved stealthily. She touched her husbandGod's feet bringing down her forehead like she had seen revered sati Sita did to her murjada purush Lord Rama with all her holiness in the dance-dramas— Sita Bibhaha held in the village fair. She rubbed the little dust from her husbandGod's feet and wrapped the same on her forehead alongside five days old red shining sacred vermillion that Dibakar had first painted in the night of their marriage amidst ritual cheering of her relations and friends, she had saved despite the water-deep bath in the Pandupur pond.

But, she found her husbandGod cool, and was still not reacting against all her previous apprehension. He seemed lied down—as if life-less—on the bed. 'Is he playing? . . . . may be?'

'He instead ought to go for the bath and pay obeisance at village Shiva temple for the best of conjugal life in the morning after their first night together as directed by the family priest after the customary fourth day marriage havan where they had promised each other to take care of each other till the last breath.'

'Of course, not accompanied by his in-laws like me,' she told her smiling.

"Ooh, my God! Ha-i-e-a, you're still on the bed? Cha, cha . . . . so lazy. Get up! It's already morning," mildly screamed obsessive Bhagyabati. Still, there was no response. She was confused with priority. What to do? Time is running away—fast. And, she was shivering badly in cold. She poked at his armpits and later his waist; subsequently, her love-wrapped fingertips ran over her husbandGod's half bare body in vain. 'So cool!'

Pulling and pushing replaced poking and body teasing. She in renewed vigor pulled and pushed her husbandGod like he did last night to her that she was craving for since the day of marriage-life's thought forced into her tiny mind by her sister-in-law jocularly during her seven days long puberty celebration some three to four years ago. She continued to do so not realizing that her luck had already left her unnoticed. Her non-stop and hard try became noisy slowly but steadily as her newly adorned bridal attires made up of glittering gold and silver metals joined her breaking the calmness of morning in the Choudhury family's abode.

Little later her in-laws reluctantly entered the bed room and joined her to find out Dibakar was too cool to respond. Everybody present was found dumbstruck. 'Hushed!' Looking at each other.

"He is no more," declared village baidya. Bhagyabati was stunned, unspeakable . . . . and fell on her motionless and lifeless husbandGod like a hapless tree cut by its root.

By the time, she got back her sense uncared . . . . unattended, she heard a mild commotion and crying in the spacious Choudhury courtyard. Her husbandGod wasn't by her side. There were a large number of unknown faces along with members of Choudhury family around. Preparation was in full swing amid crying, and abuses of in-laws directed at her. She found everybody had an inimical look at her, and sister-in-laws were scowling. None was saying, 'What is her fault?' Hostility was all around.

"Throw this witch out of our house—She is a she-devil—She is poison-lady—she shall eat whoever comes to her sight."

The durbhagyabati was watching all these going-on like the mud-made deities at puja dais to be immersed after the pious worship—speechless and motionless. Only breathes were doing to and fro journey keeping her alive.

The cruel agents of Jama Raja, the four pall bearers found readying the bamboo stretcher little away to carry the dead body to cremation ground. Later, they came to her husbandGod sleeping coolly—unconcerned of the pain and sorrow of the lady he'd played with so heartily just a couple of hours ago and promised the heaven—at the feet of Holy Basil plant, and drag the body to the stretcher. They loaded the body on the stretcher and tied that mercilessly covering his face with freshly made hay rope. The slogan—*ram nam satya hey*—in chorus from the cruel agents of Jama Raja, ranted the air signaling the start of the last journey of her husbandGod.

'How could my husbandGod leave me? He was very please with my body, beauty, elegance and virginity. He had promised me so many things—just last night. He had promised to live with me his full life. We've decided to have two beautiful children—one son and one daughter. And, he vowed by the side of havan and in front of priest to protect me from encroachment of any lewd intruder. No, he can't leave me. And, I shouldn't allow the pall bearers to snatch from me my very own reverend husbandGod.'

She rushed to them uncared of her ill-clad bathing clothes, which had in the meanwhile dried on her body, caught their legs begging to allow her very husbandGod to stay with her. She was however driven away, cruelly. She pleaded her sister-in-laws, who were just a few hours ago, were all praise of her and were so dear and overtly confessed, "We're proud of our bhabi."

Sarcastic taunts started striking her like the praises just a few hours ago. The entire world for her changed in just a few hours. And, she was no more 'a lucky girl'; her father was proudly saying every one.

"She is no more a bhagya-bati," she heard Bulinani telling her sister-in-law sarcastically.

"Bichara bhagya-bati!" announced another little far. She could hear from a little distance a comment from one of her sister-in-laws, "O ho . . . . Sati Sabitri! Allow her, she can get back her husband's life . . . . fighting with Jama Raja," followed by, "Throw her in the pyre! At least, she can be a revered sati; we'll worship her raising a grand Sati Temple with her statue inside."

The whole world became so inimical to her, so soon. The pall bearers didn't listen to the devastated durbhagya-bati as the further detention of dead body would delay the village temple daily rituals. They followed the instruction of village elders' unconcern of cursed lady's heart-rending wailing.

"Her life became meaningless! How could she, a woman live without her husband in this hostile inhuman world?" Karan Mishra soothsaid.

Later, the wife of village barber was summoned and ravaged durbhagya-bati was pulled to the village end pond where just a few hours ago she was applauded and she had her first bath as a daughter-in-law of majestic Choudhury clan, at the eye distance of cremation ground where the fire was eating the princely body of her husbandGod— seemed to her—'merrily!' She saw the cremators' cruel poking of her husbandGod's pyre with bamboo stick 'purposefully!' assisting the fire for quick consumption. She wanted to stop them. She wailed beating her chest with prayer—'What more a destitute can do in an environment of hostility?'—but to no avail.

Soon, she was stripped off her bracelet, bangle, ear-ring, necklace, girdle, nose ring, nupurs, and all other bridal costumes. The red vermillion, the proud possession of Hindu married woman, painted on her forehead by none other than her husbandGod—'so affectionately!'—was rubbed with her own sari veil by the lady barber as if she was undeserving of all these. None opposed and even had no word of sympathy. 'The whole world was unanimous.'

'All these happened even before Dibakar body is reduced to ash. The world is so inhuman. A blossoming flower just in her teen and before could charm the world and delivered the fruit to run the family's next generation is forced to fade beyond recognition for her no known-fault,' lamented Karan Mishra, unable to help remembering the founder of the village, Jittu Pandu's deed ages ago.

Her accompanied in-laws seemed happy with the turn of the event in Bhagyabati's life with those valuable bridal costumes in their possession. 'It's blessing in disguise for them.' They were grabbing the ornaments as soon as they were removed from durbhagya-bati's stony body like broad day-light robbers—amid mild-quarreling among them for the booties. Nobody around was ready to listen her heart-rending wailing and chest banging echoing loud and clear in the bathing ghat and around. She looked at them awful.

And, she was declared, "A widow!"

'Now, she is a widow . . . . for rest of her life. And, her bhagya and karma sink her to remain so for ever.'

Back in Choudhury abode her room address was found changed. She wasn't allowed to the room she had just yesterday decorated with her very colourful presence, and where the bridal havan was held, and where her husbandGod had promised to take care of her for life. She, as if a refuse, was pushed to back house, to compete for a few yards of space along with the domestic beasts, who were staring at her unaware of injustice done to their new companion.

Her father, who rushed to Pandupur, was refused a simple one-to-one talk with family patriarch with whom he had struck a family relation, 'widely adhered— stitches for seven generations.' Hostilities were all around. The aged and meek father took her back to their family against her wishes. The majestic in-laws didn't stop her as if they had a vested-interest and were eagerly awaiting for an opportunity to get rid of the refuse which they got in this evacuation.

"She is another widow who needs the intervention of the likes of benevolent Jittu Pandu," Karan Mishra spoke to the like-minded in the village alleyway and heard from a distance Bulinani jeering, "Why don't you be another Jittu Pandu?"

"He would have been but for his wife," mocked a Pandua.

The parents were in pursuit of getting her remarried—again, against her wishes. But, Bhagyabati's vomiting that followed within a few days that those— mostly the aged widowers—came forward to accept her didn't turn up to proceed further.

"This was quite obvious. Why should one take care of other's child?" remarked her sister-in-law, full of detrimental aggression, unseen of before. She even didn't refrain from casting doubt sarcastically on the character of now vulnerable Bhagyabati instead of organizing celebration associated with the conception as custom demand from a maternal aunty.

Bhagyabati knew of her body sanctity and she didn't agree to the advices of elderly ladies of her village to get rid of her husbandGod's seed growing inside her. Lately, her mother also joined the village ladies in persuading her for abortion by using the service of village quack. Some advocated with justification, "Why should she give birth to a child whose blood is so heartless and ungrateful and so conveniently forgotten the age-old believe of—marriage relation is made for seven generations? Is it nobility?"

'No body found thinking about the innocent gene growing inside my womb,' cried the cursed would-be mother. Nor even her parents—such was the mindset in the social circle. However, she conceded, 'What the old parents can do? They've in their mind the well-being of their daughter uppermost.'

However, she disagreed. She wanted to give birth to her husbandGod's seed, her husbandGod had trusted in her. 'I'm a Hindu married woman.' She wanted to save the life of God's gift, a pious atma and her husbandGod's identity, ... now growing in her, crying for birth—'for to prove that I'm carrying none other than my husbandGod's seed, as I alone know what had carried-on between me and my husbandGod during those few hours of that auspicious night every virgin bride dreamed up.'

She was asked to leave for Khandi Pandupur by her elder brother at the insistent of her elder sister-in-law with two daughters at home. Sister-in-law argued forcefully with highlighting her worst fear of their family might be maligned in the presence of Bhagyabati, 'a so-called one-night mother.' And, that might hamper the marriage of her daughters. 'Or . . . . she might have been guided by who would take the life-long burden of a destitute and her child?' as thought by Bhagyabati's only sympathizers in the living world, her aging parents. She was advised to claim the share from Choudhury family by her sister-in-law, "If she's certainly carrying only the seed of her husband." With each passing day the peace in the family started getting shattered. Even two little nieces—unaware of the complexity in the so-called civilized living world—were persuaded not to mingle with her.

She could very well see the pain in the eyes of her aging parents, unable to help her with their fast declining authority over the family affairs. She decided to leave them in pursuance of her fate in Khandi Pandupur—itself a victim of being the savior of an innocent widow—although she could guess what was there in store for her. She was ready to take risk and drew her action plan.

She returned to Pandupur village with her aged father as escort instead of youthful brother who escorted her in her first journey to Choudhury family proudly, but shown no interest this time and avoiding.

"He is young and a very short-tempered and may cause more damage to Bhagyabati's cause if there'll be an argument," justified her sister-in-law.

Parents however grudgingly agreed, but not her villagers. "He had a vested interest then, but not at present. He is no more the brother-in-law of influential Dibakar Choudhury," gossiped the villagers.

Bhagyabati and her aged father reached— 'unwelcomed and unwanted'—at the spacious doorsill of majestic Choudhury abode. "Alo . . . . alo . . . . ! Where did you come? To Choudhury House! They'll reduce your life to hell," forecasted Bulinani. "However . . . . try! What is wrong in trying?"

Her in-laws refused to accommodate her, she was standing in the alleyway. "What a fate of Choudhury daughter-in-law?" they heard a passers-by saying. Even her aged father was not told to seat and offered a glass of water; forget about of her care and honour of their family's daughter-in-law. 'What a family my parents had chosen? Once they were all praise of getting for me a bridegroom from the majestic Choudhury family, even persuaded me to abandon my school study for sake of marriage. I was told—I'm really a bhagya-bati, a lucky girl for getting a princely look husbandGod in widely known cream-of-the-crop in the Choudhury household. Dibakar and Bhagyabati will be perfect jodi, so I should give up my study in favour of marriage. I can't believe my so human husbandGod's parents can be so cruel and critical to their own daughter-in-law.'

As a last resort, her father pleaded before her in-laws revealing clan's seedling in her womb—only to be heckled and hissed and humiliated further more.

"Hello, old-man! How could this happen? And, if there is any, that may be an illicit one, planted before the marriage or after the death," roared Choudhury elder rejecting the revelation.

Later banging the door on their faces, he shouted behind the door, "This is nothing but an excuse to enter my house. Sorry to say . . . . so shrewdly designed!"

To their further despair, the father-daughter heard busybody Bulinani saying, "How can they allow a teen and a just widow to their house with a bachelor brother-in-law?" She buttressed his view quoting an example of an unpleasant incident happened just a few months back in neighbouring Pahalla village—that a widow retained on sympathetic ground in similar situation, eloped and married his younger brother-in-law against the wishes of her parent-in-laws, shamefully registering in the court. The elderly people present concurred with the view.

"What's wrong if at all this happen in this case? When we accept and adore widow marrying brother-in-law in widely revered epics Ramayana and Mahabharata why this shouldn't be acceptable in the real life in this age? Is Kaliyug more pious than Tretayayug and Dwaparyug?" Karan Mishra asked the village elders and chided, "You people use to say Choudhury elder is a learned man. But, how he simple doesn't know and understand this?"

"Alas, certainly intelligent to use his talent for his convenience . . . . opportunistic!"

However, there was no dearth of compassionates ready to share widow's sorrow. Among them, there were the likes of Jittu Pandu as well as lewd offenders of defenseless and destitute woman's modesty and sanctity in the disguise of extending a helping hand. She got lewd and competitive proposals including monetary and material assistants at village pond, at water pool, in the evening darkness while returning from abode of village stony deities after evening aarti, and in houses, where she worked as house maid.

"A destitute is everybody's sister-in-law!"

In the night, the lewd knocks at her door was a regular feature. Knocks used to continue till her aged parents coughed, informing their enduring presence.

"Sasura is there!"

Occasionally, Karan Mishra confronted the idiots and faced their ire boldly despite opposition in his own house. Gossiping was in the air as the natural sequence of event linking him with the Bhagyabati, but he was undeterred.

Bhagyabati rejected all those proposals, and in the process, denied her body the biological desires that a nun could at best ignore at her age. She turned to a biological and social unacceptable nun-hood at an age when others were enjoying with their bridegrooms. She wedded to the position of pious karmajogini which the society wasn't ready to accept; and although she knew she was vulnerable in view of her flourishing beauty in the beginning of teenage.

She felt bad about her beauty that gravitated Choudhury family to get her as their daughter-in-law. Her beauty and teenage were no more any assets for her. They were curses and liabilities, to be brushed aside at least for her peace. She recalled what she had read in the history books, about beautiful girls and women and war widows blemishing their bodies with black tattoos in order to prevent mauling lecherous invaders' imminent sacrilege of their pious body, fully devoted to the only pleasure of their husbandGods and platform for gestation of their gene, in Medieval and British India.

Even she thought of that option but was strongly disapproved by her parents 'who might have been still thinking that with the passage of time the cursed might reconsider her resolve, and would agree for remarriage. How will she manage in this hostile and lecherous world, all-of-alone? And, it is still not known what is coming from her fast swelling womb—son or daughter, or none with high infant death rate in rural India, even after decades of self-rule?'

Also, it came to Bhagyabati's mind, 'How long my fast aging parents would continue to protect me? . . . . However, I have to retain my pious Hindu woman identity for the sake of my husbandGod's seed growing inside me—nevertheless, unceremoniously.' She wanted to be a proud mother, the mother of the child her husbandGod planted in her so confidently and lovingly. She was determined, 'Whatsoever, I can't betray my husbandGod gene.'

Over the days, weeks and months the lecherous elements grew with numbers. Vulgar and lewd comments poured at her. "Zamindar Choudhury's daughter-in-law is on the road. She is a beautiful apsaraa. She is a queen. Just a few minute of bed-sharing is life-making! Who has such a luck? Bloody Karan . . . . spoiling!" ranted the calm surrounding of Bhagyabati's tiny cottage in the darkness of night. Some even were found making round of her cottage day and night elevating her to the status of a queen bee by default. Bulinani lamented with display of sympathy at a hearing distance, "How could she manage her so stunning body without infecting gent's caresses at this age? Or she has somebody visiting her in seclusion of the dark night? Let's guard who that lucky man is?"

And, all these came to the knowledge of village elders. They're disturbed. "This further spoils the image of the village languishing from the benevolent act of the village founder," discussed among them a few. Those, who opposed her returning to Choudhury family, repented. They urged the Choudhury elder in vain to take her back.

In a bright full-moon evening, her ballooned womb tickled, followed by the flow of saliva softening the path for arrival to 'the cruel world' the majestic Choudhury clan's GenNext, the Krishna of Khandi Pandupur. She cried with pain as sholla-dwaraja started expanding and opening. Mother was too old to attend her poor daughter crawling on the muddy floor with pain and father was a father, left with the only job of caressing her head and hands. The village mid-wife, assured to assist, told being requested, "Just coming!" which didn't happen.

"She may be fearful of inviting needless trouble from powerful Choudhury elder," cried among them the old feeble parents. But, Choudhury gene didn't take much time troubling much to his uncared durbhagya-bati mother.

The unborn wasn't that much troublesome during his stay inside his mother's progressively puffing up womb except occasional mild kicks and gentle inner movements that the Bhagyabati was instead enjoying, blissfully. She had been on most of such blessed occasions thinking about her husbandGod. 'Had he been there he would have caressed my expanded tummy with all pity—ticking it, kissing it and dropping down his ears to track what his gene is doing inside. He would have been very please with me for taking care of his gene to retain his family linage to the next generation despite all the pain out of extra load for which he is solely responsible. He wouldn't have allowed me to work or even walk carrying me in his hands to bed. To keep me happy and jolly for healthy growth of the child inside, he'd have taken me to Puri Sea Beach for fresh and clean wind and to Cuttack for a boat ride in the river Mahanadi. And, for God's blessing, he would have taken me to the sacred sanctum sanctorum of Lord of the Universe—Lord Jagannath. He'd have fought with his siblings for their assigning me any work at home. He'd have certainly admitted me well in advance in city nursing home for a smooth delivery. And, in case of slightest complication or difficulties, he would have liked to go for caesarian delivery.'

The child hurriedly landed on the muddy-earthen floor in the one-room-cottage and tasted the hard life that awaiting him as his destitute mother stood up being unable to bear the pain in the absence of an expert hand.

The baby's cry ranted the village skyline.

"What a pity?" The sympathetic Pandupurias lamented and Bulinani cried, "Majestic Choudhury family's child landed in a muddy cottage."

"An illicit child had taken birth. Alas, what will happen to this village?" chattered the Choudhury elder's camp followers.

There was no sweet distribution, no celebration and no folk dances such as palla and daskathia usually associated with new arrival to Choudhury's majestic abode. And even mamu-uncle didn't come on the fifth day of the birth with basketful of murri to munch by the ears of new born to weed out the possibilities of deafness, an age-old ritual. Every near and dear, even from her parents side, had already shunned her. Bhagyabati had forgiven them and consoled her poor crying parents saying, "I'm happy. If what's happening is written in my bhagya what can you do?"

"The child is none other than Dibakar's duplicate, a chand-ke-tukkuda," the village loudmouth along with the elderly village women, who out of curiosity stealthily visited her cottage in the darkness of new-moon night, were heard whispering among them.

Bhagyabati's claim found justification.

"But, who would bell the cat? No doubt, this is their child and it's up to them to take care. Why should we bother?" Bulinani murmured concurring with a few cautiously, out of fear of Choudhury elder. But, none came forward from Choudhury family even to see their GenNext.

She named the new born: Rabi, the rising sun—the son of Dibakar—'the Lord of the Day.'

Her single most objective in her life henceforth to make Rabi something any villagers could envy up without letting him ever feel dearth of any basic like many other such fatherless child used to encounter in this inhuman society. And, to show those villagers, and most particularly her in-laws, who had casted doubt on her physical chastity—as happened to any destitute widow leaving alone,—and propagated, "Rabi is an illicit child, an urchin, a guttersnipe, sonofabitch and whatnots."

The Primary School headmaster refused the child his father's name and Choudhury title in the admission register, arguing, "What's the proof that Rabi is the son of Dibakar Choudhury?" Bhagyabati could only plead.

"Yes, she has but . . . ."

"Bichara school headmaster! What could he do . . . . so scared of furious Choudhury elder," lamented a few with all sympathy to the destitute.

The broad-minded, and over and above, the rock-solid durbhagya-bati marched ahead as if she was unconcerned of all those castigations discarding them—'the by-products of frustration out of Rabi's performance and scholarship.'

"Or else what can she, a poor and abandon woman aspiring to be a Mother India, do?" Karan told to his small followers.

Khandi Pandupur

Pandupur is one among the countless villages dotting predominantly rural geography of coastal Orissa. This is the village which hadn't given birth so far any prominent social workers and nationalist who could help built its image, and so to be highlighted in the Orissa map akin to Suando or Bidyadharpur nor it had the size of Bhuban to be recorded as largest village of the state nor the village was producing world renowned handloom sari like Barapalli or appliqué like Pipli nor any of its resident had ever been occupied high position in state or national bureaucracy like Biranarasinghpur or Birapurusottampur or even its neighbouring Chabishpur.

However, it had a history, unparallel with other villages, its' inhabitants were proud of. Yet, it hadn't got the recognition for that. Instead, unfortunately, the villagers were hounded and humiliated for that by its neighbours.

Khandi is an Odia word—means incomplete. Pandupur was an incomplete village since its birth. So, the neighbouring villagers nick-named it—Khandi Pandupur, which was unbearable to its younger generation.

Puri is the abode of Lord Jagannath, Lord of the Universe as the name itself portrays, and all Odia social, religious and cultural activities have been in one way or the other attached to Lord Jagannath irrespective of caste, sect, race, etc. This is there since the day of arrival of Lord at Puri in mythological India followed by the visit of Adi Sankarachharya and construction of gigantic Lord's abode, a couple of centuries ago, which is still standing tall and intact that surprises modern architects.

Pandupur wasn't an exception. As per the tradition in the medieval period, many Puri Gajapati Maharajas, who were regarded as the highest servitor of Lord Jagannath, after winning war or annexing new territory with their then Orissa used to found a Brahmin village in his or in his main strategist's name contiguous to Puri as a memorial of victory, importing Brahmins from Kashi, the city of ancient India's Hindu religious learning, culture and Sanskrit literature and had assigned the task of protecting, preaching and spreading Jagannath Culture and the essence of The Rig Veda all around under the guidance of Pundits' of Mukti Mandapa located in the Lord's temple compound and Gobardhan Peetha's Sankarachharya, the official custodian of The Rig Veda and Jagannath Culture. Insipid Pandupur owes its origin to this practice.

Jittu Pandu, the founder of the village, wanted the village, that was to be set up in his name, was to be at a place which was equi-distance from the highest place of warship of Lord Bishnu, Jagannath temple at Puri and Lord Siva, Lingaraj temple at Bhubaneswar. The place identified was on the bank of once brimming river Ratnachira, inhabited by Jabans. They were requested to shift to not much far of a place to Danagohiri to facilitate the wish of Jittu Pandu. The Jabans obliged in the spirit of give and take respecting the religious sentiment of then ruler and his faithful lieutenant. The spirit of give and take and fellow-feelings were so intense that there was hardly any religious enmity in the area co-inhabited by both Hindus and Jabans for ages. Even they had been participating each other's festivals and social ceremonies. The world acclaimed appliqués designed and produced by Danagohiri Jabans adorned the sanctum sanctorum in the temples and exhibited as regular decoration stuff in village car festivals. It wasn't that both the communities were not aware of what had happened during Aurangzeb rules, in nation's eastern and western borders in the eve and wake of nation's independence and what had been happening in post-independence India in Hyderabad, Ahmadabad, Delhi's Chandini Chowk, Kanpur, etc.

The place had its own scenic beauty and charms with heap of white sand, tall sticky coconut trees, bulky banyan trees, thick mango and jackfruit orchids, screw pine bushes, vast plan and futile agriculture field on the bank of river Ratnachira among others that Jittu Pandu was looking for. But, Pandupur wasn't allowed to be a complete Brahmin village and was deprived of designated title of Sasan with non-establishment of all requisite religious institutions. The Bishnu and Siva temple weren't instituted and Shakti temple was half complete, mandatory for a Sasan village. The village wasn't inaugurated with a grand havan with offer of mahahuti by then Gajapati Maharaja of Orissa in the presence of Chief Priest of Lord Jagannath, not allowed to be noted in the Madalapanji, the official Gazette of Jagannath temple like other Sasan villages, and its inhabitants weren't allowed to seat in the Mukti Mandapa. Gajapati Maharaja of Puri, who sponsored the setting up Pandupur village in the name of Jittu Pandu, refused to accord such status because Jittu Pandu, his one-time confident, Chief Minister and Chief Strategist married to a lower caste widow 'allegedly infatuated?' by her beauty against the wishes of him and the Pundits of Mukti Mandapa, and lived in Pandupur.

Thus, justifying the neighbouring villagers to mock Pandupur derogatorily Khandi Pandupur and to its inhabitants Khandi Panduas even though in the government record the village name was Pandupur. And Panduas tried to explain those mockers saying what they had been hearing from their predecessors that 'Jittu Pandu wasn't infatuated by the beauty of the widow and so got married but he was moved by the pathetic condition of deprived widow forced to prostitution against her wish for her fault of being beautiful and captivating which she mightn't have chosen, had she been given an opportunity with the forecasting of her later on-life state of affairs.' Legend says, "Jittu Pandu fought with the marauding offenders of the widow's beauty and modesty, and rescued the poor defenseless lady. And, had he not married the destitute, she would have fallen in the hands of those offenders of her modesty, again."

But, all these explanations as if had no significance to the mockers who got in the background of the village an opportunity to embarrass and tease Panduas whenever they defeated Panduas or Panduas were in the verge of defeating them in any competitive sport or cultural programme. The opponents openly used the words 'khandi' to demoralize Panduas. This was used as a weapon to bring down the moral of Panduas. Even in one volleyball tournament the organizer printed Khandi Pandupur instead of Pandupur in the invitation letter, so Panduas refused their participation in protest which was viewed, "Panduas are running away to face opponent out of fear of defeat." The village lads sometimes hovered around the thought, 'Had Jittu Pandu guessed that his act of being savior of a cursed poor widow would be nightmarish to his successors in the village, he wouldn't have pursued that.'

Still, the languid Pandua lads never feel apologetic for Jittu Pandu's brevity. They were proud of him and of his act of brevity against steep odds. They were hopeful, despite repeated failures, that they would one day get rid of this humiliating tag.

'Who's there their that powerful Krishna?'

And, this type of behaviour was found spirited after India's freedom from British rule followed by land reform.

The snot-nosed Karan Mishra alike his other compatriots were digesting the humiliate tag of 'khandi' as there was no options and surrendered to live with the mucks till such time when they would be successfully repulse the humiliation. So, it was obvious that whosoever showed the sign of bringing honour to the village became the messiah for Pandupur GenNext.

The repeated losses or defeats in sports, cultural events and academics mainly due to poverty, illiteracy and backwardness had killing effect on the self-respect of Panduas. They were pondering among them, "Why the so-powerful Choudhury elder is silent over the issue? Does he never feel humiliated?" They found their answer in Karan's analysis, "Is our state leadership feels humiliated when they hear 'Orissa is the poorest and the most backward state despite blessed with all the ingredients of thriving state.' They've a vested interest in keeping the state backward and illiterate, and its people under-nourished. This serves their personal and family interest. Our leadership are scared of facing well-nourished and literate citizens of their own state."

There were some social, economical and cultural backgrounds. Once Pandua Brahmins owned most of the agriculture field; coconut, betel-nuts, mango orchards and other cash crops land in the area, leaving other villages around the radius of two kilometers for share-cropping. But, the situation changed with advent of nation's self-rule. The age-old protection, establishing their supremacy over other castes, Pandua Brahmins were enjoying under the aegis of Gajapati rules followed by the Zamindari System during British rule, vanished. With the latest development in the administration the supremacy of Panduas reduced and the vengeful surrounding villagers engaged as share-croppers for generations had taken over the ownership of the land as per new decree of government of Independent India igniting conflicts and ill-feeling between Pandua and their neighbours.

However, the Zamindari of Choudhury family having ownership of largest land holding wasn't much affected which left the Panduas intriguing. Many of them suspected of foul play. "The Choudhury family has relation and friends in Revenue Office, Collectorate Office and in the state capital. They might be used to retain Choudhury's large land-holding by some dubious and under table power play," the father of Karan Mishra used to say to the surprised villagers.

The village elders hadn't yet forgotten the dirty role of the father of Choudhury elder in closing down the village High School and exiling Biswanath Mohapatra from the village. And before that collaborating with British Police to get arrested the ill-fated High School headmaster in a fabricated charge of 'that he is instigating young school students to join anti-government movements.'

The elderly villagers also had witnessed the overnight switch over of the Choudhury from pro-British India to pro-Independent Democratic India on the 15th August 1947, surprising the entire village and its neighbours. Choudhury, neatly clad with khadi dhoti and punjabi and a Gandhi cap on the head, which could blindly rival any national level Congressman, organized Independent India's first flag hosting in Pandupur before the villagers even thought up how to celebrate the Big Day, a newly designated pious day not yet listed in their revered Mukti Mundapa approved Kohinoor almanac. Even they hadn't yet seen the design of the National Flag.

Choudhury, self-invited went to the stage and hosted the national tri-colour and delivered an eloquent speech resembling patriotic rabble-rousers the villagers had heard during Gandhi's stay at the nearby village Berboi, a couple of years ago. He praised Gandhi, and rose infected Nehru he had himself denounced not long ago saying 'the self-rule under these inexperienced and rowdy politicians, well-versed with emotive speech, would lead to social chaos and administrative disaster.

To the villagers' utter surprise, the Gandhi capped political leaders from Puri and the state capital started visiting Choudhury House after India's Independence. Of course, there was no neat and cleaned spacious cement veranda with chairs in any villager's threshold to treat the sophisticated khadi clad political gentlemen. Choudhury's was the only house in the entire village made up of burnt bricks and grey cement with wide painted pairs door, and white washed walls amidst khaki mud raised and dry hey thatched houses with narrow portico and entrance in entire Pandupur village. Thus, Choudhury elder had the overarching advantage over the others that Panduas reconciled with grouse.

"What a somersault and travesty of fact," the villagers looking at each other lamented in silence and disbelieve. Again they wondered, 'How could he replicate freedom fighters speech which he had never attended?' The elder Panduas had seen Choudhury persuading them and his share-croppers not to visit weak-long Gandhi mela. Even he had gone to the extent of cruelly punishing his share-croppers by way of withdrawing land from them who had secretly visited Gandhi's meeting out of curiosity that 'how a half-naked man like them with a stick in hand could attract such a huge movement against the century old mighty feringhee rule.'

The things started reversing in favour of Pandupur younger lots with Rabi along with his mother Bhagyabati taking over the responsibility of village lads' education. In Rabi, Karan and his small like-minded found their Krishna. He had to liberate the village from Khandi Pandupur to Pandupur. First of all, they had one objective in their mind to remove the humiliating prefix of Khandi from Pandupur. And, they had all concluded that 'it's only through education and occupying high position in bureaucracy they can achieve their objectives.'

Flying Hawk

He wasn't much tall, not that fat; a medium built man with pot-belly, bald head and fair colour, neat and clean, mostly wore spotless white dhoti often folded and a red stripped long napkin used to adorn his shoulder: a typical peasant. But, his mind was sharp; he was bold, cunning and confidence; and above all, he was capable. He had built a good network of like-minded followers in Khandi Pandupur and in the neighbouring villages vis-a-vis Choudhury elder. "For him, nothing was impossible. And, in order to achieve his wishes, he could go to any extent," Panduas used to talk among them. Although not much educated, yet he could fool at easy university degree holders, and judicial and government officials like a typical desi-politicians.

His name was Raghu Rath and he was the only one of his kind of personality in and around Pandupur village. And lately, the jokey opposition politicians from district headquarter town and state capital were found bee-lining before him like ruling party politicians did to Choudhury elder, the Panduas noticed.

"If there's any person in the entire village to whom the Choudhury elder be bothered for and visibly afraid of, he is certainly Raghu Rath . . . nobody else!" the peasants acknowledged on several occasions.

In the recent past, whenever there was any social strife, land and property disputes, and dispute concerning temple affairs, which were very common in any village in the locality, and during campaigning for Parliament, Assembly and Panchayat elections, the villagers were either in Choudhury elder's camp or in Raghu Rath's camp.

He even attended courts as hired witness and helped people charge-sheeted with criminal cases and rescued some of them from the long-hand of the law of the land. In one such case, he even gave witness placing his hand on sacred 'The Gita' in the court of district judge—'the Panduas used to discuss among others with grouse'—that an alleged murderer charge-sheeted by police was with him in his village away from the alleged site of murder, thus helped the murderer released.

He had proved his acumen ship in a land dispute case in which Pandupur village was certain to lose some joint land property to the neighbouring Palang village. He advised the techniques of getting adjournments of hearing, in one after another date, in one pretext or the other for indefinite period in the Temple of Justice. Raghu's logic was very simple, "If we cannot win the case; let the case not be judged, denying the hearing."

All these characteristics had established Raghu Rath as one of the most sought after legal consultant in civil and criminal disputes in the entire locality. Even, he had established himself as one of the most sought after adjudicator of family, property and land disputes, for out-of-court settlement, for some remuneration in and around Khandi Pandupur. This, in the meanwhile, had become one of his major source of income.

He was also ahead of his time on many social and developmental issues. 'He is a strong foresight.' When the proposal for building Panchayat road connecting Chabishpur bus-stop in the east to Delang railway station in the west through Pandupur alleyway with two lines of houses already existing on both sides came from the Panchayat Office, Raghu could foresee the deceitful intension of neighbouring villagers keen to humiliate Panduas. "Once this is there, the inimical neighbours would get legitimate right to pass through the village and would indulge in all such nuisance which would be difficult to tolerate, would spoil privacy of Pandupur village and destroy its age-old sanctity."

"In addition, there will have scope for accidents involving neighbouring villages which would heighten flow of bad-blood further," soothsaid Raghu Rath. The villagers appreciated his foresight and opposed the road plan irrespective of camp following. But, their efforts didn't work. The villagers had to file a petition to BDO and DM. They again turned to Raghu Rath. The proud Raghu Rath smiled with display of acumen ship, and shuffling his napkin between his left and right shoulders with privilege pride resembling Choudhury elder, told, "Again, this has to be done by Raghu Rath." He used this opportunity to taunt the Choudhury elder's camp followers, "Why not you go to that great Choudhury elder?"

"Pandupur is a closely netted village. The lane is narrow. The scope for further widening of road with increasing traffic in the future—as the road connects the major bus-stop and railway station in the area—will be limited in compare to other villages where public roads have been constructed in the village inner alleyways. Due to deep density of population and congestion the scope of accident will be high which may create law and order problem in a deeply caste-driven society. This will be another headache for administration which can be eased with ahead-of-its-time policy of today," he dictated.

Still, BDO was reluctant. Raghu had the reason, "How could a non-Brahmin appreciate the feeling and sentiment of Brahmins?"

Panduas agreed. They petitioned to District Magistrate with active leadership of Raghu. Finally, to the surprise of inimical neighbours with Panchayat Sarpanch and BDO in their side, and vowed to cause damage to Pandupur villagers' ego by hook or by crook, the plan was found altered and by-pass was drawn.

In Pandupur, nobody dared to challenge Raghu Rath and used to think number of times before doing anything which was one way or another concerned him and his interest. He was feared; and he was hated; and he was respected for his acumen ship, brain and knowledge. Even the powerful Choudhury elder on several occasions succumbed in front of him.

'The sacred matrimonial relations decided in the heaven are made for seven generations.' This was what the village elders used to propagate and reminded to Pandupur's prospective bridegrooms. And therefore, getting a bridegroom for a bride having no brother was a difficult job. This was a blessing in disguise to Raghu Rath. He went on marrying Prema, Preeti's mother having no brother and sister. His village mates mocked, "He is born to rescue such unfortunate bride."

"He is doing so, might be for some hidden reason," Bulinani however went little further jeering at him.

His acumen ship humbly calmed down the critics by rationalizing, "Should such girl remain unmarried, the brothel could be opened in the village for some lewd characters' illicit entertainment, and in the process, spoil the village's peace and healthy social environment?"

Whether what Raghu meant was his greatness or for a great cause—'which he alone could say'—yet he could make a good fortune in the form of dowry in a dowry infected society, none of his villagers had ever acquired in their living memory; and the right to inherit movable and immovable property of his parents-in-law after their passing away. Many in Khandi Pandupur were in fact envy of Raghu for such a great fortune that he knew. So, he used to ignore envious comments paying no importance to them. Once in a rather irritant moment, he commented, "When an elephant walks in the market, dogs bark; does the elephant looks back?" Thus, he hushed the critics of his judgments.

Like many others in the Pandupur village, mostly the believers of son-cult, Raghu didn't spare his wife till she gave birth to a son. In the process, he reduced his beautiful wife Prema, a show piece of beauty in the entire village at the time of her marriage and as admired by Raghu's mates, could rival the beauty of Prime Minister Indira Gandhi and for the Pandua women-flock, she was a replica of Goddess Parbati—to a perfect leather clad skeletal demonstration piece in the school science laboratory.

Raghu, by the time of reaching second decades' of his holy marriage, had fathered four children comprising three daughters and one son; the son was the youngest. In between, there were several abortions with the help of village she-quack—as per forecasting of soothsayer that this and that pregnancy might or might not bless them a son with one let passed—the village ladies lead by Bulinani used to gossip at the bathing ghat, water pool and in the religious gathering at temples pedestal.

For Prema, Raghu Rath wasn't just a husband but a Godly figure. She, an obedient and devoted Hindu housewife, obeyed her husbandGod, unquestioning. 'Well, how can I ignore my husbandGod's dictate, who did a great favour marrying me, when great many simple rejected my candidature just because I didn't have a male sibling?'

"Whatever, the son is a must," discoursed Raghu, "because, it's the son who would offer the funeral cake and water to us and my clan forefathers' souls, and run the clan further to the next generation."

"Or, he mightn't like to encounter the embarrassing situation like his parents-in-law while searching a bridegroom for his daughters," reasoned Bulinani.

When the family planning officials visited Pandupur, Raghu Rath successfully led the majority of villagers against educating in favour of small family with two children norm irrespective of son or daughter to the dismay of minority school dropout few. He went on quoting the famous statement "Population is the wealth of the nation" of the first Prime Minister of India who rebuffed the illustrious industrialist J R D

Tata's appeal to tame the burgeoning population which was draining economic progress of the nation. And, he convinced the gullible villagers giving the example of large family of Lal Bahadur Sastri with one short of half dozen children that he had overheard from the lawyers discussing in the bar of the court quoting newspaper report during one of his several visits to district judge court as a haired witness.

As usual, the vulture's preying eyes of Raghu spotted academic excellence of child Rabi as he was doing extremely well in his Primary and M. E. School studies, even without external support of tutors like others', and he recognized Rabi's result was due to the teaching skill of his mother Bhagyabati. In the meanwhile, he'd gathered the information that Bhagyabati was class topper at High School level. Hawkish Raghu plotted to take advantage of that for the benefit of his children at no or little cost.

In one fine afternoon, the busybody Bulinani found, the branded sonofabitch Rabi was playing with Raghu's daughter Preeti at his doorsill and the village refuse Bhagyabati was passing pleasantry with his ascetic wife, at their backyard. She rubbed her eyes in disbelieve and broadcasted the news in no time throughout the length and breadth of the village. Peasants rushed to the sight to check. They were united with their view that Raghu must have something in his mind for his do good to.

'A social space is provided to the mother-son, they were denied so far,' Karan Mishra waiting for the moment told self. He was enthusiast as he had already identified in Rabi the character he was searching for for his scheme of things.

In due course, Rabi was allowed the free interaction with Pandua tots, and played along with them. And, the sponsor got for his children free academic help, guidance and tuition. The mother-son too were enthusiast. They got a new lease of life, and hope—'unaware of the clever Raghu's hidden agenda that they may be dumped at easy—exhausted very similar to left wing extremists and right wing fanatics have been by the nation's jackal-clever political outfits.'

The plan worked and his children including Preeti, a batch mate of Rabi, started improving in their studies.

Rabi transformed from a guttersnipe to a 'rising sun' and participated being part of village teams in the events and contests organized in Pandupur, and against the neighbouring villages. With his inclusion, Pandupur started shining that Pandupur lads were dreaming for since long. And, the mother Bhagyabati too was allowed to participate in different religious, cultural and social activities in the village albeit guardedly.

PAPA'S LESSON

The village elders wanted Rabi, the best ever of Khandi Pandupur, to go for higher study in Revenshaw College, the Pandua peasants believed the best college of the state where the state's revered and the world renowned scientists, educationists, barristers, politicians and freedom fighters had their education.

"The best deserves the best!" Everybody had one opinion. So far no Pandua had ever got a chance to enroll and study in Revenshaw College whereas the boys from neighbouring villages—Chabishpur and Palang had been studying there. For the Panduas, this was a prestige issue. Karan Mishra, the moving spirit of Pandupur's GenNext, without loss of time gathered admission data of previous years and checked whether their golden boy would get an opportunity in Revenshaw College along with hostel seat with his matriculation marks. He worked with renewed ethos as he saw in Rabi's result the scope for execution of his scheme for emancipation of his loved native village from Khandi Pandupur to Pandupur.

"Ooh yes," Karan jumped up, over the moon with his finding. "Rabi will get admission in Revenshaw College," declared Karan Mishra. But, regarding Preeti, he was silent. Rabi was eager to know as Preeti turned to him dewy-eyed, restless. Yet, he couldn't ask as he thought, 'Who I am?' However, he stared at his revered mentor asking but down his head as soon as Karan Mishra turned to him. In the golden boy's silence and uncomfortable up and down of head, the sincere mentor could read the anxiety, and with an affectionate smile, cheered, "Our little girl also has done extremely well," and rued, "but, I doubt, ... sorry . . . . whether she can get a seat in Revenshaw College? . . . . So what, if not Revenshaw, she'll study in BCS College, Puri; equally a very good college."

"Preeti is a girl. What she'll do with her college study? She can better be admitted in nearby UMG Mahavidyalaya at Satyabadi if at all Raghu wishes for her higher study. She may not be required to go to distance city and stay in malicious hostel or mess," advised Bidiyadada.

"You're very right, dada," happy Gandua seconded and Dukhi, Vallu, Sarua and Hadu, the slackers applauded as if their consents were very much in need, while another elder opined, "She'll get a good bridegroom with her First Class matriculation degree. Let her college education left to the discretion of her would-be in-laws."

And, the golden girl ran away almost crying as Dukhi suggested, "Bidiyadada is right. It'll be better if she studies at Satyabadi. She can stay at village. This year, Intermediate Science course is opening in UMG Mahavidyalaya and graduation after two years," and continued looking at Karan, "Let Rabi read wherever he likes. He is for our village a non . . . en . . . ." and stopped abruptly as Karan started munching his teeth.

Upset being unable to find a comfortable solution for his golden boy's companion and bombarded with uncalled-for suggestions, the snot-nosed Chanakya turned to Preeti's unsolicited mentors—Dukhi, Gandua, Vallu, Sarua, and Hadu—and yelled in order to relieve him from pain, "You've all this information? Why don't you go for your own study instead of wasting time gathering all these uncalled-for information?" silencing the unwelcomed mentoring to the greater relief of disturbed Rabi.

Rabi was too unhappy about the pouring suggestions of Panduas, and he had all sympathy to the poor girl. Furthermore, he wasn't in a position to rescue the girl, he loved so much, placing his opinion. He started silently praying to Pandupur presiding deity for the girl's higher study at least in BCS College, she deserved. 'And, if I'm admitted in BCS College where she can get admission, it would be so far so good.' He was interested to place her opinion. 'In fact, for what I'll offer my opinion? And again, who I am? Just a friend—for the villagers—to say the least.' And, another thought, not the least and much mind-bending was, 'Can I manage at distance Cuttack without Preeti around me? She was no doubt a big inspiration.'

Rabi went on evaluating all those pros and cons in his little mind. He was feeling weak to the girl, and for her causes. And, this was growing faster. He was melting psychologically. He was nervous. He also recalled the reaction of the golden girl when he just mocked her saying WHP. He was disturbed but silent; he mused, 'Again, the elderly people talking. Who am I to intervene?' He concluded, 'No, ...' And, he kept quiet.

'She fasted day long on each Friday for me for my better result during this hostile summer. She loves me so much. What I've done for her?'

In the meanwhile, Raghu Rath arrived from nowhere in the venue. Debate stopped. All present turned to him. From his body poise, the debating Panduas could understand, there was something in his mind and he must have decided as he used to do in several other issues in village affairs. The peasants were apprehensive.

He had a piercing glace at the small peasants' congress. And, Gandua walked towards field, Galu slipped towards Sandha bazaar, Vallu crawled towards bushes, Sarua marched towards nearby fence to drain body's watery waste, Hadu towards the shop to light a time-pass and Dukhi downed his head to clean his nose with napkin. In short, all the unsolicited well-wishers did get something for ready engagement, frightened of jackal-clever sharp-talker. And, Karan Mishra had a grudging smile.

Raghu imposed, "So what, if not Revenshaw College, there are many others, equally good, where 'both' can study together, and help, and take care of each other like they did in their schools."

He declared in his trademark authoritative style paralleling the practice prevailing in India's grand old political outfit built by the hard work and sacrifices of crores of party workers over a century, but now literally owned by the celebrated widow and her son with subordination of a handful of spineless opportunistic family sweepers.

"Ravi and Preeti will study in BCS College, Puri."

He hijacked the proceeding as he had come prepared for that and he was so forceful and situation was such that his decree had to be acceptable to the major stakeholders: the mother-son twosome and the peasants of Pandupur who started seeing the future development of their village in Rabi's academic performance.

And, he left the venue leaving the Panduas clean-bowled and awful, and drained all the studies they had done on the issue in the thin serpentine water flow in the river Ratnachira.

In this imposing decree, Karan Mishra although felt disappointed like the other well-wishers of Rabi present there, yet another thought that cropped up in his mind that if the jodi culminated in their marriage—'possibility of the same is very much there with continuous togetherness of the two away from parents'—Khandi Pandupur can retain two gifted talents instead of one. And, the thought—the Choudhury elder can be better contained with jackal-clever Raghu Rath in their side—overwhelmed him.

Rabi, who was observing the unfolding happening sitting quiet, found reason to rejoice with Raghu uncle's dictate. He wanted to thank Pandupur presiding holy patron deity, for her kind to listen to his prayer, for Raghu uncle's bold decree.

'Mama will certainly agree to go by the decision of Raghu uncle,' he talked to him.

'Why should I not tell the blessed news to the disheartened girl? She'll be happy,' thought Rabi but not before paying a thank homage to Maa Garachandi. Jubilant future hope of Khandi Pandupur walked . . . . walked looking back . . . . and checking . . . . and ran—as the overjoyed mentor looked at. He stopped in front of Maa's temple and paid the obeisance before running to the doorsill of Raghu uncle . . . . but struck off finding the door shut up on his face by none other than revered Prema aunty. And, Preeti wasn't even seen at the window, nor her any siblings.

'Is it that the mother-daughter not happy with my silence when the village elders were debating my future almost ignoring Preeti? May be? Sorry aunty, sorry Preeti! What I can do? Don't you know I'm a small child? And that I am son of a poor widow. In future, I promise, I will certainly talk for you. Please forgive me this time! I have a good news . . . . a big news for you,' he went on talking self.

He knocked the door . . . . he waited there. Notwithstanding, the door didn't open. And, he was soon sidetracked as he heard from mama, "Rabi, you've not eaten anything since morning? Come and take your breakfast."

And, to the Panduas, Raghu's decree meant something else. "Has Raghu decided to keep the jodi together for a future relationship?" Bulinani started blabbering where not.

"Not impossible in case of opportunistic and futuristic Raghua," the peasants concurred with Bulinani. While one Pandua growled, "Hawkish Raghua knows very well—without talented Rabi by the side of Preeti in her study, she is a big zero." Others nodded in agreement.

———◈·❦·———

However, in Rath abode, the patron mother wasn't happy with the decision of her intelligent, clever and judicious, and revered husbandGod as she was praying to house tutelary deities for an early opportunity that could separate Preeti from Rabi, the son-of-a-widow, not recognized in the village community, like many other humble mothers with grown up daughter back home opposing tooth and nail their daughters' any interaction with the boy.

She was apprehensive of the relation between the pair at this age. For her fear, there was no dearth of instances at her parental village as well as at here in Khandi Pandupur—of grown boys and girls misusing the softness of their liberal parents, maligning their parents and family and village images. Even she'd quoted the suggestion of her parents who questioned Preeti's evening stay in Rabi's house. She even dictated Preeti what to wear when going to Rabi's house. She forced the girl to wear tight bra, and full length salwar and kurti or full length sari with bodice, blouse and petticoat to the utter discomfort of her in tropical humid climate.

She had tried to convince her husbandGod on several occasions soon after the matriculation examination was concluded to separate the pair. "This is enough! For school study, they were together. Now, since this is over, let's stop their whiling away together," she requested, and protested before her husbandGod. But, her husbandGod wasn't listening and simple ignoring 'as he has another agenda and is waiting to accomplish that.'

With the publication of the matriculation result, Prema saw an golden opportunity in her hand. The result was a blessing in disguise and she bent on to utilize that. She wanted to stop the further study of Preeti. "Or, if she'll go for higher study, she can do so at nearby Satyabadi, travelling from village on daily basis," Prema told.

"What's your problem if Rabi studies at Revenshaw College, Cuttack," speared highly disturbed Prema to her husbandGod as he descended on the low stool for dinner. As if this was the first occasion in the living memory of their children—this ever submissive Prema was so stern in asking her husbandGod that she was almost resembled the look of Mahishamurdini Maa Durga, the children had seen in village dance-drama Mahishasura Badha.

"Baap . . re . . e! Where was her this form!" They were abacked—being prompted by their grandma—and looked at their reverend mother, surprised.

'What is cooking in the mind of the reverend mother?' Preeti pondered awful. 'During the last few days, mama is itching at the sight of aunty and Rabi. They're so good and so modest and so knowledgeable. My outstanding result is due to them. They worked for me so hard. The villagers are all praise of them. Now, aunty is the most sought after tutor of the village kids. Even the neighbouring villagers started inquiring whether she could spare sometimes for their children at higher fees. But, she is so dedicated to Pandupur cause that she refuses as she wanna concentrate for Pandupur children. Once's an outcast, she is a demi-Goddess for the Pandupurias now,' Preeti went on evaluating and acclaiming.

Raghu smiled and went on taking the dinner without any tress of worry, displaying. Reverend mother appeared irritated and fumed.

Raghu again smiled.

Grandma, Preeti and her younger siblings were terrified.

'Latest Raghu's smile seemed little mischievous!' The children felt and so they were awful. A stressful situation.

Breaking the silence, the respected father elaborated confidently with visible display of his acumen ship, "So far, you ninnies have not understood me. Have you ever thought that Preeti's success is purely due to Rabi and his mother? And, Priya, Pinki and Pradeep are doing well simple because Rabi and his mother have been guiding them. I don't want this setting to be disturbed."

After flinging a satisfactory glance at Preeti, he justified, "I'm just using Rabi and his mother. Do you foolish understand?"

"Wha . . . t?" Preeti retorted instantly lifting her head. She was in anger and pain.

'Quite displaying! She is lost and broken.'

"Let's accept the fact that none of us are doing any favour to anybody. Rabi and his mother became socially acceptable in village milieu because of us when their own blood shut up their doors on their faces. And, our children got free and quality teaching and guidance in return," reasoned Raghu and concluded contentedly, "I don't find anything wrong in this arrangement—morally and ethically. I believe—this is clear, and understood to you all."

This was like a sharp arrow piercing her heart and destroying her life-valve beyond recognition. She couldn't believe what she heard. And, she couldn't hold her. Her heart started bleeding. She thought, 'How could I be so treacherous to someone so dear to me and helped me so much without any expectation?' She asked to her and questioned in her teeny innocence, 'Is it the civil world we live in?' She wanted to rush to the golden boy and her revered aunty to reveal before them what is going on behind them, and to pray to village deities to rescue her innocent and affectionate aunty and love from her double-crossing papa.

"Now, you decide, both will go to study in the same college residing at distance Puri," fumed Prema not being so convinced with the reasoning of Raghu while serving dinner to the children.

"So, what? Now, Preeti needs an escort. We can't send grown up Preeti to Puri or to elsewhere . . . . all-of-alone. And, I know, we cannot get anybody so faithful than Rabi . . . . No doubt, Rabi is a jewel, but born to a wrong mother . . . . he is unrecognized one," replied Raghu convincingly.

'Whatever that may be, Rabi's talent and virtue are acknowledged. What more one should expect,' Preeti felt elated despite all the agonies. This was the best comfort that the girl could draw. 'This is a feeble light at the end of a long dark tunnel,' Preeti comforted her.

However, she couldn't eat. She wasn't with her father on so far as the exploitation of innocent Rabi and his poor mother, who were crying for their social existence, were concerned. She'd all sympathy to them. Her hands trembled. 'Food refuses to fuel the daughter of a traitor.' She could't collect the food from the plate . . . . She strongly felt in her. However, she gobbled up whatever her thin crane hand lifted to her mouth as there was no other way out. She was trying to hide her feeling. She didn't like to expose her feeling against all these filthy and irrational thinking. She wanted to leave the place as soon as possible, at least to rescue her from hearing the filthy scheming.

But, she wasn't so lucky to hide her feeling from her vigilant mother for the moment. The reverend mother's on-guard eyes caught her taking a full size hard red chili—certainly unmindful and disturbed. The mother frantically bawled widening her eyes with fire, "Hey, hey ghungi . . . ., what are you taking? Have you lost your good sense?"

Everybody's attention zeroed in on Preeti's crany hand.

"Don't be crazy. Don't be stupid! This is the reality. Think for your future. A bright career is awaiting you. You're born to a socially respected family . . . . unlike that boy, who after all a son-of-a-widow . . . . origin not recognised, and branded—guttersnipe. I want my golden daughter marry to a prince like a princess. And, I promise, I will ensure that. You just cooperate," the reverend father soothsaid.

Preeti kept on thinking day and night. For her, there was hardly any difference between the darkness of new-moon night and the summer bright sunny days. On occasions, she strongly felt to reveal what was going on behind her Rabi and her dear aunty, but failed as if someone was pulling her.

'Wait! Don't be hurry! . . . . fast thing fast!'

She thought, 'Won't this disturb and hurt my Rabi and my dear aunty?'

Again, she was also hunted by the thought of, 'I'm no different from my papa, hiding the truth for my own selfish end.' And, she continued to think, 'No, let the truth prevails. And, let the consequence has its own naturally course.'

Yet, she failed. 'I've a selfish end to accomplish like my papa . . . . Yes, I have . . . . so what?'

"I'm no different. I'm on a par with my papa—a traitor," she cried in her sleep necessitating sympathetic Priya and grandma's kind attention. They were indeed cooperative.

THE VILLAGE IMAGE

'How could she refuse the suggestion of the person who had helped her and her son to be part of the village society denied mercilessly for long by all powerful Choudhury elder and his henchmen?' The obliged Bhagyabati accepted the suggestion of Raghu Rath without questioning. She agreed to admit Rabi for higher studies in BCS College at Puri. 'Reason: Puri is comparatively much nearer than the distance Cuttack and where her obsession, the little girl Preeti can get admission.'

Again, Raghu Rath justified his suggestion by arguing, "How could a sixteen years old child so far not exposed to city life manages himself all-of-alone in a big city like Cuttack?" The mother found solid merit in Raghu's latest argument. She didn't rejected the advices of the villagers, who seemed to her were envious of Rath children's academic excellence, yet she did not go by them. She consoled them, "Bhaia, you know, Rabi is a little boy. And he, except studies, plays and whiling away time with friends, doesn't remember and know anything. Even, he often forgets brushing teeth and bathing, and eating in time. He'll be completely alone in Cuttack. If it is Puri, our Preeti will be there with him. Further, how our little girl will manage alone in Puri. She is our village image. I am very fond of her. She is such a beautiful child."

She went on speaking as if Preeti had been her major obsession. Mentor nodded with approving smile and privately told, "Why bhabi don't you say, you see in the golden girl the persona of your would-be daughter-in-law? She would be a perfect match to Rabi; there is no doubt in it. The jodi looks like Radha and Krishna."

Bhagyabati smiled with reservation. 'But, will Raghu Rath agree? A big question? Still . . . . ,' Bhagyabati hoped for the best, confining in her.

The other aspect which was uppermost in the mind of Bhagyabati and hunting and demoralizing her since the matriculation result was published and the boy's going to city for higher study was almost finalized, was her fear of losing Rabi, her soul, her eye pupil, her chand-ke-tukkuda, her husbandGod's avatar, and her only reason of living in this hostile world—to the city girls. Although she had full confidence on her object-of-fondest-regard, yet something somewhere in the remote corner of her mind was pulling her; and alarming her every now and then.

"The city girls are like she-witch, jinn. In their eyes, they've magic wand. They're glamorous. They wear naughty dresses . . . . exposing. They bathe with intoxicating perfumes to pull the gullible but talented village boys' like queen bees. They can go to any extent to grab their choice and targeted prey," prefigured Bulinani furthering Bhagyabati's fear.

'And, my Rabi is cute, humble and talented and looked princely like his father, can be impressed by any girl. And, he is so simple and so gullible! . . . . Ooh my God, what I'll do? Bulinani is cent per cent right!'

Whether she was thinking of getting Preeti as her daughter-in-law as talked so often by the village ladies at the bathing ghat, temple pedestal and evening chatting these days—"Preeti and Rabi could be a good match to each other"—or not, was a different matter altogether. The village ladies too were also susceptive of Raghu Rath's mind that they gossiped, "If Raghu could marry Prema against all oppositions of his parents and relations and he can get that justified, why he can't get Rabi as his son-in-law although—'whose child Rabi is?'—hasn't yet been recognised and accepted?"

Once Bhagyabati had opened her mouth being repeatedly ambushed by the village ladies, and opined, "A so-lucky can get our lovely, educated, talented and beautiful Preeti as her daughter-in-law." And, she left everybody guessing. "God knows whether the durbhagya-bati is so bhagya-bati . . . . !" taunted Bulinani.

She had also thought of, 'What is wrong if Rabi will study at Satyabadi? I would be free from city girls tension,' but got conducted with the thought of, 'will it be correct to curtail the fate of the child to study in the district best college because I fear I may lose him to other?' She was inconclusive. She, a poor, a destitute, a harassed, and after all, an abandon woman, and a mother couldn't be able to decide.

'Rabi and Preeti should study together in the same college. Both will guard each other.'

'The villagers are ecstatic. They wanted my son to read in district's best college, if not state best, so far none of the village lad got this opportunity. Who I'm to frustrated them? After all, it is their blessing which help my chand-ke-tukkuda to achieve this milestone. No, I shouldn't disappoint them,' concluded confining the destitute lady within her.

'After all, Preeti is our village girl. How will she, a little girl live at Puri alone,' thought Bhagyabati by recalling the ugly behaviour of city bridegroom companion to Pandupur girls on the day of village girl Gita's marriage. 'Again, if it is Puri, the little girl will be all along with my Rabi, and can report back to me any move of jinn city girls,' the thought comforted her. 'The little girl is my agent and this is what I should expect for my service to her study.' And also, she was padded with idea that 'it could be the wish of Lord Jagannath to grow Rabi in his lap, and would give me a reason to visit the Lord.'

Rabi had to go to Puri to submit their admission forms; his first ever visit to any city. Karan Mishra, the inspiration and the mentor of Rabi, and their shield against the formidable enemy—Choudhury elder and his battery of sycophants, tutored the Khandi Pandupur's future 'hope' and 'aspiration' all that required to be done for filling the forms in the full attention of the golden girl and Bhagyabati. The girl was repeating every step of mentor's illustration for better recollection of Rabi like a palla palia because she knew Rabi used to forget like Lord Shiva aka Bholanath, she once heard aunty shouting at him saying, "You're a Bholanath," for not bringing the stuff from the market she had assigned him, forgotten.

Later, she picked up a piece of paper and a pen from the rack, and requested Karankaka to draw a rough sketch of Puri city indicating the route Rabi would pass through and got the list of the works to be done so that Bholanath could understand better and would get the assignments done without missing.

The elderly two looked at the girl with appreciation. Overwhelmed Bhagyabati however couldn't stop with this much as if the affectionate little girl deserved something more. "Our little Preeti is really a jewel, an intelligent girl like her father. Isn't it Karan?" she acclaimed the golden girl straightening out her long and thick waterfall ponytail and adjusting her necklace dangling at her neckline. She embraced the little girl pulling her to her broad chest with affection, kissed at her forehead caressing—all that for Rabi's envy.

The sight was itching to the boy. His eyes widened. In addition, the little girl's stealthy frowning pushing out of her slim red clean tongue proud of being cared by none other than her aunty while still on the lap of her, and of course, to itch Rabi which were certainly unbearable.

"She is my mother," Rabi cried and shouted, "You motti have slowly but steadily stolen my mother from me."

Another frown blasted him in no time.

"Mind, you're my mama," later Rabi roared at Bhagyabati. He was almost on fire. He pulled the little girl from his mother's hug with all the prowess of Dhitarastra's son Dushasana. Soon, there followed free flow of fisticuffs, palm-slaps and pillows dashing as Karankaka looked on. He didn't interfere—seemed enjoying the heavenly play of two blossoming birds, free from any social curb.

But, the mama-aunty had to act. For her, they were no more small kids. 'What the villagers will think? What the parents of the girl will think,' she envisaged. Some of them had their piercing look into their tiny cottage through the revolving door as always, she noticed. She wielded her guardianship. She warned with words alongside raising her hand with a stick, kept to weed out the invading stray dog, cat, and crow into the cottage finding the door opened on occasions, in order to bring order in his tiny cottage. "Rabi, you're very jealous and naughty. Has she taken away your mama? She is a good little girl. Mind, you are not anymore a small kid. You're grown up. You must keep in your mind what other people would think about you," and later grabbing bolshie Rabi, she despaired, "I doubt how you'll manage away from us?"

"I'm not a small kid . . . . but she is? Aah ha . . . . what a great comparison? This is all because of this motti?" cried Rabi. "Always cajoling my mama. Don't you have your mama? Go . . . go to her."

"All your fault! Most of the time you don't stay at home," taunted the mentor lightly. He laughed as if he was confident that this was just a game. "Don't worry bhabi; they're before us small children, playing. Once they're out and away, and on their own, they'll make up and manage themselves," Karan assured foreseeing. "This used to happen."

Rabi dressed up and gathered all the documents required to be submitted along with forms with full subordination of the little girl. He touched the feet of his revered mother and walked out hanging the bag by the left hand.

Preeti reminded, "Have you taken the note?"

"What? I don't need this. You better keep this to check on my return; you brainless, dim-wit, suspecting lot," Rabi replied briefly and walked confidently, non-stop unbothered. As Bhagyabati insisted, the little girl run to Rabi and forcefully pushing the piece of paper in the boy's chest pocket, buzzed in his ear, "Ooh . . . my Lord, please don't be angry at this poor servitor," scripting an envious sight that could hardly be ignored by preying eyes of Sarua, Hadu and Gallu hawking at a distance.

An irritating huge sneeze from malicious Sarua blasted the Pandupur skyline. And, the little girl cried, "Shit! . . . . Saruabhai, your cursed nose-goo will never stop? What a bad timing? Where you were? You can't wait a little more? Do you not know, Rabi is going to Puri to fill-up forms for admission? . . . . you sneezed! Don't you know this heralds bad omen?"

And she prayed in her, 'Hey Maa Garachandi, kindly take care of my Rabi!'

"Your Rabi? These days you are saying my Rabi!"

'Yes, my Rabi.'

"No, not your Rabi. How he is your Rabi? Say your friend Rabi. Your . . . . friend!'

'Sorry, my Rabi. What's wrong in saying my Rabi? He is my Rabi, my Rabi, my Rabi . . . .' Fight went on in the peahen's mind as her eyes were running after the flying peacock with new enthusiasm. Rabi climbed to the height of the canal bridge past the river Ratnachira and before descended to other side invisibling him to the peahen . . . . till the evening, raised his hand and shake, Preeti crying for.

The bad aspects of city that Rabi had overheard from his seniors in the village and heard from his school mates having city exposures, and he himself viewed in Odia films let-loosed before him one after another. A half pant and half shirt clad with slipper in the feet, the gawar Rabi however gathered confidence and got out of the crowded bus on Puri Grand Road amidst leg biting and body fighting from co-passengers. Half naked rickshaw pullers, throwing semi-munched betel nuts with each word pronounced, and spraying intoxicating red betel-juice intermittently in all directions, swamped him like wasps almost blocking his existential breath. They competed among them to serve unsolicited the poor and awkward peasant. But, the clever peasant didn't believe rickshaw pullers as he'd heard that rickshaw pullers cheat passengers, most particularly new comer from the villages, with exorbitant charge.

'Again, how do I pay my mother's hard earned money to cheaters for a just two kilometers ride, a distance I had been covering for my High School study along with mama's little Preeti bare-footed on rutted road during the last four years?' He thought and decided to walk to BCS College guided by Preeti's sponsored and Karankaka's prepared note in one hand, and asking passers-by on the other whenever he got confused.

He appreciated mama's little girl for her acumen ship. 'Really, she is an honest, caring and intelligent girl, true to her papa. I may be Topper but she is . . . . I shouldn't have pulled and slap her for a small thing. And, I should not chide her saying motti. Really, she is not that fat!'

He felt indebted to the little girl in absentia. 'How much does she take care of me? Mama is right. Sorry Preeti, please forgive me! And, but, you shouldn't frown at me. Really, very irritating! She is no doubt—very beautiful too. Who has such a bhagya to marry such a beautiful, lovely and intelligent girl?'

He went on comparing Khandi Pandupur's little dancing beauty with passing pompous city girls on the way in this new world. He searched in them the beauty, innocence and character of the gawari Preeti. 'No, these girls aren't any match to our Preeti. For sure, they looked attractive, glamorous and sophisticated. But, these are sweet less pumpkin flowers.'

As he entered the college campus, he felt he was lost in abundance. There were long queues of tall buildings on both side of alleyway. As he was pushed checking with passers-by to reach 'Form Sales Counter,' he found one more row of deep red structure. Seemed there were hundreds of class rooms, inside the class room large numbers of long table-chair benches, so many laboratories, a big library and thousands of students and hundreds of teachers. The students, teachers and staffs were all busy. However, there were some exceptions, he noticed.

The exceptions—appeared seniors and quite aged—were whiling away their time hurling comments on passing girls and teachers. He heard, "This is Raju's girl friend." And, yet another revealed, "You know that smarty Economics lecturer, adjudged Miss Vani Vihar, 'What is her name?' Right Madhu Parija—now-a-days, wearing a gushy gold ring and always found along with English lecturer that romantic Ranjit Mohanty. He has Dharmendra's figure. Perhaps, finally, she exchanged ring with him. Alas, what a long chase from GM College to Revenshaw College to Vani Vihar, and finally, to BCS College!"

While another reminded, "The oldie Kesabkaka was asking for the preparation of this year's Miss BCS list."

"Just wait yaar! Let the admission of First-year Intermediate is over. See . . . . last year being in hurry, we had missed some real beauties and smarty in the list!"

The peasant was ill at ease and amazed. He checked in him, 'Whether, I can manage myself in this environment? Quite alien!'

In the meanwhile, he reached the 'Form Sales Counter' in the first floor. There was a long queue and mild commotion. Rabi looked around. He was no doubt an odd-man-out, appeared had come from a different world. This strongly reminded him what Prafullasir used to tell while explaining lessons from social science subject, "There's a clear divide between India's seventy five percent ruralities and twenty five percent urbanites despite several years of self-rule."

However, the odd-man in Rabi gather confidence, and stood in the long queue, and moved unconcerned of teasing comments of, "Don't push this gawar; he'll cry!" and frequent boot biting at his slipper clad foot from front and back. Also, he had to hear a middle-aged man—'most probable a guardian,' Rabi thought—crying and breathing hard, "These gawars are grabbing the seats from our children."

"What to do? This is the policy of government . . . . to allot seats on merit!" lamented another.

The gawar too found in this some justification and thought, 'Why should our villages have no good colleges like cities? We must restrict ourselves in our domain.'

In the meanwhile, Rabi turn came as the long serpentine queue moved on, and while paying money he spelled out names—Rabi Pratap and Preeti Rath—for issue of two admission forms for Intermediate Science.

"What Rabi Pratap? What's the surname," asked sarcastically the pan chewing salesman sitting inside the counter behind the pigeon-hole, words half-missing. He, it seemed to Rabi, had allergy toward him and his likes, and was in unison with the man spraying venom against the handful few uncharacteristic gawars' present in the queue.

"Sorry Sir, ... no Sir, ... yes Sir," fumbled Rabi. "My mother doesn't cite. I write Rabi Pratap. This is there in my certificate Sir!" replied nervous gawar progressively gathering confidence in this hostile alien world.

"May be an urchin ... yaar!" He heard the sardonic flak from behind in the queue.

Rabi turned back, despaired, and speechless. He was teary. He heard the rubbish. He bore the flak as this had been part of the mother-son's life since the days he started understanding these rubbish as a child at Pandupur, and in its surrounding villages he had so far ventured out. However, he went ahead filling the Forms, seating on half-damaged class room bench in the long and broad college corridor forgetting the past and forgiving those small. But, while pasting the photograph of pretty Pandupur little girl on her application form, a passing-by bullied senior akin to Bollywood's bad character, grabbed the photo, lecherously kissed the photo, and commented, "What a beauty? A rose, an angel from muddy hamlet."

'Yes, she is a rose. She isn't only an angel but an archangel. What more you bloody scoundrel says?' was instantly in the mind of the poor peasant.

For Rabi, this was his first of this kind experience in the city. He was unspeakable. He was in the midst of a hostile environment without knowing the means how to face them. Nobody was there to guide him; nor did he had the prowess of film star Amitabh Bachhan. In the nutshell, he wasn't in a position to seize the photo from the physically strong villain. He was weak and deprived. And, at the same time, he couldn't leave his dear mama's little girl's photo to the offender. He questioned him, 'Am I that Rabi who on the day of Gitadidi's marriage chased the city bridegroom companions' for their filthy comments to Pandupur girls, for which Pandua elders' were all praise of me?'

An unfortunate and bichara gawar run past the offender of Pandupur image with soaked eyes, almost begging, till the grabber was kind enough to throw the photo to be cruelly booted in the crowded corridor.

'Each mount of shoe on his village image's photo was like kick on his face.' He collected the photo risking booting on his bare tender fingers. He cleaned that with soft cotton napkin he was carrying in his bag like Preeti cleaned her face with her dupatta with all care and sincerity on the day of result publication.

'Paid back!'

"Place a lovely kiss . . . . yaar! She is so beautiful . . . . mind-blowing," he heard another passers-by prompting him.

A remote thought—'Won't this be again vandalized if pasted on the application form by the counter clerk and his colleagues, so hostile and rough?'—agitated the gawar further. He didn't like to paste. He repeatedly read the instructions printed at the bottom of the form to check whether the application could be processed without the photo. He wasn't satisfied with his finding. The indebted Rabi went to the sales counter pushing in the crowd to cross check with inimical counter clerk risking some more sure-short flaks.

True to his assumption, he was heckled and particles of semi-munched betel-nuts wrapped with red pan juice dotted his white shirt as the city biased counter clerk went on bellowing, "Well! Don't paste! We'll reject the Form to feed our hungry dust-bin!"

Finally, he surrendered to the dictate of 'heartless' uncompromising 'Rules and Regulations' governing admission process.

As the gawar was leaving the campus, he looked back to the red building. It was awful red, the signal of danger; and was saying to him a bold 'No!' This echoed in his thought machine, and he concluded, 'Not for us—we peasants. Let's study in UMG Mahavidyalaya. We can cycle from our village. Both Preeti and I can go together. Again, we can stay in our village with parents. Not very risky some! And, the cost will be much less. Same syllabus and same university. I must propose this to mama, Raghu uncle and Karankaka.'

On the way back to Pandupur, in the bus, the meek gawar considered what to say to mama, Preeti, Karankaka, villagers and friends who might be waiting to him impatiently, to listen from him his first city experience. He was undecided whether to say the truth or not.

'Saying the truth may cause damage to my self-image, and possibly hurt Preeti. Is she so broad minded to bear what happened to her photo? She may possibly question: What a man you are? You couldn't save my photo from vandal? She may question my ability to protect her in distance Puri, a responsibility will certainly be placed on my shoulder? Or, she may be scared of going for higher study at Puri. Will her parents and well-wishers trust me? Won't the village mates question my inaction against the photo grabber? Sarua, Gallu, Hadu, Dukhi and Sallu bhais will certainly laugh at me in coming to know these. So also Bulinani! They together will make me a laughing stock. . . . . Again, how could I not say, what happened, to those who love and adore me so much? And, Preeti who fasted for my better result. Such a beautiful friend, I'm gifted with.'

'Whatever; Preeti will never mind, so understanding, so accommodative! She know—I'm a child and new in the city. She'll have all sympathy to this poor boy, if not other!'

This and that confused him. He was at complete loss. In the midst of this chaos his shattered head rested leaning on the front seat; in fact, relieving him from incontestable thought for the time being. He almost slept . . . . The bus conductor's loud call, "Chabishpur, Chabishpur!" waked him up, and again, he was pulled back to that undeniable thought. A guilt-ridden and morally lost Rabi, dropped down at Chabishpur bus-stand, sheepishly.

Rabi, the self-infected guilty, wanted to go straight to the custody of his mother stealthily covering his face very similarly to the criminals and politicians—cut red-handed—used to cover their face while taken to custody by police. He wanted to first apologise to his mother for his inaction against the offender of her little girl's modesty in the paper photo. He slowed down his walk from Chabishpur bus-stand to Pandupur, and even skipped probable cycle lift on the way hiding him behind the banyan and mango trees, and screw pine bushes whenever whatever was available, aiming to reach home in the cloud of evening darkness.

However, all his efforts went in vain. He perhaps hadn't comprehended: how could he, the future hope of Khandi Pandupur and the very soul of lovely little girl, be remained undetected from all of them?

He didn't look at any body and even didn't listen to anybody's call, being caught in the sprinkled waxing crescent moon light despite his every sincere effort to remain reclusive. He locked himself inside his tiny hut, lying down on the cot covering his ears with thick pillow.

Nobody in the village had ever seen such a Rabi since he was socially accepted in Pandupur village, years ago. The mentor was disturbed. A shocked Preeti waiting to him sitting on the steps of Maa Garachandi temple looking at the slope of distance canal bridge since early afternoon, rushed to aunty, away at Lord Gopinath temple on the other side of the village for evening aarti.

And Gandua overflowed happy, Galu coughed teasing, Vallu growled jeering, Sarua swelled taking satisfaction breath and Hadu shuffled napkin between his right and left shoulders sneezing. They were rapturous seeing pain in their queen bee's face. And spicy Bulinani was not far behind, "Alloo . . . . , alloo . . . . in one visit he is so changed. God knows, what will happen to this girl when hero will continue to stay in city for years?"

The little girl escorted by her dear aunty entered the tiny cottage—concerned and despaired. Rabi begged the girl to spare him, the first of its kind which was beyond the girl's anticipation. A dewy-eyed little girl couldn't believe what her ears heard and what her eyes saw. The deer eyes turned to the motherly aunty in deerly innocence. The mother too couldn't understand all that was going on in front of her. Bhagyabati pulling Rabi to her lap on the cot—messaged him, consoling. A chilling silence rained the cottage, which used to overflow with talk of study, game, cozy chit-chat, mock, grimace and occasional fighting whenever these two budding flowers were inside the cottage inviting envious peeping of lewd peasants and Bulinani through the cottage's revolving door.

All kept quiet with their respective obsession in their mind. A pin-drop silence rained inside the one-room-cottage for a couple of minutes.

"He is tired. Let's message him!" Bhagyabati murmured. And, Radha in no time caught hold of Khrishna's feet as if she was awaiting for the green signal for the service and started messaging. Services went on till the self-infected guilty melted.

The despair mother in search of opportunity to break the silence found the bag carried by Rabi in his trip to Puri bulky. She asked halting, "What's there?" But, Rabi was silence. Preeti stealthily got the bag to aunty. To her surprise, Bhagyabati found there were sweet packets, and so she asked, "From where, you got the money? What happened? Have you not purchased the Forms? Have you not taken launch? And the questions went on one after another being asked."

Rabi, twisting his body, told, "No, no, I walked from bus-stand to college and back. And, I saved money for . . . ."

"So, to purchase Preeti's favourite sweet rasogolla? Ooh, you had slapped her before gonna Puri. And so?" the mama-aunty ran off looking at the sulking little girl, flattering and continued, "This is okay. So, you're tired."

"Rasogolla is your favourite. I've bought it for you," the apologetic Rabi tried to convince. But, he was caught lying as the sulking girl in slowly but steadily changing comfortable milieu in the tiny cottage let dropped, "Aunty's favourite sweet is laddu." This provoked the snotty to blast, "Okay baba, this is your favourite. You gobble up this! Mama, there is another packet. Don't show that to this motti. We'll share that with Karankaka."

"That must be laddus!" claimed the jubilant girl.

The ecstatic mama-aunty acclaimed, "See, how much he likes you? This is a good boy." And, the peahen poked at the peacock's leg.

"Ahh!" the peacock screamed and kicked the peahen shouting, "Mama see, she is munching my legs. Hey motti, you munch the rasogolla, not my legs."

Bhagyabati, gently slapping the boy, told, "Don't always say motti to my little girl." And spattering the girl, she added, "She is so lean and thin, fasting for so long . . . . my chul-bulli!"

"Mama do thou know, she was fasting for my good result . . . . such a mad girl! What uncle and aunty would be thinking?"

Preeti peeping at the revolving doors told, "Nobody knows!"

Bhagyabati embracing the girl told, "Priya knows this and has told me. She's so nice a girl like you. Your parents are so blessed!"

Rabi resting his head on the lap of mother reluctantly illustrated the bitter experience he had gone through in the day in the new world. And, later, he appealed not to go to Puri for study and requested mama to allow him to get admitted in UMG Mahavidyalaya, where Karankaka had done his

Intermediate. And, he continued justifying, "The Purians are right when they say we, the villagers, are grabbing their children's seats in their college. Tell me, where their children will study?"

"Again, if I study at Satyabadi, I can stay with you," he pursued justifying. "How you'll alone live?"

The pensive mother consoled, "This is the world where we were living yesterday, we're living today, and we'll be living tomorrow." And, she went on saying and exhorting, "That, who leaves scared, is a coward, and have no place in this world which otherwise is a very beautiful creation of Lord Jagannath, the Lord of Universe. Look at me! What I've not experienced in my life? Still, I am here; I have not run away. And I hope my Rabi is a Rabi, the Rising Sun and a beacon of 'hope' and 'aspiration' of Pandupur, and your departed father. Mind, what will your papa's soul think, and what will I tell him when I'll join him after you've grown up and manage your affairs? Shall I tell him that his son is a coward?"

"You're a small kid, and ergo, regarding the choice of college, you must go by the elders' wisdom," she advised him.

Preeti contented with Rabi's fellow-feeling for her and concurred with aunty's counsel hiding her happiness and ecstasy while messaging the tired legs of Rabi replicating Gopapura's love-stricken devoted Radha in bower of creepers, which has been illustrated in innumerable Odia literatures and has been sung by folk dancers with lively demonstration that she used to watch as she enjoyed them the most, with her soft palm and thin fingers, and occasionally piercing Rabi's legs with her enamel painted sharp nails, along sparingly slapping with excuse of keeping at bay hungry mosquitoes as and when she found aunty's eyes were away.

With the third round of howling of she-jackals at distance screw pine bushes on the cremation and big tank mound reminding passing of time from evening to night, aunty asked the little girl to get back to her house, she wasn't very keen. Bhagyabati had to escort her to her door step with a lantern in hand. As they started walking out, Rabi shrieked hiding his face in the pillow, "Mama, I'm sorry . . . ." They halted and looked back, questioning. "I've not submitted motti's, sorry WHP's, sorry your little girl's admission form."

"What . . . . ???" the mother reacted, as if the sky had fallen on her head, in disbelieve.

"You know our village elders are against her study at distance Puri. Again, what will she do with her college education? She is a WHP. As and when the train will come she would board them dropping a few drops of pretending tears. And as you told, we must go by elders' wisdom . . . . Don't blame me. Sorry! I can't help."

Bhagyabati was stunned and locked up with the revelation. She couldn't believe that her very eye pupil—she was so proud of, and so also Pandupurias— could think and do what she heard? 'What the parents of the little girl would say?' she thought. She was scared, breaking down. She looked at the little girl in fear, and in repentant. But, to her utter surprise, the little girl cried hugging her, "Aunty, listen! Rabi is teasing me repeatedly saying: motti, WHP, and whatever comes to his mind."

And, the poor mama-aunty was in quandary: in one side there's the fickle son, and in the other, a lovely girl hungry for 'love' and 'affection.'

The aunty-mama was in arctic silence. She appeared stunned, disturbed, and was almost in pool of sweat. But, surprisingly, the little girl wasn't that disturbed. She smiled as if she was least bothered, and responded with display of determination, "Whatever you do that doesn't matter much to me any way. I'm accompanying you to Puri to ensure my dear aunty that you aren't trapped by city's Supanakhas. Is it okay, you smart?" And turning to aunty, requested, "Aunty, let's go. He's playing and trying to fool us." As Rabi twisted back on the cot being surprised hearing the bravado in the girl despite sky-falling news, the girl frowned him pushing out her narrow tongue, and genially told, "I've seen the form deposit receipt thou buddu have kept on the rack. Bye . . . . good night! Ta . . . ta, ta, ta . . . . !"

"Thanks a lot, my little girl. You've saved me! What a mad talk? Rabi, you've nearly killed me!" the aunty-mama breathed happily.

As the twosome walked one by one in Pandupur alleyway with matching jingle of nupurs on the little dancing legs, they were blasted with sneezing, coughing, spitting, howling, chattering, yelling . . . . and whatnot's breaking the silence of tiny hamlet's skyline. 'Might be from Gandua, Sallu, Baia, Galu, Patia, Vallu, Hadu and Sarua,' they recognized with grouse but moved on alike two huge elephants with all sympathy to poor guys.

However, the aunty's little girl couldn't have an easy walk despite the caring escort; and couldn't have a comfortable dinner despite the reverend mother's assiduously cooked dishes; and could not have an easy sleep despite Priya and grandma's consoling and sympathetic talk.

One thing that echoing in her mind, heart and thought, all the time and all the while, was: 'What's a virtue rules in that tiny cottage of the mother-son and what is there in our sprawling house with grandpa and grandma, papa and mama, we siblings and innumerable relations—manufacturing a living bereft of LOVE and fellow-feeling.'

THE GUARDIANSHIP

'Who I am to decide about my future?' thought self-effacing Rabi and continued, 'How can I refuse the advices of my fellow villagers who are so happy of me; indeed, a great acknowledgement. They started seeing in me the future of our so insipid village, crying for development matching with others . . . . Now, I ain't of my own. Nor, my mama's only. I am of the entire Pandupurias. I have to lift the Khandi Pandupur to Pandupur in the mouth of mockers. I've a task ahead.'

He reconciled with the reality and agreed to go to Puri to pursue his higher studies. Further, he imagined, 'If I'm not going, Preeti, mama's little girl and her obsession, too may not. And, Pandupur's hope of getting one of their lad studying in district's premier college will be scuttled.'

Excited Bhagyabati broke open a few baked clay money pots packed with fifty paisa and one rupees coin, her years long saving for the great purpose, buried under the floor in one corner of the cottage in the petty thief infected village. Rabi and Preeti were surprised. As directed they soon got into the lengthy act of counting of those small denominators in the sweaty summer guardedly closing the doors, scared of anybody's notice which might lead to shoplifting. Total, there was rupees five thousand, three hundred, forty rupees and fifty paisa only, not enough to finance even two years Intermediate study, forget about financing up to graduation which could qualify the golden boy to appear for the most rewarding and villagers' dream job—OAS or IAS, the job if achieved could make them proud like Chabishpur peasants.

'Am I dreaming high that my child is undeserving? Will he not be able to accomplish the villagers' hope and aspiration?' the destitute mother went on thinking in desperation.

A dark pale cloud invaded the tiny cottage. Bhagyabati was disappointed. This was beyond her presumption. She sat down with a heavy breath, two hands over her head . . . . hopeless. She was dumbfounded.

'Was I not rubbed by my in-laws all my jewelleries on the day I was destined to the widowhood, those would have been a great use today. I should claim those from Choudhury elder; I'm the sole owner as the jewelleries were gifted to me by my parents,' she thought. But, she was too scared of mighty Choudhury and his furious firing eyes and thunderous roars, she had seen on the day, she and her humble and simple old father were at Choudhury's doorstep begging for a just space. She was also afraid of the man's political and social clouts. She'd seen the visit of neat and clean Gandhi cap adorned politicians escorted by large number of bulky and heavy mustached people resembling film villains and occasional visits of khaki dress costumed smart Police Officers along with heart threatening red cock-hooded constables to Choudhury abode. In no time, she gave up the unfeasible thought leaving the matter to be decided by Lord of Universe, the last resort of a poor deserted woman, many of her kind had gone down the level of selling their body for peanuts, and living a hellish life.

The mama-aunty looked at her chand-ke-tukkuda and the little girl alternatively, speechless and breaking as she couldn't find out any suitable and dependable way out at her hand reach. 'Should she give up the dream of sending her scholarly child to study in district best college so far had been a dream to any Pandua? Should she allow the rare achievement slip out of her hand?'

The little girl analysed, 'This is like the end of the road for the mother-son. And, Pandupurias' hope! Even Rabi wouldn't get government monetary assistant distributed to reserved categories students by the democratic, socialist and constitutionally vowed welfare government as Rabi is born—allegedly!—to an unrecognized caste. His economic condition is worse than the many reserved category students.' She resented the government policy with all sympathy to poor golden boy.

'Will the brightest perish under the shroud of poverty?' Preeti cried in her. Alternatively, it came to her mind, 'I should request my parents . . . . ,' but stopped short up proceeding further as an after-thought dictated, 'Mama won't even if papa agrees. For mama, this is a sure-short blessing in disguise to execute her plan.' She closed her eyes in desperation . . . . her eyes dewed that in no time got noticed by aunty who embraced her consoling.

'What a cruel joke of the All Mighty, our age-old social system that our elders are craze to preserve, and the democratic governance that our leadership developed and force us to feel proud of?'

In effect, the much maligned city culture infected Odia films came to the rescue of desperately searching and breaking up Rabi. He examined in his tiny memory cell the scenes of Odia films poking his head and curling his heir with his fore finger spreading his body on the cot. He got up, he walked-out, and walked-in in the tiny cottage. He examined in him his capacity to tutor school students in the city setting. In the village, whenever his mother was sick or got herself engaged in household works or attended to any call he took care of the children his mother tutored. The mother Bhagyabati, the most acclaimed tutor in the village also appreciated his teaching. And after all, he also guided Preeti that Preeti and her father appreciated, acknowledged and acclaimed. The village girls including Lilli—demonstratively envious of Preeti's academic achievements—hadn't spared any conceivable opportunity to disparage with comments. "Preeti's better performance in matriculation examination is due to Rabi's tactical guidance. Alas, what a life-time mistake! Had I glamour Rabi, the thing would have been different? . . . . Again, what to do, the parents didn't allow? Preeti is surely very fortunate one, to born to a very wise parents," he had overheard on occasion.

Confident Rabi looked at distress mama and Preeti, and flashed a self-assured smile. He was displaying . . . . displaying his confident as he grabbed an easy and simple solution to a very unsettling problem. He wanted to tell but hold back blinking his eyes till to be asked. He left his pitiable audience guessing and questioning. But, not for long. His audience was so dear to him. Mama and Preeti's poignant eyes melted in him all his just gathered jovial mental strength. He gave up, and he revealed, "I'll take up home tuition of school children during my college off hours."

The audience heard him in apt attention but didn't flaunt any excitement. Preeti and Bhagyabati were found reserved and thoughtful; and even surprisingly, they were found in league not to cheer the jubilant boy for his hard find as if they knew and had studied the option before hand and found this was not viable. Both had their own reasons, unknown to Rabi. However, they couldn't spell out.

Preeti, fearful of city girls, wanted to reject the proposal on the very face of the proposer but failed. 'How, I, a prospective traitor in making, could do so?' The thought pulled her back. She caved in and buried under the burden of thought her hawkish papa infected in her mind. And the mother wanted to foot down the just discovered financing formula as she recalled the much maligned city culture infected Odia film in which she had seen the gullible but gifted village lads were stolen from their crying near and dear by the city based thinly clothed smart, glamorous and pompous girls.

All at once, the excited Rabi was very dear to them. They were as if unanimous not to spoil the boy's excitement if couldn't cheer, remained silent leaning their heads down, and at times, looking at each other in suspense and telling something to each other in their silence. 'How could they, and that too, when they don't have a ready solution to the problem,' they were thinking.

Rabi looked at them astonished. He couldn't understand why they seemed not in league with him and asked inquiring, "What's wrong with you people?" Still hushed. They exhibited studied silence; they were unanimous. He leisurely hanged around inside the little cottage sparsely looking at them. He thought, 'Perhaps, they aren't confident of my ability to earn for my study!'

'Whatever they think, I'll prove that I'm right and they are wrong.'

Later, he shrugged unhappily and folding his dhoti above the knees and shuffling the towel between left and right naked shoulders, left the cottage, indeed satisfied with his finding, leaving behind the suspicious to burn their time and mind.

They had to move to Puri with the arrival of pink intimation card, which had evaded their mentor, a victim of social envy prevalent in the village, informing college admission date and commencement of class. In the meanwhile, the preparation for admission and shifting to Puri started in full swing under the supervision of their enthusiastic mentor, the first ever village grown Intermediate from nearby UMG Mahavidyalaya. Tin box, lock and key, dhoti, napkin, slipper, mosquito net, bed sheet, etc. etc. were purchased from Athasanka weekly market. Order for one pair of shirt and trouser were placed with tailor at Chabishpur.

Besides, Karan Mishra had another task to perform as the head of Pandupur Youth Club and the mentor of Khandi Pandupur future 'hope and aspiration'. He had not forgotten the act of sabotage of insipid Khandi Pandupur's post-master, a camp follower of malicious Choudhury elder, and the father of half-a-dozen children—none could go up to seventh standard, which could helped him to retain the post-master job in the family, despite his every sincere effort that he occasionally used to rue in public in desperation. And Karan although was unhappy and angry, reconciled and reasoned with all pity, 'What the poor man at last could do . . . . out of frustration, and at the mercy of Choudhury elder for the bread-earning job?'

Post-master delivered the pink colour intimation letter carrying the message of admission date on the last day of admission to Karan Mishra though the same was posted two weeks ago. Although Karan could arrange the admission fees in such a short notice, yet he couldn't reach Puri traveling more than thirty kilometers from Khandi Pandupur, in time. That sabotage of post-master, many in the village alleged could have been done at the behest of Choudhury elder, killed Karan's childhood ambition of studying in BCS College. He used to deplore, "Might be for my fault of being born in insipid Khandi Pandupur which I wouldn't have chosen, had I given an opportunity before my birth. Let's bear blaming the nature which has deprived us scrupulously to choose our place of birth."

And Karan didn't want the same should revisit in case of his 'bow and arrow', so far the brightest of his village, and the future 'hope and aspiration' of Khandi Pandupur. He strictly instructed the golden boy to remain vigilant from the time of post-bag bearer reached the post office to till the bag was opened and all the letters were checked, stamped and shorted before sent for distribution.

"Bholanath will forget!" the mother screamed with fear. And, true to the presumption, he had simple forgotten and had been somewhere far from the eye-reach of her at the scheduled time. But, the little girl was in full attention. She used to be there before the time so also Sarua, Vallu, Sallu, Hadu, Dukhi and their likes with their all luffadami requisitioning aunty's picketing from a distance.

"Karan must have suggested for this," shrieked Bulinani and spiced, "check all the letter one by one. Or else you'll lose lifelong opportunity to roam on the sea-beach cuddling together with urchin away from eagle eyes of suspecting mama."

"Bulinani, you're great! You know beforehand everything, you are a Kalijug sheSahadeva," screamed the loafers.

Bhagyabati thanked Raghu Rath for his right foresight. 'He is certainly convinced that Rabi cannot manage without the little girl by his side . . . . so he insisted Rabi's admission in Puri . . . . may be? Certainly, he is very caring of my fatherless child . . . . if so, is he eyeing Rabi's hand for the little girl?' The thought revitalized in her mind.

In between, in one fine evening, Rabi returned home excited to share a very important piece of information with his esteemed mother and dear Preeti.

'Pandupur Volley Ball Team under his captainship and revered Karankaka's guidance won the match against their arch-rival Chabishpur team, captained by his tormentor of peace in Chabishpur High School, Lalu Sarangi.' This was a big success and so this was a big news, first of its kind in the history of Khandi Pandupur. That too closely after he had topped the list of Chabishpur High School matriculation result.

"The bad days of Pandupur has started receding," Karan Mishra predicted. In Pandupur, everybody agreed that this win was because of Rabi and his solo performance and so he certainly deserved a special treatment. The mentor, who accompanied the team as team manager, illustrated bit by bit the match progress to the surprised Pandua elders. "Rabi's 'Topspin serves' were perfect and 'Passer and Outside hits' completely destroyed the formidable defense of Twentysixpur team. He had completely hijacked the match with his brilliant strategy and maneuvering. And, the audience was spell-bound and cheering, despite vengeful presence of furious Bishu Sarangi, were almost by the side of our team hardly seen in history of Twentysixpur Volleyball Tournament in last ten years."

Rabi rushed to mama and Preeti as soon as he and his team landed at Pandupur with the trophy, leaving behind the celebration the village lads had organized as directed by the mentor. He wanted to tell them how his team tear-downed the myth of Twentysixpur team, which had been champion over the years with all the matches in their pockets.

Besides, he had a special information for the sweet girl: that one of his 'ball hit' had broken Lalu's mouth— he was expecting a special treat from the girl for this—, that used to spit foul comments and ugly rumours over their friendship, spilling out blood.

But, to his utter surprises, he found him unwelcomed. 'This too when all the villagers, but any body from Choudhury address, are erupted with joy, and mad with celebration.' But, the much loved instead were found deeply engaged in a talk under the shade of dim she-devil lantern light and this was as if, it seemed to him, they'd lost something or were sure of losing something in near future, very dear to them.

He wanted to say to his mama, 'Yours chand-ke-tukkuda's team, which yours chand-ke-tukkuda himself coached and gloomed, have won, and so, I, yours chand-ke-tukkuda deserves a Special Treat from you too.' But, the pensive atmosphere in the cottage subdued the excitement in him. A depressed Rabi started searching, 'What's going on in the mind of his affectionate?'

He correlated this situation with many such repeating during last few days. His searching mind however reconciled, 'Mama may be thinking: how I'll manage in distance Puri without her for days, months and years. Since my birth, I have never been away of her eye reach? This kind of thinking is quite obvious on the part of a mother. After all, she is a mother. And she may be sharing what's there in her mind with her little girl . . . . Or, are they scare of intriguing silence at the ever active threshold of fearsome Choudhury address since the publication of result?'

———◈◈———

With fast approaching admission date, Rabi became more and more serious and growing mature with approaching responsibility. He wasn't alone to go; he would accompany Preeti, his village girl, his friend, his mother's little girl, and most importantly Pandupur image. He was more concerned for Preeti, the grown up Preeti—no doubt an archangel—the village lads used to admire; a few even had gone to the extent of throwing lewd and envious comments: 'The guttersnipe, the urchin has stolen our angel. Our eye refresher!' which Rabi didn't appreciate, and detested but stop short of protesting in view of his prevailing social status. He was very scared of hearing the cursed word 'guttersnipe', 'urchin' which had been an adjective to his name. Lately, the frequency of use of these adjectives had been little less in view of his all round performance bringing laurels to the insipid Khandi Pandupur, and being protected by the snot-nosed Karan Mishra, who didn't spare the teasers, on occasion with physical challenges.

Rabi was fully contented with the fact that for his mama and villagers, the safety and honour of Preeti was very important. 'She is the image of the village.' He recalled the incident that beautiful angel's simple paper photo could stir up the eyes and the mind of city guys. He was scared of repeat of such incident physically. 'Maa Garachandi, please give me the massive strength and capability to preserve our village sweet sweet little girl's safety and honour, I'm going to shoulder,' he silently prayed to Pandupur presiding deity. Simultaneously, he hadn't spared the nature, and questioned the same in his childish innocence, 'Why the nature has given Preeti, the angelic beauty—the major reason of aggression of lewd elements against her modesty?'

'Again, she is so simple and childish; she may be carried away by displaying superfluous people as conducted in films.' He wanted to advise the little girl to remain cautious about her costume, and her dealing with city guys alike Indian police officers, administrative authority and politicians who used to advise college going girls and working women in the cities and metros being unable to guard their modesty which was a simple law and order problem despite stately prowess at their command, and they were mandated to protect as per the law. But, the thought 'that he may be considered weak by the girl' pulled him back. Again, he notion, 'Am I really so weak that I can't protect the modesty of Pandupur image and my friend who loved so much to me, and whose father had come forward risking possible wrath of powerful Choudhury elder in providing me and my mother social space in Pandupur social setting?'

On the day of their departure to Puri, the Pandua lads like Sri Ram's Banara Sena was at the doorsill of their village star's tiny cottage, ready to help in whatever way, small and big, ignoring his background and bad-mouthing of Choudhury elder's sycophants, loafers, and above all, the village busybody, Bulinani's. Some of them even defied their parents. They'd in their mind: their hero, coach, guide and future 'hope and aspiration' and their icon going for his higher studies. They had full confidence on him as he had already exhibited his capability and commitment. They wanted Rabi to grow in all spare of human activities and bring laurels to Khandi Pandupur—relegated by deprivation, backwardness and humiliation—help boosting its image.

"Rabi, on coming puja vacation, we'll launch cricket team in our village. Chabishpur and Palang villages have already got their cricket team," told school drop-out Satya Pani. The ever inspiring mentor promoted, "Rabi will learn the Rules and Regulations and the techniques of the game in his college and will guide you during his visit to village in coming puja vacation. Don't worry, this has already been assigned to him. Shortly, we'll arrange funds for purchase of bats, balls, wickets, globes, ..."

Since early in the morning, the mother Bhagyabati was busy. She plucked the flowers before the sun raised. After the pious cleaning of her body in the village weeded pond and wearing pious sari kept reserve for special prayer on special occasions she was hopping from Maa Garachandi temple to Lord Gopinath to Lord Banamber and finally to Maa Mangala temple located on the different side edges of Pandupur—presumable protecting the village from the evil spirits—with basket full of china rose, tecoma, jasmine and stramoni flowers, and diyas with pure ghee purchased exclusively for the occasion. She offered Special Prayers to all the village deities kneeing before them with all her devotion and sanctity repeating the act she'd done on fifth day morning of her marriage at Maa Garachandi temple. She prayed for all the blessing for her chand-ke-tukkuda and for her obsession, the little girl, indiscriminating.

Preeti too was almost eager. The golden girl, with Rabi's choice white churidar, green kurti and white dupatta along with engaging jingling nupurs on her tip-toeing legs, was flying between Rath abode and her aunty's address amidst sneezing, coughing, chattering . . . . ; and instigating papa and Rabi to be fast. She found her reverend mother Prema was sulking; and not so enthusiastic and cooperative. Preeti thought, 'Let's simple ignore her! Time will tell who is right and who is wrong?' Of course, she was not disrespectful. Priya and grandma were cooperative; however, guardedly. "So didi, finally, you're going to be relieved . . . . ," Priya mocked checking whether anybody was at the hearing distance.

The mentor supervised the departure preparation. Banara Sena loaded the little cargo on cycle carrier and tied them with coir rope. With the arrival of Raghu Rath at Rabi's doorsill sneezing, coughing, chattering at a distance stopped, and Sarua, Gandua, Valu, Baia, and their likes receded towards village alleyway in no time. Finally, Rabi and Preeti kneed before the mama-aunty and touched her feet. The mama-aunty embraced them and put on their foreheads the sacred vermilion brought from the village presiding deities and offered them sacred prasad to eat and worn out flowers to carry as the protective shield from the evils at the distance address. Later, aunty was found telling something to the little girl at her ear—'seemed very confidential.'

"The booking is over. Sarua, Gandua, Valu, Baia, ... you loafers, now look for some other," Bulinani murmured.

And the mentor murmured smiling, "This little girl has become an obsession of our bhabi. She is so caring." As they started moving following Raghu Rath and Karan Mishra to Chabishpur bus-stand on their way to Puri, the drop of tears started rolling down on early wrinkled cheeks of the mama-aunty. She controlled her, and waved her hand till her eye pupils scaled down at her eye distance, to the other side of high canal bridge beyond the river Ratnachira bordering Pandupur village on the east.

But, the absence of Prema at Rath's threshold was intriguing. Suspense hunted the mama-aunty, 'May be, she isn't happy to send her little girl for higher study. Or is it, she doesn't like her grown up daughter to accompany Rabi?'

'These days Prema isn't so frequently speaking to me . . . . avoiding!'

Karan Mishra and Raghu Rath helped the children board the bus with their luggage to the land of Lord Jagannath, the patron God of Orissa at Chabishpur bus-stand on the Jagannath Road.

Finally, Preeti accompanied Rabi, her long wait dream, free from the preying watch of reverend mother; irritating sneezing, coughing, chattering . . . . from omni-present Sarua, Gandua, Valu, Dukhi, ... and blabber mouthing of Bulinani. Together, she travelled to a different world to deal with and to live in. She was in the custody of her most affectionate persona in this living world: her dream boy, her heart-throb and the Pandupur's rising sun—Rabi.

"In Puri, you're new. You shouldn't go to anywhere alone without informing me. You do not know the people in the city and their mind," Rabi, the guardian buzzed at the girl's ears hitting his chest at her shoulder in the jam-packed bus and continued, "You're gro . . . . w . . . . n . . . . ," but stopped short of completing as he got a smiling reply in low voice, "I'm grown up. Okay baba, Okay! You're my unquestioned guardian, bodyguard, escort. And why do not you say you're my that famous cow-boy Krishna!" Further, she bowed her head confirming that she agreed to all his commands.

The overwhelmed guardian looked at the preying eyes of co-passengers in confidence and wanted to tell them, 'I'm this girl's omni-present Krishna. You can't simple disrobe her. If ever you dare, you will certainly have an embarrassing fate of the mighty hundred children of the blind emperor—Dhrutarastra.'

The girl was in a different world. She wasn't in a mood to be disturbed by the unsolicited advices of her guardian and frequent killing air-horns of speeding bus vying to reach next stoppage overtaking fellow buses to catch waiting passengers. She wasn't scared of accident like the other passengers of the bus in view of the carrier's hysterical speed. Again, she was thankful to the standing mustached driver for his heroic speedy and applying of frequent breaks on narrow pot-holed road that gave her unpleaded opportunities to hug her heart-throb with excuse of fear of sliding down.

The humble guardian was in fact uncomfortable with the girl's frequent 'contemptuous' body hugs and caresses—provoking wild sensation in him—and that too under public's lecherous gaze. He checked for any known face from neighbouring villages including Chabishpur, frightened off bad-mouthing back in village. 'Good Heaven, there are none!' However, he controlled him contenting with the fact that 'the girl is a first time bus traveler. She must be feeling insecure in this mad speed.'

Preeti wished, 'This journey shouldn't end. I wanna live in the present as the present has everything for me that the luckiest under the sky can ever get. I'm a freed bird; just freed from the preying eyes of suspecting mother and traitorous and clever papa. Now, I am in the custody of the world's most gifted personality—'Rabi, the Rising Sun.' Now, I can fly in the blue clean sky of Spring, the prince of all seasons like a just released bird from a cursed cage; I can swim in deep water of Satapada like a pretty dolphin; I could sing in the deep mango orchid like a cuckoo and I could dance to the flute-melody of the God of all lovers, in Gopapura's mimusops garden."

They reached at Puri bus-stand. They had to rush to college admission counter as scheduled time for admission was approaching fast. The girl was little nervous as the bus approached the new world—the guardian accepted. 'Understood!' And, he helped her getting down from the bus holding her pretty golden fingers like a bridegroom helps his bride to get down from church pedestal after engagement ceremony that Preeti, although nervous from top to toe, enjoyed. Rabi instead got the luggage down-loaded with help of bus cleaner. Although she wanted to assist with all sympathy to her profusely sweating heart-throb in tropical approaching rainy season, yet she couldn't move and standing stunned as she was fast melting under the preying eyes of the lecherous onlookers.

'Here too there are plenty of likes of Sarua, Gandua, Valu, Baia, etc. Am I a tree-ripe Alfonso mango to be eaten,' she was thinking. 'Do they have no sisters? Is the city dearth of girls? Or, am I so beautiful?' And, in unison, she acclaimed Rabi for his wise counseling just an hour ago on their way to this new world.

They boarded with their luggage a cycle-rickshaw to BCS College campus and after finishing the admission formalities they moved to college off-campus Paharpur Ladies and Gents Hostel located side by side on the sea front.

On the way to hostel, the guardian found the juvenile girl was cool and silent. She wasn't so enthusiast as she was in the village and in the bus. 'She was asking this and that about the city, college, class, hostel, new friends, college cultural programme, sports, ... and whatnots, a never ending list after it was finalised that we'll go for Intermediate study in BCS College,' he recalled, and wondered, 'What happened to her . . . . all of a sudden? Now, she's in this very city—the new world. But, silent! Has anybody harassed her? Even for a minute, I hadn't left her alone as advised by mama.'

Hitting fading girl at her shoulder, he inquired, "Are you tired . . . . Preeti?" There was no instant response as before. 'Is it once-in-a-month problem? May be? . . . . Why girls have such a problem? Why not boys???' worried meek guardian thought and looked at her, and later pulled him unanimously to silence although in despair searching as he couldn't see her in pain and forlorn; so much was the liking and fellow-feeling. 'The poor girl has no one in this new world to tell her problem and to take care of her but me, a boy.'

". . . . no, but Rabi, I think this is a very cruel world. Where on earth we go, idiots are all around there with all gears . . . . ain't it?" asked Preeti looking desperately at the worried face of her heart-throb.

Rabi looked back at her. He pondered and wanted to say something. As if he was unable to retain what was there in his mind—overflowing, he looked at Pandupur golden girl and told, "If you please don't mind, I'll tell you, 'You're indeed very beautiful. You're pretty . . . . Lovely!' So, people's eyes run after you. Ergo, there's nothing to surprise?"

The word 'Lovely' and ecstatic acclamation from the mouth of her heart-throb had an electrifying effect on her. Her entire nerve system got activated. All the harassments from the preying eyes in the bus, on the road to college, in the college campus and elsewhere since their start of journey on the day, vanished in no time. It was as if she was waiting for the promulgation of this magnificent description from her very someone's humble mouth for a long time.

"Wow! Is it so? You have already compared me with city girls. Rabi, really, I'm very very happy. I was hungry to hear this from you. Thank God . . . . although much late!" rejoiced Pandupur queen bee hitting shied Rabi at his shoulder amid chring chring noise from cycle rickshaw.

Again chring, chring . . . . followed by, "Bachho, this is Paharpur Ladies Hostel," from the old rickshaw puller. This full-stopped their intensive soul-searching talks. Rabi carried Preeti's luggage up to the lobby of Paharpur Ladies Hostel, the maximum limit or Laxman Rekha for gents in the ladies hostel amid comments of some—seemed senior—girls, "What a cute boy? He must have been trapped much early. A good escort!"

"The bichara gawar would be kicked out moment a glitzy companion is available in the city."

However, the guardian went on carrying out his assignment unconcerned of all these unsolicited forecasting.

He handed over the custody of his village girl and its image to Ms. Caretaker of Ladies Hostel with all other formalities completed very similar to other guardians doing there. And, he had to leave to Paharpur Gents Hostel next gate with an assuring glance at—not so happy—his 'indeed very beautiful Pandupur girl.'

But, Preeti couldn't move into the hostel. 'I'm not like an opportunist girl-friend using the boy as the carrier of bag and baggage or for the sake of soft body caress and time-pass. Or, what my father meant too?' She followed Rabi down up to her new abode gate and continued to stand there allowing her crying eyes to run after her dream boy, walking slowly but steadily to Paharpur Gents Hostel with his luggage on his shoulder.

And, the by-standers eyes followed the envious scene.

As if this was unbearable to a few envious creatures like Pandupur's Lilli, Dalli, Reena, ..., she was interrupted with teasing comments from the first floor, "Lovely pair! Don't worry, sweetie Madam! Your hero is at the next door. Well . . . . will be available as and when desired for any kind of service."

Drops of tears rolled down from the blue deer eyes as she raised her half-naked hand overflying with dupatta to say good-bye for the moment. The guardian Rabi twisted back but resolutely walked ahead to settle down with the fact, 'We're two different creation of nature, and time hasn't come we two to live together if luck has such a design.'

'. . . . no, no, this is an absurd thought. What's she and what I am? An urchin!'

KANYAKUMARIES

Preeti entered the Ladies Hostel like many other fresher. A different feeling, longing and aroma confronted her. She looked around. 'Everything new! A completely new environment, a new setting. There is no known face. And Rabi, my only near and dear, I know in this new world, is in a different quarter—and seems not so easily approachable. Such a high, cruel and bold wall separating us.'

While she was pushing towards her allotted Room No. 025 her legs slowed down at the very first door as her eyes read the name plate—"Dr. Mili Padhi, Warden, Paharpur Ladies Hostel"—in bold letters. As her eyes were progressively running on the name plates, a fierce feeling tinkled through her nerve system although she didn't have any early exposure to the lady represented before her by her name. 'She must be very strict and rigid . . . . like mama.' Next to that, there was a notice board hanging on the wall. The wording IMPORTANT with bold underlined letters on the top of a notice caught her attention. She read, "All the fresher are 'asked' to gather in the Hostel Common Room 'sharp'— the word appeared to her a razor sharp weapon piercing her heart—at 6.30 PM today 'without fail'," with the signature of Dr. Mili Padhi, Warden, Paharpur Ladies Hostel. A fear started overtaking her, 'If the Warden is like my grousing and sulking mama?"

"Baap..re..e, here too . . . . hey Bhagaban, save me!"

However, she had to move, and she moved on dangling the new tin box, not yet abandon the enamel paint smell and crying "curr . . . . curr . . . ." with every step she made, in her left hand in the corridor, profusely sweating. In fact, she had no prior knowledge where was the Room No. 025, still she didn't ask anybody and was pushing indiscriminately with her own obsession, the stealers of her freedom—mama and Warden. However, her indiscriminate walk stopped at Room No. 025 as that was wide open and the inmate was ready to welcome, even though none of them knew each other.

"Welcome friend! I'm Seema Pati from Rourkela," the designated room-mate in boyish costume—smart and dashing—introduced her 'unasked' simultaneously extending out her hand for a shake.

"Preeti Rath from Pandupur," the nervous gawari replied halting. And, they shook their hands, however coolly, but laid the foundation for a lifelong association although they were born and brought up in two different worlds, not matching.

'Shall I be able to live with this girl in the same room—looked from a family of well-up and city upbringing in appearance, approach and mannerism?' A big question mark stirred the gawari's mind.

Soon, she got into the act of settling down on her allotted bed and little furnishings. But, her mind was elsewhere as she was obsessed with the boldness of brick-cement wall standing like the giant Meghanada Pacheri, she had heard from her grandma that exists around Jagannath Temple complex guarding the complex from any intruder,—bold and high—not only separating Ladies Hostel from Gents Hostel but also her and her heart-throb. She was time and again staring at the wall, releasing heavy breath that the room-mate noticed.

The city girl smiled and murmured, "Might be being failed to find out even a just pigeon-hole."

'………………'

"So close, but so far! What a bad luck?" murmured the city girl repeating, teasing.

Preeti looked at the teaser with pity. As far as she remembered, 'This is the first time in my life that a bloody wall separates me from my very own heart-throb, physically.'

'Was she cursing?' Seema went on thinking. 'May be?'

"Bloody heartless Berlin Wall, you'll crumble down under your own weight one day," jeered the city girl again. "I curse you for the sake of my friend."

Preeti didn't react, however. This wasn't that she did not understand, directed at her.

'………………'

"Who is that cute boy?" the irritant asked breaking the short silence spreading her sporty body on the bed with a 'gauche film magazine—seemed to gawari' in her hand. Preeti after a quick survey of the determined intruder of her privacy went on thinking, 'What a shameless girl; wears a skinny boyish T-shirt—Oh my God, even without bra—exposing the shameful standing apple boobs with pointed nipples. If my mama finds me in this costume, she would roll the rolling pin on my chest, leveling it to a boyish one. And reading . . . . gauche magazine?'

'………………'

'Who is she to ask all such questions, and that too, so early? Nothing but interference! What is her interest? Why should I attend to her questions,' the gawari resolutely kept quiet literally feeling hurt.

But, the intruder was unstoppable.

'The city girls are like this!' she viewed. And, she displayed her uncomfortability. The nervous gawari read in the eyes of the intruder, 'Nothing doing, you've to not only tell but also reveal all details.'

She succumbed and spelled out, "He is Rabi Pratap, my . . . . ," but stopped short of completing, as her tongue started shyly shuddering with.

'May be trying to hide something . . . . very confidential,' Seema told self.

The gawari stared at the irritant with anguish and searching words; and, but, still, succumbed to complete, "boy friend!"

"As he has been allotted boarding in Gents Hostel, certainly he is a boy. And, again, I have also checked his shyly up-and-coming mannish symbol on his chins. But to my sweetie good buddy, Miss Preeti Rath, I wanted to know, how he is related to you? Surely, not your brother or cousin? Am I right?" asked the naughty pushy girl tickling melting gawari's sloppy lion tummy but trying to help her to feel easy and getting homely.

'Awful! . . . . What a force? Why she is after us? What is her interest?' the thoughts hunted the ghungi gawari. No response volunteered.

And, after a while the intruder maturely continued, "I understand. And I can read from your body language and eyes. Go easy!"

The caved-in rustic lass and a first generation girl collegian from the village Khandi Pandupur looked at confident and overbearing city girl in despair—frosting fast.

The city girl smiled. She patted the nervous gawari's back and assured, "It is understood. I am your friend, not a contender of your 'hard find' . . . . can trust me! Of course, the decision is your privilege."

After getting them refreshed followed by late launch, both incompatible room-mates from two different worlds got into a short and further 'knoweachother session' preceded by an exhaustion relieving siesta.

However, the siesta was found reluctant to absorb the gawari although the room-mate's lively and ever talking apparatus for the time being had been silenced. It was her Rabi's latest talk on a topic very dear to her on their way to Paharpur Ladies Hostel on the cycle rickshaw that kept her mind obsessed. The thought of his acclamation on her 'beauty' overwhelmed her. 'So, Rabi is for sure thinking about me, appreciating me.'

Later, a quick survey of the city girl's belongings, rucksack, dresses, shoes, her make-ups, and in comparison of that with her own belongings within a small tin box, coupled with the city girl's aggressive get-up and approach created a strong ripple in her mind. 'What I'm and what she is? No match! How could I accommodate with this girl in the same room,' reverberated in her little mind. Besides, she feared, 'Shall my cute Rabi be able to resist these stylish and the overbearing city girl? . . . . Aunty was right in her observation.'

'And, what Rabi would be doing in his hostel? He must be encountering these bloody, arrogant, interfering city guys in his hostel too. They must be asking him about me—many of them staring at us like Dukhi, Sarua, Baia . . . . while we were parting at the gate.'

'In fact, he is very accommodative—unlike me, a ghungi. Ooh my God! Who would be taking care of my aunty's Bholanath? Once he is among his friends— chit-chatting or explaining lesson to friends or starts reading or playing—he uses to forget his bath, food and everything. What to do? Aunty, I am sorry! I am helpless! See here, this bloody strong and bold Meghanada Pacheri.'

But, to her utter surprise, she found the city girl was quite comfortable, sleeping . . . . and snoring.

She started questioning the wisdom of her papa, Karankaka and the villagers pushing them to city college, and her own, accepting the proposal. He appreciated, 'Rabi was right. We, the villagers, have no place in this city setting. We should have taken admission in UMG Mahavidyalaya. We should be there where we're comfortable.'

As evening approached, both the incompatible inmates got up. Seema twisted her body lazily and later checking her wrist watch, she jumped, "Yaar, it's quarter-past six now. Hurry up! We've to attend the meeting with Warden and Caretaker."

"Go to be squeezed by Maa Kali and Maa Asantidevi," they heard seniors forecasting at their back as they were walking towards Hostel Common Room, side by side.

"Maa Kali! . . . . Maa Ashantidevi! . . . . squeezed! What are all these? What are they saying," hummed the panicky stricken gawari staring at her un-compactable buddy. 'So far as my knowledge on almanac goes— today is surely not the day of Maa Kali puja,' and thought, 'Is Maa Kali deity there in the Common Room? And, is there any Goddess in the name of Ashantidevi in the Hindu long pantheon of thirty three hundred crores Gods and Goddesses?' She was utterly confused.

"You, gawari . . . . dim-wit, just follow me," the city girl commanded instead.

The gawari was not pleased by the offensive trimming of the city girl. Yet, she bore and religiously followed to the cuing of her ring-leader like a dancing monkey in the village fair.

'But, where is the revered deities?' The astound girl's eyes ran all around the common room to locate but in vain.

Seema occupied a chair in the last row and offered another to the awkward and nervous gawari.

'Why Seema preferred to seat in the back row!' the thought virtually kept engaged the mind of the trimmed gawari. This pushed her to wonder, 'Seema is smart, sharp, intelligent, seemed scholarly and brought up in a modern city. Why then she preferred to sit in the back row instead of in the front? And that too, when front row isn't fully occupied?' She was surprise to witness the virtual fight for occupancy in the back row instead of front row. She recalled, 'In the Chabishpur High School, intelligent and scholarly students were mostly sitting in the front row. And, the front benchers literally hijack the proceeding. And, I was a proud front bencher there.'

'Yes, of course, Rabi wasn't a front bencher as he was treated as a pariah and he used to keep him away even unasked.' She had all sympathy, and once, she accompanied him but he refrained her to follow leaving him to his fate, 'which might not remain unfavourable all the time to come that he used to console,' she recalled. 'He is such a great boy.'

'Is the city girl such a pariah? And like Rabi, she keeps away. But, unlike Rabi, this girl has her family title following her name?'

The tired and disturbed girl sat down resting her head on the left-hand palm peeping at the dais and other occupants. And, she stood up as she heard her ring-leader whispering, "Her Highness, Maa Kali badharrahia!"

Maa Kali's arrival was followed by the hostel Caretaker and the attendant with the registers and a bunch of papers.

Portly Maa Kali, Dr. Mili Padhi, Warden, Paharpur Ladies Hostel, BCS College occupied her designated chair on the dais followed by her lieutenant slimy and looked oldie—the Hostel Caretaker, designated Ms. Shantidevi.

The gawari found none of the ladies adorning the stage had sacred vermillion on their forehead. Yet, they were wearing printed saris. 'Are they still spinster? Or widow? Or they are displaying their modernity.' She compared them with ladies with similar costume occasionally visiting Choudhury abode in her village Pandupur. And, she had heard peasants passing mocking comments about them, "Modern Ladies!"

'Chie, chie . . . . very bad! This isn't there in our culture. I won't be like this. I'll adorn the vermillion, the proud possession of a married Hindu woman. And, after all, if I won't follow the prevailing social custom what my so dear Rabi and so dear aunty will feel?' 'And, this is why Choudhury elder is against modern education in our village? He is right!'

She went on analysing till the city girl buzzed, "What a combination? What a kind of creatures? Friends, get ready to be chewed by Kumaries." This distracted the sulking gawari. The ridiculous comment buzzed the tiny hall instantly like a wild fire igniting a mild commotion which was later brought under control by the snappish looks of Her Highness—Maa Kali and her lieutenant—Asantidevi, presiding over the event in the evening.

The attendant counted the heads and told to the presiding deity all but one present. 'But, surprisingly none is talking—why the absent one hasn't come till now,' Preeti thought. 'She may be sick or not reported so far.'

Anyway the session started with a big bang as Ms. Warden hammered the shattered table with her fist in a proud display of authority which instantly stopped the chattering in the room.

"Good Evening, Girls!"

"Good Evening, Mam," responded the audience in choir.

"I'm Dr. Mili Padhi, Warden, Paharpur Ladies Hostel." She told with heavy tress and tone authoritatively. "With me, here is Ms. Shantidevi, Caretaker." Ms. Shantidevi shook her hand, seating. She has a look of faded Maa Durga, ready for immersion in the river Brahmani at the end of four days exhausting saradiya havans of devotees. She looked worn up and disgusted.

"We together have been shouldering this responsibility for last ten years. Do you know, why have we been trusted with this most critical task for such a long time?" the proud custodian of Paharpur Ladies hostel told flexing her plump mouth.

"No Madam! Please tell," pleaded the fresher with pretending enthusiasms and cry with suspense.

"No lucky bridegrooms might have been available to grace them! Certainly, it is a good engagement and time-pass," Seema buzzed provoking a subdued flutter in the hall which invited another hammer of fist that brought the discipline to the hall at once.

Preeti noticed Ms. Caretaker passing some words to Ms. Warden pointing at back row, in all probability, at her and the city girl—the epicenter of commotion.

"Stop, stop Seema! For God sake, please! We're identified," the apprehensive and frightened gawari whispered hitting the bubbling city girl at her leg gathering confidence despite the recent past trimming.

The city girl kept quiet, maintaining intriguing stony silence—'As if she knew nothing. Fully innocent!' The gawari felt the city girl was evading. She looked at her, surprised. After a pause as Ms. Warden returned to her business, the city girl, hitting the gawari's at her feet, screamed, "Shut up, you dim-wit—maffu, stupid fool! You'll get me to them in a platter. Don't talk me when they are fixed at us."

"Thack . . . . thack . . . . thack . . . ." The presiding deities and participants turned their eyes to the entrance as the sharp pitched sound of high hill shoe invaded the hall disturbing the proceeding. However, the presiding deities returned to their business, unconcerned. This was followed by a sharp chair screaming as that was pulled roughly. A heavily built girl—resembling physical build-up of Supanakha, the sister of demon king Rabana in The Epic Ramayana that came to the mind of Preeti instantly—threw her body on the poor wooden chair with full display of privilege arrogance.

But, to the very surprise of gawari, the presiding deities were silent—not concerned. "This is nothing but rowdiness. Was it Chabishpur High School, Prakashsir would have blasted the girl on her very face," the gawari went on buzzing.

"But exempted here! She must be a daughter of a Big Gun," the city girl whispered closed to the gawari.

Soon Ms. Warden returned to complete her flamboyant lecture packed with rare achievements, "Because, we don't compromise on the matter of discipline."

"It seems so . . . . loud and clear!" reacted the city girl confining among them. The gawari recognized some justification in the city girl's comment.

"During our stewardship, no vagabond has ever been able to scale the boundary wall of the hostel as it happened in other colleges. Girls, it is very unfortunate to say the very truth that the girls, at your age, are like ripe jackfruits. And, our city has no dearth of wondering lecherous bears. Do you like to be licked by them? Certainly not! You've a bright future."

And, the city girl whispered putting her forefinger on her chin, "What a beautiful comparison? This jackfruit must have been rejected by the bears . . . . full of sweet less gum."

"What do you mean Seema? They aren't married," the dim-wit asked poking her head.

"Go through the hostel 'Rules and Regulations.' Take this as your living bible at least as long as you're here. I expect you, the grown up girl, understand what I mean to say. Mind, no violation will be tolerated." Ms. Warden told with force hosting a piece of paper by her hand.

"Let's see!" re-acted the city girl.

Ms. Warden ordered to Ms. Caretaker to place a bunch of printed papers on the table.

Ms. Caretaker announced, "You now come one by one to the podium and introduce yourself in brief and collect a copy of hostel Rules and Regulations."

The introduction process went on without any hitch till the turn of the back benchers Seema, closely followed by Preeti and Rekha, together constituting the stealers of the gathering, came.

"I'm Seema Pati, Intermediate Science. I'm from Rourkela. My father is Mr. Achiuyta Pati, Director (Plant Modernization), Rourkela Steel Plant. Mother Mrs. Sikha Pati, a Senior Manager in RSP. One brother, Shri Prasad Pati, student—standard IX. I passed matriculation from Rourkela English Medium School this year with 75% marks," the statuesque stunner in her skin tight Levi blue jean pant and collar necked

T-shirt and Reebok shoe with neatly combed cascading hair tied with hair band on the back announced at the podium to the full attention of not only the fellow fresher comprising mostly ruralites and a handful of urbanites but also celebrated Misses on the dais, with eyes blinking and brows raised.

"What a fluency and stunning presentation? The stealer of the gathering," the audience buzzed deservingly.

Ms. Warden called the girl nearer to her—to the surprise of the audience as that was the first of its kind since the start of the event—and surveyed her like a bear used to do to a jackfruit as illustrate just before and certified with announcement, "Smart girl." Later, she allowed the girl to get back to her seat mumbling something unheard up to the audience and target.

In the meanwhile, a mocking buzz from Supanakha, "Daughter of Director, RSP. Special Attention!" echoed in the hall.

The gawari was surprised with the comment. And, as her turn came, she walked to the podium.

"I am Preeti Rath, Intermediate Science," the gawari read out as her deer eyes run over the prepared note. She was trembling in her jaded salwar and kurti with tattered dupatta, struggling to hide her overflowing curvy chest. She continued in hurry, "I am from Pandupur village. My father is Mr. Raghu Rath, farmer. Mother is Mrs. Prema Rath, housewife. I have two sisters and one brother, junior to me; they are studying in school. I have passed matriculation from Chabishpur High School, Chabishpur this year with 76% marks."

"What . . . . Twentysixpur High School! Ha . . . ha . . . ha . . . .!" jeered Supanakha.

Sooner the profusely sweating—despite the cooling evening blow of natural air from the gracious Bay of Bengal coming through the widely open grilled window and the service of ceiling fans—Khandi Pandupur beauty's introduction was over, she was about to run to her seat in one breath like other typical ruralites had done before, frightened off piercing look of Ms. Shantidevi fixed at her.

"Come here!" she stopped on her way back to seat as she was caught hearing a loud and sharp volcanic eruption from Ms. Ashantidevi.

The nervous gawari turned to Ashantidevi with fear in her deer eyes and display of misery on her rosy babyish face, and as directed, walked to Misses head down with phat, phat noise of her plastic slippers in the pin-drop silence of the hall.

"You are looked very innocent. But, actually, not of that kind! I'm damn sure," fired Ms. Ashantidevi with misgiving.

"In which room, she's staying," the presiding Miss asked while reading some documents.

"They're staying in Room No. 025."

"They . . . . mean—this ghungi and . . . . that smarty. That girl from Rourkela, jean and T-shirtwalli . . . . Yes, I think so, they need Special Attention, Madam," advised the presiding Miss distracting her from the reading, 'appeared worried.'

Supanakha buzzed, "Bichara gawari is caught between the ever-destined Misses and Miss Smarty from modern city. What a pity?"

"I believe her's, I mean Preeti's boy-friend stay in the Gents Hostel. Is it so Preeti?" Ms. Shantidevi jeered raising the eyebrows.

"Room No. 025, a TROUBLE ZONE! Underline, Madam," Ms. Warden advised to Ms. Shantidevi peering at the melting gawari on the upper border of her narrow golden frame spectacle. Pramiladidi handed over a red pen to the lady having a shivering impact on the girl. Preeti, in her thought, blamed Seema for ring-leading her to her present pathetic state of affairs.

She couldn't hold back her tear; she literally cried and broke down being ambushed with bothersome criticisms unexpectedly so early on her arrival in this new world. 'And she did so as if this was required to expedite the process of release from the solid grip of marauding Maa Kali and worn up Maa Shantidevi on the dais.'

Once back on her seat, the ring-leader in her sincere display of camaraderie hugged the melting girl and cleaning her teary eyes with her handkerchief whispered in her ear, "You foolish, you don't know how to handle these celebrated proud Kanyakumaries? Just think, why they couldn't even pass any comment on me even though they surveyed me like bears?"

Despite all these consolation, Preeti wanted to appeal Ms. Warden for change of either her room-mate or her room. But, she dropped the matter for time being to be finalized after consultation with her guardian— her dear Rabi. She wanted to place the matter before him as soon as possible.

The last was Supanakha. But, to the audience, she wasn't the least from many points of view. She was in her short gown and translucent top—'exposing and revealing—resembling a whore in search of her prey in the red light market' viewed in the Bollywood films. She was neither naturally gifted not grown up with elegancy; but, all at once, full of arrogance and displaying and disregarding, it appeared to the audience.

'Why not? None in the audience has the background and family stature of her,' it appeared she wanted to throw. She caught the attention of all present as she rose on her turn pushing the poor wooden chair back producing unpleasant noise to the utter discomfort of all those present including the presiding Misses. Many including the slipper clad Preeti tested her high hill foot wears' irritating bite on her way to the dais. However, she preferred to remain hushed as she had heard not much long ago the verbatim, 'She must be the daughter of a Big Gun.'

"Rekha Mohanty from Cuttack. Passed out H.S.C. from Convent School. Percentage of mark—53. Daddy Mr. Debasis Mohanty, Sr. OAS. At present, ADM, Cuttack. Soon getting a transfer to Puri as DM. Mummy Dr. Swati Devi, Professor in Revenshaw College. One sister and one brother. All studying in Convent School. Allotted Room No. 036."

"Wow! Convent School! What a smartness?" the gawaris in the audience buzzed although they were not pleased with her attitude, her make-up and get-up, and very particularly, with her dealing with them, and her way of presentation. Many were also found buzzing after her announcement of H. S. C. mark, "How could she get admission when the cut up mark is 65 percentage?" Some of them thought complaining but couldn't go further. 'How could they; and again, who they're when the presiding deities swore to maintain discipline at any cost as announced flamboyantly not much long ago and witnessing every bit of daughter of a Big Gun's display of vanity and disregard to the chair, even were maintaining studied silent?'

The city smarty growled with anger, "What a get up and what a brought up?" And with all sympathy to the boarders and Misses, predicted, "She'll be a spoil sport here."

CAGED BIRDS

Room no. 025 in Paharpur Ladies Hostel was in tense. 'Quite obvious!' Seema could deduce what was going on in the mind of her room-mates, who was avoiding. She tried her level best to cool down the gawari's anger by taking all the responsibility to her for all that happened in the common room, "I'm sorry, my dear Preeti!" But, that had little impact on the sulking girl, not speaking anything.

Preeti had already concluded, 'The city based smart and flamboyant girls can't be trusted, dependable . . . . and they're cheaters. They use their smarty look and their smarty costume and their flashy background and their vast exposure to get their wishes materialized by hook or by crook. This is what have been scripted in the several films. And, here too, I'm experiencing now . . . . Aunty is right. She is an experienced lady, can't be faulted for her conclusion.'

She wanted to maintain distance from the city girl; and if possible, avoid completely, before shifting to a different room.

Whatever, Seema was equally stubborn, wasn't ready to be cornered. She had to bring the normalcy in the room. 'Or else, how can I leave in this city, far away from my near and dear and my beloved,' she thought. She schemed of a trick lying on the bed.

Pulling out a photo from her pillow cover, she announced, "Here is my Prince Charming. What a look? What a body? The baby face of Kenneth Edmonds, athletic body of Flying Sikh Milkha Singh, kind eyes of Paul Newman and perennial smile of great Kishore Kumar. Ooh . . . . such sweet sweet cheeks and chin! In our school, he was the most shout after boy of all the girls. But, I grabbed him. He is far better than your muffasali Rabi."

Later placing a huge kiss on the post-card size colour photograph, and subsequently, lowering down the same to her bosom and embracing, she pompously announced tickling, "I love him so much and he too . . . . to me. Wow!"

Her trick worked. This made the room lively. The ghungi gawari coiled her body spread over the bed like a cobra. She, combing her cascading uncared hair—obstructing her eyes—with her naked golden slim fingers, raised her hood at the city girl—hissing and fishing.

"Is it?" she screamed. "Let me see!"

"So . . . . for what? I'm extremely sorry, Miss Innocent. I can't part my hard find to a spinster," the smarty refused brusquely hiding the photograph between her two flowery soft peeping hills decorating her heart container, protected by tight but cotton soft mercerized Rupa bra under her skinny T-shirt, the most secured place that she could find out instantly.

The now-nosy gawari was unstoppable. Again, how could she keep quiet when her own Prince Charming was compared and appraised badly with another boy? That too whom she hadn't seen? Soon a wild fight broke out between the two love-stricken birds. The ghungi gawari pounced on city smarty, with the force and ferocity resembling the wild lion pouncing on a cheetah to rub its' just caught prey in the African forest. But, the cotton soft Rupa bra trusted for last few years protecting the smarty's teenage blossoming feature failed to save her most affectionate something closer to her very heart for the moment. She gave up. "Baap.. re..e! What a force? Gawari is so strong and forceful."

Preeti flushed out the photograph from the bra wrapped pigeon-chest crawling on the Seema who was in fact giving in, and after having a quick survey of the photo, reacted, "Wow, what a fascinating eyes, cute face, dark oily hair and stealing smile? What a young man? Seema, you are really very very very lucky. Well, you're a good pair . . . . Madhubala and Kishore Kumar! God bless you!"

Still, she continued her concentration on the photo, studying it again and again as if she was not satisfied with her observation. After a while of musing over the photo, she, shrugging her shoulders with confidence, appraised good-humouredly, "Still my Rabi . . . . no comparison . . . . is the best, a sparking Karna. Yes, there is no comparison . . . . Please don't mind, I'm proud of my Rabi."

As there was no response to her critical observation, she looked back to her ever twittering room-mate and found her sitting on the bed hiding her face by two bare palms. Warm tears started filling the narrow gap between the fingers. She was surprised . . . . scared too. She couldn't understand what happened to a so tweeting bubbly so sudden.

A feeling of camaraderie invaded her. She asked pulling the girl to her broad plump chest, trying to comfort, "Ooh my God! You're weeping. Have I hurt you . . . . friend? If so, I'm very sorry. Very . . . . very sorry! God promise!" Touching her own gullet, she continued, worried, "I don't have any wrong intention . . . . No, no, yours is the best! Yours is the best!" She went on cajoling Seema, caressing her head and curling her un-frizzed long hair elderly.

"No Preeti, I don't mind what you say. I'm just thinking, how will be my Sambit?" cried the girl hiding her face and cuddling over gawari's broad soft chest like the fatherless child Rabi was doing in anguish and sorrow over Bhagyabati aunty's being humiliated and harassed by Sarua, Gandua, Sallu, Gallu in village Khandi Pandupur. The stunned gawari despite having reservation against the smart city girl, in no time, turned a sympathetic mentor, caring and sharing. They were two comrades in distress.

"Why, what happened?" Preeti asked instantly in surprise to halting response from the city girl.

And, thus started the illustration of a story of sorrow and frustration:

The girl narrated to the apt attention of Preeti, "Can you imagine that I'm in exile and brutally dumped in this proud Kumaries' cage? I'm punished to clear the path of my father's promotion. Sambit, my fiancé, is the son of the most powerful Managing Director of the Rourkela Steel Plant, now pursuing his 1st year Bachelor in Civil Engineering in Regional Engineering College. We were studying in the same school and he was my senior by two batches. We love each other. But, our liking and loving each other doesn't mean anything to our ambitious and career oriented parents' and their bloody heartless high society. When my papa nourishes the ambition of to be the MD of RSP; Sambit father wants to be Chairman of Steel Authority of India. Their methods to reach their professional objectives are ruthless and they don't mind if that is accomplished in whatsoever means. The present Union Minister for Steel and Mines, who incidentally was the college mate of my fiancé father, wants my Sambit to be his son-in-law. Sambit's father can't take risk of his career for sake of his son's love although he liked and appreciated our relation before minister's proposal came. So, also my papa supported by my mama pursues their professional ambition. And, the victim is this bichara Seema Pati, aged sixteen, dumped here at a distance of about seven hundred KM, far from her very near and dear—exiled, caged, and in the custody of 'may be cursed' Kumaries . . . . What . . . . an awful fate!"

And she laughed . . . . and laughed till that was overtaken by a cry with flooded eyes breaking all the boundaries of patience; and uncontrollable. Preeti, while thinking, 'Sooner or later I may be—Good Heaven, save me!—a victim of parental ambition and ego,' embraced the inconsolable smart city girl closed to her soft bosom.

Both the caged birds, hungry of flying free with their loved one, went to give rest to their dog-tired mind with ring of bed time-bell in the first night in the safe but 'cursed!' habitat of 'might be ever waiting Kanyakumaries.'

However, Preeti couldn't sleep well. How could she, a first-timer in the city, and when the issues such as the jackfruit, bear, Kanyakumaries, scaling of wall, Seema's exile, Room No. 025—trouble zone, Pramiladidi's bold red pen, Supanakha's buzz of special attention, hostel rules and regulations, and how Rabi would be, a first-timer like her in the city ran competing one after another in her little mind? And all these had taken place so rapidly in just few hours of her arrival in Puri which she'd never thought of before and prepared to face. There were no near and dear, no known faces to talk about. 'All strangers. And, Rabi is neither audible nor visible although physically being not much far.'

Again, her promotion from mud-thatched house with soot and spider nets co-inhabitated by cat, rat, mole, cockroaches, lizards, mosquitoes, and above all, with grandma, papa, mama and siblings to cement plastered building with one room mate that too from a different world, were so unfamiliar. There was no bed time chit-chat and fighting among her siblings for the space along side lovely grandma on the bed and there was no grandma's chiding for their disturbances and never ending tales of prince and princess, forgot about very dear and ever considerate aunty. Along with the first day's happening in her city life, there were echo of her Pandupur life, and all these were in league and unanimous in pinning and spoiling her sleep.

The issues were so disturbing that they kept her simple rustic mind pre-occupied in the most part of the night under the zero-powered bulb spraying moon-light in the tiny room.

BIG TANK

Preeti woke up to the sweet morning Vedic chant over the loud speaker at distance temple and paid her pious homage to city's presiding deities sitting on the bed in buddhic position. She looked at the city girl still sleeping, snoring and occasionally raving; seemed to Preeti, she was completely unconcerned of anything like her. She felt unaccompanied and lonely. And she went out to toilet to deplete her body waste and had a crying look at the Meghanada Pacheri, disappointed.

After one raving followed by childish cry of the city girl, the amused gawari hesitantly pushed, sisterly slapped and jocularly pinned the city girl at her slim waist and fleshy armpits cheering, "Hey, maa smarty, stop dreaming! I bless you, your prince will be your; nobody can snatch him from you."

However, there was no response. Instead, the city girl pulled the chaddar further, covered her face, turning the side keeping back at the intruder of her morning sleep.

In the playful mode, Preeti thought of a trick to play with the smarty, and to wake up her. She took some time. Later, she little by little slipped out of the room and standing on the threshold asked mildly, "Pramiladidi, please check, who is that boy in the lobby? Is he from Rourkela?"

"What? Sambit! Sambit has come? I know he can't stay for a moment without me," the dreaming girl broke open. She jumped and about to rush to the lobby in no time, only to be stopped by the triumphantic but the apologetic gawari standing with two hands at her ears, twisting and begging, "Sorry!"

Certainly furious, the smarty was about to pounce at the gawari but hold back and exploded with laugh bear-hugging her room-mate. Both laughed at each other in league before the smarty left for evacuating her body waste.

The gawari, curling smarty's uncombed statuesque hair, asked with pleasantly, "You love so much to Sambitbhai. So nice to hear! I enjoy all these sweet-talk; I don't know why I'm so homely with all these," and heard the city girl appreciating, "I'm very happy and I thank God, for sending thou for my company during my these days of pain and despair."

As directed by Ms. Warden at the introduction session, they had to read the hostel 'Rules and Regulations' and acquainted them with that so that they wouldn't knowingly or unknowingly and willingly or unwillingly ever dared to ignore, and thus would invite punishment which might include rustication from hostel.

Preeti was indeed very afraid of rustication as she feared, 'This will end my study. Where can I stay if rusticated from hostel in this hostile new world? Of course, Rabi is there. Yet, I can't stay with him, a boy and we're grown-up now. Studying together in the same college and moving around are different matters than living together—in day and night—in one room or in one house although Rabi could be trusted. The suspecting mama, prompted every now and then by susceptive maternal grandpa and grandma, wouldn't at all agree. So also, the Pandupur peasants and spicy Bulinani would not miss opportunity to bad-mouth our living together making a mountain of a mole-hill. So, the scope of full-stop of further study is almost certain . . . . Further, Rabi might continue his study and gets himself exposed to these gauche city girls . . . . these girls will skyjack him.'

'If that, what'll happen to me? What'll . . . . to my simple aunty? What'll happen to Pandupur and its hope and aspiration?'

The frightened gawari picked up the pink sheet and lying down on the bed started acquainting her with the content. But, Seema snatched the paper from her and commanded, "Leave this bullshit! Let's go to the roof and enjoy morning cold sea breeze and 'watch half-naked monkeys and bears loitering in our' neighbourhood beyond this bloody bold and strong Berlin Wall."

The caged and disgusted gawari, who had thought up a free mingling with her heart-throb on their arrival in this new world free from preying patrolling of reverend mama, envious Lilli, Dalli, Manju, busybody Bulinani and lewd watch and chattering of Sarua, Gallu, Vallu, Dukhi and their likes but dismayed with Ms. Warden's warning, was fired up with the idea. In fact, she wasn't concerned with already revealed motive of Seema to walk to the roof.

Obsessed with thought of to see her heart-throb, who had been out of bounds during the last few hours and she didn't find any chance to see him even on the day, so far the longest period since her papa allowed her free mingling with the boy, the gawari reacted with ecstasy, "Wow! What a great idea? You're really The Great, Seema. You're really Smart." She virtually saluted the city girl.

The smarty was in her printed slack and pajama and gawari was in her red jaded salwar and kurti and tattered dupatta over her shoulders and thriving chest. The divas were just out of their bed, looked like progressively ripen fleshy tomatoes awaiting ready appreciation in the morning vegetable market. Their customers were just beyond the strong and bold abused Berlin Wall that sincerely and boldly stands between Paharpur Ladies and Gents Hostels, guarding.

At the pick of ecstasy, the gawari followed the smarty to the roof jumping the steps two to one, and at time, three to one. 'Such was the enthusiasm.' She poked fun at obstructive heartless Meghanada Pacheri, mimicking—'Bloody, get lost! You bold and strong. Who cares you?'—unknowing that their present venture was short-lived one, and this one was once for all times to come. She had forgotten for the moment that she was in the custody of celebrated Kumaries.

Once on the roof, the budding flowers unfolded their arm petals wide upon facing at the gracious broad and generous breezing from the sprawling Bay of Bengal. They wanted to be embraced by clean and cold morning breeze and inching sunray.

"Wow! What a beauty! This is the beauty of nature for all of us, we beauties—unfortunately cursed to the

Kumaries caging," Seema jeered. She started jumping, dancing and humming with Hindi song, 'thanda thanda hawamay mastee karan chahiyaa,' sparingly pulling and hugging Preeti—rivaling blossoming marigold swinging with mild spring breeze to impress the honey bees. Seema was intermittently glancing at the Gents Hostel lawn which was in fact her prime target in order to enjoy the funny looks of the gents hostel inmates and Preeti started searching her radiating Karna in the thresholds of Gents Hostel numerous rooms, in the empty verandas and in the front lawn: at times, peeping, leaning and kneeing. Slowly but progressively, the smarty's defined funny characters filled the empty veranda and lawn; some were in their half pant or trouser and banyan, and some even were in their underwear covered with just narrow stripped towel below the waist.

All of them as if had one sight to see—the two beautiful divas—unknowing that one of the divas and master mind of the staging was making fun of them. There were fighting—that the smarty could notice and was enjoying—among the funny items for the clear viewing of the two budding divas, who were dazzling under the morning shining sun with its inching rise on the eastern horizon in the clean sky of the gracious, broad and the generous Bay of Bengal, for their morning eye feast, which had been out of bounds since the installation of solid iron grill at the entrance of the roofs of both the hostels stairway and increase of height of the boundary wall at the beginning of last academic session as suggested by Ms. Warden as she noticed in the preceding session that the inmates from Gents Hostel were making vulgar comments to inmates from

Ladies Hostel relaxing on the roof and she apprehended this might led to unpleasant situation in future.

The smarty played hide and sake with the boys sometimes swinging between the northern and the southern edge of sprawling roof playfully coming to the eye reaches and hiding from them. But, the gawari was searching for her heart-throb, for the sight of whom she applauded the smarty's idea. But, she was surprised not finding her heart-throb in the crowd. Instead, she could locate her eye-sore—idiot Lalu-Kaaliram in his black banyan and later with red banyan. 'Why he changed? . . . . Has he changed to red banyan to be better identified in the crowd,' guessed the gawari. 'What a combination? Pooh! Deep red over deep black'—waving his hand stealthily at her. She noticed Kaaliram moving towards a corner away from the crowd looking at her.

'What a spoiling sight? Bloody Kaaliram spoiled the moment and polluted the eyes,' Preeti cursed. She ignored him. Her searching eyes went on scanning every face at all the doorsills, in the wide and long veranda, and in the sprawling lawn of the Gents' Hostel from the distance unconcerned of competing chattering, jeering, peering and peeping of half-naked creatures.

'When almost all the inmates of the Gents Hostel were out of their rooms, where is my Rabi? Is he sick?' Unable to tress and so frustrated, many thoughts invaded the girl's mind. 'Did he not have a good sleep yesterday night—might be thinking about me and aunty like I was and still sleeping to compensate the loss? Or, in the worst, has he left for home? Not impossible in view of his homesickness. Since his birth, he had never gone to bed without the aunty's caress. Both talk to each other before going to bed.' Later, hitting her head with her palm, 'Shit! What non-senses are coming to mind? Rabi can't go home without informing me. He has taken the guardianship of me in this new and hostile world. He has promised me to escort wherever I'll go.'

'The classes are scheduled to commence from tomorrow,' Preeti thought and built up confidence in her, discarding all the non-sense thoughts.

Soon the crowd led to mild commotion, and to hubbub with comments, jeers, lip-whistle which flushed out the Wardens and Caretakers from their respective addresses in both the hostels.

Once out of the caves, Kumaries wanted to know what was going on beyond the high boundary wall. Ms. Warden called to Mr. Warden over phone.

But, what she heard she couldn't believe. She roared. She roared resembling a wild lioness in Gil forest. Instantly all the office bearers and a few students loitering in the corridor reached at her room.

"How could two girls reached the roof? Where is the key?" she pounced on Caretaker and Hostel Attendants, shouting. Before anybody attended to Ms. Warden's flare-up, all, however, had started floating like a mass towards the stairway on their way to roof.

On their way, Ms. Warden noticed 'TROUBLE ZONE' was locked from outside. She stopped. So also, all others crashed on each other, staring at the door in surprise. 'Where are the inmates of Room No. 025? And, where can possible they go so early in the morning?' Pramiladidi had no answer but she was sure gate hadn't opened so far, the key was with her. She looked at the Warden and Caretaker in pity, and told, "Gate is locked . . . ."

'Now, everybody could figure out—none but the inmates of TROUBLE ZONE—are there on the roof.'

Both the Misses looked at each other, now convinced. They struggled to reach the roof top forgetting that they were in their night costume as if the matter they were going to deal with was much important and serious than anything else. Ms. Warden, who was very sensitive to her costume and make-up whenever they were out of their respective addresses— that the senior inmates had noticed—was found ignored this aspect.

After a long and persistent search, the gawari could locate her sparking Karna standing alone at a safe distance of the jeering crowd. 'He appears stunned, nervous and dumbstruck,' seemed to her. 'Why so? Does he not like to see me? No, no, he wants to speak to me. Again, if he speaks that can't reach me in the commotion.' Later, she felt, "Rabi is saying what you mad girls are doing there?"

'I'm here to have a look at you, to talk to you and to inquire how are you? You buddu, do you not understand?' Preeti wanted to say. But, the telepathy didn't work.

Rabi desperately tried moving his hands up and down 'signaling to go down and get back to the room.' As he didn't get the desired response, he pleaded joining his hands on his forehead like he used to do when he failed to convince her on certain issue in the village in disgust. Notwithstanding, Preeti pulled Seema and guided her to have the darshan of her cute Karna and told, "See, there is my Prince Charming, my Karna; so cute and princely that your eyes will get fixed, and refreshed."

"O, your sparking Karna is there, hiding! Very clever! I was searching since long. Indeed, a good eye refresher!"

From the body language of the boy, the smarty could understand his desperation. "Preeti, he is not happy in this jeering crowd. We must respect his sentiment." She waved her hands and told, "Okay baba, Okay! Agreed! We're going back to our cursed cage."

She raised her hand and signaled him, "Ta . . . ta . . . . ," and turning to Preeti, told, "Let us go."

A satisfied and happy statuesque stunner winked at the gawari and applauded, "Surely, you have a praised catch!" and quickly turned her eyes to exit as they heard of huge murmuring and rush of few heavy feet, quaking the stairway . . . . and they got ambushed with a sight that they couldn't ever forget in their life-time.

A marauding elephant followed by a hungry wolf and a pity looked Pramiladidi, and a few jeering seniors. While the elephant was fuming to crush the twosome under her meaty weight; the hungry wolf was crushing her teeth as if polishing them to munch her preys at the earliest. And, there was no escape route. The two victims had no words to face the trespassers of their morning time-pass and eyes refreshment. Their throats and tongues got dried despite cold sea breeze's sympathetic washing blow. And, all at once, they couldn't ascertain why they were under fire? None spoke any word. A pensive but unbearable hush rained for a few second.

'Grill was wide open and we've come to view the sea and get refreshed. And that's all!' the victims thought. In this new and unexpected setting, the gawari started melting. And, the smarty too got nervous as she lately comprehended why Rabi was desperately directing them to get back to the room. The smarty in the meanwhile thought, 'Is there any restriction to come up to roof in the Ladies Hostel? May be?' However, her smart and at time naughty mind immediately manufactured a way out to rescue them. She walked to the denial mode very similar to veteran and artistic politicians, who denied at easy when they were caught on the wrong foot.

"Eh, the grill was wide open and we came here to view the beauty of sea being tempted by the roaring of morning sea waves," she told however confidently and assertively. There was no instant response, but the eyes of the Kumaries were burning and firing at them.

No response helped build-up confidence in smarty. 'Blessing in disguise!'

She broke the silence and told with a lighter vein, "Mam, do you know what this dim-wit, at the first sight of sea, told? . . . . What a Big Tank?" and laughed poking armpits of the sulking gawari standing with her head down in the pose of complete submission, almost iced from top to toes.

Seniors standing behind the Kumaries in the stairway laughed. And she could see Kumaries were struggling hard to hide their laugh too.

'Or who knew whether they were speechless being embarrassed thinking how easily they could be outsmarted by a fresher from modern city Rourkela. Or they were thinking-up means: how to manage we naughty girls in days to come,' the smarty thought and also concluded, 'the right time has come to say good-bye to Kumaries and get released from their grip.'

She went on cajoling, "Really Mam, yours big sea is very beautiful and generous. We must enjoy the morning sweet, clean and cool breeze; good for health! Mam, how could we resist not getting embraced by these available so freely? You know these aren't there in Rourkela—Ees, a dirty city, full of black smoke and dust and suffocative pollution. You Purians are blessed!" and after a short pause, lightly and cozily told, "Shall we go now, Mam?"

"Shut up! Stop all these non-sense bravado. Get back to the room and get lost, you over smart stupid girls," embarrassed Ms. Warden shouted in the full view of senior inmates.

Instantly and obediently the city smarty bended her head pretending complete surrender to the mighty of Her Highness Maa Kali.

Ms. Warden ordered the instant shelling of stairway to roof and advised Ms. Shantidevi to keep the key in the keyboard in the hostel office, locked and secured. And she ordered her lieutenants there and then to have Special Watch at the TROUBLE ZONE.

"Yes, Madam!" obliged Ms. Shantidevi and Pramiladidi instantly.

The lovely birds while getting back to their address, heard Rekha jeering, "Bichara Kumaries . . . . completely stomped. Smart girls! What a look? What a style? What a pretending innocence? And what's the presence of mind? And, the courage! Hats off girls!"

And, the seniors found wailing, "What we couldn't do to the Kumaries during our last few years of stay these girls could do on the just second day. What's a brevity? Whatever, this is great!"

Back in the Room No. 025, nervous but the happy ghungi gawari stretched her just flexed body on the bed flat, and with a long breath, acclaimed, "Thank God, we're saved. Nice drama! Seema, you saved." The smarty bolting the door from inside, promised confidently and assuring, "Preeti, have faith in me and enjoy the life and study. This should be our mantra in this corrupt world full of cheaters and betrayers, and bears and monkeys."

The gawari nodded as if she could find some solace in smarty's proclaimed mantra, and accommodating.

"However, Seema we must read and thoroughly understand and remember the Hostel Rules and Regulations," pleaded the humble girl but heard from the smarty, rejecting, "I least bother all these non-sense, the bullshit 'Rules and Regulations' meant for under-privileges, and you dim-wits and pigeon-hearted. You read but don't remind me. I'm a free bird." She dropped down on the bed with a heavy bang, "Aah . . . . satisfied!"

Preeti wondered, 'Why is Seema apathetic to the Hostel Rules and Regulations?' Many reasons soon invaded her unexposed and inexperienced pondering mind.

'Is it because she is the daughter of a Big Gun like Rekha and could be spared for any punishment? Or she is doing so just to keep her busy to avoid the thought of her Prince Charming at a long distance? Or she is of funny type and easy goers? Or she is so confident on her presence of mind and acumen ship like my papa? . . . . even if Seema and Rekha are the daughters of Big Guns; I'm not just fallen like a drop of water from the sky to be soaked in the dry Thar Desert—unnoticed. I'm also a daughter of a Big Gun—Raghu Rath; everybody knows him in Pandupur and its neighbourhood; respects him for his presence of mind and acumen ship; fears and scars for his cunningness and pays obeisance for his intelligence. Even powerful Zamindar Choudhury elder uses to pay reverence to my papa. I'm certainly proud of my papa,' forgetting for the moment what once social science teacher in Chabishpur High school highlighted, "Although majority of Indians are muffasali, yet they don't carry much weightage in comparison with saharis in the matter of the nation's affairs in our proud self-ruled country."

Preeti went ahead reading the printed whip of hostel supremo and grasping them, which she strongly felt might mar or bar her future, unconcerned of the smarty's refusal and her own thought of—'I am too a daughter of a Big Gun.'

Rules & Regulations

(For the boarders of Paharpur Ladies Hostel, BCS College, Puri)

1. No boarder is allowed to go to college alone and return alone. Minimum two students.
2. Entry and exit times, date, name and signature in 'In & Out Register' by the boarders is mandatory.
3. No male visitor is allowed entry into hostel premises on any pretext.
4. Female visitor is allowed entry with permission from Warden or Caretaker up to 6.30PM. If it is beyond 6.30PM in special circumstances permission from Warden is necessary.
5. Outing for marketing and recreation are allowed only on Sunday and college holidays in group of minimum of five boarders with special permission from Warden/Care Taker.
6. Boarder can meet the male visitor at the lobby outside the inner grill.
7. By 6.30 PM all boarders should be inside the hostel premises.
8. The names of all male visitors are to be recorded in the visitors register. And he can stay in the lobby for maximum of about half an hour.
9. Male visitors' time: 5 PM to 5.30PM.

10. Locking of room and suitcases are must. No valuable and money above Rs. 500/—are allowed to be kept in the room.

11. Last date of payment of mess due is 5th day of the month. Rs.1/—is to be levied as fine from 6th of the day till dues are cleared.

Any violation of above Rules and Regulations will be viewed seriously. Violation will be intimated to the guardian with copy to Principal Office. Up to three violations will be tolerated. If it's beyond three, violator may be asked to vacate hostel. However, in case of severe violation, boarder may be asked to vacate hostel after proper investigation and as per the recommendation of inquiry committee and with the approval of Principal. More rules and regulations may be added as and when required.

By the order of the Principal
BCS College, Puri

Dr. Mili Padhi
Warden
Paharpur Ladies Hostel

She found the presence of feared Ms. Warden and Ms. Caretaker in the bold two words of 'Rules' and 'Regulations' respectively and of Pramiladidi in the word '&', the new tormentors of her freedom away from her reverend mother.

Preeti scanned the pink sheet repeatedly. She looked at the ceiling fan busy in discharging its duty sincerely seriously. She found everybody and everything were sincere and serious except perhaps her room-mate knotty, smarty, city girl—Seema.

'So, I can't meet my Rabi as frequently as I was in Pandupur. I can't even talk to him at my wishes as I was doing in our village occasionally pretending mama, in disguise of clearing my study doubts. I can't look at him as closely as I used to do not much long ago in Pandupur. Who'll guide me in my study? And again, I can't keep track of Rabi as aunty had advised me before we left Pandupur.' And, many other thought cropped up in her teeny mind and continued to disturb her.

And she acclaimed the booted suggestion of Rabi, 'It would have been better, had we taken admission at Satyabadi. If we, studying at Chabishpur could do well why can't we repeat the same performance at Satyabadi? The same course, the same university and the same certificate.'

Seema was busy in reading Filmfare. She turned to deep in thought gawari. As if she understood what was going on in gawari's mind, she asked turning, "Over! This is bullshit, nonsense and awful stupid! You have seen me how easily I could bowl out our celebrated Kumaries and they caved in, embarrassed. Have you not seen how Rekha could disregard them at easy in the common room in the introduction session?" She repeated her mantra, "Enjoy and study or get lost!" and continued putting down the magazine, "This is what my Prince Charming has taught me. And I salute him for his acumenship."

Preeti recalled the verbatim pronounced by her heart-throb during their latest company aboard the cycle rickshaw day before which was still fresh in her ears. She wanted to discuss with him again and again all those topics Rabi initiated along with monstrous 'Rules and Regulations' from the Kumaries. And, about the most disturbing living style of her room-mate.

"But, only at 5 PM and that too, only for half an hours. Disgusting! Isn't it, Preeti?" taunted Seema still poking her nose inside the pages of the magazine sleeping flat on the cot that was crying with her every twist.

SMART GIRL

Around 5 O'clock, afternoon. Window was wide open allowing free entry of pleasing land bound cold breeze from the generous Bay of Bengal. The two girls were still on the bed after an extended siesta, and whiling away their time talking and poking jokes over hostel seniors, Kumaries, each others' fiancé and half-naked inmates in neighbouring bachelors' castle they had viewed during their short but exciting morning escapade. Seema was mostly leading the talk as Preeti hadn't yet fully recovered from the morning shock and echoes of her reading of Kumaries' Rules and Regulations. And after all, she hadn't been fully accommodated in this new world. Besides, she was thinking about her heart-throb and looking for means to meet him. 'This is the time when we can meet. But, how does Rabi know our hostel visitor's time? Again, Bholanath must have been lost among his friend. So accommodative! He must have completely forgotten me.' But, as an after-thought dictated, 'No, no . . . . whatever, he can't forget me; I'm sure! Thinking negative about such a selfless and humble boy will be great injustice.'

"Thack . . . . Thack . . . . ," somebody knocked at the door of Room No. 025. Both the inmates got up, cleaned their eyes with dupattas and adjusted their wears and their burdensome long and thick hairs. First knock at their door since their arrival. Seema guessed of a Special Tuition followed by warning from the Kumaris for their morning—in fact, by default—transgression of forbidden area whereas Preeti was thinking of her heart-throb's visit. 'Rabi must be equally uncomfortable without meeting and talking me for so long. He must have come. I'm dead sure!'

Seema soothsaid, "Kumaris may tuition us, for our morning misdemeanor," and went on guiding, warning and assuring to the gawari like a responsible guardian, "We've to be very careful. Don't worry, I'll be doing the most of the talking!"

With the forecasting of her room-mate, the new found excitement of 'the daughter of a Big Gun' from Khandi Pandupur deserted her in a flash. She looked at 'the daughter of a Big Gun' from modern city Rourkela with apprehension. Even, she wanted 'the daughter of a Big Gun' to inquire who was knocking, and also unchain the door. Seema understood surveying the gawari's melting appearance and told, "Okay baba, okay! I'm opening."

She told self, 'I had led Preeti to hostel roof and so I'm morally responsible for all that follows. I won't run away from my responsibility for whatever consequence. Let's be a good and honest friend!'

The statuesque stunner smiled with display of confidence and responded to repeated knock, meekly, "Who? Just a minute!" She, true to her responsibility, rose from her bed and blinking her lotus eyes at the gawari, walked to the door: confident and steady.

"I'm didi, Pramiladidi!" they heard while Seema, displaying her confidence, unhooked the door. "One, Rabi Pratap from Gents Hostel has come and wants to meet Preeti Rath," she quickly delivered the news and left before the inmates could see her, face to face.

"What? Rabi!" the gawari shouted and jumped from her bed, electrified as if she got a new lease of life in a rather captive and fearsome environment like the might river Mahanadi with release of flood water from gigantic Hirakud Dam, and about to rush to someone she hadn't meet for ages. She proudly proclaimed, "I know he can't stay without talking to me for long," and she jumped to the door. But, she was stopped at the door by the mischievously smiling city girl.

"Hold on, hold on! I know why he has come? He'll tuition you. Let me cool him first. You wait here for a few minutes . . . . or shall I lock thou here!" demanded boldly the statuesque stunner. The gawari was reluctant; nevertheless, she bowed before the self-appointed guardian obediently despite her impatience.

The stunner walked to the lobby confident, upright and bold. The ghungi gawari's eyes followed her: awful. On reaching the lobby, Seema checked looking back and around to know whether anybody keeping watch on the venue where she was going to stage a drama.

"So, you're Mr. Rabi Pratap, our Preeti Rath's shining Karna, she is mad to see and talk," asked the bubbling stunner almost throwing her at the humble gawar—appeared highly disturbed—with her smartly scripted dialogue.

For Rabi, the gawar from undescriptive Pandupur, this was his first ever encounter with a unknown and smart and aggressive teenage girl—such a situation, he wasn't prepared to face. Still he held on and stealthily staring at the ladies hostel corridor leaning left to right and right to left through the half-opened bold steel grill ignoring the city girl's piercing eyes—disturb and agitated. He could notice somebody looked like his village girl Preeti at a distance in the hostel corridor— seemed leaning to check what was going on in the lobby, impatiently.

'Yes, she is certainly Preeti!' He was sure as he heard Preeti nupurs' sweet jingles, he was familiar with. The statuesque stunner went further closed to him and blocked his impatient stealthy stare of corridor and yelled, "Hello mister! Can you not see me, hear me? Is it right on the part of a boy to sneak a look into the ladies hostel corridor? Shall I call our Kumaries?"

The gawar stopped; he was terrified, and so also, anguished. Though agitated and in hurry, he came to his own with sudden deluge of threat and heat of strange word 'Kumaris' at his eardrums. He fondled. He looked at the statuesque stunner in sorrow and despair, couldn't speak. The girl guessed, 'The gawar wanted to spare him.'

She being unable to control her triumph, laughed with all sympathy and fellow feeling. "Okay, Okay! You are Mister Rabi Pratap. Preeti's . . . . ?"

"Friend! I am Preeti's friend from her native village Pandupur," replied the gawar humbly before the stunner could finish, and later prayed, "Can you kindly help me informing Preeti? I've so many things to tell her. Time is running away. You know she's from a village; don't know how to manage her in the hostel and in the city. Today, she committed a blunder!"

Later, halting with a notion, he dared, "You were with her too! Why didn't you prevent her going to hostel roof?"

"Ooh, you've come to teach her manner! Are you her guardian," inquired the overarching city girl.

"Ye . . . s . . . . ! No! But . . . . Still . . . . ," fumbled the gawar.

In the meanwhile, Preeti couldn't hold her back so long leaving her heart-throb waiting for her. Again, the city girl menace . . . . 'After all, Seema is a city girl. She could have said a fabricated story about her own fiancé in order to hoodwink me in her bid to get an access to my simple dreamboat, and subsequently, elopes with him leaving me high and dry. How can I trust such a dashing smart city girl so early? This will be nothing short of baikubbi,' the gawari after-thought. 'Aunty has also advised not to trust any city girl and don't allow any of them come close to Rabi,' the gawari recalled with apprehension.

She, in the meanwhile, quickly removed her tinkling nupurs and walked to the lobby. She stood behind the door—calm and quiet, could be seen by Rabi—and watched the smart girl engaged in dialogue with Rabi. She heard her dreamboat asking her standing in front of the stunner, "You girl, why did you go to the roof? Did you not hear how our hostel boys commenting, jeering and heckling? Do you not know that I'm staying in neighbouring hostel?"

The statuesque stunner was struck with this sudden outburst of a so far meek gawar. She was astonished, 'How could a typical gawar from an undescriptive village, still in his worn-out school uniform of blue half-pant and white half-shirt, and seemed not yet relieved of his village hang-over, got so much of guts to shout at me, the most stylish and smart girl among all the Paharpur Ladies Hostel boarders as established last evening introduction session, and to the daughter of future Managing Director, RSP, the largest PSU in Orissa or in short, the daughter of a Big Gun.'

"What are you saying?" she shouted as she couldn't believe her ears. She pushed her left and right little fingers in her left and right ears and shaking them with an apparent display of cleaning them of unexpected intrusion. 'This is an unexpected loss of face.'

The stunner was in her display of pretending fury hiding her all the sympathies to the angry gawar. She caught the gawar's wrist hard and while pulling him with all her strength towards the empty curved wooden bench waiting at a corner, and used to cry instantly with every loading and off-loading of fleshy stuff as if this lifeless creature had been assigned to inform the attendant of the hostel the arrival and departure of each visitors to the hostel lobby, shouted stopping short of sitting, "Cool down, cool down, angry young man! Other may be hearing you," and asked in low but in firm authoritative tone, "First of all, tell me, who are thou to shout at me? I've to live my own life in my own way."

For the gawari, what was going on in her very presence were too much to put up with. She couldn't hold up seeing her very someone in such a pity and uneasy state of affairs, and heckled by an allergic city girl. Sympathy, sorrow, fear, anger, jealousy, fellow-feeling besides Bhagyabati aunty's advice started bombarding her thinking appliance with their full vigor from all directions. She strongly felt, 'She is fast loosing. Her all senses wanted her to act before it was too late.' Her village hang-over vanished in no time. She dived to the epicenter of activities to establish her right over her very someone who was bursting out drops of sweat with nervous and fear and in distress; she stood between them 'rock solid' snatching the hand of the city girl locked with her heart-throb's wrist.

The surprised statuesque stunner turned and saw the gawar trying hard to say something to her pointing his finger at the gawari almost down with apprehension, "Sorry sister, I didn't mean you! In fact, I mean Preeti!" The guardian in the city girl turned to the indiscipline gawari and after a teased look, demanded, "What yaar, you can't wait for a few minutes?" and quickly softening her tone certified, "Truly, yours 'catch' is a nice guy," and announced, "Well, the drama is over!" Soon she introduced her unsolicited, "By the way, I'm Seema . . . . Seema Pati from Rourkela and your heart-beat Preeti's room-mate—caged in Room No. 025." And, jocularly advised jumping her eyes, "Note, never try for whatsoever reason to forget that our custodians are celebrated Kumaris! Don't ever try to trespass the high Berlin Wall guarding we ripe jackfruits. Madams have promised us, they won't spare any intruder."

She extended her hand for a handshake. However, the awkward gawar was seemed hesitant. 'How could he shake hands; again, this was the first of its kind, with a bold and smart city girl, just introduced, and that too, in front of Pandupur ghungi?' He looked at the ghungi, disturbed; undecided with the city girl's latest gesture. The city girl understood. Patting both along with an assuring smiles though funny but serious, she started walking to cage no. 025 leaving a few beautiful and pleasing words, "By the way, I had persuaded Preeti to the hostel roof with my own personal agenda. Please forgive me and have a nice time and a few sweet sweet words. I'm extremely sorry to spoil your very limited but precious intimate time. Sorry! I'm little naughty! Thank you very much for your noble advices. Nice to meet you and speak to you. You're really impressive! Preeti should be proud of you," that having lasting impact on the suspecting girl's mind.

Both the peasants looked at the departing girl with interest.

"Smart Girl! Good room-mate! . . . . ain't it, Preeti? But, seems little childish and funny," Seema heard lately confident gawar defining her to Preeti.

As the time was running fast, they noticed the intensification of Pramiladidi patrolling of the lobby with red covered visitors register in her hand, and seemed saying to them boldly, 'Time is over!' She had a gesturing look at them.

But, the gawari thought, 'Is it because I'm from TROUBLE ZONE? Special Watch? . . . . May be?'

The submissive gawar apprehended and told, "Continuance of my stay in the lobby any more on the just second day might be troublesome." Still, the gawari was reluctant. She wanted to see her Rabi and ask and deliberate with him on all issues that she had encountered during her last few hours of stay in this new world.

Rabi got up, looking at Pramiladidi at the grill, with shy comforting pat on girl's clean and thin lovely open palm and with reminding words printing on that, "Don't be childish anymore! Follow the 'Rules and Regulations' of the hostel seriously and sincerely. Don't go by what other say. Go by what you think is right. Be in your own self!" While leaving the lobby, he reminded like an oldie guardian, "Remain ready for college at half past nine tomorrow, the first day in college."

Preeti bowed confirming to Rabi his unquestioned guardianship over her and followed him up to the outer gate; however, looking around scared of anybody's watch and repeat of yesterday's acerbic comment.

And she hummed, "Yes, my Lord! My sincere guardian!"

MISS BCS

'Attending lectures from lecturers; hopping from one class room to another at the end of each class; lab classes and practical experiments, no teacher imposed compulsory home works; no need of carrying ass load of books and notes, only a note book would do; large numbers of students in the class and scope of attendance duplication; no uniform, no detention for not completing home-work, no physical punishment from teachers. Full Freedom! An obvious promotion from rigorous school days to leisurely college life! Besides, free mixing of boys and girls, and lewd comments. Class tests, not compulsory; only course completion examination at the end of second year. No yearly promotion problem!' These were what all the new collegians admitted in the Intermediate had heard from their elders at their home or from their neighbours in their native place or in their villages having college exposures. They had to experience all these happenings in the college. So, they were in their life-time aficionado.

The day was significant as it was to herald a new chapter in their student life—'a big leap forward!' Preeti got up to the ring of the morning bell with a new hope, dream and imagination. They got into the preparation in full vigor, helped each other in combing their frizzy hair, a burdensome affair for any girl. As Preeti wished to braid her hair Seema suggested, "We must take up to easier and quicker practice," and handing over a hair band, she suggested, "Take this band and start using this. You'll feel more comfortable and relax. And, above all, you'll be looked more gorgeous and dashing," and passing a lovely wink told, "Don't worry! I'm confident, Mister Rabi will appreciate this. Or else, I'll take care of him."

"In fact, he is quite modern and pragmatic. This is what I find out; unlike you, a ghungi gawari!" observed the city girl after a short while. "Change you quickly! Or else, he will look for other. There are plenty in the college and on the city streets."

Seema opened her classy packed leather rucksack on the bed. This had ringlet a different aroma, unique to the gawari Preeti. And the gawari opened her half empty tin box pulling that from under the bed on the bare floor, noisy and crying. She was uncomfortable, and had a feeling of embarrassment but still pursued in her preparation with just a pair of churidar and kurti, chemise, panties, bodice—purchased from nearby village weekly market and home made coconut oil and collyrium; occasionally staring at the city girl's accessories.

Seema picked up scented Laxmi hair oil, Pond powder, Rupa bra and panties, brand new Reebok full shoe and Levi's navy blue jean pant and deep yellow collar T-shirt. "This costume is Sambit's favorite. Sambit had got this for me from Calcutta and gifted me before I boarded Utkal Express at Rourkela railway station on my way to this cursed exile," she revealed showing the sulky gawari the costume. Picking up her dreamboat's photograph kept inside the T-shirt, she planted a huge kiss and announced with a laugh, "With this pair of dress, I would look like a perfect Ratnagiri ripe Alfonso Mango and lecherous two legged chimps will beeline around me. Wow, what a kind of site! We'll enjoy Hanumans and Jambubans chattering and howling on the way to college and in the campus." And turning her side to Preeti, she asked, "What are you wearing on this Special Day?"

'What is there to say in comparison?' Preeti thought and kept quiet pulling the upper cover of the box down hiding the small belongings within that. Seema could understand and hugging Preeti sympathetically, consoled, "I'm sorry Preeti. We've to accommodate in our own world. Yet, Preeti, I'm very much at home with you. Please promise . . . . never part me so long as we're in Puri . . . . at least!"

In time, they got themselves ready for their journey to the new phase in their students' life. At exactly half-past nine all the new collegians queued up in the lobby to sign the register under the watch of Her Highness Ms. Warden's First Lieutenant, Ms. Ashantidevi. Seema located Rabi hanging around outside the Ladies Hostel gate amongst rickshaw pullers with a note book in hand; dutifully in a bid to provide much needed escort to his village image on her way to college.

"Madam, your bodyguard is ready in full gear!" Seema whispered at the ears of Preeti and acclaimed patting her, "You're so lucky! Alas, I've done a blunder not hooking a class-mate."

The shy gawari looked around—'probable checking whether anybody was watching'—, displayed her privileged smile. She gently patted at the stool-pigeon for the kind of information before she guardedly flew to peacock like a peahen.

Seema followed and in her trademark bubbly style pleaded, "Mister, I don't have any bodyguard to escort. Will you please allow me in your custody," and added, "I believe, we three could make a formidable squadron, for anybody to ever dare to encroach upon us and even wink."

But, Rabi jocularly directed the applicant to the crowd of rickshaw pullers vying for newcomers' attention with competing ear-biting "chring . . . . chring . . . ." rings. But, to no avail as the applicant wasn't so keen to his suggestion.

"Ooh yes! Why not? But, can you city grown well-heeled walk such a distance? During our school days, we used to walk barefooted double of this distance on the rutted clay road. In comparison, this distance here is very short and better. Besides, you know we can't afford the luxury of rickshaw riding on daily basis," and jeered, "we take this as an excuse for physical walk out that these rickshaw pullers understand better, and hence, they're very selective in their approach to customers. Further, I'll certainly not like them to lose their income by inviting you to our squadron. They may curse us. Besides, this isn't good for our social economy."

"But, still, you can take your own decision, and if so desired, you're most welcome!"

True to the gawar's observation, the experienced rickshaw pullers—strong in marketing sense—were forming their bee-lines after Seema, Rekha and others appeared came from well-up families—the social divide was markedly visible—ignoring Preeti, Rabi and of their kinds.

"This is the day the rickshaw pullers use to build a bond with new comers for long business relation. And the young, smart and libertine few market themselves for realization of rare dream, like in films," Seema told recalling what she'd heard from one of her friend's elder sister. She skipped the appeal of rickshaw pullers, and accompanied the walking squadron.

"Shalla gawars are spoiling our business!" the walking squadron to their much discomfort had to hear from a young and displaying smart rickshaw puller, failed to entice Seema.

"Or, for something else, smart bha . . . i . .a!" the outspoken Seema returned wittily. The marching squadron laughed covering their mouths with their palms to the discomfort of smart rickshaw puller who returned with equal vigor that the marching squadron refused to content with as they had a much important issue to deal with at their destination.

On their way, Seema delivered an interesting time-pass—the technique of a smart auto rickshaw puller who eventually ran away with his passenger, the daughter of senior plant officer and married in the court in her native city Rourkela. She explained, "You can see the horde of young and smart rickshaw pullers aren't roaming in front of Gents Hostel," and predicted, "and many of them will disappear over next two to three weeks if they failed to impress upon us this year leaving behind a few oldies."

Comments such as: 'the gawar brigade,' 'aah, rose from muddy village' . . . . loud lewd mare lip whistle were heard from bears and monkeys at the tea and pan shop on both side of the road, in front of widely opened college entrance decorated with colourful pamphlets and painted slogan of numerous political parties' students affiliates, and the appeals of the candidates aspiring to contest the upcoming college students union election welcomed them. Some students who were vying in the election approached them with small cards with their names printed.

However, the most surprising was Rekha's sudden appearance from nowhere and out of the blue applauded Preeti literally ambushing her on the campus alleyway, on their way to first floor office Notice Board, the fresher were supposed to march to collect the class time table on the first day. Before this, the gawari had a very little acquaintance of Rekha, that was what she'd heard at the time of introduction in the hostel under the tutelage of hostel's celebrated Kumaries just day before yesterday evening. 'Yes!' the gawari could instantly recalled, 'I had tasted her shoe-biting and heard her comments on Seema, and vice versa.'

Rekha forcefully strode into the horde straight to the ghungi gawari—walking flanked by her two faithful companions as she was nervous progressively being found the target of lewd growling and chattering of bears and monkeys on the way to college, at the entrance and that forth. The fleshy Rekha blocked the gawari's walk standing in front of her like an un-evadable Kumaris' Hostel wall. In adding to that she, lifting her hand for a handshake, cheered, "Congratulation! Congratulation, Preeti!"

The gawari was stunned, and so also, each member of the horde to the showing of smart and well make-up, the city grown daughter of future Puri DM, the aggressive Rekha's sudden and un-predicted flare-up. The confused gawari stared at her heart-throb who had promised her the uncompromising guardianship and guidance not much long ago on their way to this strange new world.

The equally uncomfortable gawar was clueless in this sudden outpouring from a very odd quarter. He felt awkward and embarrassed. As the gawari didn't get any answer from her very trusted guardian—a typical gawar not yet gloomed up to city standard—she turned to the other option she was fortunate to have at her arm's length, the city grown Seema for apparent succour, who was readily found to rescue her. She patted her with an assuring and maturing smile and later nodded her to accept the congratulation; of course, she wasn't aware what for?

Rekha's outburst was so sudden and so unexpected that nobody could get time to ask what for, even. More to the point, her personal posturing was so arrogant and irritating that they would like to avoid.

Rekha wasn't pleased with the gawari for her addiction to smart city girl. She frowned at the city girl and went on cajoling the un-cooperative gawari and her accompanied dreamboat as if she had a vested-interest that anybody could deduce.

There was a big crowd at the entrance of Office-cum-Arts Block that the marching squadron could notice. Rekha led them to there, unsolicited. What they could see from a little distance was: A black and white printed pamphlet with bold and underlined headline 'List of Miss BCS' and a few names listed below, which were not that legible, was found pasted on the entrance wall beyond anybody's hand reach. Literally, there was a huge commotion. Students, most particularly boys were found jumping and peeping over one another to read the mysterious content in the pamphlet.

The gawari found the situation similar to what she had seen at Chabishpur High School when their HSC Examination result, which was nothing less than lifetime achievement of examinees, was published on the school notice board. Humble and nervous with the strange happening, the two peasants preferred ignoring what was going-on there under guidance of the city girl—seemed confident to their satisfaction and pushed towards the college office.

'Certainly, there was something very very important published there,' the gawari however thought. To her surprise, she found there was no seriousness on the part of her new guardian. However, she neither asked nor questioned the wisdom of the city girl and followed her with equal footings like her heart-throb.

Not much they had walked, they were again ambushed with another announcement. This was gauche Rekha again. "Our hostel diva Preeti Rath has been voted Miss BCS. What a great feat? We're proud of her. We must celebrate. Hip, hip hurray! Congratulation Preeti! Congratulation, once again! Rabi, you too celebrate! Your village girl!"

The latest announcement was hard to ignore although many including the gawari Preeti and the gawar Rabi couldn't comprehend what was what although Rabi could instantly recall what he had heard on the day of Form Fill-up some seniors discussing the issue? The feet of everybody in the herd locked as if just crowned Miss Universe was among them, and they were so fortunate to see her and congratulate her so closely and celebrate. But the smarty guardian could guess what was going to follow and so she guided the pair to quickly move to first floor office Notice Board and from there to class room telling, "Be fast! Leave this rubbish here. I'll explain you."

The utterly confused and nervous peasants followed their confident and smart guide like the Hindu devotees in the sacred Lord Jagannath temples leaving behind other mates despite Rekha's desperate bid to stop them. Now, in the smaller squadron, the gawari and the smarty were found more exposed to the bears' and monkeys' growling and chattering, and their bodyguard—a typical gawar, breathing hard to accommodate in this new world—pushed him to further embarrassment.

Moment they reached the Physics gallery after collecting the time-table both nervous but curious peasants, plunged on their 'All Knowing' smarty escort, wanting to learn what she'd promised them to say before they rebuffed Rekha's bid to stop them at the entrance.

Seema was found serious and thinking, and later amusing. She, blinking her ever crazy eyes at the gawari, confirmed, "Our Preeti is now the college's queen bee . . . . the most beautiful girl! She is Miss BCS," furthering the peasants' interest with this strange feat that the gawari had no knowledge, forget about her participation.

In a pretending unhappiness and later with a sarcastic smile looking alternatively at the peasants—as if she was afraid of their frown ambush on her—she continued, "I was fully confident of cornering this feat for me like I was adjudged in my school but," and poking the gawari at her sloppy stomach, "this Pandupur sundari has run off with this rare crown from me. What to do in this old model city? Anyway, let's put up with whatever is available."

A completely pondering environment. All were hushed. The peasants were in their worst confusion. Intermittently, they were staring at each other and their guide.

'Perhaps, they were searching the answer on what's going on in front of them in the campus,' Seema guessed. She let them purposefully to remain in this state for fairly sometimes.

But, for how long? She was impatient. "Ha..ha . . . ha . . . . ," she laughed; . . . . very peculiarly provoking the peasants to think, 'Has Seema turned mad, not being awarded with this mysterious crown? . . . . may be?' Still they were in their pondering silence.

And, it was again the city girl who had to pull down the curtain of the confusion.

She lectured smiling, "That is nothing but some luffadamis of some loafers may or mayn't be the students of this college, to say the least. There's nothing official about it and deserved to be discarded at its face value. They published this for fun and amusement, and in some cases, with hidden agenda of cajoling gullible girls, and to trap them for their bawdy satisfaction. Our hostel Kumaris may be the victims of such a type of idiocy. This will be followed by unsolicited congratulations from the so-called smart but lewd loafers with scented flowers. And, after some days unsolicited offers of help with notes and books followed by love letters hidden inside with eloping message such as: I'm the son of that hotel owner, or this cinema hall owner or that officer or this doctor; so many cars and have such and many things and so many servants at home to attend; building on VIP Road or Grand Road in Puri or in Bhubaneswar, or in Calcutta or Delhi or Bombay . . . ."

"The village girls are their soft target. It isn't that our dear friend sweetie Preeti doesn't deserved to be crowned with Miss BCS title. She's gifted with natural beauty. She is intelligent. She is generous. She is one among the thousands," Seema continued appraising and applauding the shy girl.

The peasants were in full attention as they were required to learn all these city stuff for their graduation to city citizenship. Later with a pausing smile at the peasants and booting the upper slipper clad feet of the gawari on the close right, Seema applauded lightly clearing her throat, "And don't mind, but fact is our lovely and beautiful Preeti may be asked to compare with smart glittering urban proposal with low-key rustic Rabi. And what next, Rabi can guess now!" She went on teasing. "The fate of the bichara Sisupal may await our today's cute and sparking Karna . . . . Is not it, Miss BCS?"

Preeti, who was seemed totally disturbed with back to back succession of unfamiliar events and the city girl's latest disturbing forecasting of future events that she hadn't remotely comprehended in her thought ever since the proposal for her higher study in the city was finalised by her ambitious papa, was serious and thinking. Speechless, the gawari looked at the revealer and her heart-throb alternatively—disbelieved and apprehensive. And she was pondering, 'What this mad girl is vomiting at, non-stopped?'

And, the highly embarrassed, and seemed uncomfortable with all these forecasting, Rabi turned to her and snapping her in her teasing eloquent dismissively appealed, "Please for God's sake, stop all these non-senses! What are you talking? This is too early to indulge in such type of stupid talks!"

"Sorry! Sorry, Baba! I shouldn't have gone so far," nodded the statuesque stunner instantly looking apologetic at the aggressive Rabi.

Rekha, appeared not so happy, later coming to class, occupied a seat behind them in the Physics gallery, and was found grumbling and uttering something directed at Seema not so pleasant to hear.

In the meanwhile, the lecture arrived and after a brief introduction of him to the gallery packed with more than hundred overjoyed new collegians started Physics Theory class.

"Bloody, thinks she is the most smart and intelligent girl in the entire college. Let's see!" an inferno having huge potential to ignite a destructive clash between the two daughters of Big Guns hit the eardrums of the trio as soon as the Physics lecturer vacated his position on the dais. Humble Rabi, scarred of a clash caught the hand of Seema by-passing Preeti in a bid to pass the message to remain cool ignoring the fire, and requested hurriedly, "Let us move fast to Biology Block."

"Okay, baba! What to do? I'm in your city," the statuesque stunner complied trembling with anger.

"That's a Good Girl! I appreciate," the gawar thumped up, and the little squadron marched fast.

The gawari, who'd already reduced her to the level of obedient dancing monkey in the hands of her handlers, shy of her undesired elevation in this new world, followed the guide and her own heart-throb—flanked by them on left and right, and occasionally in front and back—without asking any question in the crowded corridor, she was best saved from any kind of trouble. She trusted them.

On the way to Biology Block, they heard bears and monkeys standing by the parapet of the long corridor and talking pointing at their prey, "Who is that Preeti Rath—Miss BCS? Ooh, that one in the middle in white churidar and green kurti, next to that deep yellow T-shirt and blue jean diva! Looked like a peasant. Wow! Indeed, an angel from muddy hamlet!"

"But, the yellow T-shirtwalli . . . . not bad yaar! Modern, smart, gorgeous and dazzling; seems from a modern city," another applauded. Yet another went on acclaiming, "Her eyes could rival the legendary lotus eyes of dashing Gayatri Devi."

The theatric was closely followed by unsolicitated revelation, "She's the daughter of Director, RSP, Rourkela," from gauche Rekha, walking just behind them. And, the smarty's quick glance at the audience, twisting her statuesque body to back along with furling of her T-shirt collar by her naked gorgeous fair skinned right hand, made the environment more vibrant and amorous—promoting further chattering, buzzing, growling and lip-whistling from lecherous loafers.

Nevertheless, they moved as wished by Rabi non-stop to reach their destination pretending, they were unperturbed of unpleasant and envious vomiting on the way.

"Wow, what a style? What a look? What a walk? Really, rather this T-shirtwalli should be voted Miss BCS than this ghungi gawari. Now-a-days, the gawaris have overtaken the urbanites in the beauty selection," rued the loafers on the way. And the trio later heard, "What a beautiful sight, the pair of Miss BCS and Miss Smarty-BCS make! They're drawing room show piece. We must capture them in our camera."

This was another feather on the cap of three member squadron. And, Rabi didn't lose time and cheered, "Congratulation, Miss Smarty!"

And, he was immediately attended with a huge wink, the first of its kind that the gawar blasted with from Miss Smarty. He was stunned and thought, 'Why should the gawari mama and the gawari Preeti not be terrified by the city girls? So prompt!'

But, these were very pinching and discomforting to Rekha, following them foot by foot. She was—seemed—burning almost resembling a burning coal in the hostel's oven which provoked Miss Smarty to mock, "Perhaps, the daughter of a Big Gun was expecting a place in the college beauty list but got rejected by bears and monkeys."

The peasants were uncomfortable with the Rekha's hostility with their accompanied virtual guardian, Seema. The question of 'why Rekha is inimical to the girl, and again, why she's showing so much of interest to Preeti,' puzzled the peasants the most. They wanted to discuss among them in this regards but failed to do so with back to back classes with very little break time. Besides, in most of the time Seema was close with them. To their surprise, she wasn't found that much disturbed. Instead, she was enthusiast and bubbling, as if she was enjoying even every turn of the college uncouth time.

'Is the city society shameless? Certainly, ours' is better—at least there's no open and quarrelsome vulgarity,' the peasants evaluated among them remembering their village society.

In the canteen, there was the echo of that so-called Miss BCS pageant. At the threshold, as they were about to enter the canteen, they heard from inside somebody invisible, proclaiming, "Her Highness Miss BCS and Miss Smarty-BCS badharrahia," and requested, "Kesabkaka, please prepare something Special! Two divas guarded by their Prince Charming have been pleased to grace your stinking canteen on the very first day of their crowning, that too uninvited!"

"Now, Kaka's canteen will have good business," yelled yet another.

True to the observation, there were a mad rush to the canteen followed by a virtual mild fight for space.

"Ooh, this is why Kesabkaka pays so much interest in publication of Miss BCS list? No doubt, Kesabkaka deserves salutation for his business sense."

"See, Chottu instantly follows the trio!"

The reluctant trio shyly occupied a space in one corner, desperately trying to be away from the lecherous gaze. They heard some—appeared seniors—discussing among them the issue too.

'This is like the college has no other business on the day,' the peasants were thinking.

Miss Smarty jeered, "What a farce of the situation? Bichara Miss BCS has a status but unable to celebrate?"

And, they heard the debates:

Some were against while many other were in favour of the publication of the list of Miss Beauty. Those, who weren't so happy and against, were advocating to ban the publication of this so-called list of college beauties.

"This is putting a very bad psychological impact on the girls, the majority of them coming from lower middle-class background in our not so-upgraded society. This is the handiwork of some repeaters and roaming loafers, and also some oldie and frustrated element still hanging in the campus through back door means. Need to be banned! This issue should be raised during the College Students Union election," one vociferously howled.

Kesab Swain with red pan juice wrapped teeth smiled at the proposition and frowned like the epic Ramayana's Lord Hanuman did to the Rabana's guards in the Panchabati Garden. All presents turned to him. However, another senior reasoned, "Even if college administration will ban this stupidity, the question of implementing the ban is next to impossible as the campus is free for all!" Many concurred.

Whereas a few other were in favour of the Miss BCS publication and argued, "What's wrong in this? This makes the college more vibrant, lively, exciting and interesting.

We're no more mere small kids . . . yaar! Grown-up and matured! Let's have fun and study together."

As if this view was very amorous to Miss Smarty's ears, she winked at the gawari and kicked at the gawar.

"We should be broad minded. This will encourage our college girls to participate in Miss India followed by Miss Universe . . . . Miss World competition," and lamented, "So far, no girl from our state has been crowned with Miss India title and only one Indian accomplished Miss World crown. And, in Miss Universe pageant, India till date draw a shameful blank. Is it not a great tragedy for about eighty crores strong Indian population?"

The trio were hearing the pros and cons debate in rapt attention while lifting to their mouths hot piaji-pakadi, unconcerned of its taste and aroma. Ever interested to make fun, the bubbling Seema couldn't keep quite when the debate on India's poor status in beauty pageant was going on. She, while looking at Rabi with smile, nailed Pandupur houri at her soft narrow lion waist and amusingly whispered, "We must propose and encourage our lovely Miss BCS to participate in Miss India pageant. Why not? She's this year Miss BCS, next year Miss Puri, then Miss Orissa, and so on, so forth. Alas, what a great feat! Preeti, you have Sophia Loren's eyes, Brigitte Bardot's cascading hair, Faye Dunaway's rosy high cheeks, Regina Taylor's luscious plump lips, Barbie Doll curves, Betty Brosmer's pin up era hourglass figure, Kate Moss's legs and height!"

"Besides you have gifted with the personal distinctiveness of Reita Faria, so far the only Indian crowned with Miss World title. Are you ready? I'm ready to coach you. Mind . . . . free of cost!"

This was too much that the ghungi gawari from a remote typical Indian hamlet—Khandi Pandupur, which was even after more than three decades of liberation from centuries of alien rules, didn't have an all season road and school beyond VII standard, could tolerate any more. Pandupur ghungi hissed, "You non-sense, the shameless city girl, stops these miss . . . fiss . . . brigi . . . . kate talk! Had we been in the room no. 025, I would have pulled out your naughty tongue and smashed your fluttering jaw bone," and roared, "Stupid, what a disgraceful proposal you're offering? And, that too, in front of Rabi! Have you ever thought what he'll be feeling?" And, snarled munching her teeth. However, at the moment, she restricted her to just kicking smarty on her fully covered leg, which boomeranged hurting her. And she screamed with pain, "Um, the smarty has a hard shoe!"

"Sorry, yours Highness Miss BCS, let's go to the next class if not interested in my plump proposal at your own loss. You would have got opportunities to interact, mingle and body caress with glamorous film stars, film producers and directors from Bollywood; and advertisers, writers, editors and who's who of glittering Bombay city. And, they would have got you surveyed of your pompous body, to check your suitability for heroine role in their upcoming films or for modeling in advertisement campaign for promotion of panties, bra, body lotion, lipstick, vanity bag," smiling glamorous Seema went on humouring sulking gawari raising her palm to her own bowed head of Moghul durbar's jhampanna style.

FIRST OUTING

After two days, there was the first college holiday for the fresher in hostel. They were waiting for this blessed day since their landing in their new habitat. They could move around in Puri—side by side with their boy-friends 'if any?'—in its sprawling Grand Road, in its huge markets; could visit Lord Jagannath temple and could walk in long and broad golden sea beach free from any family restriction imposed on grown up girls at their native places, away from the patrolling eyes of their suspecting near and dear.

Preeti had her plan: she to accompany her very own humble and cute sparking Karna—sweet-talking, curling hand by hand, foot by foot—wanted to walk to Lord Jagannath Temple and would pray to Lord for a very lovely life with her heart-throb. She had full confidence on Lord Jagannath, an avatar of Dwaparajug's legendary great devotee of eternal-love, cow-herd and flute-singer Lord Krishna that he would certainly listen to her prayer. Besides, she had to beg to Lord to give the good sense to her papa and mama, who were nourishing a double-crossing intention in regard to her heart-throb and her revered aunty, and to see reason in the mother-son's personality and honest attitude. Besides, she wished to sit next to her heart-throb on the Golden Sea Beach and would talk openly opening all the chapters hidden in her heart—suffocating her time and again—looking at length and breadth of the open, broad, endless and relentlessly waving great ocean.

"So, on coming holiday what is your plan, Preeti?" Seema inquired while the trio were walking to college.

As it was uppermost in her mind and Preeti was longing for fine-tuning the programme since long time, she instantly started, "We'll first visit Lord Jagannath Temple and then . . . . ," as the smarty interrupted with her jeering laugh, "Ha . . . ha . . . . ha . . . ," and commented, "to the shore of Big Tank. Isn't it, Miss BCS?"

Gawari stared at smarty, her eyebrows raised and eyes flashed. And smarty turned to Rabi, who looked surprised, and asking. He was eager to know what the matter was—'it appeared.'

"Guess!" advised the smarty looking at the boy, smiling, ... and later supplemented haltingly, "This is Preeti's Big Tank that saved us from marauding Kumaris that day morning on the roof of the hostel." The gawari looked at the smarty with threatening fire in her eyes— might be assuming that this clever city girl wouldn't spare her and certainly rake up fun of her here in front of her heart-throb.

But, the funny girl was unmoved, despite threatening poser from the ghungi gawari, gurgled, "Preeti at the first sight of sea, applauded, 'What a Big Tank?' This was the bramhastra that cooled Kumaris down with all sympathy to our Miss BCS."

"Ha . . . ha . . . ha . . . ," Rabi busted with laughter and was uncontrollable. He was equally keen to enjoy the moment furthering the momentum. "Hallo, Miss BCS, is it true? . . . . shame, shame! I'll tell to all our villagers, mama, uncle, aunty, Karankaka and Priya," he announced comically and clapping the smarty's hand, applauded, "What a presence of mind! You're really 'The Great'—Miss Smarty!"

Humiliated, the ghungi run to the spoiler of her image with raised fisticuffs, and as the target speeded up looking at the attacker in her bid to rescue self on the narrow lane connecting VIP Road with College Road, came crashing a cycle rickshaw. She was however saved from the jaw of the mauling rickshaw as the alert rickshaw puller applied the sudden break.

But, what followed the incident was mind-bending and was hard to leave aside by any self-respected human-being.

"Hey, so-called Miss Smarty! Rourkela beauty! Don't forget that this isn't your city," they heard from about to fall and appeared disturbed kitschy Rekha, the envious and bothering comment. That didn't end there. As the rickshaw puller started pedaling, she went on throwing the unsolicited advices to the humble peasants, "Mr. Prince Charming, remain save of this modern city girl! Bichara Miss BCS, God knows what's there in your fate?" And, she vanished with speed of tri-cycle leaving the bichara gawari crying with unavoidable fearsome thought.

"Whoop, what a mad creature! Bloody, doesn't have a minimum sense of humility and decency. What a cursed by-product of the privileged arrogance, a true replica of Supanakha," Miss Smarty—fired but not injured—reacted with a huge rejecting laugh, "Ha.. ha..ha . . . ." Even so, they marched—amid ungracious pouring of lewd chattering from flying passersby on their bicycle, rickshaw and bikes—after the bloody skirmish.

"I believe, she is a rejected Supanakha, and in exile; and must be in search of her next prey," Miss Smarty as if not to lay aside, breaking the stillness considerably, roared what was there boiling in her mind,

'..................'

"Now, I understood why she was so cozy to Miss BCS on the very first day of our college," she black-humoured thought-provokingly.

The humble gawari stopped. And her co-walkers felt, 'She wanted others too to stop.' As if the latest disclosure from Miss Smarty apart from Supanakha's advice to her and her Prince Charming were warning bell to her, she tear-looked at her heart-throb in panic and despair. Her deer eyes were asking, Rabi felt, 'My Prince Charming, my soul, my heart-throb, what am I hearing here? Sorry, I can't live my life without you. I want an assurance from none other than you. And you have to attend or else be sure, I am not moving an inch!' Her eyes prayed without fall of eyelids.

Although Rabi was disturbed yet he'd no alternative but to attend the query of the poor girl, obsessed with love. 'What to do with this mad girl?' Yet, he smiled in desperation, assuring. He attended with a self-assured display of confidence, and rejecting Miss Smarty's prediction, chattered, "Smarty Madam, I believe, you're an avatar of Pandu's son Sahadeva in this Kaliyug. With all regards to your valued prognostication, I wish to suggest you to please stop all these wild and absurd speculation and non-sense viewing. I don't find any merit in all these points. Let's concentrate in study. Bury and forget this matter here itself. Leave this as if this was just an accident without any scared injury. So, nothing to remember. And, that's all!"

Seema could understand the pain in the gawari's heart. She had all sympathy to her. She went close to her and hugging on her shoulder she told assuring, "Well, I'm with you. Just have faith on me! I repeat, 'I'm not your competitor.'"

But, the gawari was hardly convinced as she remembered aunty's advice, 'No smart city girl is dependable. What I would do now?' She felt insecure and fast losing confidence in her own self. She was more concerned for her heart-throb than for her own security from lewd preying eyes and lecherous tongues.

This had ended their holiday's outing planning abruptly as they, in the meanwhile, reached the class room.

That was an afternoon. They were returning to hostels. Preeti's mind was pre-occupied with the thought of holiday's outing plan.

"Reach at 12 noon at our hostel gate after taking launch. No excuse for whatsoever reason," she ordered her bodyguard. "Our dear friend smarty has already spoken to four inmates who will go for outing at that hour so that the formality of five inmates going out together can be solved. We will first go to the temple, from there to Miss Smarty's (with her fore-finger at her lip, comically smiling, looking at the targeted girl) Big Tank and back to hostel by afternoon nasta."

Rabi looked at smarty with blinking eyes as he found her standoffish on the subject. 'She is part and parcel of our team,' he believed and wanted to enforce.

"Sorry Rabi, I don't like to disturb my good friends' very intimate hard found time and privacy . . . . Alas, I have to suffer my exile! Let my parents succeed in their career . . . . my penance! Please leave me in my world," replied, the despaired and dejected, ever bubbling statuesque stunner looking skyward with late bursting tear in ever promising lotus eyes.

Rabi couldn't grasp what he heard, so abrupt and alien.

'Exile . . . . parents' career . . . . penance . . . . leave me in my world . . . . what are these, the girl is saying,' he analysied. The verbatim couldn't be so easily milled in the mind of the peasant Rabi, who hadn't yet relieved from his meek muffasali hang-over. 'Is ever-funny Miss Smarty in trouble? But, till now, she isn't appeared so? She is beautiful, helpful, humble, funny, elegant, considerate and sweet. How could such a beautiful girl be in such a pain and sorrow? Whatever, I enjoy her company.' Rabi went on thinking. 'Without her, the outing won't be that interesting!' he concluded. He wanted to know instantly all her pain and sorrow.

But, his appeal was met with drops of tear flowing down from lotus eyes to her cheeks and chin. Her tone was locked. The gawar, being failed getting the answer, turned to Preeti. Their walk back to hostels was slowed down till Preeti had finished the girl's 'tale of sorrow' with all sympathy and pain.

"Regrettable!" was the shocked peasant's spontaneous outburst. He was dumbstruck as he was fixed in disbelieve. He looked at the sky thinking, 'Has my papa been there, would he have been so self-seeking and callous? But, my mama is different!' Cleaning his sweating face pulling out the handkerchief from his trouser pocket, he came close to the distressed girl. He placed his brotherly hand on her shoulder, assuring and sharing.

As they came nearer to the custody of Kumaries, the down-spirited girl run away downing her head as Rabi announced authoritatively, "If Seema isn't accompanying us, tomorrow's pilgrimage is cancelled." Though the ghungi Preeti wasn't very happy with her Prince Charming camaraderie with the city girl— courtesy aunty's warning and her own fear—, yet she couldn't protest her dear's verdict and decree.

They had to mount a cycle rickshaw on their way to Lord Jagannath Temple, the patron deity of the city. The smarty insisted to seat in order of Rabi, Preeti and she despite the gawari's—intentionally or unintentionally that she only could say—pushing the smarty following Rabi that forced him to flash a teasing smile. He was about to open his mouth on the issue but stopped hearing a huge black-omen sneeze on the back. The trio turned to the Gents Hostel gate.

"Shit! Yours good friend Lalu Sarangi," Preeti cried and shouted at Rabi, "You buddu must have discussed our outing plan in your hostel. Or else how did he know our plan and timing?"

"Bloody blackish-Kaaliram, the black-omen, garbage from Twentysixpur septic tank has been omni-present. Idiot spoiled the auspicious moment," cried Preeti and instantly ordered, "Friends, let's get back to hostel lobby. After sometimes, we'll go."

Before the other two think anything, the ghungi was already inside the lobby in a few hops. Her mates followed her as they'd no alternative but to respect the sentiment of their commander at the moment.

In the lobby, she wasn't ready to listen anything from her mates. Later, she came out of the Kumaries' safe cave and surveyed like the mongooses do at the threshold of their hole standing on their toes, checking before venturing out. Satisfied, she came out and signaled Ramuchacha san words. She wanted they should quickly mount the tri-cycle and leave. But, the branded bad omen again re-appeared.

But, this time, Miss BCS was defiant. "This is too much! Let's move," the impatient ghungi shouted. She—appeared fired—threw her body at the rather dull gawar that the gawar and the city girl were enjoying—smiling at the every act of her frenzy—on the cycle rickshaw frowning Lalu Sarangi, as he looked-see. 'Crying!'

The three pilgrims had their own issues in their mind to place before the revered Lord of Universe. When Rabi was thinking to pray for a suitable tuition to earn for his study and his now lonely mother's health back home; Seema, the victims of her parent's selfish-end, was thinking to pray for return of her happy days. And, Preeti was considering begging the Load to forgive her for being so unfaithful to humble and simple Rabi and her lovely aunty, not revealing before them what she knew about her papa's hidden agenda. As they were busy in their thought, there was a pensive silence on the cycle rickshaw except 'surr . . . surr . . . surr . . . .' noise.

As they moved towards Laxmi Talkies alongside noon-show goers chattering on glittering Bollywood stars by-passing BCS College Campus Hostel gate, the lewd vulgar growling and chattering from bears and monkeys started pouncing on them.

"Wow! What a sight? Miss BCS and Miss Smarty are in fulsome display," one standing in front of pan shop cheered. While another acclaimed, "What a beautiful combination? But, who's this cute boy? Is he their fiancé or escort? What a catch? A lucky guy!"

While another shouted, "Who knows—he wouldn't be another bichara Mister Bachelor—Kesab Swain?"

Virtually, the trio were star attraction on the city street. Everybody's attention was on them.

Some followed the rare combination, refreshing their eyes, hungry of beauties—mounting on their cycles and bikes, and occasionally, resorting to vulgar comments.

For the gawar Rabi, this was unbearable. And, he felt impotent in the presence of two girls. He pondered over the thought of 'how could the brother, the husband, the father and the relations accompanying their sister, wife and daughter manage on this city streets?' He closed his eyes in rejection and later wanted to cover his face unfolding the handkerchief in pain and resentment, and told him, 'Were it our Pandupur village, I'd have taught a good lesson to these loafers?'

The sulking gawari covered her head with her dupatta and offered to share the same with the smarty, who was in her trademark T-shirt and jean pant. The smarty could understand their male buddy's pain, and so peering at him, she gestured to hold down and keep cool, and resentfully rued, "This is the hell of the social life for any naturally gifted girl, and extremely painful to their male companions. You know my grandma and grandpa blame this to advent of modern cinemas plenty of vulgarity in the disguise of artistic expression. Awful! We've to live with this as part of our social life, the living-hazards!"

But, the gawari wasn't in league with her. She was assaultive and told blaming, "All at once, we shouldn't wear exposing attire . . . . provocative! We girls are partly responsible for all these."

"That means only boys have got the license to wear their wished attires . . . . why? And you, a girl, support them. Chie . . . chie . . . . ! This is very unfortunate . . . . very bad!" the stunner screamed. The debate went on and on without the active participation of Rabi although he was provoked occasionally by the stunner with body poking and stunning winks by-passing the ruing ghungi gawari sitting in the middle.

"But, my dear Preeti, I'm very comfortable in this wear. What to do? And again my 'would-be' is fond of to see me in this wear only. You know, one day, I was in your costume—churidar and kurti, and he, on sight of me, kept his eyes closed till I changed to his choice one. And, next day, he was at our doorsill with two pairs of Jean pants and T-shirts . . . . Sorry yaar! You must support me," she pleaded. "Since then . . . ."

"Hey Mister, you check, any part of my body is exposed? Isn't it fully covered?" shouted the stunner standing up tall on the non-hooded rickshaw to the instant applause of chattering monkeys following close behind, "What a sight? Rare! Stunning! Keep it up! Keep it up! We're recording."

But the ghungi, unmindful of unsolicited applause, shouted, "What's this non-sense? How can a boy check? The city girls are very clever—instead of asking me . . . . !"

"Sorry . . . sorry . . . . ," cajoled the girl sitting down and embracing.

Yet, again, they weren't spared at Lord's abode. Pandas and pujaries crashed on them for one or other reasons. While the half naked oldies were after them to purchase their flowers, ghee-diyas and prasad; the younger lots were with their smarter display of traditional half-naked get-ups. And, some were competing among them offering the temple guide services. To the surprise of the peasants, they were found the younger lots were giving more concentration on them.

"Why not? We're such materials!" the smarty whispered at the ears of the uncomfortable peasants. She narrated what she heard about the nefarious acts of these elements of Lord in his own abode from her beloved Sambit, who'd in the recent past visited the Lord along with his grandpa, grandma, and sister, and vowed not to visit the Lord; they were so ashamed of the Lord attendants' lecherous behaviour. She, now the virtual guardian of the nervous peasants, declined the attendants in all her boldness despite irksome heckling very similar to the one the lecherous rickshaw puller displayed on the first day of the college in front of hostel gate, that the peasants appreciated. The smarty herself took the responsibility to guide the uncomfortable and dispirited peasants to various part of the temple complex paying obeisance here and there. But, in the sanctum sanctorum of the Lord, the ghungi was found awfully upset, and about to break down. She was melting to the surprise of her accompanied escorts as if she was rebuffed by the Lord for the blessing she appealed. Her closed playmates looked at her asking but in vain as the girl was found evading.

They guided her to the Laxmi Mandir's platform nearby. As she wasn't forthcoming with her revelation on her reason of being upset so sudden despite their curious digging out glance, they preferred to leave the matter to her for the time being.

"Let's move to the shore of the Big Tank," Seema told looking at the ruing ghungi in her bid to lighten the pensive moment and philosophically concluded, "Let the huge and broad tank of our dear Miss BCS washed out all our pain and sorrow by her ever clean and energized waves if not the Lord of Universe in his expansive abode."

On the way, they ignored repeat of frenzied growling of bears, chattering of chimpanzees and prying stare of vultures hungry for teeny flesh as if they were advised by the Lord to be sympathetic to the poor creatures—seemed deprived—, and to move ahead bold and steady and undaunted, forgiving as they were born for something great to pursue. 'They're huge elephants marching on the street unconcerned of barking dogs.'

That was the tropical rainy season's afternoon. But, the sky was free from any usual dark cloud and afternoon sun was reflecting on the sand enticing the atmosphere to very pleasant and lively one. The big sea was unrelenting in embracing with waving kisses to the lovely but shy sea-lines veiled by the shadow of beach-walkers under the setting-sun in the western sky. The sea beach was bursting with crowd of all age brackets, substances and intents. After getting down in front of Puri Hotel they'd to refresh them freed from tight sitting of two people's capacity cycle-rickshaw for about two kilometers ride in half an hour on crowded chattering city narrow lanes.

"What a great relief?" Rabi reacted jumping down, and instead of extending a helping hand to the crowned beauty of district's premier college reflecting an envious glitter under the descending sun-shine, like he did at Lord's Singhdwar on the Grand Road hour before, he run to the shore-line shouting, "You, motti, you should start dieting, at least for Ramuchacha' respite; if not for your lean and thin bichara co-passengers. Am I right, Seema madam?"

"Nothing doing! I'm not going," sounded the ghungi smiling assertively after a long time.

Seema paid the fare, and before walking to the shore-line, advised provoking the enchanting beauty, "Don't get down! Let him come . . . . he has to come. Don't worry, I'll ensure!"

And, there at the shore-line, she pulled Rabi and directing him to see Lalu Sarangi walking towards glittering diva on the cycle rickshaw, asked him, "Go and get her! Or else, Kaaliram is ready to fill the vacuum."

Bichara Rabi had no alternative but to rush to the pig-headed diva. As he extended his helping hand to the self-enthroned diva, proud of pulling the adamant boy to her knees, Seema, following closely, bubbled, "Lalu! Lalu!" And in no time, lovebirds were together: they were together descending one over another in the sequence they were just before—houri's frizzy free hair on Rabi, invisibling his head; forehead to forehead, eyebrows to eyebrows, eyes to eyes, nose to nose, not lip to lip (nose huddle), chest to chest (asymmetrical), hands to hands, waist to waist, thigh to thigh, knees to knees; and the viewers could undisputable claim complete dash—body to body—envious sight—and the mad girl, not ready to release.

The cries of sympathy were all around—down-pouring like Kalla Baisakhi thunderstorm. Many came forward, rushing. Lalu ran but stopped short of reaching the pair's body contours as Seema's service made him surplus. And, the fluttering girl while pulling Preeti, yelled, "Baap..re . . . e! You're so open! . . . . Who wouldn't cry, forget about bichara Lalu?"

They walked to shore-line—two girls busy dusting the sand over Rabi's hair and sweaty body—but not without the bubbling from Seema, "Sorry yaar! I had to check physical equation between you two."

The enthusiast Preeti looked at her, searching and eager to know—'felt the smarty'—the finding.

"What a great matching? No doubt, you're born for each other. I forecast, 'You would be a great pair . . . . physically like Veeru and Basanti. From waist to up, Preeti is just two inches short and waist to down again

224

two inches short.' Not bad! World standard! But, you are below world standard in age, 'Same age bracket, is not it?' There is certainly some problem in this area."

"No, no! . . . . I'm one year junior to my dear Rabi," the cheerful diva corrected.

"Had I asked you?" shouted the stunner, piercing. "Ideal standard age gap is three years, you dim-wit don't know. My Prince Charming is fully matching in age and in height with me."

"Sorry, my dear Miss All Knowing! No, it's half of boy's age plus seven years. Of course, I agree, we are matching on this count at present but wouldn't remain so with passing of age," shouted Preeti. "In this area, you must think twice before challenging me."

"It means you'd pre-designed the staging," Mr. Innocent shouted. He wasn't happy with Miss Smarty that Miss Happiest could apprehend. And, ergo, before Mr. Innocent pounced on her like-minded and supportive smarty with more verbal attack, the happiest initiated the long forgotten childhood game of water and wet-sand throwing on the sulking innocent, they were once indulging in on the bank of the river Ratnachira at Pandupur village, abandoned in the past couples of years as her reverend mama opposed such indulgence since the commencement of once-in-a-month problem, saying, "You're grown up now!"

Later, Miss Smarty joined them.

The trio played with the rhythm of dancing sea waves supported by tinkling of Pandupur beauty's singing nupurs attracting envious and stealthy glances of beach-walkers comprising the likes of Khandi Pandupur's Salu, Galu, Sarua, Gandua, Baia, Dukhi, ...

and the city's licking bears and chattering apes. Once exhausted, they walked northwards on the land edge in search of a place free from crowd, talking and joking and picking up issues starting from Miss Warden's talk of jackfruit to possibility of the reluctant ghungi gawari's participation in the Miss Universe pageant, to Supanakha's bursting at Miss Smarty, to Kaaliram's crying look and to temple pot-belly half-naked Pandas' unsolicited guide service. They discussed everything they'd experienced during the last couple of days in hostels, in college campus and in Lord Jagannath's Puri.

And Miss Smarty pulling Miss BCS away from the Mr. Innocent asked searchingly, "The cow-belly Pandas' must be a big burden on their partners on the bed . . . . I've all my sympathy to their bichara patnis. But, we're blessed. My Sambit is sound in health. And also yours! Ensure, Mr. Innocent remain so." And she went on in her eloquent till she was elbowed and advised, "You must get married early. You've so much of research on the subject."

However, Rabi's question to the enthusiast Preeti searching the reason of her upset at Lord's sanctum sanctorum paled the situation as the beauty slipped to ghungi state and found musing. A dark cloud invaded the small squadron again.

Seema and Rabi looked at each other, stunned. Both looked at fast fading beauty. After a while, she broke the silence requesting, "Let's get back to hostel. I'm not feeling well." As a matter of fact, there was nothing unusual in it for the boy as the girl used to ask shyly for such abrupt end of their study or whiling away on several occasions before in Pandupur during the past couple of years.

Seema smiled looking at the ghungi gawari and Rabi looked away, distancing. She, a cursed bird enjoying beauty of the nature and playing with the like-minded buddies, wasn't ready to go to Kumaris caves so early. And, as natural, she wasn't very pleased with Preeti. However, she accepted the fading houri's request as if there was no alternative; but not without a teasing scream, "You, dim-wit . . . . could not wait for another one hour," and playfully advised curling her hand with the cute boy at Preeti's arm distance, "Better, you go to hostel. We'll go later."

"Do you think, I can't go? I can manage without ye people. But, I'm sorry to say, I have given words to aunty, not to leave her cute chand-ke-tukkuda (winking at Rabi) with a smart city girl. What to do? I'm sorry."

"Or, bichara Rabi has been assigned to escort the beauty in this not-so female friendly world," provoking a thinking look in Rabi's appearance.

But, back in the room no. 025, Seema was surprised to find nothing abnormal in the Preeti's activities. She fired, "What for you ghungi, stupid spoiled our beautiful whiling away?"

As Preeti left for the lavatory in hurry, the guardian Seema concluded, 'There's something that the ghungi is hiding.' And, she resolved, 'I've to dig out. I should as we are now close-friends. We must share each other's pain and sorrow. And help each other whenever required—relieving. This is friendship! Or else, how could we pass the time comfortable in this cursed Kumaris cave? And I'm not ready to live in depression as I have promised to Sambit. I need friends; friends—free, frank, sharing and above all, humorous and funny.'

"Nope, nope . . . . the business of hiding isn't acceptable," Miss Smarty announced fluttering as the ghungi entered into the cave no. 025.

After the dinner when the ghungi laid on the bed with the class note, the witty Seema murmured exploring, "I prayed to Lord to give my parents some sense of righteousness and take care of my Sambit in my absence at Rourkela. And, my great Lord promised, he would. I'm extremely happy for his kindness to his this poor devotee."

Still, there was no response. And, she waited . . . . the ghungi was still found craftily evading. She pulled the pillow under the ghungi's head.

"Aah! Ooh! Stupid, what's this non-sense? You're always very thorny. You're interfering. I'm exhausted . . . . do not disturb," the ghungi cried with pain as her head dropped hard on the bed.

"Preeti, I'm asking what did you pray to Lord?" the statuesque stunner demanded forcefully standing by her bed side.

"Why? Why should I say . . . . very confidential!"

But, the ghungi couldn't be successful in her effort and finally she gave up, revealing. "I beg to Lord, to give my parents some sense of righteousness. But, my Lord was in his woody stillness, non-committal. I cried. Yet, he kept quiet . . . . I'm a cursed girl," Preeti sobbed with heavy breath. On determined demand, she disclosed what her father meant in regard to her heart-throb and dear destitute aunty.

"But, whatever, I can't live without him. He is my 'LOVE'; he is my heart; he is my soul. I can't think of my existence without my dear Rabi. So, this is my selfish end. I'm hiding from Rabi my papa's selfish intention. I don't know how long I can do so? I don't know what the simple and humble Rabi will think when he comes to know about my fraudulent intention? And, again, I don't know whether I can leave without Rabi in my this birth. I beg to Lord to forgive me. And he refused; he was non-committal." Preeti opened up and revealed in a few gasp.

So, both the love-infected birds were victims of their parent's self-centric mania. Thus, the poor Seema had to go to bed with one more pain and sorrow in her heart.

"Let's pray to Lord of Universe, Lord Jagannath, and this was what we could do, at best," they self-consoled, embracing each other.

MR. BCS

A shiner shines anywhere; he can't remain clouded under any cover despite the fact that in some cases the conducive surrounding is required to thrive. In the widely revered and pious epic Mahabharata too, every attempt was made with pretending intent by the vested interests to suppress the brightest Karna with excuse of his birth legitimacy. Even so, nothing worked. He sparked. In case of Rabi, the shining Karna of Khandi Pandupur, the invincible obstacles erected by the vested interests to suppress him had the resembling consequence. He shined in BCS College like he shined in village schools. And, he too grew up to as good as a city dweller within one and half years of his stay in the new world—in manner, in style, in understanding, in maturity and in dealing.

In the class room response to teachers' questions to class tests, he excelled well above others. He also excelled in the college annual debate, essay, personality test, song and quiz competition; and in the cricket ground, all-rounder Rabi mangled his opponents like Jimmy did in Third Edition of Cricket World Cup to the applause of his batch-mates and the entire Science Block which had never shined in the area of sports and games against Arts and Commerce Blocks in decades long history of BCS College. His all-round performance along with his cute Kenneth Edmond's baby face caught the attention of everybody in the college and subdued the alleged propaganda of envied Lalu Sarangi, the persistent tormentor of his peace since his school days.

The muffasalli Rabi established himself as the most shout-after boy in the college; in short, he was the college heart-throb. He was in the mouth of the college's boys and girls—seniors, class-mates and juniors—professors, principal, lab assistant, librarian, office clocks, peons, and even among the loafers, who once upon a time branded him derogatively—gawar. Besides, he was also in the mouth of the greatest survivor in the campus, the canteen contractor—Kesab Swain, popularly known with several title such as Kesabkaka or Bachelorkaka or Mr. Bachelor.

But, the girls were the most vociferous and started calling Rabi: Hero of the college, Mr. Heart-throb of the college, Mr. Heart-beat of the college, Mr. Sweet-heart of the college, Mr. Prince Charming of the college, Mr. Kenneth Edmonds of BCS, Mr. Dreamboat, ... And in the mouth of majority, in short—he was Mr. BCS.

Lalu Sarangi was shaking as he was slowly but surely losing ground and bargain for Preeti—he had been pursuing since his school days—to Rabi Pratap, a guttersnipe.

"Unfortunately, we girls are not that much smart to publish the list of Mr. BCS of the college. Alas, even, there are no oldie Miss Canteen Contractor or Spinsterkaki to help and guide us in this matter! Or else, the gawar Rabi would have been on the top of the list of Mr. BCS outsmarting the so-called smart city roaming loafers," announced Ruby alias Miss Femme Fatale, she was popularly known as, within the hearing distance of the college's two crowned beauties in the canteen. Further, she went on crying with a grumpy gaze on the two girls, "So, a few bitches are after him! They've trapped the poor orphan but a gifted jewel, early."

As if Kesab Swain wasn't in accord with the observation, he rejected the envious comment with a huge irritating sneeze, followed by a noisy throat cleaning and spitting of red betel juice to the dust bin stealing the attention of the crying girl. A terse stare of Miss Femme hit him. But, it seemed, that had very little impact on offender of her comment and he was found emboldened and disregarding, instead. "Bloody oldie, the red-faced ape, can tap anything told. He needs to be fixed," Miss Femme murmured.

Despite itched, teased, fired and provoked, the college crowned beauties however were unanimous to maintain cool. "Well, this used to happen," Seema consoled to appeared-disturbed Preeti and buzzed, "Let's forgive with all sympathy to the bichara Miss Deprived and Envious!"

And Miss Smarty later murmured with an after-thought, "Well, Rabi is such a material . . . . what to do?" She rejected the comment while another sneeze from the red-faced ape blasted flamboyant Miss Femme Fatale. To make the irritation of the deprived girl more vigor, she yelled with the Bollywood cabaret girl Helen's ravishing quirky smile, "Let us enjoy Mr. BCS's magic of hand on the crease," and they walked out.

———◈———

Although the love struck Preeti and her well-wisher Seema were very happy and overjoyed with their dreamboat's elevation with his outstanding performance in almost all activities in the campus, yet they were equally disturbed being subjected to frequent itching, teasing and provoking comments; and that too, mostly from the fellow class-mates. They heard it from Rekha in an early occasion and from Ruby in the canteen today. The sheSahadeva in Seema now could apprehend what was going to happen in the coming days in their small circle in progressively aggressive gravitation of glitzy girls towards Rabi. And, she could presume what would be the fate of an innocent, humble and devoted the Preeti-in-love, her friend and her share-holder of pain and sorrow, living with her in the Cave No. 025 if Rabi failed to resist. Seema murmured at the ear of the progressively frightening love-struck girl, "Preeti, this is a warning. We've to further intensify our patrolling over Rabi."

The guardian Seema and the ever frightened gawari—courtesy aunty's warning—discussed the subject with due diligence that the issue warranted, and concluded to guard their Rabi as far as possible. Even they'd politely appealed him not to be swayed by the privileged girls, not knowing that their Rabi was in tight spot in view of his social status.

To their surprise, Rabi was found evading. Looking at her room-mate and the self-appointed guardian, the gawari-in-love expressed her thought in silence, 'What happened? Has he already been swayed? . . . . stolen? Ooh my God, he is . . . . !'

The guardian was angry. She instantly pulled the crying girl to her caring embrace on her pigeon-chest and shouted, "I can go to any extent to protect the interest of my friend, and can go to Pandupur to speak aunty as well."

'This is the time to bare before the girls the real world they're living in,' Rabi strongly felt. He looked at the brimming guardian with a severe smile.

"What interest are you talking about, Miss Guardian Madam? After all, your aunty, you are talking about, is my mother. She is supposed to trust me more than anybody else. And, she has my well-being upper most in her mind," Rabi screamed and jeered snapping words of the guardian, and shouted in a manner anybody could doubt his intention, leave alone the simple gawari, who every now and then had been beaten with sceneries from Bollywood celluloid world, and warning of affectionate aunty. Further, Rabi good-humoured with pretending arrogance, "Rabi is talented, he is intelligent, he is brilliant, he is cute and he comes out successful in every field. Mind—rich, beautiful, convent educated and smart girls in large numbers started making bee-lines for just a talk, unsolicited. What next that you can guess?" "Wow, what a large number of competitive and mind blowing options!"

'Is it, Rabi wanted to dissuade Preeti? What's there in his mind?' Seema asked self. 'Let's settled the matter here and today itself.'

Poor Preeti couldn't believe her ears. She went on thinking, 'Is it that Rabi, with whom I've spent so many days, months and years together and walking, talking, studying, playing and sharing the pain and ecstasy, is saying? Or, somebody else?' She looked at him as if she was verifying.

'How could I believe that Rabi changed so much so soon,' the girl pondered. She tear-eyed him; she was abacked. She searched in him her Pandupur Rabi 'who was so simple, so caring, so understanding and so intelligent, and who'd promised to shoulder her guardianship in Puri, unsolicited. And, that Rabi, who used to carry me on his hands' fold unasked when crossing water channel on the way to Chabishpur from Pandupur and back to save me from leech attack, I fear the most. And that Rabi who struggled so hard to protect my photograph, being vandalized by vandal in the college corridor. I couldn't ever expect my very own Rabi could say so to me so easily—comfortably and relaxed!' She was shocked. So also Seema . . . . the beautiful sunny sea-beach which had witness their many very intense friendly plays and whiling always of time during passing days. Everybody and everything seemed very disturb and pensive.

For the guardian, this was unbearable. The statuesque stunner flared-up . . . . and volcanoed, "Hello, do you think you're the only talented, intelligent, cute and come out successful in every field under the sky? If you're something, my friend Preeti is no less . . . . far behind. She is Miss BCS. She is one in lakh. Many are also after her; mad of for her just a fleeting look! She's an archangel. Yes, she may not be as good as your knowledge, talent and scholarship, yet her stunning beauty and humble personality can shadow yours all that you are proud of . . . . Mind, you'll pay for your arrogance and betrayal. And, you will cry!"

In between the intense debate, the ghungi girl had taken an U-turn and had already started walking—'to where?'—none of the left-behind could probable guess leaving them sweating despite heavy shore bound cold sea-wind from the gracious and broad Bay of Bengal.

The loose sand on the sea-line felt getting slid under their feet—'seemed asking them'—to go and stop the sweetie sweetie innocent beauty. Afternoon's receding sun, appeared got shadowed with rare winter cloud and stopped shining early. Even wind failed to dry their bodies' profuse sweating. And the awkward eyes of beach walkers found appealing. The pretendingly proud shining Karna felt, 'All are in league with the girl . . . . leaving me alone . . . . ignoring me and my reasoning in this big world. They're blasting me: you heartless idiot selfish cruel—Mr. BCS of Supanakhas and Femmes—go and stop the beauty of our garden.'

Lotus eyes stared at Mr. BCS despite all anger, appealing as she apprehended her two best friends and companions during her these days of 'cursed exile' parting away from each other in front of her very eyes. 'I'm helpless!'

And, Rabi to Seema, pleading to help— appealing . . . . apologetic.

Both realized the need for urgent action. 'We shouldn't be late any further. There is the need of urgent action!'

Rabi had told knowing very well that 'one day this has to be disclosed.' He was feeling in the remote corner of his sense that 'longer this was delayed, critical this would be to reconcile. What to do?'

However, he ran to the love-struck girl. He stopped the girl grabbing her hand tight. The girl crumbled down on him like uprooted tree. He sat down and keeping the beauty's head on his cross-legged lap, started combing her frizzy hairs and cleaned with his handkerchief worn-out forehead, cheeks, nose, chin, throat—he was sweating—intermittently looking to the sky—to his talisman, to generous and broad sea and its relentless waves. He also glanced at the disturbed city girl, the bold and dogged guardian, equally speechless and trying hard to wrap with the tattered dupatta the jaded salwar kameez clad blossoming teenage body hungry for peacock's attention—could be envied by most beautiful apsaraas—and desperately trying to rescue that from the prying eyes of beach-walkers—the omni-present bears and monkeys.

Bichara Rabi was found himself helpless. 'What would he do with this bolshie girl sleeping, resting her head on his folded lap unmindful of his dilemma?'

Meanwhile, a strange feeling in the meantime started trickling in his mind, soul, heart and ultimately his body sensation. He thought, 'I've been with this girl for days, months and years since long. We were even together on the way to school and back, in our study, playing and whiling away time at home, in village and in Puri. All along, we were mostly two. But, I didn't have the same feeling that I have been passing through now.' A feeling of—she was intimately of him—started riding him. And, he was gradually becoming more and more caring than before. Whether that was due to the impact of 'growing age or basic impulse' he couldn't immediately ascertained but still he was feeling and tickling. He wanted to caress her from head to bottom assuring her and helping her with a spirit of fellow-feeling.

"Please forgive me . . . . Preeti," the apologetic Rabi with heavy breath pleaded and mumbled, "What could I, a son of cursed widow, a guttersnipe, an urchin do? I have been trying to let you know the fact which can't ever leave me—sooner you understand this, this is better! Let the magnetic force in the form of 'LOVE' among us remain intact taking care of each other's well-being like friends and benefactors. I don't like there should have a destructive storm. 'LOVE' has a very magnificent meaning and connotation that the true lovers in humanity could understand. I want my Preeti, I say once again my Preeti, should understand this. Your well-being is always there in my mind!"

Disciplining the disobedient hair dancing with unyielding land-bound cool sea wind on beauty's babe face and cleaning warm tears, the talking Rabi continued, "Will the society allow our LOVE, culminating to a life together, a smooth sailing? I'm afraid, it may not? So growing with this bond will be very dangerous and devastating. Once it is cemented, it would be very difficult to break. And I know, you can't bear; and so also I, and above all, my mama—your affectionate aunty. So, it is logically correct not to allow this to happen with all regards to 'Institution of LOVE'."

'…………………'

"No, whatever may be the consequence, I'm her and she is of mine," he pronounced in front of the guardian and the bolshie girl, sleeping in peace growing assure.

The girl got back to her own self. 'How could she not when she was at the care of her very someone,' the guardian thought. 'She perhaps could feel the feeling Rabi was passing through at the moment.' She slowly but steadily lifted her palm to Rabi's chin and cheek and cleaned them with care, which she couldn't see in her Rabi flooded with tears.

"I'm sorry Rabi. But . . . . what can I do? I'm so weak and so alone without you. I can't see my existence without you. Rest left to you and to your decision. I've full confidence in my dear aunty," she went on appealing and revealing.

Rabi couldn't respond in words, and concurrently, he couldn't remain so unkind to refuse an assuring hug to an innocent soul crying for the most beautiful gift of the nature manifested in the form of 'LOVE'.

He, still in the warmth of togetherness, looked at the broad and endless sea full of relentless waves and searched in it a way out. He talked sensibly, "You're very childish and tender. You don't know the road ahead. The 'Travails of LOVE' is full of lethal thorns, I'm afraid of!" To reinforce his points, he went on lecturing a few stories without knowing that there were no sincere takers.

"Look at Ms. Shantidevi, your Hostel Caretaker, still a Miss or a Kumari or a Kanyakumari you people mimic her. Her 'LOVE' has led her to this state. At this age, in her mid-forties even she waits for her 'LOVE', she embraced when she was a brightest student in Revenshaw College. For her 'LOVE', she was driven out of her parental house and reduced to pauper. What she hadn't done for her 'LOVE'? An enthralling classic novella can be written on her life—full of sacrifice, devotion and finally tragedy. Her heart-throb went on marrying for fat dowry claiming that he had no alternative but to surrender to the aging parents' pressure. Sadly, what an excuse? Still Ms. Caretaker is waiting to her 'LOVE' like Kanyakumari at Cape Comorin, waiting to Lord Bholanath."

"And Ms. Mili Padhi, your hostel Warden may have a similar story."

"Look at my mama. An awful life! How she suffers for the sake of her 'LOVE' to my papa, seemed a deceitful husband. Still, she loves him. She adorns him in her heart and soul. And, for the sake of her 'LOVE', she embraced a life of a cursed widowhood, and all abuses that followed. And her son is branded 'son of a WIDOW, a guttersnipe!' She's a symbol of sacrifice, which even the all-accomplished society, isn't ready to accept. What's her fault? Does the learned society not know what had happened to her? But, it pretends for the selfish end; for vested interest!"

"The tragedy is: our society is compassionate and adores the fiction but not the facts! My mama, who was just in her teen and from a village, swayed by her parents' overjoy of getting a bridegroom from a rich and socially acclaimed family, was cheated; yet she loves my papa and lives with her LOVE," he went on saying.

Looking at the dogged guardian with full of compassion, he continued, "Back, among us, we all know our good friend Seema's suffering. And, at one fell swoop, I don't doubt Preeti's 'LOVE' to me and her commitment, and may be if so happened—I'm confident—she will go extra miles for the sake of her sacred LOVE."

He became emotional and continued looking at the talisman, "For God's sake, please don't ever think that I don't believe and respect the 'Institution of LOVE'. I can claim I'm the greatest devotee of 'Sacred LOVE'— whether anybody accept this or not!"

Rabi was almost swollen. A pensive silence invaded the trio amidst relentless noise of sea wave heating the sandy beach . . . . watering and washing.

Notwithstanding, the beauty was stubborn in her resolve. She looked at her heart-throb. Her little blue deer eyes were appealing and were intensive and telling what her heart and soul wanted. Rabi gentle removed the dark un-frizzed hair flying over his dear's forehead, rosy cheeks, meek nose, symmetrical chin, plump lips and baby oval face. Rabi lowered his head; further bended and lowered; lowered till that reached the plump lips of his lovely beauty—his lips struck her—his own dear's resting on his buddha crossed lap with all her innocence. Steady and certain. And Khandi Pandupur beauty won as Rabi yielded. And, the spontaneity grabbed with momentum of basic sensation forgetting the very presence of the bubbling city girl, and beach-walkers' preying eyes.

And, Seema witnessed that greatest event in her living memory and the repeat of what she'd seen between Bogart and Bacall in English movie 'The Big Sleep' and reacted, "Wow! What a sight?" The astound guardian broke open and flashing a victory sign amidst pretending cleaning of the disbelieved eyes, she shouted, "Hip, hip, hurray!" and frantically searched, "Where is the camera?" From behind the abandoned fisherman's boat at a little distance, they saw a snap-shot.

And the warm tear busted out of the gawari's closed eyes, slid down her eye edges and reached the body nerve of her heartbeat piercing into him a sense of eternal feeling of unity that would never be broken despite every attempt of social vagaries.

Happy and satisfied Pandupur girl sat down. The love-birds looked at each other; went on musing and intermittently smiling.

"Let's move. Or else, I'll be envy of you and your 'LOVE'—my dearie Mrs. and Mr. Rabi Pratap," snapped the funny smarty being flattened with the long talk followed by captivating visualization. She flashed a pretending jealous glimpse activating her knotty arresting wide lotus-eyes and extended palm with a flying kiss directing at Mr. Prince Charming that the ghungi gawari could very well witness, and got provoked to react, "Seema . . . . you too!"

Preeti jocularly spatter over her heart-throb, like aunty used to do whenever anybody enviously flatter her chand-ke-tukkuda, in a bid to ward off evil spiteful look of the 'spinster' city girl, pronouncing, "Excuse me!"

LETTER BOMB

Girls approached the college dreamboat, almost competing among them, and at times, trying to outwit one another whenever wherever he was found out of the arm's length and eye reach of his double escorts, the ghungi gawari Preeti and smarty statuesque stunner Seema—which were, in fact, very rare—in the class room, in the library, in the corridor, in the canteen with flimsy excuses such as to clear course doubts, to share notes and books. They invited him for a chatting walk at Puri golden sea beach in the evening and in weekdays or on holidays; coffee in canteen, launch in Arnapurna Hotel, dinner at home with family, birth day party at Tosali Sand, film shows in Laxmi Talkies and dolphin watch at Satapada in the mouth of blackish Chilka Lake or sight-seeing in Khandagiri cave and natural zoo at Nandan Kannan or gazing artistic presentation of 'Play of LOVE' on lifeless stone on the wall of Black Pagoda.

Some even offered the most sought-after boy to take up tuition of their younger siblings for a fat monthly remuneration with a beat of sympathy ferreting out financial difficulty he, a father less child, might be passing through.

One evening, the dim-wit Preeti got a sealed envelope addressed to Rabi from the Physics note book, she had taken from him. She, true to her rural humbleness, couldn't sense anything unusual with that and kept the envelope in her hand bag to hand over to addressee next day on their way to college. But, that hadn't escaped the view of her well-wisher and sincere guardian's pierced eyes. The guardian caught hold of the envelope wide-eyed and raising eye-brows as the unsuspecting dim-wit was handing over the same, saying, "Rabi, take this envelope; I found this from your Physics note book," at the Ladies Hostel gate.

Rabi stared at piercing eyes of the statuesque stunner—almost melting. He was visible scared as if he was sure what was there in that envelope and what impact that would have on their well-netted companionship if disclosed. He was speechless and terrified not because he had cheated the girl but because he was apprehending whether the content would be tolerated by simple and dedicated humble Preeti who just a few days back couldn't even bear a simple talk of . . . . Further, what would happen if the content of the letter would ever be known to his simple and muffasali mama? He literally had gone to the extent of begging Preeti's almost fanatical guardian joining his palms for the letter.

"Seema don't be childish! This is my letter, my mama's letter to me. This isn't good to read other's letter," which had in fact contributed further aggravating the guardian's suspense. Her lotus eyes blinked at Mr. Innocent . . . . mischievously. And, the victim quaked.

She checked the envelope turning its sides before the peasants searching for sender's name and address, and with a sarcastic shrugging, jeered, "I'm sorry dear Mr. Innocent, your appeal is not convincing! With all the sympathy to bichara dim-wit, I foretell—this is certainly whatisthiscalled a bloody 'LOVE Letter'. I'm sure . . . . I bet!"

"What . . . . LOVE Letter! Whose letter? Is it for Rabi?" cried the dim-wit at the peak of her suspense, raising her eyebrows and eyes wide opened in fear and apprehension. And she checked the envelop taking that from her sincere guardian and revealed, "This isn't the handwriting of aunty," and cried, "Rabi, you've started lying me? Hey Bhagaban . . . . I can't believe!"

"Shall I open?" with a ravish quirky smile, the bold and stubborn guardian asked to melting Mr. Innocent.

"Ye-s, you can," the distressed Mr. Innocent agreed. "I'm sorry to my Preeti's sincere guardian, I had vainly tried to hide something to prevent you from wasting yours precious time for some rubbish. Since ours' well-wisher and good friend Seema wanna know, let this be opened! But, before that, I would say—I may be believed!—this is nothing but another such letter pounding on me on daily basis. I've no time for such thing and you better tore it and throw the scrap on the way side as I've been doing since long." Mr. Innocent responded gathering confidence in the absence of any alternative.

But, the ghungi gawari wasn't sparing. She was found reserved, and thought-provoking, and intriguing. Her apprehensive mind albeit didn't allow her to end the matter there itself. 'Is Rabi lying me?' she thought. She looked at Mr. Innocent as if she was asking with agony and fear. She was speechless. She came close to Rabi melting, praying, which was enough for meek Rabi to speculate—what would be milling in the little mind of simple and dear girl, 'a soft teen hungry of nectar of LOVE; after all, she was the mate with whom

I had started my early days of doll games when other village kids were avoiding and boycotting me. She has been with me during all my days of pain and suffering. She is the girl who fasted day-long once in a weak for two-three months during painful summer for my better result in matriculation. I'm indebted to her.'

Again, he thought, 'This will be a great injustice to the girl if I deny her what she wants to know. No, I can't be so unjust! Let the truth prevail! The sacred relation can be built only over the trust and believe. She deserves it!'

He turned to the guardian and requested holding the melting hand of the girls, "I plead to Preeti, not to be impatient and crazy! To read and bear the content of this letter, one needs a lot of maturity and trust. And I believe and confident, our Preeti," putting his hand over the girl's shoulder pressing and cajoling, "sorry, my lovely Preeti does have all these characteristics."

The ghungi gawari found thinking and after sometimes—appeared gathering confidence—concurred ringleting with her Prince Charming, "Let's believe my Rabi! Let's close the chapter cursing the letter in the way side as suggested, and move."

However, a satisfied Rabi happily lifted the head of his 'LOVE' with his fore-finger and with a satisfying serene smile, cheered, "That's a good girl! But no, let us read the letter without any prejudice for anything, at least for the sake of little fun. For the sake of our demanding guardian," and cheered, "Ha . . . . ha . . . . ha . . . . !"

As if this was what bubble Seema was longing for lately, she was found exulted. But, surprisingly, she was reluctant to go further to open and read although the envelope was in her hand, and told reckoning, "This is immoral to open and read other's letter, and hear too without receiver and/or sender's sincere consent. This is what I believe and cherish in my life!"

The love-struck pair looked at the sensible girl, astounded. They viewed, 'What's a worthy personality! And, see the pain and sorrow, she is passing through, and still happy, funny, jolly and bubbling.' "Really, we're proud of our worthy guardian," Rabi acclaimed.

"Sambitbhai is really a blessed one! Besides, I salute thou for your acumen ship, dear Miss Rourkela Diva. You are really The Great! And, you're a worthy friend; anybody could be proud of you and your friendship!" Preeti bustled summing up.

However, Seema couldn't resist the persistent appeal of her beautiful companions to read the letter. "Since, it's purely for the sake of fun, who could be the most suitable reader other than our lotus-eyed," observed Rabi with profound display of confidence.

"And if I'm trusted to read, I want this be enacted in full privacy," requested the stunner and conditioned, "We three only! No classes today for the celebration of LOVE letter to our dear Prince Charming. Hip hip hurray! Let's move to sea-beach and enjoy the letter reading in a calm and lonely setting under the cover of fishing boat at this hour. Don't worry, I'll allow you full privacy with all pain to my exiled heart." The ecstatic Miss Bubbly announced bubbling with a quick U-turn, and literally dancing like Tollywood twinkle toes—Vyjayanthimala.

But, her jubilation couldn't last long; she could feel a hard twist of her left ear followed by an authoritative outcry, "Hello madam! Have you gone mad? What are you saying? Mind it; no, no such non-sense at the cost of class!" Rabi rejected the proposition with the authority and cow-herded the girls to the college.

And, they heard on their way silenced bubble's murmuring caressing her flexed ear, "Ooh, what a force? What a hard twist? It is snatching yaar! Anyway, my ear got loosen after a long gap. Sambit used to do this very often; I enjoyed! Preeti, if you don't mind, may I say something what's there in my mind—freely and frankly?"

"Oh, yes, go ahead! But, I know what are you going to tell," replied Preeti confidently and concluded jovially, "You wanted to say—'were I not in 'LOVE' with Sambit, I would have stolen your LOVE'—ain't it, you knotty, smarty, city girl, my aunty's envy and allergy?"

"Exactly!"

Setting was an empty class room and time was a class break. Seema handed over the hand-bag of Preeti to Rabi to collect the letter. But, Rabi was reluctant, displaying. 'How could he, a boy, open a girl's hand-bag for anything,' he told to him, shy.

But, under the persistent pressure from the designated reader supported by unsuspecting gawari Preeti, peasant Rabi ventured to the boy-tabooed territory in vain.

"That is your letter and you've to get that and open that before you give me to read. Go on searching. That is certainly there," Miss Smarty wasn't sparing, and yelled. Still, Mr. Shy failed and was blasted by the Seema with rejecting smile, "What a man, yaar? You can't find a just letter in your beloved's bag. Open that paper wrapped packet . . . . and whatever!" Preeti looked at Seema wide-eyed and shouted, "Ooh my God! Seema, you knotty girl, what are you telling him?"

But, that was too late. And, Mr. Innocent was caught 'red-handed!' with opened lady sanitary napkin in hand—hoisting.

"What a sight? Preeti see, what your cute brightest mister is holding? Shame! Shame!" overjoyed stylish smarty shouted and added, "Had I a camera, I would have captured this onceinalifetime visual." Preeti rescued the trapped peasant with serene smile of Juhi combining her eyes, cheeks, lips and chin, "This is certainly this knotty smart city girl's handiwork. Further, I couldn't understand how you still remain so simple," and pushing his head told, "You buddu, you claim—you can manage with rich beautiful gorgeous smart city girls who in large number started bee-lining you, that too unsolicited! Chie . . . . chie . . . . ! Thank God, we have rescued you in time. Or else, the city Supanakhas and Femmes would have shown you chandmama holding you on their meaty waist. Am I right, Seema?"

Preeti handed over the open letter to the designated reader, the elegant and the witty statuesque stunner, bubbling in her trademark costume of dazzling light blue jean pant and deep yellow T-shirt, unfurled her neck collar under the busy ceiling fan.

Of course, she wasn't a professional artist. But, still—it seemed to her enthusiastic fans—she was no less in comparison for the assigned job.

The session started with a jovial wink from the ever-funny lotus eyed carbon copy of immortal Gayatri Devi at the stage and mild fist from Preeti at the zeroed in rather the dull and meek Mr. Innocent, who wasn't yet out of apprehension of embarrassing situation, and was fretful of negative consequence as because he had read the preceding letters, some of which carried the messages and presentations, very difficult to bear by a sane mind, forget about his ghungi Preeti, 'mad of LOVE'.

The host cleaned her throat with a cough and swept her eyes with her handkerchief in front of her impatience and curious audience.

"This is alright! You're a great presenter. Accepted! Don't waste time. Quickly finish before anybody come," Rabi ordered.

And the reading started with a bang on the lecture podium followed by a flying-kiss directed at the addressee of the letter by the dashing designated presenter.

"Hi Mister BCS!

Hats off, my heart-throb! Hearty congratulation to you for your achievements for cornering majority of prizes in this year Annual Function. What's a rare accomplishment? This is an exceptional feat for a 2nd year student from an unknown dusty countryside hamlet."

Bubbly reader read out with her sparking thrilled eyes and fabulous half naked hands in theatric hats off action standing on the lecture dais to the full entertainment of the horror-struck and apprehensive gawar, and the sickening dim-wit.

"I am Ruby Dash," the bubbly read brandishing a flying kiss on her white clean palm in the direction of Rabi.

"Ooooh, this was Ruby, Miss Femme Fatale," asked the surprised gawari in astonishment, and continued thoughtfully, "What's a choice of name—Ruby? Yesterday, this bloody brown motti, swinging her papaya boobs, was cajoling my Rabi to clear her doubt in Physics Paper II. Thank God, I was there. Or else, her boobs would have crushed Mr. Cute's head . . . . shameless girl!"

Poking her own head, she added, "May be, at that time, she fooled this dim-wit? Really, the city girls are very shrewd!" She laughed ruefully caressing Rabi's head hugging on his shoulder and whispered at his ear, "How soft were her meaty boobs?" And got cooled down with a hard slap.

"Ahh! Are those so solid? Thank God, your head is still intact!" she screamed.

"No further interference be allowed . . . . okay!" shouted bubbly banging the duster on the table like the Paharpur Ladies Hostel custodian Ms. Kanyakumaries used to do in boarders meetings and read pausing with occasional sneaking quick look at her audience.

"I hope you'll find these few sweet-words in a very jovial frame of mode."

Another wink hit Mr. Innocent with repeat of 'sweat-words'.

Rabi, looking at the lovely girl and pretending ecstatic, and enjoying, pushed her away. But, she, like a honeybee, wasn't ready to give up drinking the nectar of LOVE being closed with her heart-throb in the course of singing of lecherous literature from the sweet mouth.

"I am longing for you since that auspicious day of our first meeting in the Physics class. I had too noticed you looking at me eagerly as if we are born for each other. You know, many among us in our class also feel very strongly on the rationality of this thought of me."

"Hey Bhagaban, this has been going for so long, this buddi don't know," Preeti heating her head murmured. "This hasn't been informed to aunty!"

Hissing, teeth-biting and breathing of heavy air by the ghungi gawari invaded the peace of the setting at the moment, and later stopped as Mr. Innocent turned to her and putting his forefinger on his lip, stomped her saying, "Shut up, you foolish girl! You're— 'whatisthiscalled?'—a big fool! This has been proved here. Let's enjoy this bubbly jolly funny smarty sweetie stunning city girl in her action and presentation standing on her twinkle toes."

Seemed little annoyed being blasted by a provocative talk along with a lecherous wink of Mr. Innocent to Miss Bubbly, the gawari shouted, "She is bubbly, she is jolly, she is funny, she is smarty, she is sweetie, she is stunning . . . . Iamzero!" And, later, she confining within her told, "Fine!"

However, Miss Bubbly continued unconcerned of resentful Preeti's knotty punching, poking, and love-wrapped fisticuffing at Mr. Innocent.

"You're a brilliant student!" Miss Bubbly read thumping up.

"You're a jewel," Bubbly grimaced pulling out her narrow red tongue between her stunning red lips.

"You're a shining star!"

"Yeah, he is! What more . . . . read read Seema . . . . interesting!" cheered Preeti, rejoicing.

But, what followed there-after had rained a pale of gloom in the setting.

"Unfortunately, you are born to a discarded widow in a non-descriptive slummy village."

Rabi pulled-down his head.

The adjectives used fired the other two equally. The statuesque stunner couldn't proceed further illustrating and looked up to the talisman 'might be praying to give strength to the unfortunates.' And the shy, sober, relatively calm, playful ghungi gawari, Preeti Rath was stunned in disbelief.

"How could such a bitch-witch Femme say to my dear lovely aunty—discarded? What does she think about her?" the aunty's little girl hissed, and cried.

Rabi pulled the girl to him as she cried . . . . cried, un-consoled. Both shared the pain and sorrow together.

The reader plunged to silence. She silently read the remaining part of the letter followed by the aunty's little girl when Rabi was still sulking; holding his breath, thinking of, 'Why papa left mama and unborn-me so cruelly in this heartless and inhuman world?'

"I do strongly believe you are a talent; a valuable asset, can better be utilized if you're placed in the right hand, place and guidance. And I think which can be the best hands in our entire state other than my able parents' who own the largest freight of buses covering all the major routes in the state? I am the only daughter of the crororpati parents and, hence, I will inherit all that my parents own. My dad was a wise man! Like you, he was a bright student and got married to my mum accepting her advice and now enjoying life with wealth, power, fame, respect and prosperity. Who doesn't salute him in Puri, and even, in the whole state? Who will contest for councilor in which ward, who will be municipality Chairman, who will be MLA and MP candidate from Puri, and who will win in which constituency in Puri district that also have been decided in our drawing room. Besides, the state ministers consult my dad prior to posting of DM, SP, and even our College Principal."

"Many say you are in 'LOVE' with Preeti Rath, the daughter of a countryside farmer. Compare me with that bitch-witch and lean-thin hungry maffu in tattered churidar and kurti—the so-called Miss BCS of a handful of loafers! Mind, she has trapped you. What's there with her?"

"LOVE without wealth and glamorous status is meaningless in this world. A wise man, my dad could understand that better, and now enjoying the life."

"I am convent educated, smart, dazzling, gorgeous, and above all, modern. My parents are planning to send me to abroad for higher study in Business Management. I think why not you should accompany me?"

"Besides, I have some words of advice to you: avoid that modern cocktail girl, the so-called Miss Smarty—Seema Pati, the daughter of a government company Director. To run our business, we have number of Directors. Behind her smart get up, modernity and elegancy hide her wild passion and lofty desire for physical refreshment. And, you know, the girls brought up in the so-called modern cosmopolitan socialite setting are like that."

"Here, I would like to propose you to leave the clumsy hostel and stay in our specious and palatial house with all sophistication of majestic living. And, we can study together and you can take advantage of my home tutors, free of cost. My parents on my request will certainly arrange accommodation for your widow mother in any dharmashalla in Puri. I assure."

"Think! Think for your future before it is too late! I'm with you. This is my third letter. I believe my earlier letters must have fallen in the filthy hands of these evil-witches shadowing you all the time."

"See you in college canteen at 2 O'clock on coming Friday. Please come alone.

Bye Mr. BCS and bye with a sweet kiss!

Yours most warmly,

Miss Ruby Dash"

This had a startling impact on the two girls in the calm, and crowd free class room. They looked at each other, speechless and immobile. They turned to Rabi, equally disturbed and wrecked. They agreed to his wisdom and saluted him apologizing, "We're extremely sorry Rabi for our foolhardiness."

He responded them with an exhausted body shrug, and after a short while, resorted to a sarcastic laugh like an autistic child, surprising the houris.

Later, he in renewed vigor went on, "This was why I didn't like you to read this spoiling dirty paper. This is like a Time Bomb, having tremendous destructive impact . . . . beyond repair! Karankaka during his last visit to Puri had already alerted me about the possible consequence of such letters, and even, of refusals of them. I had destroyed Ruby's earlier letters and had been destroying many others' as and when they reached me, even without reading them. So, I advise to leave this letter here too. And, I appeal you to behave normally as if you have not seen this letter, and so haven't read. Take my advice and remain normal and natural. Or else, we'll be in such a problem—you know, nobody will come forward to save us—forget about our talent and skills, and our prizes and acclamations. This is the rich and privilege people's world! Remember, they won't remain lie down, cooled down so easily. Again, I don't like for me you two too to suffer. I cannot bear any trouble to you, so dear to me. What I'll tell to my mama, village friends and my conscience if anything happens to you girls? To deal with these people, we need maturity and intelligence—not emotion. And, I believe, I'm sure, we are gifted with all these characteristics." And added, "What I am? A rootless, a guttersnipe—in the mouth of privileged! If anything happens to me there is only one soul to cry whereas for you people, there are so many. At least, you must think for them, if not for you!"

Before Rabi talked further, hurt Preeti blocked his mouth with her palm and shouted, "Stop, stop all these non-sense talks," and asked, "Rabi, how can all these stinking stuffs come to your mouth? And, that too, after so many days, weeks, months and years of togetherness? Who says you have none except your mother in this world?"

And Seema blasted, "If you think I'm none for you, leave me! I'll never accompany you. I cannot manage with those who don't think I ain't one of them—part and parcel. I'm extremely sorry!"

Soon the trio sat together, looking at each other. They talked together, smiled together, cried together and laughed together around the just ragged particles of gauche letter. Later, with an assuring and confidence glace at each other they got up and moved as Rabi advised, "Let's go to next class. We must be focused on our objective and goal. Mind, in studies lies our future and career, and our benefactors' aspiration."

"Yes, with all respect to the 'Institution of LOVE.'"

And, he got up satisfied as he believed—yes, for trying his best to bring the situation where it was before the Letter Bomb exploded. So also Preeti's response hurling a cozy slap at his clean chin—satisfied.

The peasants showed the sign of let bygones be bygones but not the city girl, hiding.

BALANCING ACT

Despite all the sincere and meek advices of humble gawar, the daughter of Rourkela's Big Gun and allegedly branded 'cocktail girl' wasn't able to forget what was thrown at her in the 'Letter Bomb'. Besides, she went on thinking, 'Since, I am not what I am told about, how I could remain silent; and after-thought—my silence may be misunderstood in the long run in this complex world!' The thoughts went on keeping her disturb. Sleep couldn't soak up her. She couldn't concentrate in anything. Revenge cropped up in her mind. "A wounded spinster is more dangerous than the raging fire!" But, all at once, she rationalized, 'I shouldn't go for anything that will remotely cause any problem to my lovely friends—my only companions during these days of my cursed exile—so brilliant, faithful, simple, sharing, humble Preeti and Rabi. I've a responsibility towards them!' In night, her wounded and dog-tired mind resolved to act, 'but, in such a manner that can be beneficial to my friends—rescuing Rabi from his financial crisis and the pair, their LOVE from the potential threats. And, that should be satisfying my hurt ego too!'

The news report of Rekha's father Mr. Debasis Mohanty's promotion and transferred as District Magistrate to Puri was a God-sent blessing in disguise for the schemer.

She fine-tuned her strategy. In her scheme of thing, she planned to engage two puffed-up titans, the daughters of Big Guns and the challengers of her friends' LOVE in a fight that none of her targets could even remotely get scope to pin down.

The lunch break time. The trio along with other class mates were vacating the Chemistry Gallery in the first floor of Science Block. The statuesque stunner made a sudden U-turn and stood in front of the daughter of new DM, her other sworn bête noire. She extended her hand to the girl with a smile. "Congratulation! Congratulation, Rekha!" she shouted shaking the hand with her eye-sore picking that up, and later, patting her on her back announced, "Here is the proud daughter of our new District Magistrate." Some followed her while a few frowned.

Rekha felt blown up and thanked Seema, the news announcer with a privileged smile.

But, the incident took shape so sudden that the humble peasants, who knew these two girls were not in good terms, couldn't comprehend anything—surprised and confused.

The privileged girl was equally bewildered and stomped. Whatever, she smelled an opportunity to come close to her Prince Charming she was literally denied by his all-time accompanied escorts. 'This is a blessing in disguise from an unexpected quarter. Let's utilize this,' she concluded. 'Certainly, the right time has come, however late. Patience paid!'

Further, she thought, 'Smarty Seema may be flattering her for some vested interests due to her father's new position. There was nothing astound in it. She had experienced such things during her school days in Cuttack. The school teachers and principal, who weren't listening or not taking notice of her presence once upon a time, suddenly started complimenting her, and showing her undue interest after his father joined as ADM Cuttack after his transfer. So also, some students. Besides, the envious comments from some class-mates—mostly the children of the Big Guns.'

"Let's go for a small tea-party during this break time," Seema requested and guided the abacked peasants along with puffed-up daughter of Big Gun to canteen. 'Has Seema forgotten the content of Ruby's letter? Ruby wasn't in the class which means she most probable would be in the canteen as per the schedule.' The peasants thought and were surprised with Seema's foolhardiness. 'Nope! She can't be presumed to forget. And she isn't a so-fool! There's certainly something in her mind and may be for this she cajoled her sworn eye-sore.' They wanted to speak to the sponsor of tea-party reminding her the programme of uncouth Femme Fatale which they wanted to skip but in vain—as if the sponsor had pre-made out what she might encounter from the humble peasants in between—she didn't give them any opportunity keeping her absolutely engaged with DM's daughter asking her about her family's new status and majestic DM bungalow: How many servants? How many cars? How many rooms in the bungalow? Whether the sentry saluting her at the gate? Whether she is accompanying her father to parties? . . . . etc, etc? that the overwhelmed girl was—appeared to the peasants—enjoying.

True to the expectations, Femme adorning the designer gorgeous anarkali suit was in the canteen. On seeing the extended team of her prey, her over fleshy face got instantly paled betraying rosy make-up for the occasion. She told her, 'Has my dream boy again missed the letter or his omni-accompanied witches again stolen the letter?' She could also sense the possibility of an abashing encounter from the boy's three accompanying girls which now included the powerful new DM's daughter. And so, she was about to leave disappointed and forlorn that the tea-party sponsor and the master-mind in putting together the odds could clearly guessed. The team seated close to about to leave crest-fallen Femme around the round table. The alleged cocktail girl with pre-designed agenda for the occasion, took the seat face to face of her basher and requested her to join them.

"I offer this small party to celebrate Debasis uncle's promotion and transfer as the district's all powerful DM position," Seema announced winking at Rekha in the full view of Ruby.

"Ooooh, you come to know this reading yesterday's ' . . . . Samaj'—I believe," said Femme displaying her trademarked privileged smile and continued, "But, I've come to know this two weeks ago. One State Minister was discussing about this transfer with my dad over phone."

"In fact, this is a routine consultation!"

The proud daughter of DM wasn't happy, yet she kept quite—sulking—as Femme talked exposing DM's vulnerability. The sponsor of the party announced, "Whatever, I, on behalf of this small but vibrant team of our college, request to our generous and eminent daughter of district's official first family, to offer a dinner to us in DM's majestic bungalow on a day of her convenience."

The sulking Rekha got an opportunity and instantly nodded in agreement. She was overjoyed with the stunner's tricky flattering and told throwing her to back and forth on plastic chair in an apparent display of privilege, "What a small request you are asking for? You would have asked for something big. Anyway, let's start with this small thing!"

But, it seemed, the other important invitee to the parley wasn't so enthusiast. She was agitated in the presence of her another potential threats to her prey. Besides, Rekha's extravaganza talk and Seema's flattering of her were highly sickly-sweating and ear-biting, adding to her already crest fallen heart pain and despair. Still, she continued to be seated for the just satisfaction of the golden boy's rare—though lifeless, dull and shy glance at her gorgeous costume. She wanted to pass on some messages through her eyes and body language but failed being under patrolling watch of the cocktail girl. She felt in cocktail girl's watch something prejudiced and intentional.

But, the humble peasant wasn't happy in the congregation, not because he was the only boy among the four girls who were who's who of college and Puri city, so he was poured with sarcastic comments from friends and foes, a very common part of life for any boy omni-accompanying girls in any college campus, but because he was confused as he couldn't grasped anything in Seema's scheme of the thing—seemed rather revenging despite his all laborious counseling on the day of the Femme's letter content disclose. His steady graduation to city life didn't rescue him either. He was however observing everybody closely, with occasional pretending smile on all participants in an apparent bid to carry on with them in the absence of any scope for escape in Miss Smarty's overshadowing approach while Preeti was ruing with her head down in the very presence of two displaying, disgusting and irritating characters. She was literally scolding the fasto Ruby in her thought recalling the content of the letter which was very much present in her mind word by word, and Rekha, recalling her shoe biting in the introduction session in the first day in the hostel, and later contemptuous advices on the link road.

"So, we can say next year college Annual Function is an affair of DM's daughter, and naturally, of our batch. Again, I am thinking, why not we propose to invite to a person, who can give a good package of generous donation to our college as 'The Guest of Honour'. How is my idea, Miss Ruby Dash?" Seema asked looking at the gaudy daughter of the Big Gun with rare ravish quirky smile. Now, Rabi to some extent could understand the scheme of the thing of Seema. He was occasionally staring at her who was non-stop in executing her schemes leaving occasional stealthy wink.

The distressed and disappointed Femme found in this a perfect moment to impress upon her prey and tame the extravaganza of the daughter of DM with show off of her wealth and charity. She started with a lavish thank to smarty, "Thank you Seema for inviting me to this Mini Goal Table Meeting!" And subsequently, she, thieving a look at her prey, promised, "If it is my parents, I can assure for a good donation in lakhs!"

"Wow! Lakhs!" reacted the unexposed dim-wit gawari astonished but stopped short of proceeding further, and cried with pain as she felt a strong shoe biting at her slipper clad leg. Gawari's reaction furthered Femme's enthusiasm and generosity. She ordered coffee instead of the sponsor's tea along with special piaji-pakadi and suggested, "If you don't mind, I would suggest my good friends here to approach my mum for donation to replace these stinking dirty plastic tables in the canteen with marble top to start with. You know, my parents are planning to earmark two percentage of our business net profit for social service. This is a concept prevalent in developed countries, and some big corporates in India have introduced the scheme. The Dash Transport is planning to introduce this scheme in Orissa for the first time."

"Why to your Mummy? Why not your Daddy?" the branded cocktail girl asked exploring.

"Actually, our family property is in the name of my mum and she is our company Chairwoman," told the puffed-up Miss Femme failing to understand the cocktail girl's scheme of thing.

"Ooh, your Daddy is a Ghar Jamai?" jeered the cocktail girl provoking a sarcastic comment from the daughter of DM, languishing with grouse, "Her father is consort of her Mummy!"

"Yeah, our family business empire runs in the name of my mum like the British Empire. However, don't worry! My mummy is very generous. She has so far donated lakhs of rupees to Lord Jagannath Temple. You'll find a lot of marble plating there with names of my grandpa and ma," eloquented Femme.

"So, whomever you marry, he'll be a Ghar Jamai?" asked the cocktail girl.

"Certainly! Is it a small thing for him?"

"Who would be such a bhagyaban? Rabi note it. I believe, this is certainly an interesting subject. Ain't it, Rekha?" the cocktail girl, the ever bubble and omni-searching for opportunity to poke fun and embarrass her basher, told.

As if Ruby's extravaganza talks were itching in the ears of the canteen contractor Kesab Swain, he tried to rub the ears pushing his thick fore-finger into that. This followed by a series of mocking cough pretending to clear his throat apparently directed to banter overflowing Femme—felt the participants. However, Femme was unstoppable and un-bothering. She murmured looking at the intruder of her self-importance, "A rejected Sisupal, a living cesspit, is envy of everything in this beautiful world. What to do?"

As the coffee served, Femme opened her Gucci purse flush with few brand new fifty rupees notes. She gave one to Chottu and patting him ordered the boy to retain the balance with charitable smile flashing over the participants of Mini Goal Table Meeting mixed with envious, reserved, surprised and shocked characters. The gawari, true to her peasantry character, was about to break open at the charity of Femme but again got kicked and stopped looking pity. The brimming Femme stood up pushing back the poor plastic chair, crying being crashed down, before other could curtain down to end the talks, with satisfaction. She flashed a quick loving glimpse—seemed satisfied—at her prey that could be noted by ever guard cocktail girl, and taunted in dejection looking at the table, "This is stinking. I can't stay here anymore. Excuse me!"

As she moved away Rekha's eyes followed her and Kesab Swain activated his itching throat again. She disappeared with a turn at the wide canteen grill. Agitated Rekha hissed at fast leaving Femme while staring at ever pan munching oldie but exciting Kesab—thanking.

"Stupid generosity! Let's wait and see her charity!" Kesab Swain responded with a smile and spitting of red pan juice pulling the spittoon from under his high canteen throne, he had been adorning since his first un-ceremonial coronation years ago.

Amidst the short raining silence, the participants of Mini Goal Table Meeting for sometime concentrated in emptying the plate of piaji-pakadi so far not appreciated for their water mouthing taste and aroma. They thanked Kesabkaka for his ready services.

However, the daughter of DM was seemed not very please, agitating. And she, in her thinking, was cursing the sponsor for spoiling her moment of glory inviting Ruby to The Goal Table. At the same time, she was also happy over the sponsor as it was the sponsor, who facilitated the opening of a window of opportunity for her to reach her Prince Charming.

'Now, I can outsmart the gawari Preeti, and also Miss Smarty, the modern smart city girl, her two major competitors in her bid to capture Prince Charming,' she was thinking. She however concealed the fact that, 'This is nothing short of back-stabbing! . . . . So what? I want Prince Charming and that's all. This is the privilege of privileged. This is there in revered 'The Ramayana' and 'The Mahabharata', and history has plenty of such examples. And, there're plenty of such incidents in today's world.' She also thanked the invisible hand of 'fortune' which had given her birth as the daughter of a Big Gun, a booming bureaucrat who is now the all powerful DM of Puri district. She even didn't forget to thank the British Raj which had established this powerful position of District Magistrate.

"You're now the most powerful persona in our college. Everybody from principal to peons and from students' union president to we, the under-privileged bichara class-mates, will be after you for this or that work. Lucky Girl! A rare luck and privilege," Miss Smarty got back to the ecstatic Rekha deviously elating her.

"You're also very important persona in steel city Rourkela," the pumped up Rekha on the peak of her happiness responded in an apparent bid of undesired consoling.

"No yaar! With my papa's promotion, I was banished to Puri and now in a cursed banabasha, far away from my near and dear, brother, friends, and after all, my up-to-the-minute dear Sambit," Seema cried with display of sorrow and heart-bleeding pain.

"Oooh, this is the matter!" Rekha reacted with the make-believed sympathy. Again, as if something she had left in her response, she was found musing. And, after sometime, she returned sparking with a query, "By the way, who is this Sambit?"

So far a woody, the Prince Charming flashed an eccentric smile, and so also sulking gawari.

"Miss Smarty's fiancé! And, if our Miss Smarty permits, we can say he is our would-be he-friend-in-law," Preeti revealed with a bold wink at the chic stunner pulling and shaking her.

"Big surprise?" Rekha screamed along with satisfactorily euphoric spark in her witchy eyes. 'Yes, I'm lucky,' she asserted in her. She was found delighted as she went on concluding the deduction of one prospective competitor as she so far had been under impression that Miss Smarty was after her prey. She reacted instantly pointing at her ex-eyesore, "That means you do . . . . not . . . ."

Her artlessness and abrupt stop provoked sheSahadeva Miss Smarty for an acknowledging shrug.

Later, the smarty flashing a ravishing eccentric smile at the puffed up girl brought the matter to a satisfactory end with her response, "No fiancé in Puri!" And with a wink flash at Rabi and later at ecstatic Rekha yelled in her usual funny and mild teasing approach, "We're just friends. Yes, friends! Is it okay, my dear . . . . Miss Rekha . . . . Madam . . . . happy . . . . satisfied?"

Kesab Swain coughed pulling the attention of the foursome towards him, and he pulled the spittoon bending, leaving thrilled Rekha browbeaten.

Rabi, not so happy with the latest confabulation, shouted, "This is too much, out of substance! Let's move to class." He had by now fully understood the scheme of Miss Smarty. 'She is now all set to take revenge for all those humiliations from the daughters of Big Guns,' he concluded. He commanded with full authority straightening him vertical by the table, about to leave.

But, the lucky girl wasn't ready. She was reluctant. "Who will friend this boy, so reserved, woody and bookish?" the lucky girl proclaimed and frowned. As the squadron walked out of the canteen, she cried rejecting, "An avid bookworm! Only bloody mind jamming study, . . . and study! Life is also for other something," which offered a suitable opportunity to smarty to throw a deadly message, "Certainly! You're very right Rekha, Rabi is suitable for a bookish one."

"His matching sweet-heart is already there. Is not it, Preeti?"

Rekha witch-laughed at the belittled countrified Preeti, and confidently rejected opening her mind, "Let's . . . . !"

Rabi bended down his tired head in a bid to avoid an anticipated pity look from the scared and pained deer-eyed gawari. But true to her guardianship, Seema did take care of the poor sulking girl by a camaraderie pat stealthily pulling her back to the brimming and the proud-of-privilege's daughter of Big Gun, struggling to catch up with her prey.

"What's cooking in your mind, Miss Seema Pati? I guess you've a game plan despite my humble advice," the not-very-happy Rabi asked on their way back to hostel after the long exhausted classes and Miss Smarty's devious but—seemed—well oiled Mini Goal Table Meeting.

She smiled and told, "So, you understand! Well, let me explain. Yes, I do have! Since thou asked this I don't like to hide from my good friends . . . . and for whom my heart also bleed. I'm hurt and my ego has been blown apart by both Supanakha and Femme. But, I can say I have my best friends' best interests uppermost in my mind. I may request to be believed," Miss Smarty replied seriously and thoughtfully, confidently.

But, the submissive gawari couldn't grasp anything and stared at her two flanking guardians' faces, one by one. Again, she had in her agitated mind, why she was booted by the smarty again and again, that too, so hard? She wanted to protest. "Oooh, what a hard bite?" she shrieked, displaying.

However, the smarty in order to divert Rabi's attention floundered looking at him, "You know, Preeti is still in her muffasali hang-over. What's the need of those reactions before that bloody kidda from privilege's septic tank, looking for opportunities every now and then for exhibition of her parents' ill-gotten wealth and superfluous charity?"

That didn't evoke any response from the musing Rabi. But Preeti nodded in shame and surrendered, childishly hugging over her guardian, "Oh, that's why? I'm sorry to my ever guarding guardian!"

After a while of quiet walk Rabi again poked the issue, the smarty—seemed to him—cleverly tried to avoid with excuse of gawari's unwitting intervention, and he mischievously jeered, "Well, the reaction out of her muffasali simplicity helped you save fifty rupee. Isn't it, Miss Seema Pati?"

"Hello, hello, one minute! Should I assume you say so branding me a stasher? Mind, I have enough RSP modernization money dumped in my account," turning to Rabi, the daughter of RSP's Director flared-up and yelled.

They laughed initiated by Rabi clapping each other's hand. Before saying bye to each other for the day, the boy reminded seriously, "I've now got my doubt cleared—Miss Guardian! If you don't mind, I would rather suggest, we must know what we're doing for each other's benefit before implementing such a complicated scheme."

"Bye guardian! Bye Preeti!"

"Bye, thou too, Mister Rabi Pratap," responded the girls in chorus before they entered in to the Kumaries' safe abode.

"I don't know why I am so week to Preeti's cause. In her innocent deer look, I find her prayer to save her LOVE. You're her LOVE. And sometimes, without any prejudice, I'm afraid you are forced into the situation of slowly drifting away from her. On the other hand, lecherous offers, glamorous messages and literati letters have also been pouring on us since the day of our joining the college. The bears and monkeys want to take advantage of Preeti's gawarly simplicity and my modernity. They think we're so cheap. Preeti could be bought with modern glamour and I, for physical pleasure. As we rebuff, we are being threatened on our way to college and back and when we're alone. Even they've gone to the extent of saying that they may not hesitate to fix you as you're mostly accompanying us as a protective shield. And your by default background is a biggest boost to them. I can't tolerate any trouble to my good friends and I don't think Preeti, who is so immersed to you, has strength to bear. We're completely devastated. You two are very dear to me as you incidentally have given me company when my parents have literary abandoned me along with their ill-gotten money."

"And, we feel it's cursed to be beautiful, talented and glittering, and wish to live of our own life, independently. If we've something why should we not enjoy? So I resolve—let's use our talent and rescue us. My scheme is clearly a well spooned and calculated move to pass the time while engaging our dreaded vagaries in their own games with an uneasy friendship. I've gathered information that Rekha's mother is a very conservative as well as a disciplined lady unlike her daughter. But, Rekha enjoys her father's sympathy. With the transfer of her father to Puri her mother may get a transfer as per the government policy, which is a God-sent opportunity that we have to utilize to our advantage. My next move is to get close to DM family. With help of Rekha, you'll enter his house as a tuition teacher of her two siblings. This will help you earn your cost of study and protection for all of us. A balancing acts, although a tricky one. And I believe and confident, I'll be successful in executing my scheme of thing. I believe you understand my plan better now."

"Am I right, Rabi?"

Rabi heard in apt attention as he found himself completely bowled over. He stood in front of the guardian wordless, and saluted her acknowledging her scheme and acumen ship.

"But mind, this isn't at the cost of Preeti's LOVE and my friendship with you. I warn you again without prejudice. You've to remain guard of Rekha's every devious move. Her mother will be a great help to us in this regard," the guardian told heating Rabi's chin with envious fist that Preeti could hardly bear.

'How could she? Rabi is her . . . . absolutely her. She needs to protect him from any intrusion,' Preeti told to her. She attacked. This led to a free flow of fists followed by the game of sand and water throwing among the overflowing teens in the lap of very nature, on the rich golden sandy sea beach washed with afternoon descending sunray and energetic sea waves. Later, Rabi joined them. They were hopping and beating with hopping and dancing of the sea waves on the sea-line. 'What a beautiful panorama that the painters of Ajanta and the stone sculptors of Black Pagoda could understand.'

The beach-walkers halted at the safe distance enjoying, devouring, and at the same time, not disturbing, pretending, allowing the beauties of nature to have their moment of joy. When the two blooming girls and one cute boy play child game, the whole world halts at them. Envious scene with intermittent jingling song of flamboyant nupurs at Miss BCS's golden legs. And, many started taking shots stealthily standing behind the abandoned fishing boat in their tiny black boxes—acknowledging and recording the teens' play in the lap of nature.

"As if two just budding beautiful flowers fighting among themselves for the attention of the only honeybee at their sight. Who could resist this amazing spectacle, not to view? Even a musing saint can't remain aloof," the walkers sang among them.

SHOW OF CHARITY

No misgiving. No jealousy. No reason for eyesore. Why there should be any? There was no substantial reason. There was synergy among them. Both were from elite family, schooled in English medium, brought up in high society and cities, modern in approach and style, and had high profile parental, and above all, now, not competitor for the college's Prince Charming!

Rekha and Seema had become good friends. Rekha started talking to Seema, praising her eyes, hair, nose, cheek, chin, gentle boobs, symmetric body, structure and height; her style, her body aroma, choice of costumes and perfumes. And she certified, "You deserve Miss BCS crown. Alas, these days gawaris have been found overtaking. Taste has changed!" Besides, she was accompanying and flattering her. So also, she spoke about Prince Charming. She became an associated member of the three member squad. And, in the squad, she at times was found avoiding and ignoring the gawari Preeti, seemed openly and intentionally—leaving the poor girl occasionally forlorn. Even, sometimes, she was found leaving no opportunity to throw stinking words at gawari to the dislike of her ever flanking escorts who true to their responsibility, never forgotten to display their unhappy boldly.

"Girls from the villages are looked very innocent and non-descriptive, yet they're very shrewd. And on whomever their eyes land, they are trapped. We urbanites are far behind them in this subject. Am I not right, Seema?" opined Rekha at a hearing distance of gawari. "This isn't what I am saying alone. This is also the observation of Ms. Santidevi, we've all heard that day in the introduction session in the hostel."

"May be, but I'm sure, this isn't true in all the cases," philosophized the guardian and added elbowing Mr. Prince Charming and looking at Rekha, "I believe urbanite aren't far behind too! You see the case of your city's celebrated Ghar Jamai, Mr. Naresh Panda, Ruby's daddy. Her urbanite mummy trapped her gawar daddy."

Preeti, as a part of the scheme and as schooled brilliantly by her guardian, although was feeling hurt and dejected, was bearing obediently all these filthy pouring, surrendering before the mighty privileged. "This is part of loss and gain game." And, Rabi although was in league with Seema, yet he had all sympathy to his dear beloved, and was morally crying as and when the girl was at the receiving end of the puffed-up, displaying on his way. This was, in fact, major consolation to the poor girl.

With the transfer process of entire DM family was over and Rekha shifted to majestic DM bungalow on the VIP Road, she invited Seema and Rabi for dinner on a day of their choice. As they didn't show any enthusiasm and instead looked at each other and later concentrated cajoling the sulking Preeti and tried to convey that she was dearer to them than the grandiose dinner. This was understood.

"Yaar, I'm sorry. I've forgotten to invite our friend. Preeti, you too are invited," flashing a frown smile, Rekha—seemed unwilling—extended the invitation to the side-lined girl.

In between, Ruby had arrived at The Goal Table and was instantly got invited by Seema to the dinner. But, she showed no interest, and instead seemed took pride to reveal, "I'm sorry. I am shortly flying with my dad and mum to Madras on a business tour. Soon, our company is adding a few new inter-state routes, and for that some new buses are being purchased from Ashok Leyland. I've to experience how the business deals are negotiated and concluded. Our company Director (Purchase) is already there in Madras to initiate the process."

Kesab Swain, as if he was resolute to torment Femme's showy talks, activated his teasing sneeze and cough intermittently disturbing her whenever she opened her flamboyant mouth.

"If our dear DM daughter's dinner party defers to some other date, have you any problem?" asked Seema in her brilliant tricky teasing style.

"No, not so possible, I think—but I'll see," Femme replied—appeared—paying little seriousness, the subject deserved as per the instigator.

After a while of silence with lifting of hot and spicy mouth-watering piaji-pakadi along with fried green chili Seema, pretending that she didn't have any prior information, inquired, "Ruby, do you have any sibling?"

"No, not till now!" Femme responded with instant slip of her uncanny tongue looking at the enquirer, whose tongue fluttered, but certainly not uncannily, "This means, the attempts are still on!"

Everybody peered at the cornered Femme with reserved smiles. Mouth watering hot singhdas, just served, provided a timely relief for diversion to both canny and uncanny tongue-slippers and to their entertained audiences.

So far quiet and reserved Prince Charming took charge of the situation and shouted inhaling the aroma ringleting from the plates, "Wow! Whatever, Kesabkaka's singhdas are extremely yummy!"

"Kesabkaka, these days, is found favouring a few," they heard their class-mate Biju seating at another table lamenting.

"Why not? They're who's who of the college and also the city's," added Sasanka, the tickle boy tick-tocking.

With the passing of time along with eating the hot singhdas, although uncomfortable, the fleshy Femme, seriously inquired, "Why?"

"Nothing as such; but, I was asking . . . just!" Seema concluded, and later turning to the proud DM's daughter, she asked, "Rabi is looking for a hassle-free tuition job," and added with make-believe expression of disappointment in her eyes, "You know he has got financing problem for his study. You, well-heeled people, can compensate a hassle free good amount in time unlike middle-class people, who want result against every pie they pay, and at the same time, very irregular in paying."

As if this had bared a golden opportunity for both the struggling daughters of Big Guns for an inroad into the affairs of their common prey, they competed with each other for display of their kindness and charity to the utter amusement of the master schemer.

Rekha in her bid to grab the opportunity instantly proposed with displaying kind look at Rabi, "I'll talk to my parents and get back tomorrow. He'll tutor either my brother studying in Standard IX or my sister in her Standard VII. No need to go anywhere! And our bungalow is closed to Paharpur Hostel."

Fleshy Femme wasn't far behind. She had more striking offer although she had no siblings. She revealed, "So what if I don't have a sibling? My parents can go for providing group tuition facilities to our family servants' children. Very good social service! I'll purpose to my parents and I'm confident they'll certainly agree to this. Our Rabi can earn a good remuneration. Above all, there's a lot of difference and satisfaction attached teaching for charitable purpose than at somebody's home as a home tutor. What do you think Rabi? Have patience, I'll get back to you tomorrow. And if dad or mum so spare sometimes from their tight business schedule, I may take 'my Rabi' to my parents for a word on the issue."

And, she left the canteen in a hop with a privilege glance at the others around The Goal Table and at domineering present of Kesab Swain who was coughing, sneezing and chattering demonstrating his red teeth occasionally.

"She seems in hurry," Seema told.

"For long, my boys are left in lurch for generosity, Mam . . . . d . . . a . . m," Kesab Swain taunted in pan packed mouth. "What about the replacement of stinking dining table in the canteen?"

<hr>

The change of verbatim from 'our Rabi' to 'my Rabi' in the dialogue of Femme had a fainting effect on the foursome left behind. They were all left victimised. But, Preeti was unrelenting; out of anger, she kicked at the full-covered feet of the designer of the scheme with her slipper-shoe and cried with pain, "Aah!" being beaten back. Alternatively, she tightened her fist but sadly failed to utilize her body weapon like the one she had seen in her village strongman Pejabhaina, playing the role of Pandu's son Bhima in the dance-drama Draupadi Bastraharan. Alternatively, she wanted to question their self-appointed guardian's schemes and wisdom in coming close to Ms. Femme Fatale and the bulky Supanakha. But hold her down at the moment in the presence of the daughter of a formidable Big Gun—DM.

For Rekha, every minute was precious. After thinking for a while combing her head by her thick fingers, she appealed with a running look at the smarty and Prince Charming, "I am extremely sorry friends, I haven't introduced my mummy to you. She reported in our college today. Let's visit her in her chamber in the Department of Psychology."

As they were moving towards Arts Block, they heard Biju passing a joke looking at stadium side gate, "Bichara rickshawalla, he'll vomit blood on the way."

"Why, what happened?" asked his girl friend.

"Look at the gate! An elephant is riding a sticky cycle-rickshaw, pulled by a bony," jeered the discoverer of the onceinalifetime sight. The foursome following closely turned to that direction and saw Miss Femme Fatale hurriedly loading her fleshy rolling hips on a cycle-rickshaw, and moved out of the campus instead of waiting to her car that used to drop and picked up her as per class schedule.

"She seemed was in killing hurry. What can be the reason?" Seema provoked looking at Rekha.

This had a crippling impact on Rekha's apprehension and she was sure of an imminent competition for charity.

She took her friends to Dr. Swati Devi and the trio pay respect to her touching her feet. But, before Rekha introducing them to her mother, she told, "You're Rabi Pratap, the brightest student of our college and you're Seema Pati, the glittering girl from modern city Rourkela and the daughter of Director (Modernisation), RSP. Rekha had already told me about you yesterday. I'm very happy to see you kids."

There were no words about Preeti. She felt she was an odd-man-out, and turned towards the exit and about to leave the room bending her head in distress.

'Indeed, for her, her self-respect matter,' concurred Rabi and Seema in themselves and wanted to follow the girl as quickly as possible but . . . .

Dr. Swati Devi, it appeared to Seema, 'as she knows better about her daughter and guessed something mischievous' caught the forlorn girl by her hand running from her chair and looking at Rekha with displaying irritation, asked, "Why did you not introduced this sweetie little girl to me? Is she not your class-mate? Not fair!" And turning to the girl and embracing her, she appreciated, "A sweetie little doll! What's your name?"

"I'm Preeti Rath, a native of Rabi's village— Pandupur," the recouping girl replied.

"I'm happy that my daughter has three worthy friends. Children, now I've a class. At 4 O'clock, you come here. We'll go together in our car and will talk then. I'll drop you at your hostel. This is okay, children!"

"But mummy, I've something very urgent to discuss with you," Rekha appealed.

"You child, mind, there's nothing so urgent than the duty. Duty is God! And, at present, yours duty is to attend the class and my duty is to conduct the class. All right! Whatever is there, we will talk at 4 O'clock while returning to bungalow," messaging the head of her daughter the duty bound mother reasoned and rushed to her class with attendance sheet, duster and chalk in hand.

"If it was my daddy, he would have attended me immediately. But mummy is different and very rigid. Today, daddy has been on a rural visit. Has he been there in Puri, I would have rushed to him and got my Rabi's problem settled today itself."

"What to do? Let's wait," Rekha growled in disgust.

"Mummy, for Ratan and Reshmi you're asking daddy for home tutors. I've a ready solution in hand. I've a friend who's a bright student as well as a needy one, and stays near our bungalow in the Paharpur Gents Hostel," Rekha told breathlessly embracing and cajoling Dr. Swati Devi as soon as they crammed into the red-starred white ambassador car.

"Are you talking about Rabi? Not a bad proposal! But, how he'll manage his study? He is a bright student and a bright future is awaiting him. Again, he may play in the college cricket team in the Intra-varsity Cricket Tournament and many other competitions as our college representative; I heard this was being discussed in the HODs meeting in the Principal's chamber. This will be nothing but wrong utilization of a rare talent," rued Dr. Swati sympathizing.

"That's all right aunty. But, he has nobody except a mother—a struggling and deprived widow—to finance his study. He had to earn for his study. It would be a great help," appealed the guardian.

"Let Rekha's daddy come. In this matter, he's very hard to please. We'll decide and tell. But, I assure you, if not this, something else will certainly be found out to take care of his study. Is it okay, my children," Dr. Swati promised and ordered the driver, "Let us drop the children at their hostels first."

While the trio were about to stepped down at Ladies Hostel gate, Dr. Swati told, "I'm very pleased with you—kids. Today is our little Reshmi's birthday. You know, my children have very few friends here. And, their daddy has been on an urgent rural visit. He'll be reaching late in the evening. Has Rekha invited you? If not, I invite you to give a company to my children in celebrating the birthday at our place if you're absolutely free. Car will pick up you and drop."

"We're free aunty," overjoyed Seema replied even without consulting her friends as if she was looking for this God-sent opportunity eagerly. "How can we miss our little sister's Birth Day? We are coming aunty whether you send the car or not."

"I'll speak over phone to Dr. Mili for permission. Get ready at 7 O' clock! Okay! See you in our bungalow. Don't mind for gift," Dr. Swati told.

"Thank you, madam!" chorused the trio as the car turned back.

The guardian was very satisfied as she was confident of her scheme's output. And, Rabi was comfortable with the progress. But, the ghungi gawari was found unhappy, and she was indifferent. 'She's certainly disturbed with some apprehensions.' She rushed to Room No. 025 in hops leaving her friends blemished. And the friends were united to take care of the ghungi gudia's feeling of resentment.

"Well, you leave me your burden. I'll take care," the guardian assured the disturbed Rabi and pushed her into the Kumaris' custody fast leaving a promising look at the sulking boy. Back in the room, the guardian found ghungi was sobbing hiding her face in the pillow. She poked beauty's envious hourglass figure: she punched at her legs, at her slimy waist, at her armpits running her sticky fingers hither and thither, and later to neighbouring fleshy boobs' contours, sensitizing. But, still in vain, she told, "So woody!" She was sleepstill and stubborn. Nevertheless, the guardian, overwhelming with successive successes in execution of her scheme, was equally stubborn and wasn't ready to give up her hard found success at any cost in the mid-way. She schemed to entice the forlorn girl with a new trick—she was well-versed in inventing, scheming and executing.

"Had you noticed how the Jambubans, Hanumans, and that your Twentysixpur friend whatishisname—Kaaliram was looking at us, almost breaking and shattering, when we crammed into the red-starred car? They found them all clean bowled. Many were trying to hide their face and some making hurried U-turn . . . . frightened! What's a scene? I was thinking up to capture those creatures in their actions in camera with all pity to them," the guardian rejoiced.

The ghungi gudia got up and looking at the guardian, flared up, "Stupid, what's your plan? You mean to say, Rabi is saved from these witches. No, not at all! They're now almost after my Rabi. They've now started saying 'my Rabi'. What does this means? What I'll tell my aunty? Please explain me! Do you have any explanation?"

"Ooo ho, this is the thing! I was thinking up something else. Good Heaven!" the guardian jeered and added, "Hold on, hold on, my dearie little breaking sis," pulling ghungi's gloomy face to her compressed pigeon chest, the confident and jubilant guardian turned herself to the role of an oldie grandma, and explained, "I've already told you, Dr. Swati Devi is a conservative and pragmatic lady and had an arranged marriage unlike Femme's parents. Even if she allows your Prince to tutor her children, she'll remain averse to Supanakha's advancing to him at least on caste ground. And, this is the reason why we'll accept Rekha's tuition proposal rebuffing Femme's one in view of her caste and family background. Now, we'll keep Supanakha engaged with Femme."

"I'm sorry, Preeti. Why all these aspects don't come to your stupid mind? Is it so closed? Yours is a peculiar and outdated muffasali mentality; I'm sorry to say I am so cursed to live with thou."

The gawari's palms started banging her head. She pinned for a while and screamed, "Really! Yet, I won't accompany you to DM's bungalow. Please excuse me! . . . . I'll feel suffocated there," the ghungi, still in the mood of feeling of the odd-man-out, requested.

"Don't be foolish and maddish! Think once, what that humble lady, so beautiful and so caring, and our God-sent protective shield will think? She'll certainly feel bad which isn't good for all of us in this hostile city. Think for the highly vulnerable Rabi, if not for you. Again, for sake of Swati Mam, we, all the invitees, must visit her. I warn, this may aggravate, if there's anything in her mind, her suspense of the relation between your Prince Charming and her daughter. Keep in your mind: you've to over all the time accompany your Prince in order to dispel the doubt of anybody that he is drifting away from you. This is good for both of you. And, this is my sincere advice."

Pandua Preeti was very uncomfortable to any dresses other than that of salwar kameez or churidar kurti along with dupatta over her shoulders and chest. So also, she had never tried any other costume. When the guardian proposed her to wear for the occasion, her prescribed costume she rejected the option forthwith saying, "Shameful city costume! Sorry, it's exposing and attracts avoidable risk."

"What exposing? Do you think you're the only possessor of some rare body substance?" screamed the bold statuesque stunner and later jeered lightly as she didn't get any positive reaction, "What for then your parents appointed Rabi to guard you?" Still, there was no response! No body motion even.

"Dry wood! . . . . So you forget Rabi. He is a big chap. He can't remain underneath your tattered dupatta for all the time to come. Up-date yourself with time! Mind my advice or get lost," the statuesque stunner blasted the ghungi gawari, rejecting; but left the room dumping on ghungi's bed one brand-new pair of Levi blue jean pant, rosy Lacoste T-shirt and Reebok full shoe pulling out from her rucksack quickly to attend a tele-call as Pramiladidi shouted from the hostel office.

On her return, she found the door was locked from inside. She was surprised and asked to her, 'What the ghungi might be doing?' She knocked the door. Still, that didn't open. She stole a look through the rusty eye-hole. What she saw, she couldn't believe. Are her eyes—so far never failed to grab the right thing—gone disarray at the moment? First, she tried to rub her eyes with her bare thin fingers. She was excited and was in tearing hurry to push in. And she knocked the door, she banged the door, she hammered the door . . . . till the ghungi unhooked the door—cautiously.

The costume designer, as she entered the room, pulled out the tattered dupatta that was hiding the T-shirt covered Miss BCS's shoulders, broad chest, flowery boobs and hourglass waist.

"Wow! What a diva? What a pair of bosoms? What a waist? What a saint melting body curve? What a pair of meaty thighs? What a God gifted body? I can't believe my eyes. I'm envy of thou . . . . Preeti. Khandi Pandupur Rabi will be completely dashed today. Now I understand why you're chosen for coveted Miss BCS title by our college Jambubans and Hanumans? And why you're wearing churidar and kurti with dupatta," she oozed blinking her eyebrows.

Humour went on till the costume designer exhausted up all the acclaiming verbatim and sentences stored in her bodily in-built hard disk narrating and elating the golden girl. Later Seema, twisting diva's nose, cheered, "You'll be a big surprise to my dear Rabi; oooh sorry (touching her ears, apologetic), your dear Rabi . . . . um, certainly your dear Rabi!"

"Remain out of his hand reach. Or else, he may dash you," she advised and foretold, "and, gaudy Supanakha will be completely clean-bowled today." The costume designer went on singing praises non-stop looking at Preeti and later added with satisfaction, "In fact, this is what I want. You're now quite fit to my scheme of things. I'm sure; you'll hijack the birthday party at DM's bungalow." She embraced and kissed diva's forehead with friendly love and satisfaction with happy worm tears in her eyes, and she later exulted, "I'm now proud of living with a rare beauty, and moving around a rare combination of intelligent and vibrant friends. I long for this! I'm proud of my worthy friends."

"You know, Swati aunty had called me over phone and inquired whether we all are coming? And, she was very particular about her sweetie little girl, and checking. And was inquiring about your reason of upset while traveling in the car." And ticking at the narrow lion waist of the gawari, the stunner jeered, "I wonder why she's so particular about you? I've to double check whether she has a proposal for you? If so, I've to take care of my Rabi's, sorry your Karna's interest, side by side. What to do? I've some responsibility towards him as friend. Or else, he'll be a bichara Sisupal," bubbled the guardian with her characteristic symmetrical style till she was stamped down of her soothsaying with mild fisticuffs from elevated diva.

For a while, the diva found to her surprise the ever counseling, chatting and flattering guardian, silent, lying on the bed. 'Must be scheming something else,' concluded Preeti and asked jocularly, "What more is cooking in your mind, my dear the ever guarding sincere guardian?"

"If truth be told, surely, there's something," sounded Seema.

"I know your knotty mind," acclaimed Preeti. "This cannot lay idle. So tell, what's on the card next?"

They seated together fine-tuning a plot to fool their Mr. Cute. "Without play and fun, where is the life?" both leagued. "He'd told that day on the sea beach: he is talented, he is intelligent, he is cute and he is successful," clapped the inmates of Room No. 025.

"The idiot, stupid Mr. Cute will be dashed today," yelled the stunner.

"Hello, what you told—idiot, stupid, ... ? Say sorry," screamed the ghungi gawari pulling the ear of the stunner.

"Sorry, Maa Garachandi . . . . sorry yaar! I've for the moment forgotten that his 'would-be' is here."

The city street lights were off under the scheduled pick-hour power saving scheme of state government run power provisioner. And, the waving hemispherical uncle-moon hadn't yet graced the city street. The situation was perfectly matching for the two teens to exploit in order to play with their target—bichara Mr. Cute.

The bellowing of DM's Ambassador invaded their cave and they got up.

Rabi was already there in time, got into the front seat as the car parked in front of Ladies Hostel gate. Sitting in the front seat along with the driver, he failed to recognize Preeti in her new get up stealthily sneaking into the back seat shadowed by master schemer.

"Where is Preeti?" asked Rabi. There was no tinkling from nupurs which used to accompany the girl whenever she was out except college, that Rabi was so acquainted with and on several occasions had expressed appreciation. (He used to enjoy the jingle on the gawari's clean dancing legs. And the gawari knew Rabi's taste and she was cooperative, and had never forgotten.) But, on this occasion, the nupurs had been disciplined under skin tight jean. Seema, pretending as if not heard of Rabi's request in evening chattering of passing cycle, tri-cycles, bikes, and ever companioned envious mocks and comments from in-mates of both the hostels, requested the driver to start. As Rabi insisted for information about Preeti and later wanted to know, who's there along with her, Seema answered in feringhee language, "Preeti is not well. The same once-in-a-month problem. (Seema preferred the feringhee language to prevent the presumed little literate chauffeur to understand the gauche talk among them. But, against all the witty presumption, the young chauffeur pressed the jeering horn. And the smarty understood her limit of pretention.) So, Pratikhya is accompanying me as a replacement of your cheri ghungi Preeti. Esh . . . . very defiant! God knows, how you manage with such a girl, you have decided to partner with in life?" And halting continued, "Further, how can I, a teenaged and crowned Miss Smarty-BCS, go with a young man alone in this dark night," the stunner jeered but latter cried in pain as she was heat with an elbow from the ghungi, "Aah! Don't stab me, yaar!"(Pratikhya was the class-mate and a perfect replica of Preeti: in height, bosoms and slimness. And, her body colour was suitable to the situation. Lately, she had started copying Seema's life style which had been a talk of the hostel. And, she had on several occasions accompanied them in their team of three.)

Mr. Cute seemed reluctantly concurred but got pensive seating in isolation. 'He kept quiet, might be thinking something' looking on car's headlight flashed black top road and asked with resentment, "So what . . . . she can't come?"

'He must be thinking—I'm not listening to him. Too mulish and defiant! I'm arrogant; even have no regard to an elderly respected professor. This isn't good; not expected, and I cannot be a good life partner. How will he manage with me, such a crazy girl? I may behave in this manner with his mama? He would be crying . . . . he would be praying to Maa Garachandi to bless me with the right sense, and this and that,' Preeti told to her as the DM's car moved on occasionally bellowing, jerking and shaking its cargo.

As earlier, ever ready to help, the guardian patted the sulking peasant on his back, and assured, "I'll manage Mrs. DM. Don't worry! Or, else, what to do? This is a cursed problem with grown up girls . . . . we have to accommodate with," and clapped with Preeti unnoticed of the musing peasant.

The unhappy and grudging peasant growled, "Whatever, these days, she is becoming very pig-headed." And he settled down—'appeared highly worried.' Preeti was about to explode with a big laugh but stopped short of just opening the mouth.

Big salute from the sentry as the gate got wide open. Car entered the majestic DM's residential compound on the VIP Road. They could see, as they entered, gauche Rekha and her siblings with glittering brand new costumes standing in front of the bungalow with apt attention to welcome the valued guest of the evening.

'Who knows one of the occupants in the DM's car is the future DM in making,' Preeti told to her. As the car rammed in front of the bungalow, host ran to unzip the front door on the left and shook hand almost falling on Mr. Cute—that frightened the ever suspecting ghungi gawari—and guided him to bungalow lobby unconcerned of other invitees. The melting gawari couldn't push her out of the car; however her eyes ran past the unmatched pair till they were vanished to the lobby behind the door curtain. She wanted to follow them quickly but she found her immobilised in this new world. And, she growled at her guardian for her so-called smart maneuvering and prayed, 'Hey Bhagaban, please rescue my aunty's chand-ke-tukkuda.'

Ever understanding guardian took stock of the situation and the setting, alien to her companions she was wardening. She more or less pulled the sulking gawari out of the ambassador car, and being escorted by Ratan and Reshmi walked to DM's sprawling lobby. The gawari was so pre-occupied with the thought of Rekha's fleshy assault on her Prince that she didn't burst with her trademark reaction, "Wow, what a . . . . ?" on coming across the extravaganza in the DM's bungalow. As they offered chocolates to the two siblings of their host they heard Dr. Swati Devi—appeared annoyed—ordering Rekha from the drawing room to go out to escort the girls offering an opportunity to the guardian to update sulking ghungi saying, "See the nobility of our lovely aunty!"

"Namaskar aunty, we're already in. Ratan and Reshmi have taken care of us, and they're very cute and interesting," conveyed Seema.

The gawar instantly couldn't recognize his mama's little girl inside the new costume. He took time—dashed by strange sight—as if his eyes tucked inside his head. His head quaked. "You . . . . you were in the car? Wow! Unbelievable! You're marvelous, stunning," an unmoved Rabi reacted. And Rekha's eyebrows rose alarming, and her eyes widened.

But the euphoria didn't last long as the envied Rekha, walking to edgy Preeti ridiculed as the servant served the cold-drink, "Have you grabbed this get up from Seema?" The ever guard guardian, soon jumped to the rescue of the harassed girl, pulled her to Dr. Swati in the kitchen and requested, "Aunty, nothing is ready! Let's start preparation for Birth Day celebration. Please give us all the materials—balloons, candle, flowers, thread, ... cake."

"When our uncle is coming? Anyway, by the time he has reached we should have got ready everything."

Ratan and Reshmi joined her. Preeti, being hurt, was feeling perturb. And Rekha's coziness with her Prince Charming were aggravating her shakiness. Even she questioned her own wisdom, 'Whatsoever, I shouldn't have come to this strange setting.'

However, Dr. Swati was very caring, and with motherly affection—as if she understood what was cooking in gawari's mind in this unfamiliar setting—embraced the drooped girl and told elating, "What a beautiful and sweetie girl? You look like a beautiful Barbie Doll in this wear. Very matching! But, you seem very upset? Anything wrong? Don't hide. I'm like your mother. Come to kitchen, we'll talk and prepare the dishes. This is your house. Let them remain busy in their chit-chatting . . . . In principle, I do prepare our dishes." And, this and that, she went on talking.

Rekha had a sharp glance at the twosome in the kitchen as if she wasn't happy with their coziness—the guardian noted.

As they were talking and working in the kitchen, they heard a car jammed in the compound, and Rekha pulling her uncomfortable companion rushed out. And, shortly, they heard from the lobby she was introducing Rabi to DM, "Daddy, this is my friend Rabi. He is the brightest student in our batch. This year, he topped maximum numbers of events in our college and is an outstanding all-rounder on the pitch in your favourite game. You know, in the campus, the students and staff use to call him Mr. Jimmy of BCS," and pleaded with embarrassing sympathy to Rabi, "but daddy, he needs your help. He is very poor. He is in need of an opportunity to earn for his study. I want you to accept him as our Ratan's tutor. Mummy is waiting to your opinion. Please be sympathetic to him."

"Okay, we'll decide. Certainly a good proposal," the dog-tired Mr. DM however told affectionately cuddling his juvenile daughter. Later he, looking at his daughter, mocked, "This is all right. But, where is your trophy?"

"Oo . . . . ho, dad! Don't you know, I'm your knotty doll? Next time, I'll certainly bring at least one," Rekha assured.

"Borrowed or stolen one?" yelled the seemed dejected mother. Ratan and Reshmi laughed provoking a battle among the siblings that relieved DM to escape for washing in the bath-room.

The spacious DM drawing room was converted by the artistic hands of Seema supported by Ratan and Reshmi into a beautifully doll house; a small cake on the table in the middle flanked by candles, and by balloons from all shades of rainbow, which were dancing keeping rhythm with the slow moving ceiling fan. As Mr. Mohanty entered the drawing room escorted by Rekha and followed by Rabi they were dump struck with the setting. Seema touched his feet as Reshmi introduced her, "Daddy, she is Seemadidi, Rekhadidi's classmate. And, there is with mummy, Preetididi. Very beautiful!"

"Your didi too!" the father in Mr. Mohanty consoled as he found Rekha staring at Reshmi, almost firing.

Preeti came and touched the feet of Mr. Mohanty. Mr. Mohanty, appreciating the three beautiful flowers, chanted, "Three sweetie kids; ain't they, Swati? Very nice to see you, children. Keep on coming!"

After the celebration of the small but amusing Reshmi's birth day as designed and scripted by the artistic hand of Seema, the hosts and guests gathered for the dinner. The beautiful Barbie Doll helped Mrs. DM in adoring the dining table with neatly cleaned glittering china dishes. Everybody's eyes were at her. "Preeti has been the stealer of all eyes," Seema chanted at the ear of Mr. Cute stealthily.

But, to the surprise of three guests, Mrs. DM hadn't shown any interest to her daughter's proposal. As Rekha kept on raising the issue, the father in Mr. Mohanty patted the girl and assured, "What's the hurry . . . . my darling? We've just landed in Puri. Let's settled down first. We know, he's your good friend and you want to help him. We're proud of your compassion. This should be, and I promise, I'll certainly go extra-mile to do something for him. This is also a responsibility of DM."

"But mind, he deserved recognition, not sympathy!" advised Mrs. DM deferring the decision to the utter frustration of the sponsor and to the comfort of guest trio.

Back in the car, in the rear seat, Rabi lost no time appreciating Pandupur girl's get up bowing his head and raising his palm much to the satisfaction of the guardian, jhampanna style.

"Well, what a mistake, I committed? This is like losing the market so unwittingly," Seema chattered bubbling. And, further, she continued with a provoking hand maneuver at Preeti's fleshy armpit, "Were I not here Rabi would have flashed your body with a pompous sweetie kiss. Is not it, Mister Rabi? Further, may I request your highness Mr. BCS to repeat the scene of that afternoon on the sea beach? My eyes are hungry of that beautiful scene. I wanna learn the style to apply on my Mr. Prince Charming . . . . Please repeat once more for me, yaar!"

Rabi turned to smarty passing over ever warm Preeti, already over his body, and pulling smarty by her ear shouted cheerfully, "So, this is your design! Yours costume," and appreciating cheered, "Wow! What a crafty scripting? Here, the peasants are measurably bowled out."

Again, turning back to chic smarty as if he was incomplete, he appreciated, "You deserve the credit! And, I respect your discovery," and rued, "but my ears are deprived of sweet song of nupurs."

In the meanwhile, Rabi's muscular warm sensation tinkled as diva's body continued to heat him producing a feeling offending the cooling blow of land bound late evening cold wind from the sprawling Bay of Bengal. He had found himself in the pool of provocation; he couldn't control, and his lips busted at the rosy cheek of the beauty just rested on his thigh.

And, the man on the wheel blew the horn. 'May be envious,' thought the boy looking at Miss Smarty.

"Wow! Stunning! What a force?" Seema reacted as she witnessed the beautiful scene under the stealthy reflection of just arrived waving crescent uncle-moon's cool light.

"Idiot black box again has gone missing! What a bad luck?" the girl cried. "The scene required to be recorded."

As if this wasn't enough, the love-struck girl showed her other cheek disregarding the public civility with excuse of Rabi's initiation and smarty's endorsement. But, she had to cool down with a sharp slap from her dear Prince Charming, she enjoyed pushing out her narrow red tongue, grimacing.

"Still, I'm happy!"

Pandupur beauty wasn't selfish. She looked for an opportunity to return the generosity. She readied her fleshy lips, watering them with quick push of tongue. As soon as the 'soon to be victim' was found buried in a thought—'might be engaged with thought of being so open, public and vulgar'—Preeti knocked Rabi's cheek with her lips peering at the chauffeur busy in negotiating on the pot-holed road.

CLASH OF KIDDAS

"Tomorrow will be a very interesting day. Needed to be handled very carefully and masterly. Kiddas may clash! Hey girls' dreamboat, get ready for the feast of events," the guardian forecasted as if she knew the proceedings that were going to be unfolded. 'She was found ecstatic with the above possibility,' seemed to her audience. "Note, this ghungi gawari will be a big burden on us. She is better advised to stay back in the hostel with excuse of once-in-a-month problem," the guardian told digging ghungi at her sloppy tummy hardened with favorite regal fried rice, makhan dal and chili chicken and mouth watering rasogolla and frumenty at the birth day dinner. In the meanwhile, they got down under the dim street light, from the DM's car, the trio's new found shield, as soon as the vehicle parked in front of mighty Iron Gate of Kumaris' secured cave. But to the forecaster, the gawar was appeared not so enthusiastic, she was found in buddhic musing. 'Might be the side-effect of the latest prediction of her,' Seema concluded.

On the contrary, the gawari was in a different state. She moved closer to her musing heart-throb as the car made a back turn permitting the lovebirds under waving crescent uncle-moon's cool light a parting private moment. The overjoyed gawari stood in front of her heart-throb, unfolding her wing-hands wide open in an apparent bid to demolish her guardian's just ridicule,— she appeared hearty and confident—, and declared, "I am no more a gawari. Is it okay, my darling?"

The guardian was watching and was enjoying the unfolding newly found jubilation in ghungi. Before leaving to each other's addresses, she walked to the musing boy and cuddling his back wardenly, planted in him the valued confidence, and assured, "Don't be worry! We've now with us the very understanding Mrs. and Mr. DM. I'm sure they won't let down us if situation so warrant."

Next morning, Seema woke up early to the surprise of Preeti. There was no snoring, and there was no need of usual pulling and pushing to get her up as if she was very serious to face her forecasted happening of the day, and she was readying her mentally and physically. There was excitement and sparking in her elegant lotus eyes too. The gawari found in their self-appointed guardian the complete seriousness—true to her promise.

And, the guardian didn't find in the branded bookworm concentration in her study. To her, the Preeti appeared thinking, and sluggish in turning the pages of the book. Unseen before, she couldn't surmise any satisfaction. Her last night display of confidence was missing. 'After-thought may be,' she reached the conclusion. She couldn't remain with her mouth shut. Talkative as usual, she suggested, "Don't worry if you're not confidence, you don't go to the college. Well, heaven won't fall in one day absence. I'll explain the lessons to be taught. And I, along with your Prince, will manage the clash of privilege kiddas."

Still not being found with any reaction, she kept on watching the ghungi girl. 'Is it she reluctant to wear new costume that I forced on her last night,' she guessed.

"Well, Maa Garachandi! If you aren't so comfortable, don't wear this boyish, exposing costume," approved the guardian running her open palm over the ghungi's cascading hairs. However, the ghungi gawari got up and hanging on the guardian's high shoulder, cajoling to ascertain, asked, "Rabi was very excited to see me in your sponsored get up . . . . isn't it? And, also Swati aunty! Am I really so striking with your prescribed costume? If so, why shouldn't I adopt to new style although I'm uncomfortable? I wanna go to college with your jean pant and T-shirt if you've no objection to share till I've purchased one pair. Now, I've full confidence on my dear guarding guardian, she can ably handle any hurricane which will ever dare to assault us." "Please . . . . ," she begged.

The guardian was amazed. She pushed her artistic thin fingers on her ears pretending to clean them. "What I'm hearing?" She looked at the jubilant girl— smiling and approving. 'The gawari is changing,' she felt and she acclaimed, "I'm happy that things are running in the right direction. That's a good girl. Let us face the challenge head-on together. You wonderful two helped me keeping me engaged during these days of stressful banabasha. Really, I enjoy yours' company," praised the guardian with a satisfactory bear-hug on the jubilant girl and added, "For your information, the costume I offered to you, has been very carefully chosen by your friend-in-law after he surveyed your full size photo during the last puja vacation in Rourkela. I was just waiting for a pompous opportunity to inaugurate this. This get up is for you."

"Wow! What a nice and caring 'brother-in-law' he is? I believe, we were two sisters in our last birth. Thank you, thank you very much, Mrs. Sambit! So, my brother-in-law is very fond of jean pant and T-shirt, is it? I mean, he's your costume designer. May I be blessed with an opportunity to have a look at him and talk? Why don't you invite him to Puri?" the excited gawari requested with excitement.

"To be eloped by you? Do you want to fool me? No baba, no! Sorry, I haven't forgotten what that city breed Supanakha had opined on the other day. No, not till you're locked with your Prince Charming! Or else, I doubt, you'll elope my Prince Charming leaving me high and dry, and Mr. Cute, a celebrated Sisupal for life! Sorry, I can't take risk," the guardian jeered and later embracing little discomfit girl assured, "Don't mind, yaar! . . . . joking! For your information, I'm thinking of taking my two good friends to Rourkela after the Annual Examination. You'll talk to my Prince Charming, move around with him on his bike, eat in Mayfair eatery, watch movie in the Konark Hall, bath at Vedvyas ghat, boat in the picturesque Mandira Dam and enjoy the friendship; but, sorry not in seclusion. Is it okay, Maa Garachandi?"

"Seema, do you know what I was thinking about you after our first meeting in this room? I, the peasant from Khandi Pandupur, had almost decided to shift to other room as I was sure, I couldn't manage with a flamboyant and intrusive girl from the modern city,

Rourkela," the gawari revealed, and expressed, "I'm extremely sorry for this."

"This is okay! . . . . happens!"

At 9 O' clock, they'd to gather at the Ladies Hostel gate. Preeti was in hurry—'Certainly not to face the already forecasted marauding hurricane of the day but to place her appearance before her heart-throb in the day's bright light,' understood the guardian—even without locking the Room No. 025, she used to do on all other days. The guardian followed her with guardianly satisfaction and passion. Besides, she wanted to witness and enjoy the newly scripted enthusiasm in the love-struck girl.

"Rabi is late! My God, he is always late!" shrieked buoyant girl at the gate.

"Hello, madam! He is not late; you are fast," the guardian watered the elated girl checking the presence of anybody around. However, her search went on. The guardian felt, 'The peahen is almost readying to fly to Gents Hostel to check the where about of her peacock,' and she, to poke fun with the hysterical peahen, frowned, "Hey foolish, don't go, Kaaliram may be hiding behind the wall?"

As if this wasn't enough, she heard one passing senior from Gents Hostel goaded, "Eee . . . . ss..h, bichara Miss BCS! You're so late. DM's car has already picked up your chikini! What a big loss?" and while riding the bicycle, advised, "Better look for a substitute to tempt you in your new get up!"

The dampen girl gasped and turned to her ever ready guardian for apparent relief. And, the guardian signaled to have patience, smiling. The patience paid.

"My Rabi is coming," screamed the peahen and ran unfolding her wings, almost singing and dancing.

"Oo-er, you're again in this get up," the surprised gawar asked jumping his eyebrows.

The spirited girl shrugged and replied with shy but sweet smile, "Because, you like it! Because, Swati aunty like it! Because, Seema and her fiancé like it! When everybody like it, who I am to refuse," and later landing a mild fisticuff on the boy, told, "Don't look at me like a bear or monkey. I'm not our hostel Kumaris' ripe jackfruit or Smarty's Ratnagiri Alphonso mango. Mind, others may be watching us, you buddu, don't have presence of mind."

"In fact, you're very childish!" Rabi reacted smiling.

"You must be thinking, how will you manage with this babe girl? Am I right, Rabi? Don't worry, I'm with you," the guardian consoled.

As they entered the college campus amid teasing comment targeted exclusively on the day at the gawari, they could see from the gate, the Femme Fatale standing in front of Science Block entrance leaning over the white ambassador holding her head on her right palm, replicating a sight of Bombay's red-light harlot to trap her unsuspecting prey. She was dressed up in a brand new shimmery rah-rah skirt and a white tank-up besides silver heels in her feet with full display of affluent arrogance on her meaty body.

"She is waiting to Rabi for sure," Preeti whispered with fear at the ear of her ever ready guardian.

"Rabi has come. Bichara maffu will be roasted by Miss Femme Fatale," a boy shouted at the top of his voice at their back. While another shouted, "Wow! What a dashing diva? Miss BCS has almost overcast stylish Miss Smarty in her new get up."

"Feast of colour! This side Miss BCS and on that Miss Femme Fatale. What's going on?"

"She is almost in her vulgar get up with single-point-objective of impressing upon your heart-throb in the disguise of material comfort and overflowing fleshy tissue," narrated the guardian to the melting gawars.

The envious bears and monkeys were all around and were all active—jeering, growling, yelling, coughing, ... targeting at the showy girl in front of the Science Block. Some were criss-crossing nearby, flying on their bicycles or bikes, blowing, itching and taunting horn, and overflowing with mare-lip whistles. Despite, Femme was unperturbed as if she was enjoying them. 'As if this has been part of her campus life. Or the elements aren't worthy to be attended—dismissed as the acts of envious and frustrated substances.' "Kiddas . . . . rejecting kiddas!" concluded the elegant guardian.

"What a bloody get up?" Preeti reacted in the meantime.

"So get ready to witness a big fight. But mind, we've to take care of the dignity and honour of our dear and respected Mrs. DM. And, she shouldn't get an opportunity to even guess that we are involved in staging the quagmire. Rekha is a mad gal. She can go to any extent forgetting the common sense of dignity, and so also, sultry Ruby . . . . brought up in such a setting!" the guardian let loosed her mind and warned like a tactical war commander while leading her small squad towards Science Block entrance.

But, the humble peasants were apprehensive. They wanted to avoid the eye to eye contact, frightened from head to toe. 'They aren't coward, but certainly reluctant to encounter an unpleasant situation. "Let's skip her by entering through Arts Block entrance," Rabi requested.

"What good it will do? Will this spare the inevitable? Let us face the challenge and reality head on. In fact, her acts don't matter to us? This is her problem," the stunning guardian yelled like a veteran warrior and expressed, "Why should you go for penance?"

'Seema is right,' however thought the scared peasants. And, they walked. As they passed the Arts Block gate they heard a car jammed behind them. They turned back and as they saw Dr. Swati getting down, they walked to her and pay obeisance to her in chorus, "Good morning, Mam!"

"Good morning kids! How are you? So, let's go to the class. See you at launch break if you are free or in the afternoon. We'll travel together." Dr. Swati responded flashing a quick glance at them with her usual gentle manner with books in one hand and vanity bag clinging in another. She entered the building and melted in the crowd.

And Rekha accompanied the trio, but stopped short of pushing further—'Might be at the sight of Ruby, her mighty and formidable challenger for the college heart-throb.' The trio understood.

At the moment, Rekha had the advantage of being at the arm's length of the common target. She'd a quick crafty check at her get up—'you, the daughter of a salaried parents, can't be any match in costume to an daughter of Indian businessman,' thought Seema confining within her—and then started walking matching with her companions towards Science Block gate discussing last night party. As they approached the audible distance of Ruby, Rekha cabling her right hand with her Prince Charming's left, asked, "Rabi, how was yesterday's birth day party and dinner in our VIP Road bungalow? You must have fully enjoyed. My parents are very receptive. You know, Ratan and Reshmi are very fond of you. My parents had never refused my request. Be sure, your work is done!"

As if this wasn't enough, it appeared, Rekha was found literally pulling humble gawar as he was trying to slow down, 'might be to greet Ruby' amidst jeering of Jambubans and Hanumans at safe distances.

'Whatever, I should have greeted her. This is the civil courtesy. After all, she's a class-mate. Now, we are friend. We're together studying in the same class and taking nasta on the same table,' lamented the almost skyjacked Rabi, finding him helpless in the company of the daughter of VIP Road's first family and district's most powerful person.

The humble Rabi couldn't believe what was going on in front of him. He rejected this bloody culture prevalent in high society and cursed him for being at the gate of all these. Even, he also didn't spare his present mentor for her scheme of things.

———◦◦◦———

Miserable bowled out in the hand of a government employee's daughter, which she can't remotely thought, the proud and only daughter of the owner of state's largest transport company closed her eyes in anger, and harshly turned her side facing college ground. She was burning and found murmuring something as the meek gawar forced to disappear in the crowded Science Block corridor side by side DM's daughter.

"A clear edged out! A defeat that could hardly be envision. And, that too in Puri where her family is recognized as the first family of the city's Grand Road," yelled the anxious watchers followed by their sarcastic laugh salting the bleeding love-struck heart of privileged Miss Femme Fatale.

In no time, she was heard barking at the bichara car driver to leave. A quick start, bellow of horn and spitting of thick curly black smoke beneath the back guard, the four wheelers vanished—appeared out of scar like a defeated bull on the Grand Road.

"She is kicked out like an ordinary stuff before even touching the shore of her LOVE," shrieked with all sympathy a passing bear.

"Unbearable!" chattered yet another flying on a motor bike with irritating mare-lip.

Enjoying the aromatic sight of bleeding heart, happy and aplomb and allegedly branded cocktail girl slowed down and went closed to the proud daughter of Grand Road's first family and in her pretending bid to douse the fire with her flattering wit, she praised, "What a costume? What a style? Well, you look stunning in this designer attire! What for this today, madam? Is it your birth day? Or you're in a mission of honey trap! Who is that lucky Badshah? You look very attractive. Anybody could be envy of you!" She went on promoting despite latter's hard hissing. Further, she, lightly caressing Femme's skirt and winking at her, inquired, "It must be prescribed by a costume designer for a special purpose," and asked with Helen's eccentric smile she was competent in resembling, "How much this cost, Miss Ruby Dash? . . . . must be in thousands? What a great rare fortune? This is the privilege of children from business family. Isn't it, Preeti?"

"Whoop . . . . what a rare fortune?"

Yet, Femme wasn't responsive or even accommodative. 'Understood!' Later, Femme skidded furiously towards Physics Gallery—seemed hunting to the poor gawar or the powerful DM's daughter or both—ignoring the flattering of the overwhelmed but pretending cocktail girl, the kind she in fact was enjoying in the canteen just yesterday.

The houris followed her as they were prompted by a growling class-mate at their back, "Be fast, Madams! Go and rescue the bichara gawar badly lost in a buffer between the daughters of two Big Guns."

Femme had a brief halt in front of her stolen prey and her formidable challenger, sitting closed to each other in the first row in the Physics gallery. Kidda looked at kidda, eye to eye, mind to mind, gasp to gasp, thought to thought. VIP Road's first daughter raised her hood—victorious—while gawar, caught in a buffer, was praying Khandi Pandupur's presiding deity Maa

Garachandi to rescue him and get him out of this bloody quagmire, almost shuddering.

Later, Femme turned to frosting gawar, and fired, "I'll see you!" The poor Rabi heard the explosion bursting out of Femme's mouth directed at him.

With the arrival of Dr. Jena, a very sincere but strict and affectionate professor, the usual mild pre-lecture commotion concerning the just concluded fight between the who's who of the college subsided and the students got to their respective seats.

Dr. Jena was energetic and highly cooperative and reasonable. He had all praise of Rabi for his all-round performance and brilliancy and used to sing piano in his name in the class room which hadn't gone down well with his tormentor Lalu Sarangi. So, he was searching for opportunities to corner Rabi and had been humiliating him at every feasible opportunity.

The simple and humble brilliant from Khandi Pandupur wasn't able to concentrate in the lecture. The warning—'I'll see you!'—went on echoing in his ears, hunting him with his every inhalation. And, he was feeling suffocated and disheartened. He wasn't able to attend the first question from Dr. Jena. Even he failed to answer the second, third and so on, surprising everybody in the class as this was first of its kind they noticed.

"Is it VIP Road effect?" jeered Pratikhya. This made sworn tormentor Lalu overwhelmed. "No, no! This is out of Grand Road effect," the tormentor fired the second salvo, and chit-chat followed in the back row. Soon the verbatim "Grand Road effect! Grand Road effect!" in full vigor had a free run all around the gallery. A mild commotion with sneezing, coughing and chattering filled the usual quiet lecture's gallery. As if this wasn't enough, the tormentor fired another salvo duplicating his voice, "Sonofabitch has been completely clean-bowled today."

The lecture stopped. This silenced the jam-packed class instantly.

Dr. Jena was astonished. He was in pain and in anger. He shouted, "What? . . . . Who? Who has got clean-bowled?" No response as deadly silence rained the gallery. All the students down their heads. Waiting for sometimes, Dr. Jena hammered the podium with the duster, and cautioned, "I know how to tackle nuisance in my class. Don't forget that you're studying Science, not Arts or Commerce without practical," and went on dragging, "Alas, how could you say to your own class-mate sitting shoulder to shoulder, a sonofabitch? Shame to you! To your attitude! And, to your up-bringing."

Rabi told to him, 'Nope! I'm an odd-man-out! I've no place in this world. Nobody is dependable! Everybody has his or her own agenda. Even Seema, the daughter of a Big Gun, can't be trusted. She is pursuing to take revenge for the humiliation she had been subjected to by the privileged daughters,' and cried within despite all the sympathetic and bold talk of revered professor, 'Mama, I am coming to you. We're odd-man-out in this world. Sorry Preeti, I'm helpless! Please excuse me! I am leaving.'

As soon as the lecture was over, as everybody started walking to next class, a visibly disturbed Rabi leaving aside the DM's daughter, approached literally sobbing Preeti and telling something at her ear in broken and chocked voice, not fully understood in the humming surroundings, walked with manly fast-steps out of the gallery, then the Science Block, and lastly, from the girls' sight.

Ill at ease, Preeti couldn't understand anything, and even guessed anything in such a sudden and fastness. She felt lonely and dumped. She wanted to stop him. She walked fast to catch him . . . . but failed. The guardian was too equally disturbed with the humble boy's unusual act.

Both the girls had never seen him so disturb and hurry. 'A celebrated cool and a composed creature in our circle, and this is despite heart-stinging provocation on several occasions in the past.' Both rushed, trying hard with matching steps, towards the Science Block exit and not finding the 'by-default' cursed boy on the alleyway, went on searching in the campus.

"What happened? The beauties are crying? Is it Femme or DM's daughter, who has stolen their Prince Charming?" the monkeys and bears as well as Supanakhas and Femmes were relentless in their jeering, chattering, ... mocking the houris.

They dropped the next class. They boarded a cycle-rickshaw to Paharpur hostels. Not able to trace him in the Gents Hostel, they looked awkward and later returning to Room No. 025 sat down dumb-struck.

"Rabi is a very simple boy and not that bold to put up with all these humiliation and complication . . . . He might have gone to his mother," Preeti threw her out sobbing.

The guardian hugged Preeti like an equal partner of pain, sorrow and distress. She being unable to control the girl, announced, "Let's move to Pandupur!"

The gawari raised her head, cleaning her flooded eyes, cheeks and chin looked at the announcer astound. "What . . . . ? You will go?"

"Yes, I will. I'm too to a great extent responsible for his' present state of affairs. I won't rest till I find a logical solution. But mind, what I'm doing, I am doing sincerely for the benefit of my friends who are now part and parcel in my life; the company, I'm homely with."

"Don't waste time! Let us be fast! Pack up with minimum. I'm getting the permission from Caretaker Madam. If you like to change to churidar kurti, you get into that fast," the guardian advised with authority and left for the office room of hostel for permission from the Caretaker.

Within a few minutes, they're on oldie Ramuchacha's cycle-rickshaw, on the way to Puri bus-stand.

Calm, composed and spineless appearance. They were sans any usual funny chit-chat, unseen in the past that provoked Ramuchacha to surprise. And, Rabi was absent. In past, Ramuchacha was part of their talks pertaining to Jambubans, Hanumans, Supanakhas and Femmes on the city road, on the sea beach, in the college campus, in the Hostels, and most particularly, those roving around their ladies hostel periphery, sometimes staring—it appeared—planning to scale the Kumaris' bold and secured Berlin Wall.

He was on occasions harassed by loafers for his unsolicited suggestion. Ramuchacha even didn't spare his young rickshaw pullers colleagues who had lewd intentions.

And occasionally, they talked concerning so-called strict Rules and Regulations of celebrated Kumaris' of Paharpur Ladies hostel and violations of that at easy by senior students and the daughters of Big Guns. He shared the information about who had gone where with whom, and made fun of those elements. Ramuchacha did share information as asked. He on occasions had shared his feeling and thought like guardian and grandpa, and as a well-wisher which the occupants of his tri-cycle had appreciated and offered their unprejudiced thanks.

They gave Lord's Prasad not only to him but also for his family exclusively purchased and packed on their each visit to the temples. Even they used to invite Ramuchacha to take masala-dosas and chats with them on the Grand Road and on the sea beach, indiscriminating. He never asked for fare. And, he never checked what was paid. He was so confident that he simple used to keep the payment in his pocket as they were paid. There were never an occasion when there was dispute on payment of fare, a regular feature taking place between hirer and hired at hostel gates, college gates, bus stand, railway station, temple gate, and where not. In the past, together they had enjoyed their journey. In one way, he, like Kesab Swain and Miss Warden, was a BCS College's long survivor: many used to say—if truth be told—without any fight or maneuvering but for his honesty and accommodative approach.

But, unfortunately, that day, Ramuchacha had no information about Rabi when asked by the occupants of his tri-cycle.

"Certainly, Rabi hadn't come to hostel before leaving," murmured the guardian in despair.

Ramuchacha was apprehensive. 'How long he would remain silent?' "Betia, what happened? Anything . . . . anything wrong?" he asked breathing hard leaning over the tri-cycle handle struggling to reach fast, of course, unasked.

"Not, as such! But Rabi had abruptly left the college because you know that bloody Kaaliram abused and humiliated him. Perhaps, he has gone to his village," responded Seema coolly and continued, "We're going to Pandupur."

"Hey, Bhagaban! What's this bad mind-bending news I am hearing? How will be my beta," cried Ramuchacha along with the cry of cycle-rickshaw 'curr . . . . , curr . . . . , curr . . . .' under undue stress trying to be fast. "Why he is after my beta? God save my child!"

TATHASTU

As the bus approached Chabishpur bus stand, the eagle eyes of Preeti instantly located her heart-throb standing there—appeared to her—waiting to board a bus back to Puri. The sight of Rabi gave a new lease of life to her heart—crying since their parting in the college campus—and to her eyes happy warm tear.

The overjoyed girl pulled her guardian's head, and whispered, "Look . . . . look . . . . . , there is my Rabi—I am sure, I can bet—hurry to return to Puri . . . . back to me," and added, "It is certainly due to his late-feeling of guilty . . . . feeling of guilty of being very uncaring and irresponsible towards me at the moment of anger. This is my Rabi's greatness. This is the 'Magnetic Force' that my Rabi uses to speak! He loves me so much!"

The guardian was happy too. She flashed a confidence smile and later told, "So, this is the thing. First of all, I've to discipline him. Let me think of a plan."

As the passenger carrier jammed at the bus-stop whirlwinding red dust invisibiling the faces of the passengers, they shouted, "Rabi, Rabi!" They were in chorus and in a mood of play as the guardian advised, "Let's fool the snot-nosed first!"

Hide and seek—they resorted to being amongst the just landed co-passengers and waiting few under the mango tree. Rabi looked hither and thither, surprised. Chorus, "Rabi . . . . Rabi . . . ." repeated, till they were caught by each other's eyes. He stared at them shaking his head. As the girls rushed towards him, his eyes weren't ready to believe what those were viewing. He looked at them astound, wide-eyed, and later screamed "You!" pointing his finger at them.

"Ooh, ye-e-es, we! None but we! What's the surprise? If you could come, why we can't?" attended the happy and confident girls.

Quite an envious sight—two beautiful apsaraas (that too one with boyish attire)—dancing, jeering, mocking, joking and playing—to the peasant onlookers including Preeti's eye-sore monstrous Bishu Sarangi among them standing at a distance staring with envy.

"You so distrust me that you didn't even feel it necessary to speak before leaving the campus. Again, may I ask you at whose responsibility you left this burden-some ghungi in that hostile city? I'm here to dump your village image. You two stupids get lost! Besides, I'm to say sorry for all the pain you've gone through, and you believe they are due to me," the guardian broke open in one breathe and moved aside; 'however, reluctantly,' felt Preeti.

"I'm indeed extremely sorry, Seema," apologized the snot-nosed to the girl, getting close to her—their ally, guide and the guardian in an unfamiliar city-setting they were new at their arrival and asked, "Tell me, once placing thou in my shoe—what would be your mental state after all those filthy pouring? Neither I'm in a position to stop the intruder of my modesty nor do I bear their stinking language? Was not the situation killing? I'm exhausted hearing all these, refusing to relieve me despite my all sincere efforts."

The reasonable and understanding guardian turned to the peasants, and explained them masterly, "But, this is whatisthatbloody's name—Kaaliram's prime objective. He wants to spoil you, resentful of your performance and envious of this ghungi's unflinching LOVE to you. And you, by being so foolish, reckless and abrupt, are doing a favour to him, unfortunately not understanding the consequence—out of emotion—which is nothing but momentary fury! Your today's act was nothing—if you don't mind, I would rather brand—but foolhardiness, not expected from an intelligent and responsible . . . . "

She later told patting them in lighter vain, "Whatever, let's move to Khandi Pandupur!"

"What???" Rabi shouted, abacked. He looked at the city girl, then to the Preeti, again to the city girl . . . . as if his ears were dashed by something strange and crazy.

"Preeti, check your bag for an ear cleaner. Hey girl, please help me clean my ears. Be fast! Some strange intrusion, may taint," he asked and laughed, "Ha . . . . ha . . . . ha . . . !'" Again, he reacted looking at the city girl, "Hello! What did you tell? Repeat . . . . have you turned mad? Mind, you urbanite can't manage in a remote village. Even, we don't have a bath room or toilet or latrine; my cottage does not have electricity, forget about fan. My home is a one-room-for-all-purpose cottage, a thatched house packed with tse-tse mosquitoes, lizards, rats, moles, cockroaches, stray cats, and occasionally, stray dogs, crows, bats, mongooses and even snakes. Sometimes, they used to encroach our cottage with strength. They'll dinner your city grown, cream-lotion, well-groomed fleshy clean tissue," and added with remorse, "Again, our village people will suspect our relations and gossip non-sense linking you with me which may not be appreciated by my mama. They may even bad-mouth and tease that would be unbearable to you . . . . Apart from, my mama is a muffasali woman. She suspects the city girl. And, along side, you know my family's social status in our village."

"And, there is spicy busybody, Bulinani! She can blabbermouth anything, she is so azad," Preeti forecasted.

Further, pointing at Seema, Rabi said, "Have you checked you? . . . . in this costume . . . . Nope! I'm extremely sorry. Sorry, never . . . . impossible!" Rabi dismissed at last focusing at her attire, signally a clear and bold, "No!" He hurriedly raised his left hand signaling to stop the passing bus to Puri.

But, the city girl was stubborn, and reluctant to listen to anything other than to her instinct as usual. She was resolute.

"Nothing doing! I'll go," she demanded and appealed, "I want to talk to aunty. I want to sleep in her lap, listen to her, learn the cooking and eat her cooked food. I have heard a lot of beautiful things about her from her little girl—a worthy mother of our The Great Gawar," and continued winking at Preeti, "After all, to learn from her how to raise a beautiful child like our sparking Karna," and begged to Rabi, "please share your mother's 'LOVE' with me. I'm hungry of a mother's lovely nectar, a true mother's nectar!" She was dewy-eyed. She was emotional. She was swaying. And, she won as Preeti supported her, "Let's agree to her! All her urge will last for one night. Matter of maximum one day yaar—maximum one night and a few hours."

"But, I've a condition: don't ever say Khandi Pandupur. Our village name is Pandupur," Preeti demanded.

"Well, you promise here and now, not to place in my mama's durbar, you—as the guardian of Preeti—threatened that day on the sea-shore, against my that bravado—betraying this mad girl's LOVE?" Rabi wanted the assurance, of course, lightly.

"Okay baba! Yours Highness Miss and Mr. Khandi Pandupur; sorry (biting the tongue) Miss and Mr. Pandupur, all your condition . . . . accepted . . . . agreed," concurred the guardian bubbling at the peak of her delight, and the squadron marched-fast jumping, joking, chatting, poking, hitting and caressing with each other free from city's raunchy comments on the county pot-holed road passing through Twentysixpur village lane, and deserted mongo orchid, rice-field, knee-deep water channel, screw pine bushes, ...

"Ahh, what a beautiful sight replicating Gopi's Gopapura," reacted the guardian while walking through the mango orchid.

The guardian was guardian. She inquired with usual pleasantly, "Our very dear dreamboat, may we know what cooled you down so quickly that you were returning to Puri, even not visiting Pandupur though came nearer to it?"

Rabi remained silent and pretended to say as though there was nothing as such.

Preeti too looked at him with film star Juhi's catchy smile. However, Rabi's buddhic musing to repeated queries was quite revealing.

The clever guardian stopped, pretending the fatigue of walk on the rustic dusty road.

Preeti revealed fixing her blue deer loving eyes at her heart-throb, "I know my Rabi can't live without me. Besides, he can't give pain to me. This had been proved that day evening on the sea-line. Is not it my dear Mr. Snot-nosed? Again, he would have been scarred of my dear aunty's query about me." And, she stood in front of the snot-nosed on the deserted road passing through a mango grove. She quietly touched her boy's clean soft chin lifting with her thin palms. Warm and happy tears rolled down watering the dry and pale soft cheeks of two lovebirds, intensely gazing at each other till the guardian yelled, "Stop, stop! Mind, I'm here! Okay, I certify: the gawars are also good LOVERs! After all, the greatest LOVERs were brought up in village cow shed."

Busy Bhagyabati and sleepy Pandupurias were surprised to see their golden kids sliding down the high canal wall.

"They were so abrupt? What happened? This isn't a vacation time. Is Rabi running short of money? May be?" murmured mother Bhagyabati and so agreed her companions in the afternoon chit-chat under the big banyan tree.

But, the strange girl Seema in her boy's attire hijacked the attention of the peasants. As the trio came closer, the peasants intensified their focus on the strange girl forgetting the assumption on their golden kids.

And from nowhere Bulinani descended at the sight and found surveying the strange girl reminding Preeti and Seema the act of their hostel presiding Kumaris on the day of introduction.

'May be she is a guest of Choudhury elder? And, she is just accompanying my children from the Chabishpur bus-stand,' Bhagyabati guessed as she had seen jean pant and T-shirt costumed girl from cities visiting Choudhury abode on the days of family functions and festivals. 'But, they used to mostly come in cart sent in advance to either Chabishpur bus-stand or Delang railway station or in dry season on motorbike or jeep.'

However, to the surprise of the beholders the strange girl came close and bended to touch the feet of Bhagyabati with praying look following her buddies. But, Bhagyabati's feet were—seemed—sliding back as if they were reluctant to be touched by the strange girl, she had allergy to. Despite, the girl touched the feet which fuelled the gossiping "................" among the peasants and provoked Bulinani to react, "Aushmati Bhab-ba-ha!" And, later, she buzzed, "Prema will now be relieved from tension. Let me go, so much of works are there!"

"Where? Let us check?" joked a lady.

'This girl must be a city girl—a city witch—my family's tormentor of peace—hijacker of my chand-ka-tukkuda,' Bhagyabati cried in her and with many fearsome apprehensions such as, 'She will run away with my child—Again, I'll be alone!—God has not been kind to me—what crime I had committed in my past life so I've been condemned to such a hell—what will happen to

Khandi Pandupur children's hope and aspiration!' She lamented almost sitting down on the exposed root of big banyan tree.

'I had requested the little girl very specifically to guard my chand-ka-tukkuda. The little girl has neglected in carrying out my instruction? Or she in the meanwhile drifted away from my child in favour of a glittering and wealthy city boy and allowed my child to drift to this city witch?'

'Hey Maa Garachandi, what I'm seeing? What I'll do? Alas, why did I send my child to city,' Bhagyabati kept on pondering.

'......................,' she stood up, walked few steps and sat down on her cottage step murmuring, her chin on her knees and hands on her head. She was impatient, raised her head, dewy-eyed. She stood up, seemed resolute . . . . she wanted immediate answers.

Panduas had several questions in their mind, "What happened? Who's this girl? Why she has come? What relation she has with our village future hope? . . . . etcetera, ... etcetera?" Even, the mentor, Karan Mishra wasn't escaped from the bad forecasting in his mind. 'If Rabi will be taken away by this glamorous city girl, certainly he'll be drifted away from our village . . . . What will happen to my plan?'

'Or is there any effort from Choudhury family to patch up with the mother-son through this girl? . . . . Is the girl, a relation of Choudhury family?'

But, Salu, Valu, Gallu, Dukhi, ... were very happy with remote thought that Rabi had certainly been drifted away from their Pandupur queen bee. 'Whatever, we can now cheer up our eyes after a long gap. And, we've one more stunning beauty as bonus.'

Sneezing, coughing, chattering, jeering, ... echoed the Khandi Pandupur skyline, followed by gossiping bringing the dull and sleepy village to life.

Impatient Bhagyabati called her chand-ka-tukkuda to the backyard of the cottage, away from the nosy gaze of the city girl, the juvenile little girl and the suspicious Pandupurias. And instead of inquiring which were routinely asked on the previous occasions, "How are you? What have you eaten? How many days to stay? How is you study? How is your health? How is the little girl doing? How much money you have and how much you need now, etc., etc.," she fired with low intriguing voice—full of crying suspense and apprehension—"Who is this girl?"

Rabi checking back the audible distance of the city girl, tried in vain to clear his mama's doubt, whispering, "She—Seema Pati—is the daughter of a big officer in Rourkela Steel Plant . . . . a class mate of us. And above all, she is the room-mate of your little girl in hostel . . . . She is a very good girl and our close friend. She helps me pay my hostel and college dues in some months; very cooperative."

Like the paper boats melted away in no time in the current of torrential rain water in the Pandupur alleyway, the boy's all persuasions melted away in the current of scarred mother's raining suspense—she was far from convinced, rejecting—and in frustration, the boy cried, "I know you'll never trust me over this issue. This is why, I had requested Seema not to come," and added little loudly as Bhagyabati sat down resting her head on her knees on a exposed mango tree root frightened, "Ooh ho, what to do? How I'll convince you?"

'How could she when her simple gullible peasant mind is infected with melodramatic Odia film scripted with objective of exploiting emotion of largely Orissa's rural viewers for commercial gain,' the grown up Rabi thought, and later consoled him with all the sympathy to his dear muffasali mama looking away.

Dissatisfied aunty summoned the little girl—looked as if she had self-cooled her in the absence of any alternative—and caressing her head and back and adjusting her dusty frizzed hair, asked sweet-talking, the question she had already fired at her child. But, the answers she got were not to her satisfaction.

Rabi in the meanwhile was apprehensive of the city girl's feeling—they were so-closed—being excluded in the parley standing alone and occasionally gazing at them . . . . 'What to do? On one side, there is reverend mother, and on the other, a committed friend, and above all, a guest—*aatithi deva bhavo!*' He was in impasse. 'Whatever . . . . ; I have a responsibility towards her,' he felt strongly.

However, the bold and chic statuesque stunner wasn't surprisingly found disturbed and irritated, noticed Rabi and he felt as if the girl had prior clue of such a state of affairs and mentally prepared to face them. She surprising all walked to the trio unasked and told cajoling, "Aunty, you know, your dear chand-ka-tukkuda being bad-mouthed by some ruffians, had left your dear little girl in Puri alone and had come to you. I don't understand how could it not come to his mind—what was the fault of your little girl? And, I had no alternative but to escort your crying little girl and village image, still in her muffasali hangover, to you. But, I am having a liking for your two eye pupils. They're so nice! So beautiful! So friendly! However, if you don't like I'll go," and with depression she continued further, praying, "Aunty, I don't have anybody to share my sorrow and pain and happiness at distance Puri but these two. Please don't separate them from me!"

"I can't live," she cried.

The gawari mama-aunty still wasn't convinced as she continued to believe, 'This may be a filmy ploy?'

"The city girls are very clever!" gossiped the village girls among them.

In spite of . . . . and at one fell swoop, the mother in Bhagyabati felt elated and elevated. She was proud of her son for his overall impressive personality, studentship and above all, his physical appearance that could impress, attract and pull a beautiful, smart, rich and educated city girl to be his good friend. And, the girl could be pulled to their poor cottage. 'This isn't a small achievement. What more a poor widow and a mother could expect from her kid?' She was satisfied. She was swollen with pride of her motherhood. And she thought of her late husbandGod for planting in her such a beautiful and talented gene. She thanked him. This was the moment of joy and satisfaction amid—fear, apprehension and distrust.

Nevertheless, what all the mama-aunty heard from the strange girl regarding her child was unbelievable and embarrassing. She looked at the composed Rabi and twisting his left ear, asked, "How could you be so irresponsible and reckless?" Embracing her little girl, she shouted, "What would have happened to my little girl?

Have you ever thought what your Raghu uncle, Prema aunty, Karankaka and our villagers will think when they'll hear yours all these non-senses and stupidity? You've let down them and their 'hope and aspiration.' I feel extremely sorry and sad for your this kind of behaviour."

"Now, you promise before me not to repeat such an act ever," the mother demanded.

The little girl was in her exploding ecstasy. She hopped to the embarrassed boy and requested her aunty, "Shall I twist his ear? He isn't sparing me even for a small mistake. You see," checking all around told, "yesterday, he slapped me on my chin. There was a finger spot. Was not it, Seema? . . . . This is my turn. Aunty please . . . . allow?"

"What???" an angry and dewy-eyed aunty shouted embracing her little girl, "he slapped you? Hey Bhagaban, what I am hearing . . . . one after another? Rabi, you slapped a grown up girl! Who is there to take care my little girl? She must have cried!" And checking the face and cajoling the little girl, aunty shouted, "What your uncle and aunty will think when they'll hear your this brutality? You're still behaving like a little kid!"

But, the dim-wit, as she got back her sense late, told hugging at her so caring aunty, "Sorry aunty! I was just lying. How could you believe, Rabi will beat me there at Puri? He 'lo . . v . . . !' likes me so much," and with loss of no time, exhibiting her face to aunty requested, "check, see, there is no such spot! For sure, I won't tell my papa and mama," and touching her gullet told, "I promise!"

Seema murmured intriguing, "Preeti, you are . . . ."

"That I know and I'm confident . . . . but still, he shouldn't have slapped a grown up girl, even touch. Very bad!" reacted aunty with a contented smile.

A deprived city girl however couldn't believe her eyes—witnessing this lovely scene. 'What a lovely life thrive here and what's there at my family—full of artificialities, make-believes and deceit . . . . Shh . . . . no love? Money . . . . position . . . . career . . . . bloody high society,' she cried. She hated her and her birth. 'Indeed, I'm a pariah here.' She developed a liking of her friend's upbringing and to live in this. She was returning into the cottage, depressed that Rabi could understand. He signaled Preeti. Preeti followed and embracing their friends, announced, "You're no less a sister of us . . . . part and parcel of my aunty's extended family."

As the evening approach, the two girls seated for an endless chat sitting around a smelling kerosene lamp on a hay mat laid on dry clay floor in the one-room-for-all-purposes cottage.' A few curious village girls including Preeti's cousin, the school drop-out Lilli, were there to hear and talk to the city smart girl amid buzzing and bloodletting biting of mosquitoes, screaming of bats and daring run of moles despite cat's mew around.

The village girls were curiously watching how the city girl was sitting and walking in the boy's attire on the floor mat. Even a few followed her when she went for pee by the side of cottage backyard bushes. Before, they'd seen such smart city girls in the Odia film, and in the reclusive Choudhury abode but they hadn't ever talked to them one to one and that too sitting side by side. The Pandupur teens used to rue, "Choudhury elder doesn't allow his guests to mingle with the villagers as if this will lower their noble and high social upbringing."

Again, the Pandua girls, fuelled by Bulinani's forecasting, were also suspicious of their heart-throb's compatibility with this city smart girl; and so, they were curious to explore, 'Has Rabi drifted away from Preeti, if so . . . .'

In the nutshell, the city girl was at the center of their attraction.

In the meanwhile, the aunty had suggested Seema to cover her T-shirt adorned pigeon-chest with a dupatta borrowed from Preeti which the girl instantly obliged earning aunty's appreciation. And after that she had never forgotten to ignore the dictate although that wasn't a matching attire. Besides, she was very particular as soon as Rabi or any male person was entering the tiny cottage and when she was going out of cottage.

It seemed despite all the tearing pain in this new world, the city girl was enthusiast and was enjoying every moment of life in the village.

Lilli suspected. So also, many others including Dalli, Chandi, Malli and Manju who joined Lilli later. And, they gossiped, "There's something. Or else how could a city brought up and a daughter of big officer from the modern city Rourkela surrendered to such an oppressive life in one-room-for-all-purpose cottage made up of raw clay hooded with dry hay."

Seema had heard about the villages' natural, physical, social and cultural environment but hadn't got an opportunity to experience its' life physically being in it. She had heard her papa was born and brought up in a village. She had persuaded her father to visit his native place but to no avail as he became more and more career oriented and ambitious, so dearth of time.

"Papa had almost forgotten his root," she rued and moralled, "This is not good," and had expressed her displeasure to the much dislike of her parents as and when she had got opportunities in Rourkela.

But, it seemed, the Pandua mosquitoes weren't ready to allow the city girl to accommodate easily. "Your dupatta is flying like frizzy-free tail of our Balia bull," jeered Lilli focusing at her, and Dalli clapped with her to the chuckle of others.

"Yours too!" Seema jeered.

"But not like yours! . . . . Is not it, Preeti?" shouted Lilli.

Despite the perceived ill feeling towards the city girl, the aunty however had all pity to Seema for her discomfort in the village environment. She occasionally was waving her sari veil around the city girl to weed out mosquitoes sparing her little time from cooking dinner at the cottage back veranda over shifting chulla earning crook smiles from village girls. And the Lilli commented, "Aunty is found very caring of Seema."

She was busy preparing extra menus for her chand-ka-tukkuda, the little girl and the so-far resented guest. 'Daughter of a Big Officer! Will she eat my cooked food? At her home, they might have expert cook preparing number of delicious dishes with special favours. Occasionally, they may be visiting restaurant and hotel for change of taste . . . . even so, let's try for the best!'

They heard Bulinani had now and then been jeering on the street, "She'll vomit eating widow's food . . . . Let's see, where Rabi is sleeping tonight." As another told, "May be in the Club House," she rejected, "No, not at all! Club House isn't a night shelter for village outcast."

Alongside, Bhagyabati thought, 'Bulinani is right. Where the girl will sleep, change her dress, take bathe, etc., etc.? Already, she has problem for pee.'

"Hey Bhagaban! Where my laadla will sleep?" the girls heard their aunty murmuring on the back veranda.

"Hallo, where is Rabi? He is almost forgotten and thrown out from here," Seema asked and jeered, "is it we, so many girls are here, so he is in banabasha? Friends, you must go now. It's so late! Regarding Rabi, nobody is thinking about?"

The girls were surprised seeing the expressed worry of the city girl for Rabi when Preeti and aunty were silent, opening a long awaited opportunity to question the city girl for her reason of cosiness to the boy. Lilli taunted with suspense, "Ooh Madam! Why are you so worried for our village boy?"

"What is wrong with you, yaar? Since the arrival nasta in the afternoon, he hasn't taken a drop of water and you are saying why I'm worried. This isn't fair!"

"He is such a guy, whenever he comes to village, he has so many works," Preeti picked up. "He has the heart-beat of our village. Now-a-days, everybody except perhaps Choudhury family wants to speak to him whenever he comes to village."

"Since he mauled Chabishpuria in matriculation examination closely followed by the big win in the volleyball match, he has been elevated to the position of the most sought-after persona of our village," Lilli rued following Preeti.

"Bholanath must have been feeling hungry. But point is, he won't ask for, suppressing his hunger whenever he is with his friends, with Karankaka and with village elders," Preeti reminded and added, "but, when he is at home, he orders aunty for this and that as if aunty is a hotel boy and quarrels with me for . . . ." Later Preeti, walking to street door threshold, shouted, "Rabi . . . . Rabi . . . . , where are you," and jeered, "Meal is ready, come!" And, they heard sneezing, coughing, crying followed by doubling-up of the tone of the boys to the surprise of the city girl who asked in low voice, "There are no dearth of bears and monkeys, even here."

Rabi returned and shouted at Preeti, "What you told: Meal is ready! Is it a hotel or restaurant? What the villagers will think? Brainless girl!"

"She is right! You have reduced your house to a hotel, only grace it at the time of eating and sleeping. Am I right, aunty?" Seema screamed to the envy of village girls.

"This is all you see and experience," the aunty told.

And, the gathering reduced to three plus one as Lilli, Dalli, Chandi, Malli and Manju had to leave—however reluctantly that could very easily be recognized by the city girl—with heavy breaths, ruing, "So, we have to go now . . . ."

On the alleyway before parting each other they abstracted, "Preeti will be the biggest loser. Rabi will certainly drifted away from this dim-wit. Such a flamboyant, smart, rich and also accommodative girl . . . . to be hard to resist! Cha . . . . cha . . . . bichara Preeti," and wondered, "How does she allow?"

"Preeti may have trapped another boy. She knows Rath family may not allow an urchin.................," Bulinani told.

As Rabi walked to mama-cook still busy at the back veranda preparing dishes by-passing the two girls in the cottage, Seema observed in the ears of Pandupur queen, "Here too hearts churn for the Prince Charming. They left almost crying! Indeed, Preeti, you need to be saluted for your praise catch in this cut-throat competition. Rekha in fact is right in her observation," and added mocking, "Sorry, I won't allow Sambit to meet you till we are locked. You're a master grabber! Hats off!"

"Are you far behind in this subject?" Preeti reacted lightly with a wink.

The girl had to change her dress in the one-room-for-all-purposes cottage. Either Rabi had to go out or the girl . . . . high tension as the girl picked up her night wear from the rucksack. Aunty pondered, 'How a young girl—whoever she may be?—will go out, and that too, to open place, although there's deep darkness invisibiling anything in which sometimes I change my wears too?' And, she was in confusion and moral aching.

Preeti took control of the situation. She told to the odd man, "Well, Mister Rabi, you better understand, you're the odd-man here," and ordered, "So, may I ask you to 'Gate out!' for a moment? And you remember, never enter the house without a knock. Your free entry henceforth is banned and this diktat will remain in force till Miss Rourkela is here in Pandupur."

The mother looked at her chand-ke-tukkuda, speechless. The odd man shrieked pretending helplessness at his mother, "See mama, I am asked to 'Gate out!' from our own house. Great injustice! Nothing but didigiri!" The mama-aunty however kept quiet and slipped to back veranda with contented smile—it appeared she was enjoying the babyish play—concurring with the diktat. The insider heard their mama-aunty murmuring at veranda, "Did you not know this? Why did you bring her? Take this as your penance! . . . . if you have sister?"

And, the poor mama's son followed the decree bowing before the interloper and walked to street veranda. And, he came back later knocking despite the advance permission, "Now, you may enter."

"That's a good boy! Keep it up," Preeti applaused.

Dinner time. Mouth watering aroma ringleting from freshly cooked dishes and conducted all around in the small cottage for immediate attention. And, the happy mother thought about her share of fun. She laid special dishes: khechdi, dalma, coconut cake, green leave fry and chutney, all favourites of her little girl in neatly cleaned sparking bell-metal plates.

The eagle eyes of the odd-man-out after having a quick survey of the dishes, shouted at revered mother, "Where is my fish curry?"

No reply! And, to his further irritation, the mama's little girl yum-yumed taking chutney to her frowning narrow tongue and cheered throwing herself over her aunty, "You are my great aunty! For long, my tongue has lost its sense of taste grinding Kumaris' junk menu. Thank you Seema for your scheming that facilitated this visit to aunty's menu."

"You've prepared all the favourites of this large mouthed fasto, forgetting me. I won't eat," cried pig headed Mr. Neglect throwing him on the cot.

"Where were you? Have you told anything for preparation? Late comer has no right to claim of his choice. I'm sorry. What to do? Seema and Preeti had eaten the fish pieces as soon as they were fried," the mama challenged him as she wasn't ready to spare, and subsequently, in a lighter vain cajoled, " . . . . small children. Forgive them this time!"

"Wow! What was the taste? Mind blowing!" hummed the girls in chorus, further irritating.

"Children, let him enjoy the exciting perfume. I'm hungry," the mama sat down on low stool to start.

"So far, she had never eaten the food before I started. But, today, what mantra you two have sprinkled over her that she even has forgotten me . . . . She has started speaking for you. Forgive them, small children, as if I'm an oldie like Lokidada," grumbled Mr. Neglect.

"Aunty, you told you're hungry but you aren't eating? You don't keep your words? Sorry, I would rather say this isn't fair? Three, two, one! Get start!" the knotty Preeti demanded.

In the meantime, Seema had got the fish curry plate hidden under the rack. "Hello snot, come on! I've saved something for you," the city girl revealed and the eagle descended in no time, and the mother coughed pretending to clean the throat peering at her chand-ke-tukkuda. While engulfing delicious fish curry along with khechdi, Rabi grabbed the little girl's favourite coconut cake and shouted at mama, "You're responsible for fasto's overweight, a big burden to our skeletal Ramuchacha."

After the dinner, Rabi accompanied Preeti with the only lantern to drop her at her house amid deprivers' sneezing, coughing, chattering, ... in the Pandupur alleyway. In the darkness, the city girl grabbed aunty's lap on the cot and slept resting her head on it as if she was hungry of it since her birth, being brought up by ayahs—the hired mother in the high society. The mama-aunty couldn't deny nor protest to save her only lap for her 'eye pupil' as she slipped to universal motherhood overflowed with selfless love and affection resembling the greatness of never complaining mother earth.

On his return, Rabi found his mother's lovely lap was stolen. And his mother seemed deep in a thought caressing the interloper very similarly she used to caress him, and waving out the mosquitoes.

The mother-son as a practice used to review day's study, talk games, talk about friends, ... and also play pleasantry. Lately, they had stopped talking about the filthy branding of Rabi with verbatim 'loafer, urchin, son of a WIDOW, shame of the village, sonofabitch, guttersnipe, etc.' poured on him indiscriminately from the elements inimical to his existence and successes.

'Who sleep where?' the decision was hunting the mama-aunty. She was also disturbed thinking, 'What the ever bad-mouthing villagers will gossip about the compatibility between Rabi and the city girl when they'll know that the twosome were together in the same room in the night?' Also, she recalled her little girl's declaration just a couple of hours ago that 'Seema is no less a sister of them'. She soothed with the fact that, 'Of course, I too will be very much here. And were I a daughter, we would be staying in the same one-room-for-all-purpose cottage.'

As if Rabi had thought about the issue before, he requested his mother, "Let Seema sleep on the cot. We'll sleep on the mat below. Just a matter of one night!" But, the girl wasn't ready to relieve her aunty. She thrust her head on cross-legged lap and pretended deep sleep and started snoring. Rabi hanged the lantern at the nail on the wall and screwed the light dim till that was looked like she-devil light from a distance, and drew the mosquito net on the cot. And the mama-aunty felt another head on her lap. There was a mild pushing and pulling for little space on the mama's precious lap reminding her of such fights with her youngest brother during her childhood. Her two hands started spraying nectar on the two heads hungry of mother's 'LOVE'. Finally, the mama-aunty's kids settled down for the rest of the night on both side of their mama-aunty as she unfolded her legs, stretched her body . . . . and retired for the day—assured and confident, talking and passing pleasantry.

With crowing of cocks from distance drummers and the washer men habitations and cawing of crows from the overshadowing mango tree, the mama-aunty woke up and saw her lovely children in their deep sleep enjoying the same as if they were starved from time immemorial, their bodies laid by her left and right side occasionally cuddling her, snoring and raving competing with each other.

She sat down on the cot straight up and pulling her legs to lotus position, prayed to estranged in-law's family deities and Pandupur's patron Goddess Maa Garachandi joining her palms over her face with all pious reverence. She prayed to give her children all their blessing. The mama-aunty didn't discriminate between her chand-ke-tukkuda, the little girl, and latest grudging addition, the city girl. Then she had to caress Rabi before she left for morning household works. Today, there are two. Who to be caressed first, a mother in her, was in moral quandary?

The jingling of nupurs and the peeping shadow through the window followed by frantic knocks at the door: "Thack, thack . . . . ," and cry, "Aunty!"—"Thack, thack . . . . ," and cry, "Aunty!" "Thack, thack . . . . ," persisted in quick successions, unrelenting.

Rabi guessed, the cry wouldn't stop till the knocker's aunty had obliged. Although the little girl rescued quandary mother, yet she wasn't allowed to attend the knock as Rabi trapped her waist. And, the city girl joined—seemed to aunty the naughty two were in league to harass the little girl. 'Certainly preventing,' thought the mama-aunty. 'Nothing but children's game!'

"What, yaar? She can't sleep? Aunty, see wherever I go and stay with your Rabi, she follows me like a leech," Seema growled in her sleep.

"How long a grown up girl remain waiting at the door? What'll the villagers think? This isn't fair! You two are very envious of my little pretty daughter," protested the aunty and forcefully slipped down the cot.

"Daughter or daughter-in-law!" Seema buzzed at the ear of Rabi as the mama-aunty open the door.

A crafty elbow heated the bubbly cooling her 'certainly, an intentional talk.'

Preeti was shocked to see Rabi and Seema on the cot together, side by side, and snoring competing among themselves. She couldn't speak. She was stunned with the sight. To instigate the melting girl further, the city girl drop her hand on Rabi slipping little closer to him. 'What's this non-sense? How could they sleep together on one cot? Has this smarty city girl been hoodwinking me all these days? Is it for this she insisted for coming to Pandupur? Aunty is a simple muffasali lady. Has she been swayed with the witty and rich talk of the chic city girl? I am simply edged out by this smart city girl. I'll soon be an odd-man-out in this cottage,' aunty read from the little girl's appearance and heard the murmuring, "Bulinani is right."

And, the snoring became vigorous and irritating—focused to provoke the little girl—seemed quite intentional to aunty. Aunty decided, 'Let the children play their game.' She, leaving the sleeping pair in the custody of the scared little girl, went to backyard with a pot of water to wash her face. On return, she saw her little girl was almost crying, tears in her blue deer eyes; she was still standing motionless amid competing snoring and breathing on the cot. She, a mother in heart and soul without any prevailing pretension, couldn't bear her very affectionate little girl's blood frosting further. She melted. She smiled. She embraced the little girl, cleaned her sweating with her soft cotton sari veil with all sincere care, whispered in her ear, "Have you not told: Seema is your sister? . . . . Yes, she is! She has proved your confidence on her. I was between them on the cot. Is this not all right?" aunty revealed and asked, and snoring stopped. And cuffs, fists and pillows started flying as the pleased aunty-mama left the battle ground to pluck flowers for stony Pandupur presiding deities, who—she recognised—although late, started listening to her prayers.

"That Bulinani isn't a good lady. Always instigating! You know, last night, she told Priya, 'Rabi and Seema will sleep on one bed.'"

"And, you turned mad! Seema, see her eyes . . . . so swollen! Not slept last night, cursing the Goddess Night for her preventive darkness."

"Sorry, sorry yaar!"

Like his previous visit to Pandupur since his joining in BCS College, this time too the golden boy was busy with his village lads including seniors and juniors. The village elders were talking to him regarding his study, and what were going on in the city, sparingly. Every gist in his college life starting from cricket match in which he single-handedly led his class to defeat the seniors to mauling of arch-rival and tormentor Lalu Sarangi in debate competition to letter from Femme Fatale to the city girl's engineered dual between the daughters of two Big Guns were talked, chatted, critically reviewed and commented with drop-out ex-class mates. They were enjoying with occasional jeering, sneezing, chattering, blinking of eyes and teasing throat pretending to clear cough. Some were envious, displaying doleful cry at their mouths and were found repenting with verbatim, "What's a miss? Why didn't we study well?"

Eventually, the matter concerning jean pant and T-shirtwalli, the strange diva, the city girl accompanying them this time became the central topic of their chit-chat as the issue was in every body's mind. And one heard floating, "Rabi is trapped. The smart city girls will elope him. He'll forget us. He's a big chap now, even bigger than the Choudhury!" Yet, Saroj couldn't evade the truth and eloquent, checking the presence of dreaded Choudhury elder's any sycophant around, "After all, Rabi is a Choudhury. Whether anybody accept this fact or not. I've heard this from our village elders, talking. He had got the body and facial appearance, colour, height and personality of his father Dibakar Choudhury. A carbon copy, a ditto!"

However, belying the peasants believe, Rabi wasn't elusive. He was cooperative and answering every prying question fired at him by the curious peasants as regards to the city girl. Rabi tried his level best to clear their suspense regarding his personal equation with the city girl and his relation with her. And, even, he went on clarifying, "Who I am? A rootless son of poor widow! And she, the daughter of a Director of RSP, the Orissa's largest PSU with thousand crores business . . . . we're just friend, yaar!"

But, those explanation—looked—as if didn't help to break the ice, the peasants were not ready to be swayed by Rabi's clarification and looked at him blinking their eyes and brows, far from convinced.

"Rabi has become very smart and glamorous these days," opined Gundhia.

"Bichara Preeti, alas . . . . !" Dukhi buzzed.

Followed by passing Sallu's rue, "He has now two queens around. It's all lucks! How many will follow . . . . God knows!"

"What's wrong? Rabi, please don't mind, but I'm happy. I'm with you. You keep on bringing this city girl, and if possible, some more. At least, our village girls will be inspired. The days of old style, thinking and mind-set have to go. In other villages, the girls have started wearing modern dresses. Ours' have been left behind with this old model frock and oldie sari," Saroj appealed sarcastically. "This is all due to bloody Choudhury elder. Had our village the High School during our parents' schooling days, they would have been educated and got placed themselves in higher government position in cities opening opportunity for all these advances to our generation?"

There at Rath's abode, the ever suspicious and questioning reverend mother of the golden girl was very blissful by the sight of the dashing and smart city girl. She was exulted with her husband's witty maneuvering.

"We have got our child's education in the safe custody of the son-of-the-widow. Rabi is certainly trapped by this city witch," opined Prema and heard, "Just wait and watch! . . . . just matter of time! I'll pull the princes all the way from cities to our doorsill begging for our Preeti's hand. We'll hold her marriage ceremony with equal extravaganza and fanfare of Choudhury family. Preeti is talented, educated, beautiful and no less a princess. One day, she'll be a big officer. Do you know the village lads were talking—our Preeti has been adjudged the most beautiful girl in their college defeating large number of city girls and this smart girl? What's there at Choudhury's doorsill? Our doorsill will overflow one day." Raghu Rath bubbled shuffling his towel over his right and left shoulders alternatively displaying his superior intelligence over his dim-wit wife. And happy oldies came closer to each other but stopped short of just stealthy winking as they felt of somebody walking towards them from the neighbouring room.

The Rath abode's princess heard his clever father saying, "I'm proud of you for delivering such a beautiful daughter—one in lakhs. I'm proud of our considerate daughter. She is no less intelligent than me. She'll certainly deliver to our expectation and satisfaction."

"She's your gene. I have just carried her to grow," replied the reverend mother in appreciation, and later joining her palms over her forehead with all the reverence, she prayed, "Maa Garachandi, please bless my child; I vow to sacrifice a black sheep after my apsaraa marry a prince of my choice."

Chipkali applause, "Tik . . . . , tik . . . . , tik . . . . !" supplemented their ecstasy. And the reverend mother repeated, "Tik . . . . , tik . . . . , tik . . . . !" So also the reverend father pronounced, "Tik . . . . , tik . . . . , tik . . . . !"

'One day prince will certainly come—tik . . . . , tik . . . . , tik . . . . !—but that prince is of my choice,' Preeti constrained in confidence for the moment. 'You'll be proud of him.'

Rabi guided the village lads studying in schools, a responsibility he had taken over as per the scheme designed by the President of the Pandupur Youth Club and the mentor, Karan Mishra in their effort to lift insipid Khandi Pandupur to Pandupur. He also visited village Primary and M. E. School along with Karankaka, and discussed with the teachers regarding academic progress of some brightest students, and the trailing few. In the afternoon, he was in the playground with cricket enthusiasts, coaching village lads aspiring to retain the winning spree inaugurated by him one and half years ago against arch-rival and dreaded Chabishpur in their own backyard. In the evening, in the Pandupur Club House, he was the star speaker and discussed strategies how to maul hostile neighbouring villagers in education and sports . . . . leaving the city girl and Preeti chat with the curious Pandua girls—and their aunty as and when she was free—any issue that came to their mind and were appropriates.

But, the golden boy's study and extra-curricular activities had drawn special interest of their aunty. For her, this was the most satisfying. She felt proud of her chand-ke-tukkuda's academic and extra-curricular performances in the college as the two girls went on illustrating breathlessly—occasionally competing with each other. The little girl was found highly puffed up while comparing the golden boy's performance with the bloody Kaaliram, the tormentor. Aunty felt assured that her chand-ke-tukkuda would bring fruits to her labour. 'Yes, I'm a proud mother,' she felt elated.

And as an after-thought dictated, the aunty asked, "Preeti, you aren't talking about your performance?"

"My study . . . . what for? I'm just a WHP! I'll be a teacher—A for Apple, B for Bat, C for Cat . . . . ," cheered the girl and added embracing her aunty, "But, aunty, I'm not going to anywhere. I'll teach in our village High School that Rabi and Karankaka promised to set up."

"You're a mad girl! You pagilli . . . . you won't change," aunty screamed.

And, the ever jovial city girl wittingly added some feather stressing Rabi's personality, and guardedly told, while stealthily poking the little girl's sloppy tummy, "These are the characteristics in your Rabi that attract me and the other college girls, the most."

"The other college girls?" shouted aunty almost shaking, instantly. She appeared alarmed and crying.

"Ooh yes, there are many from the big families of Puri town, including the DM and the rich Dash family. And, for your beautiful little girl, there are hundreds; literally begging for her just splitting looks," eloquented chic statuesque stunner in her characteristic pleasantry.

"Hey Bhagaban! Hey Maa Garachandi, what I shall do?" she joined her two palms and raising them over her forehead, prayed and begged, "Maa Garachandi, please save my eye pupil and my little girl."

'What more she, a bichara abandoned widow, can do to save her object-of-fondest-regard,' the city girl with all her sympathy and fellow-feeling, thought. "Aunty, Rabi is your son. Truly, he has all your noble upbringing and characteristics . . . . personality and culture. I'm sure; he won't do anything that will ever hurt you. Rabi is very careful while dealing with the city girls and don't allow any such girl to come close to him. And, your little girl is there. She even didn't allow me to be alone with your Rabi (frowning at Preeti pushing out her tongue like a tortoise head and pulled in after being slapped at back), you have seen today morning. Rest assured, I'm honestly guarding him. I won't allow my meek brother to be stolen by any girl that my lovely aunty feel sorry about," Seema consoled aunty hugging her while sneakily winking at her little girl.

"Yaar, you've almost stolen my aunty," cried the little girl.

In the afternoon, along with Lilli, the divas went for a round of Jittu Pandu's Khandi Pandupur. They walked to Lord Gopinath, Maa Garachandi, Lord Banamber and Maa Mangala temples located on the different edges of village and paid pious obeisance everywhere. They went to rice fields, village ponds, water pools, mango orchids, and swayed backward and forwarded by suspended big banyan trees' aerial roots. Preeti illustrated how they as small kids were playing monkey games in mango orchid and whoever was found lost in the game were jerked on the earth being suspended by their legs up-side down by the winners as a measure of punishment. They passed through the high and thick bushes where village lovebirds pass their intimate times craftily away from the guarding eyes of their relations and the prying envious during afternoon siesta time and twilight hours. They walked on the sandy bank of dry, thin and serpentine Ratnachira river chatting the crowning of Preeti's Miss BCS title and many other issues, a herd of teenaged supposed to talk when they were together. Later, they whiled away seating on the parapet of canal bridge while watching Rabi's skillful coaching to his fellow village tots in the playground. The gawaris narrated at length the proud story of Jittu Pandu and the fall-out of his brave acts that the city girl appreciated and enjoyed.

Everybody including passers-by were appreciative of star's techniques and skills. Even a few were halting to watch the game and the expert coaching by a princely boy. There is a big crowd around the ground unlike the other day. The village elders including Karankaka were there cheering the star and his team. And, some were lamenting, "What a travesty of fact? It isn't understood why Choudhury elder is so adamant in not accepting such a jewel and his beautiful mother to his family?"

"It is all Zamindari egos! Choudhury elder never takes back his word once he pronounced," murmured another.

"The sun has started peeping on the distance horizon of Khandi Pandupur after long years of eclipse," Lilli buzzed to the attention of Preeti and Seema.

Preeti understood and preferred to keep quiet. But, the unfamiliar guest felt something unusual with latest revelation from interesting and classic gawari Lilli and looked at her with interest. And, the gawari went on unfolding the sorrow of Khandi Pandupur and its lateral successes with arrival of the deprived Rabi in the village affairs. And she acclaimed, "Rabi's success in matriculation examination has been the long needed prelude."

Preeti was looked elated and satisfied. How could she not when she heard her Prince Charming was being praised, and saw him in action on the ground? Seema and Lilli checked Preeti's eyes almost fixed at the distance play ground. And she was—seemed to her companions—not liked to be disturbed.

Lilli comically running her figures on the Seema's shoulder and later to her armpit and cautiously digging at the contour of her boob, buzzed, "My sis is mad of Rabi. She, the laziest among us in entire Pandupur, is studying with interest only for Rabi."

Preeti looked at her envious cousin. The guardian in Seema too wasn't in accord with the view and realised the presence of jealousy, and had all pity to bichara gawari Lilli. "What's wrong with this? Both are so nice, so friendly, so sharing, so studious, so intelligent and so beautiful. Rare combination! You, the villagers should be proud of them," Seema counseled and advised, "If they're inspiring each other, they must be encouraged instead of . . . ."

Suddenly, they heard a fierce bellowing at a distance on the lower bank of the river Ratnachira with cloud of dust ringleting to the clean afternoon sky. Nothing was clearly visible in the thick curly dust. The city girl was terrified—stood up—seeing the furious whirlwind.

There in the ground, the coaching halted. Passers-by on foots, bullock carts and cycles stopped. Every body's attention directed towards the whirlwind as if there was a rarest of rare event being staged. To the surprise of the unfamiliar city girl, the boys on the playground started giving a round of applause resembling the audiences of a boxing ring.

"Is it our Balia fighting his rival from Palang or Chabishpur," asked Lilli. She was found excited to dig out who were there, not clearly visible. She even asked the passers-by coming from that side checking, "Whether Balia was there?"

Seema asked, "What's going on?" 'How can so sudden there staged a fight? And, the fight that can create so much of furious noise, dust and whirlwind? And the bellowing were so strange, certainly not from two-legers.' In no time, she saw a big bull with sharp horns—similar to many roaming on the Puri Grand Road, and engaged in occasional fighting and uprooting poor shop-keepers cabins—found chasing furiously another out of the whirlwind. Her companions rejoiced while she breathed in relief.

Balia hounded the vanquished till that crushed the knee deep watered Ratnachira river bed and canal walls, the southern border of Pandupur which was Balia's territorial limit on that side, with applause from its audiences in the field-padia.

"Amazing! This is Balia, you're talking about? Ooh my God! I was thinking the duel was between legendary Bhim and Duryadhan, the trainees of Lord Balaram!" the city girl cheered releasing a heavy breath. Balia's win invited applause from the two gawaris. Lilli revealed with extra euphoria, "Preeti, do you know, last week our Balia had mauled Twentysixpur bull which has been donated by that Bishu Sarangi to their village Shiva temple."

"What? What are you talking about? Is it so? . . . . definitely a matter of great satisfaction and pride for Pandupur," Preeti exulted, and informed Seema pulling and shaking her, "Do you know, Bishu Sarangi aka Gabbar Singh is the uncle of idiot Kaaliram?"

"Balia's success stories can be counted as another feather in Pandupur's cap after Rabi's mauling of Kaaliram in matriculation examination, and subsequently, Twentysixpur volley ball team in their own backyard," shouted Lilli with satisfaction.

"It seemed from your exultation, Balia pahalman is your papa's donated bull to your village Shiva temple," taunted Seema with provoking smile.

"No, no! This is donated by Bhagyabati aunty's father-in-law," snapped Lilli.

"Rabi's grandpa!" Seema told.

"Not exac . . . t . . !" Lilli wanted to say but couldn't complete as Preeti stared at her with fire in her eyes. Preeti's clean and rosy spotless cheeks in no time turned to a ball of fire, and about to burst. She was angry and disgust. A pensive silence rained over the small entourage for a while. The offender diverted her attention to distance playground as an excuse although Preeti's burning eyes were almost fixed at her. And, Seema was sharing her time peeping at Preeti, Lilli and in-between at the distance ground.

Later, as they were returning back to Rabi's cottage on the advent of twilight, ever-interesting and talkative Lilli in her bid to bring back normalcy among them whispered with her usual cynical smile, "Our Balia is a worthy husbandGod of our village cows."

"Stupid, what are you talking? Lilli, you're very loose-talking and going out of limit sometimes," Preeti fired at naughty girl while the astonished city girl was looking in bewilderment.

The sharp and intelligent city girl was taken aback with latest inflow of information that she couldn't understand. She was found defeated before the school drop-out village girl, like the cursed Indian Shakespeare, the celebrated Kali Das, defeated by an illiterate fisherman at Kashi, the seat of ancient India's rich knowledge, culture and literature. She looked with blinking eyes at her companion in curiosity and suspicion. This was perhaps for the first time during their companionship Pandua Preeti found the city smarty in acute intellectual distress. And Lilli wanted to explain with due consent from grudging sister. Seema looked appealing at Preeti and Preeti obliged with reservation, "You know, she is talking too much. I'm not happy. Yet, ... I let her . . . ."

Lilli explained expertly and playfully with stunning body and eye poises the-theory-of-survival-of-the-mightiest and two-bulls-can't-live-together in one horde mystery of Balia. And, she also went on explaining how Balia could be ruthless to push to exile his own bull children posing potential threats to his hegemony over the village cows, and running his empire like monster for last half decade. Later, Lilli pulled the city girl and directing her towards the relaxed Balia pahalman, buzzed, "See, the size of piston, he has below his bulky belly; furiously dangling! One single shot of this is sufficient to get any cow pregnant."

"Wow! What an observation," the statuesque stunner fisted at Lilli as Preeti looked on, angry as well as amazed.

However, Preeti smiled poking Lilli at her armpit for such a vivid dramatic illustration she was indeed shy up to listen forget about to speak. And, the city girl felt aghast. She acclaimed, "What a valued specialist study you have done on this topic? This ain't seen in our ghungi Preeti. A virtual dry wood! Only Rabi, Rabi and Rabi! Her day start with Rabi chalisha, and doesn't end even as she raves singing the song of Rabi while on the bed in the night. Her everything starts in Rabi and ends in Rabi. What yaar! There are so many—cute, smart, attractive, generous, wealthy, ... ready for any service, unsolicited!"

"What else we foolish school drop-outs would do in this tiny and dry Khandi Pandupur. These are some of our time-pass," Lilli mildly cried with display of deprivation.

"Why? What about the village bears and monkeys . . . . sorry, what about your village lads? There are so many," Seema buzzed with itching fun.

"Who are there . . . . left behind? These are by their name Gandua, Valu, Galu, Sarua, Hadu, Dukhi, ... They're all useless, are only after cheep time-pass, roving around the bushes. Bloody ugly donkeys and chimp . . . . rejected items! There's no life in the absence of the brightest and shining Karna," lamented Lilli in a single breath and looked skyward as if somebody had stolen her Prince Charming.

Preeti could understand the agony of the girl and bended her head pretending to check the potholes on the alleyway in an apparent bid to allow the depriver's fire to pass with all the sympathies that deserved. 'What else she could do,' Seema observed in her thought but preferred to keep quite. She had in all these very interesting moments of her short but lively village time, the first of its kind in her life.

Second day had gone and so also third day was about to pass. Rabi was busy with his friends, Karankaka, and even small school going children from morning to late in the evening till the third round of howling from distance bushes reminding him the arrival of dinner and bed-time. He had forgotten that he was a student of Intermediate Science in BCS College, and the annual examination was round the corner. He had forgotten his daily work and was even found unconcerned of teeth brushing, bathing and food in time and performing them being reminded. This was nothing new to his mama and dear Preeti. In the past, Preeti used to remind Rabi to brush his teeth and take breakfast and bath and launch. She was almost working like a personal assistant of Rabi, not appointed and unpaid, reminding for everything. She was acknowledged for all these good works. And she was enjoying this, and thus helped otherwise busy aunty despite mother Prema's opposition.

Mother Prema wasn't happy, and on several occasions dissuaded her advising, "Mingling with a son-of-a-widow, an unrecognized child demeans the family image and this may affect your marriage." But, to no avail. 'I want that to happen,' Preeti wanted to say but kept quiet.

Seema and Preeti were equally busy enjoying their village stays and whiling away their time, far away from clumsy and crowded city and campus life. And, the tedious college time-table and cruelest Rules and Regulations of the celebrated Kumaris in the hostel. They were in the company of motherly aunty and the interesting village girls, and above all, with envious and talkative Lilli with her animated teasing comments and funny village romantic fictions. The city girl was also enjoying aunty's delicious foods; and once she acknowledged frowning at the Preeti, "Now, I understand why the gawari is Miss BCS and I'm a runner-up?"

And, Seema heard about the early life of aunty in her village and later at Pandupur—after marriage. She was also assisting her aunty in cooking food unasked like a bride-to-be and an under-trainee which provoked gossiping among the envious village ladies initiated by Bulinani that Bhagyabati heard at the bathing ghat, water pool, during afternoon chit-chat and at evening aarti at temple stage. "How is your boyish, would-be daughter-in-law, cooking?"

Besides, she heard teasing comments, "Has Rabi eloped her? She must be from a rich family. She'll bring good luck to your home, at last!"

"Or God knows whether she'll elope your object-of-fondest-regard leaving you again high and dry," jeered Bulinani, glaring.

Unexpectedly, the city breed Seema found accommodated in the one-room-cottage belying early forecasting of her friends. And, the adult Rabi whenever at home cooperated going out of the cottage when required. And, on occasion, the city girl didn't feel shy of requesting Rabi, "Rabi, please!" And the mama-aunty enjoying as if she got a daughter in Seema.

Aunty started liking her. And, she compared the city girl with her little girl. 'Both are equally good: beautiful homely accommodative jolly elegant intelligent and studious,' she concluded in her. All the same, she was selfish to acknowledge openly; in fact, she was scared of the city girl menace. She restrained herself.

'None of the trio was talking about their return to college. Is there something else other than what they have said for which they aren't talking about to go back. Are they lying and hiding?' the mentor thought, and so, he was worried. So also, in the Rath abode, the hawkish Raghu Rath and the overwhelmed reverend mother Prema. But, at the tiny cottage, the mama-aunty was mama-aunty. In contrast, she wasn't looked worried, enjoying the lovely presence of beautiful children—playing joking laughing dancing commenting fighting . . . .

'How could she part away her chanda-ka-tukkuda and the two lovely little flowers so early? Her children have come after such a long gap,' the mentor concurred and he was sure that the children were taking undue advantages of their mama-aunty's emotion.

On the next day early in the morning as usual the little girl knocked the door and as she entered, she was found running short of breath. The mama-aunty was surprised as she found her little girl highly disturbed and looked as if she hadn't slept last night.

"What happened? Have you seen bad dream in the night? Or Bulinani has told you anything? From today onwards, you better sleep here," the mama-aunty suggested embracing her little girl.

"No aunty," told the intruder of morning peace in the tiny cottage hugging on her aunty's shoulder and taking breath, cried, "We are asked to pack up."

No response. She repeated . . . . The aunty-mama looked unhappy but compromised with heavy breath, "Yes . . . . you've to go!"

"You pack up. I won't. I'm not going so early," Rabi shouted covering her ears with the pillow. And, they heard Seema started snoring with increased volume and frequency.

"Your dad told, you pack up. We are n . . . . o . . t!" later Rabi whispered taunting.

An ear twist by the presiding deity, Rabi stopped his brevity abruptly and he cried to a round of applause of the trespasser of morning cold sleep.

"Now, your mother says, you too pack up. Okay, Mister!" the trespasser blasted throwing her hips on the legs of the boy on the cot.

Seema was still snoring. Aunty pulled her little girl's eyes to snoring creature by moving her hand.

"Aunty, just wait!" the little girl buzzed at the ears of her aunty. She picked up the carry bag of the city girl and pulling out a photo, aped, "Aunty, look at this ugly boy. Seema says—this brown, fat and lofty boy is the most beautiful guy in this living world!"

"She has a poor choice. Isn't it?"

The city girl twisted in her pretending slumber and in no time, raised her hood and pouncing on the trespasser, grabbed the photo. She shouted with screwed up face, "Your Rabi isn't better than mine!"

All present were aghast. She pushed out her narrow tongue, and was apologetic for slip of tongue. The mama-aunty hurriedly looked through the opened street door, she was looked frightened. 'Perhaps, she is checking whether there is any body in the threshold, and has heard this sudden outburst. She might be scared of Raghu uncle and Prema aunty,' guessed Rabi.

"Aah! . . . . Ooh! Will you idiots kill me? Aunty save me," cried the city girl with pain as the lovebirds pounced on her with slaps and fists as soon as the presiding deity of the cottage left. "Sorry yaar! This was a slip-of-tongue, unintentional. You idiots are feasting on my Sambit's belongings . . . . so hard!" and cried, "Alas! Were he here, he would have smashed your bones like he once did to a loafer who passed a lewd comment on my stunning body at Rourkela." And, she begged holding her ears, and added surprising the dim-wits, "But, mind one thing, aunty has given her consent in her silence," and she kept quiet till musing rained on her attackers . . . . and shouted, "Hip, hip, hurry!" She reversed the situation in her favour bowling the peasants out. In no time, the love-pair cooled down and sparked like tube-light looking at each other with satisfaction and nodded in agreement. "Maa Miss Rourkela, you're The Great!" they saluted in chorus kneeing in front of the Rourkela diva resembling the pose devotes play before the reverend Maa Garachandi in Khandi Pandupur temple stage.

"Tathastu," the diva flashed raising her right palm with Lord Brahma's poise.

Preeti reminded her Bholanath the final of Inter-class Cricket Match, scheduled to be held on Saturday.

"Oh, my God! Fasto has another salvo! Is it last or some more are still pending in your kitty," the relaxing Seema shouted.

"Yes, we've to go!" Mr. Jimmy obliged.

Mentor Karan Mishra suggested, "Let be aggressive in study, sport and extra-curricular activities instead of defensive vis-à-vis the tormentors of your peace." He inspired Rabi picking up iconic examples of politicians, social workers, renowned legal luminaries, scientists and educationists who although were born in villages could be successful in their respective fields and professions bringing laurels to their place of birth. He counseled, "They achieved their prominence simple because of their knowledge, talent and perseverance with honest objectives. Since you are gifted with all these right qualities, I don't think you will be unsuccessful ever. All you want is: have control over your emotion. Dr. Swati Devi and Dr. Jena will be your messiahs and mentors. Don't ever annoy them! But, all at once, remain guard of idiot Lalu; naughty, arrogant and privileged Rekha and Ruby, and their likes from the privileges' cesspits."

"As soon as you reach the college campus, you meet Dr. Swati Devi and Dr. Jena and beg pardon for your abrupt missing. And, you don't repeat the mistake that you had committed this time. You shouldn't simple forget our little girl and leave her alone. She is our village image, a very good girl. Let the frustrated elements go on scripting their schemes and enjoy dialoguing their scripts. How long, they'll do so? When an elephant pass through the market place the dogs bark! Does that stop the huge elephant and its march? You're a huge elephant. So, the dogs bark! What's new in it?"

They're about to march with their little backpack. The mama-aunty loaded home-cooked cakes and marked their forehead with vermillion drawn from Pandupur reverend presiding deity. They touched the feet of the mama-aunty and hugged her together. But, the city girl turned back and again hugged her justifying the villagers gossiping. She was almost crying. Everybody looked back, and was abacked. Both had tears in their eyes. It seemed aunty had a lot to say but concluded with, "You're a good girl. I like you. Keep on coming. We'll seat, talk, cook, eat and sleep . . . . all together!"

'Is the little girl not happy with her aunty's bonhomie with the city girl, and her revelation? The sight is such,' the spectators thought. 'The little girl is musing. She appears upset.'

And Sallu, Gallu and Patia, watching at a distance, were found sneezing, coughing and chattering as they were at the peak of their delight seeing their already stolen queen bee crying in suspense and pain. And, they could entertain their eyes with the stylish city girl visit in the future. And, the envious Lilli, Malli, Dholli, ... happy with the presumed loss of Preeti.

'Is there something that should be noted seriously? Aunty has never been so emotional with any other girl before except certainly me,' the ghungi gudia thought but kept quiet as dictated by an after-thought, 'No . . . . I shouldn't read everything prejudicial.' However, she looked at the city girl with piercing eyes and shouted with privileged authority, "What's going on . . . . ? You've almost stolen my easy-to-fool muffasali aunty."

"Bichara Preeti . . . . what's there in her mind?" Bulinani reacted in confusion.

Rabi was found unconcerned of what was going on behind him although he was very much at the hearing distance that made the aggravated aunty's good girl uncomfortable. He was loaded with the thought of how to face Swati Madam, Jenasir, friends and team mates on his arrival in the campus. 'They're so nice people . . . . They must have given up their trust on me.'

The trio walked without any pleasantly . . . . chit-chat, quite unusual. They walked with their respective thought milling in their mind. They crossed the river bed and climbed over the canal bridge, the village edge from where they could see their village and the important of all, their affectionate mama-aunty and near and dear. From over the bridge, Rabi waved his hand to his mama still standing under the banyan tree for the last glimpse, and the two girls to their affectionate aunty.

But, the crying utterance of the good girl, "I'm sorry aunty, I cannot keep on coming. I am failed to be a good friend of your little girl. I don't like to be the reason of her pain," that followed, caught the attention of so far unconcerned Rabi. He looked at the crying girl, asking and later the relaxed and smiling little girl but found none of them were forthcoming with explanation. Smiling and hissing; hissing and smiling went on unperturbed.

The bichara Rabi was caught in-between; he was searching for answer. "What happened? Two girls can't leave together," he jeered.

'Can they keep quiet? It was okay for seconds, but not for minutes. They were so sisterly.' And, the setting wasn't conducive for their rare buddhic silence to continue for long. They had to cross a water channel with knee deep water. Preeti reminded the leech attack on Rabi, they're very scared of, on their way to Pandupur. Last time, both were lifted to this side by Rabi, the brave boy.

As the sulking city girl struggled to fold her skin tight jean up her ankles, Preeti ordered, "Rabi, please take care your mama's good girl! Or else, she would curse your home for ever. She had already stolen your mama. And, you know, aunty won't spare us."

"And while being lifted, you Miss Good Girl should keep your eyes and lips shut and hands on your body, not on Rabi's shoulder like last time. These are the terms and conditions. No compromise on this issue!"

The girl religiously obeyed and as she was being lifted by the shipper, she asked opening her mouth, "Is it okay, Mrs. Rabi Pratap? Don't worry, I won't dilute his satitwa! . . . . remain assured!"

"Well! That's a good girl!" Preeti certified and added patting at Rabi, "You boy look straight to the water not at her body. These days you and your mother are found very caring of this smart city girl. Is there anything cooking behind me?"

"Baap . . . re..e, so many conditions and clauses! Who'll lift this Waiting Hall Passenger?" cried Mr. Caring.

On reaching the other side, Rabi taunted, "Sorry, I can't carry the fasto. Her weight has doubled during the last few days of emptying my mama's dishes. Let the leeches suck her blood," and added looking at the good girl, "Let's walk." He walked but not the responsible guardian . . . . And, he yielded to the pressure of the guardian.

As Rabi shipped the fasto crossing the water channel, the guardian scanned his legs for any leech. And Preeti embracing Seema revealed, "I'm sorry Seema. I'm still suspicious and envious of all smart city girls despite my every sincere attempt to exempt you. Whoop! What to do? I'm a ghungi gudia. Please forgive me!"

STRATEGIC COLLABORATION

Rekha's suspicious hobnobbing with Rabi and Ruby's display of anguish at the entrance of Science Block and in the Physics Gallery followed by Lalu Sarangi's comment and Dr. Jena's outburst in the class spread like wild-fire in the campus. 'Why not when matter concerned with who's who of the college: Mr. Jimmy of the college cricket lovers, and the daughters of the first family of city's VIP Road and Grand Road?' Their every activities had been closely watched, discussed and analysed. This was aggravated further with the abrupt eclipse of the famous 'teen murtis' from the campus and their respective hostels. In the class rooms, common rooms, library, corridors, campus alleyways, cricket ground, canteen, outside magazine and stationary stalls, tea and pan shops and in the hostels; every where the issue had a lively presence among the students. This was the talk of the day and the week.

Mr. Jimmy's class mates were much worried for the Saturday's cricket match. This was a big match against formidable B. Com. Seniors. They were last year's Inter-class title holder. For the first time in the college history, the unofficial chronicler of college, Kesab Swain revealed in the canteen, the First Year Intermediate Science won the Inter-class cricket match. This was possible due to the all round performance of one player—that was Rabi Pratap. His performance helped him acquired the title—Mr. Jimmy of BCS; everybody was singing piano in his name.

"Who will lead their team if Mr. Jimmy isn't made himself available by that day?" was in the mouths of his class mates and the fans from other branches of studies, besides college faculties and staff. And, Lalu Sarangi was singled out and boycotted and abused. Some had gone to the extent of threatening Lalu Sarangi for his incivility. Although the acts of the daughters of VIP and Grand Road were primarily responsible as witnessed by the class mates and the bears and monkeys, yet they were escaped the wrath of cricket fans for obvious reason.

And, the Students Union Sport Secretary, who had promised students before the election for better performance of their college in the Inter-college Cricket tournament during his tenure, and the PETsir were worried lot because Inter-class final match would be followed by the college team selection and the practice sessions for Inter-college Tournament under Utkal University to be held at prestigious Barabati Stadium after two weeks. 'Batting, bowling and fielding coaches from Shahid Sporting are requisitioned to impart coaching from next week.'

As the last resort, the Sport Secretary proposed to the PETsir to defer the final match date and college team selection by at least two days, and in the meanwhile, to send an emissary to Pandupur with messages from Principal and Dr. Jena, Rabi's affectionate teacher and also an ardent cricket lover, to pursue him.

B. Com. students, smelling a smooth sailing for their team in the absence of the star player in the last year champion's team, didn't agree for deferment.

"After all, they're seniors. A defeat in the hands of juniors is humiliating. Why will they agree?" PETsir reasoned.

"PETsir is sympathetic to seniors," Mr. Jimmy's batch mates gossiped. "This isn't fair on the part of a teacher. He is expected to remain neutral and promote quality game."

In the afternoon, Dr. Swati found the missing of trio at the appointed time. "Where are your friends?" she inquired staring at her daughter. 'Even, neither there is any ethos nor interest to speak about them in the eyes of Rekha,' she noted, and so she was surprised.

'Is there anything wrong among them? Rekha is surprisingly silent,' Dr. Swati thought and was aghast. Rekha, who was so spontaneous, very particularly about Rabi, and advocating for his cause so keenly, was maintaining studied silence that Dr. Swati clearly found out. She guessed for some mischief. And, she suspected if there was anything as such Rekha's hand could not be ruled out. A serious and sensitive Dr. Swati, who had met the trio the day before and the day morning, had found in them so much of humbleness, characters and civility that she wasn't ready to accept them to be so abrupt and disregarding. She, looking at her daughter while boarding the Ambassador, tried to dig out the possible reason but in vain as latter was found evasive. Now, she suspected Rekha's hand in the trio's abrupt missing.

Psychologist Dr. Swati craftily asked in clear display of rejection, "How can we engage such an irresponsible, unstable and disregarding chap as our children's tutor," forcing Rekha to smell trouble.

'Certainly a warning . . . . hardly can be ignored,' Rekha analyzed and concluded. She was moved. And she answered, as their carrier rolled ahead, looking outward as a reflex of action, "They were last seen in the Physics class . . . . missed the other classes! Perhaps, they've gone to hostel early."

Psychologist didn't talk anything further. However, she had peeping glances at the evader.

Later, Dr. Swati could learn talking to Dr. Jena and Wardens of Ladies and Gents Hostel the rest of the things. She fired her daughter and blamed her for all the problems that Rabi had been passing through. Further, she advised as well as warned her daughter, "You should keep in your mind your parents' positions. Since you're the daughter of District Magistrate and I'm in your college as a Professor, your every move is noticed and noted seriously by everybody in the campus. We love you, and at the same time, it should be in your mind that we shouldn't be let downed by our loved one. Besides, I would like to tell you that this is the world of moneyed people. They can go to any extent on the strength of their money. This is the cardinal truth that we've to accept. Today your papa is here; tomorrow he may be transferred to remote Kandhamal or Kalahandi or dumped in a department, where a just chaparashi may not attend him for a glass of water. You're a grown up child! Mind one thing; you shouldn't ever do anything for which people shall deduce conclusion that you're misusing your parents' position. Again, you have two younger siblings who look upon you for inspiration and guidance. You're expected to keep all these possibilities in your mind while you're out in the society. I, as a teacher and a guardian, can't advise you to compromise on moral aspect. Whenever there is anything as such you must face them with all the verve. For this, we'll certainly feel proud of you." And, she announced seriously looking at Rekha, "Sorry, we haven't been able to decide whether to engage Rabi as Ratan's tutor."

Girls were crying, "Where is our Prince Charming? Where he has gone widowing us? Such a bright and cute boy! Bloody blackish Lalu-valu Kaaliram, how can he brand such a bright guy, a sonofabitch?" One girl aired: "Perhaps, Lalu is hell-bent maligning Rabi being failed to lure either Miss BCS or Miss Smarty. Each of them is such an item, no boy can have a sleep without dreaming them." "Alas! They're God gifted and rarest items under the sky," another deprived girl screamed dirging.

And, the bears and the monkeys were weeping, "Whatever, in the absence of rosy Miss BCS and flamboyant Miss Smarty, there is no life in the campus. The campus reduces to a dry and lifeless desert . . . . we're certainly coming for a bath of our eyes!"

The news on arrival of the Prince Charming of the college girls, Mr. Jimmy of cricket fans and Mr. Brilliant of faculties—all-in-one in Rabi and along with his two accompanied beauties spread like wild-fire in the campus. They're in everybody's mouth. This had made them overwhelmed. The faculties in Science Block in particular were highly enthusiast. They were expecting: this year their college lad will certainly grab the top position in the Intermediate Science University Examination which had been elusive for the college during the last one decade. They had all praise of their star performer.

The final cricket match would be held as scheduled; B. Com. Students were nervous. Enthusiast Dr. Jena announced cash prize to Rabi if Rabi's team won the match. This was followed by the Commerce Department HOD Bimalsir's announcement. A pre-IndoPak match fever had almost swayed the campus.

So also two beauties welcomed to campus by bears and monkeys. "Please don't deprive us, we poor guys yours' darshan so long as this is possible! Rabi is a blessed guy. You're so blissful to him. Are we so bad?" they went on lamenting at the hearing distance of the beauties, applauding their Prince Charming practicing in the net.

Classes overflowed again, getting back to its old packing. Professors were found enthusiast with record attendances of students in their classes. In the students' attendance review meeting Principal was surprised to note heavy ebb and flow in attendance of students in Section 'A' Intermediate Science during the week.

"This is due to more or less three students, you know better Sir," cited Dr. Jena.

———◦◦◦———

"But, Lalu and Ruby aren't so visible in the classes," Rabi told to Preeti at a hearing distance of Seema. 'Must be cooking for some dirty schemes,' the guardian felt in her but wasn't outspoken. She was afraid of aggravating mental agony that might revisit her dear friends who were in fact trying hard to accommodate in relatively sympathetic campus environment.

They along with Rekha called on Dr. Swati in her department chamber and begged pardon for being so abrupt and irrespective. As she was busy in preparing for next class she wished them to visit her during the launch break. However, she informed her family decision to engage Rabi for Ratan's tutor. And requested, "If you've anybody you can suggest his or her name for Reshmi's tutor." After the announcement, she very carefully observed the foursome like a typical psychologist and later looking at Rabi told, "Do you have any objections? . . . . happy? You, Preeti . . . . Seema . . . . Rekha?"

A jubilant but foolish Rekha thanked the talisman looking up. Later, the unsuspecting child hopped to her mother and planted a huge kiss hugging her. "Thanks a lot, my very dear mummy; you're so understanding and kind," she celebrated. But, she didn't know that her jubilations and enthusiasms hadn't gone down well with other present.

Mother Dr. Swati picked up a fifty rupees note from her carry bag and giving that to her daughter advised her to offer friends sweats and tea in the canteen. "You must invite Ruby to the tea, and accept her as a good friend," Dr Swati advised as Rekha was packing up fast. Again, she repeated, "Be a good girl, my child!" and she returned to her class-note preparation. But, Rekha was unconcerned.

"Don't worry Mam! We'll take care of Ruby," the insightful Seema picked up and assured.

As the foursome entered the canteen, they saw the tormentors of their peace engaged in a parley—they were never seen indulged in this manner before—that they the victim of their previous act could hardly take so easily at its first sight. 'The defeated Femme is seemed not ready to lie down.'

'Have they started scheming to take revenge?' suspected the frightened peasants. They looked at their guardian with fear and dismay. But, to their surprise, the guardian signaled Rabi to join her to invite the tormentors to tea. Their guardian in confidence greeted their offenders asking, "How do you do?" But, she was rebuffed beyond her civil expectation. It appeared as if the war-line had already been drawn 'for a bloody clash to finish.' As the tormentors got up to leave the canteen in a hop, the privileged Rekha found celebrating.

This followed the aged thuggish canteen contractor's sarcastic comment bathed with teasing chattering over his ever pan munching face, "Alas, bichara maffu will be finished," and later turning to others, he forecasted, "Only God can save him!"

Rabi looked at him scared and so also the gawari and the guardian. Their new found jubilation faded away in no time. 'We're back in square one!'

"Bichara guys!" whispered the while awayers in the canteen.

This prompted Rabi to recall what he had overheard some days back, the seniors talking about canteen contractor Kesab Swain's forecasting to a not-so-stable jodi of final year graduation, "You'll have the fate of Kumari Dr. Mili Padhi and our city's celebrated Ghar Jamai—Naresh Panda."

"Kesabkaka is the chronicler of BCS College and is also the respected Kalijug Sahadeva on any subject in the campus," told another guy and all seniors nodded in agreement, "Whatever he forecasts, that happens in due course. He is such a soothsayer although he doesn't know A, B, C of horoscope."

The thuggish Kesab Swain, still a bachelor, was one of the few greatest long survivors in BCS College history. Hundreds of students used to get admitted in Intermediate or Bachelor or Master course every year but a few, who either failed in the examination or fell in LOVE, left the college within maximum of two to four years of their admissions. And, those who left behind mostly males hanged around in the sprawling college campus or its' surrounding—designated as loafers—for another one or two or even little longer till their loved one complete their course and got married ignoring them. Or, in some cases, till their parents had drained of their saving. The principal, faculties and other staff could stay for three years or for the period they could grease the palm of babus and Minister in Dept. of Higher Education through the most powerful 'Gang of Four'.

However, the case of Kesab Swain was an exception. For him—it was talked every now and then in the campus—only his death could curtail his tenure. He was a skilled manipulator, and heard could go to any extent including entertaining the principal, who was the final arbiter of approving annual canteen bid, and using the services of college Students Union President and General Secretary from whichever political party's students wings they might belonged to. There was allegations of his use of the service of the most powerful 'Gang of Four', he was closed with. At times, there was charges of he employing the service of underground elements to refrain the other prospective bidders for canteen contract.

He was the college's one of the early student, admitted in Intermediate Arts. Since then he had been in BCS College, first as a student, followed by ex-student appearing to clear back papers unsuccessfully for a few years and till his father exhausted of his patience to see his object-of-fondest-regards graduated with bachelor degree, often called as loafer; and finally, as canteen contractor where he could comfortable accommodate him in view of his all round qualification and skills for the job for such a long period.

The search on question of what made him love so much to BCS College revealed that he was also a victim of mysterious LOVE. His shrewd girl-friend pretending that she loved him, exploited him of his time for her safe escort and time-pass, and his father's sweaty money. As happened in many of such cases in such a type of associations, a devoted and innocent lover in Kesab Swain still was in his muffasali hang over failed in the graduation examination providing his lover an opportunity to desert him with a plea that 'how can she hang around with an under performer, shaming her prestigious university degree?' She went on doing her Master Degree in Revenshaw College and latter married her new found boy friend who couldn't live with her for reason still in shroud. "Kesab had gone to the extent of advising his offender of LOVE as being gossiped in the campus, 'Either you marry me or embrace the fate of Kumari leaving me a celebrated Kumar for life. But, mind, not a Sisupal, I hate!'" He didn't marry as he couldn't cheat his LOVE like his girl friend. He is such an ardent devote of 'Institution of LOVE'! Many used to appreciate and adore him for his such a dedication.

The statement of the canteen's celebrated Kumar in regard to Rabi and his forecast to the seniors a few days ago found their echo in the mind of the trio necessitating their deliberation on what did all those mean to them and mattered to them.

What their persistent investigation revealed was difficult to digest and couldn't be simple kept aside. They felt pity to Dr. Mili Padhi. They felt pity to their own attitude towards the lady. They were also surprised to learn her devotion to the institution of 'the Sacred LOVE' and her sacrifice for her heart-throb who cheated her. They saluted her in their thought. They evaluated among them whether they would be so devoted to their LOVE.

"I can very well endorse the life of Mili Madam if cheated," Preeti jumped declaring.

"We know this. Don't advertise it anymore, people will be envy of it," Rabi shouted down Preeti winking at Seema.

Ms. Mili's cheater was none other than Mr. Naresh Panda. They belonged to the same village and came to Puri for their higher education. They loved to each other. But, their fate wasn't on their side. The financial difficulty of Naresh Panda forced him to look for a part-time job. And he knocked the door of Dash Transport. Impressed by his talent, Ruby's grandpa engaged him as the tutor of Ruby's mother Priyanka Dash, then studying as his junior in the college. And she trapped the humble gawar getting herself pregnant. Like Kesab Swain, Dr. Mili Padhi was a devoted lover and didn't cheat her LOVE and remained till date a Kumari. She refused all attempts made by her near and dear to go for marriage. She was also another great survivor in BCS College although she had been transferred on several occasions to government colleges in Bhubaneswar or Cuttack. On each such occasions, she went on leave and continued staying at Puri till the transfers were overturned. The rumour mill flashed the story that 'there's a powerful hidden hand behind her continuance in BCS College.' All known were sympathized with her and were supportive too.

The love story of Mili madam and Naresh Panda further frightened the trio delaying their confirmation to the tutor proposal from VIP Road first family. Rabi although was very confidence of him and of his determination, yet Rekha's aggressive approach towards him and hunt of innocent face of the frightened Preeti kept him disturbing. However, all along Preeti was keeping quiet and sometime found thinking closing her eyes and looking up when the matter was being deliberated among them. They're in dilemma. And, on the other hand, Rabi's pocket was drying fast of the little saving of his mother and inconsistent earning from the tuitions. They were now caught in a vicious circle—unable to get rid of.

As usual, the guardian had got a solution, and without any loss of time she confidently proposed, "Let's request Swati Madam to engage Preeti as tutor of Reshmi they are looking for. If she agrees, you two together could be a formidable team to withstand the nefarious design, if any, of Rekha. And I may accompany you with some excuses." Preeti found some consolation over the proposal despite the possibility of Rekha's unpleasant wrath she had already experienced.

Rabi met Dr. Swati in her department chamber and after keeping quiet for sometimes he gestured to speak. Busy in preparation of class notes, Dr. Swati however signaled and Rabi carefully spelled out the guardian's script, "Madam, that day you're asking for a tutor for Reshmi . . . . Preeti is equally facing some financial problem. May I request you to engage her? She is a good student. It would be a great help to both of us. Besides, together we can go to your bungalow."

For a while Dr. Swati kept quiet but later found considerate. 'Rabi is in league with us,' she told to her. After sometimes, breaking the silence, she replied with a smile hiding what was in her mind, "Rabi you've relieved me from a big dilemma. Thank you very much!"

'She didn't consult her husband like earlier proposal?' It seemed to Rabi: she found in his proposal a respite. And, the message was loud and clear. 'Whatever, Seema is right! She is really intelligent and has a mind to reckon with.'

Rabi wanted to speak to Kesabkaka privately to get clarified on his comments directed at him days back. He hanged around in the canteen unaccompanied by his two omni-accompanied girls and made attempt to establish rapport, but, in vain, as he found Kesabkaka was always busy and surrounded. He was very talkative. His talks covered all aspects concerning BCS College, Puri city, state and national politics; even included who eloped with whom? People from all walks of life in the campus were comfortable with him. He was so sociable and had so much of information. Even the college girls found compatible with him to chat, play joke and pleasantry and pass comments. So, it was near to impossible to find him alone for a private talk.

But, the veteran Kesab could guess what was there in Rabi's unusual hanging around in the canteen. 'He is looking for some help.' In the past, many such students had come to him to consult when they were, in particular, LOVE related trouble. Many wanted Kesab to work for them as spy for some consideration which he used to rebuff, blasting them on their face. But, he was always sympathetic to 'poor lovers' among the peasant lots, and volunteered to collect the information and inform as if he had weakness towards them. As per the rumour mill, he had mediated some loves on the verge of breaking down and solemnised some marriages. In some cases, he didn't hesitate to employ his powerful contacts in both over ground and underground administration to bring to line some idiots. And, he was proud of that. As he had all sympathy to Rabi, he called him and advised him to visit his house on coming Sunday at morning hour.

Canteen, located on the one side of college ground and behind the stage, was the college's un-official key centre of debate and discussion concerning almost all college affairs. "In short, this is the college's Legislative Assembly," the students and staff used to mock. But the major difference here was that there was no restriction to its visitors, free for all. Although the canteen was officially meant for college students, faculty members, staff and visiting guardians, yet its' visitors also comprised local petty politicians, love-locked loafers, ruffians and who-not's of the city. And they got free assess in the disguise of back papers students or the guardians of existing students or this or that work; and argued, when caught being found by some snot-nosed oldie professors red-handed indulging in unpleasant activities, "This is a public institution!"

Even many elements used to claim they belonged to this political party or that. It wasn't that there was no ban on such elements. And, there was strict instruction to canteen contractor and his staff not to entertain such elements. The loop-holes in the system, as the similar were abundantly seen all around in administrative affairs of the nation, were cleverly utilized by astute and crafty Kesab Swain for his commercial benefit.

At times, it seemed, Kesab Swain was the presiding deity of this assembly house, unofficial and un-elected. He also contributed in the debate with his valuable suggestions and analysis. And his suggestions and analysis every now and then were given due importance as he was only decades old veteran, and had long experienced mind on college affairs. This made him privy to debates, many accept with some reservations.

The very powerful 'Gang of Four' comprising three faculties and one office clerk, who were as per many the un-official rulers of college, irrespective of whoever may be on the Principal chair. They used to sit every day evening in the canteen for their parleys along with Kesab Swain. They had good contact with red-tape infected bureaucrats in the Dept. of Higher Education, which enabled them not only in rescuing them from their own transfers, but also used to get transfer of faculties and staff inimical to their hegemony even before the due dates. Even they had got for some faculties and staff dreaded kalapani transfer to remote Kalahandi and Phulbani Colleges. And, also they had well-oiled netting in major political parties. They had been visited by the municipality corporators, local MLA and MP and the future aspirants before every Municipality, State Assembly and Parliamentary elections, and they, the 'Gang of Fours' was the known link between political parties and college Students Union President and General Secretary. In a nutshell, it could be attributed that they were the major arbiter of the college affairs.

Besides, the canteen had witnessed many loves that had been made and many that had been broken. And, it had witnessed the heart rendering appeals and cries of lost fellows including Dr. Mili Padhi. It was alleged that the list of Miss BCS had also been prepared in the canteen with glamorous Kesab Swain's active participation and his proposal for starting publication of Mr. BCS from the coming session was under due consideration. Besides, who would win and who would loss in Students Union elections he could forecast correctly. He also was aware of which political party funded how much to which candidates. For college related information, the local representatives of Fourth Estate used to keep contact with him. Even he dictated which news concerning BCS College was to be prioritized for publication and which news was to be placed in which page.

On several occasions, he was approached by the local police station to share information for lead in investigating the cases of violence, suicides, thefts and murders in the campus and in the city in which there were slightest tress of involvements of college students and staff as it was believed that canteen was the place where many such issues might have been discussed and hatched by the offenders. Even, it was doing the round that, once he was called to nearby Sadar Police station and threatened for information by a newly joined Police

Inspector, and he got the transfer of the snot officer within weeks.

During natural calamities like floods and cyclones, a regular feature in densely populated coastal Orissa breaking the economic backbone of the state, he used to lead college students and staff in arranging relief materials including cooked food neatly packed for distribution. During the world famous Car Festival, he used to be on the Grand Road along with Scout and NCC Cadets.

He was equally admired for good works and abused for alleged dubious activities. In short, he was a non-ignorable part and parcel in the college. So far as his dubious activities were concerned, they were hardly discussed in open for reason best known to all.

As scheduled, Rabi and Kesab Swain met, and he was found very sympathetic to Rabi's cause and told, "You're a bright student with endearing characteristics which can impress any girl. Mind, you're a rare gifted child!" He went on length telling how the girls exploiting the gullible boys as well as boys exploiting gullible girls which ended in several cases of socially non-sustainable love destroying life and also families. He even gave example of Ms. Mili Padhi and Naresh Panda.

He warned Rabi to be very careful while dealing with Ruby, Rekha, Seema, Preeti and their likes.

"They're rich, influential and privileged. They can go to any extent to satisfy their lust. And, they can get support from their so-called high civilized society as well," warned Kesab. And he went on advising Rabi to concentrate in study ignoring all these so-called LOVE and ROMANCE suitable for film productions and theater houses.

All the explanations Rabi placed before Kesabkaka regarding his two endearing entourage were brushed aside as he went on saying, "They're nothing but bullshits, childish games and socially non-sustainable, and part of the one-sided fabricated so-called LOVE, ROMANCE and time-pass of rich and privileged children—have been cleverly woven!"

On Rabi's persistent query on Kesabkaka's comment and forecasting on the other day in the canteen—"the bichara maffu will be finished. Only God can save him!"—he revealed bringing to mind, "Ruby seems has joined hands with Lalu Sarangi, the nephew of Bishu Sarangi, the petty politician from Chabishpur. I personally know Bishu, an ex-student of our College, failed to clear his graduation, joined politics as a last resort. I could understand from their discussion that Ruby loves you and Lalu loves Preeti. For their love, it seemed from their talk, they're plotting some dirty schemes and can go to any extent, and they're capable. And, I guess they've the blessing of their families. So, it appeared to me that they have got into a strategic understanding for their mutual benefit. This is very confidential! As you approach, I tell. Or, else, God would have saved you!"

Again, he went on assuring Rabi for all possible support in future and told, "This is part of my personal mission to help the innocent one. And I'll continue to do so so long as I'm here and I'm trusted. Many, who have listened to me, have been benefited and those, who have ignored, are suffering for their life."

He went on telling a number of ex-students names as examples (including present DM) who had after completion of their graduations from BCS College went on doing their master in UU, DU, JNU, etc. and later got through the tests and examinations for Civil Services, Bank Services, OAS, Defense Services, etc. successfully.

On learning from Rabi that he along with Preeti joining as tutor of Rekha's siblings, Kesab had some words of caution, "Never go to DM's bungalow alone and avoid moving around in the city in the night. Also, you advise the same to your friends to follow. Ruby is seemed mad of you. So also a few loafers including Lalu mad of Preeti and Seema. Your joining along with Preeti as tutors of DM's children is a wise decision. I know Mr. Debasis Mohanty and Dr. Swati Devi, they are two good personalities. But, despite this, one shouldn't forget that they're parents, and parents are parents of their own children first. And, there is hardly any benevolence Utkalmani, who can be expected to sacrifice their children's cause in the worst case for sake of others' children. Take these advices as sermon!"

HanumanGod

Preeti wasn't feeling well. She had pain in her lower tummy. Keeping her hand on her slimy tummy with reflection of pain on the face, she requested, "Seema, I'm not feeling well. Let's buy the stationeries tomorrow and prepare the practical note then only. Jenasir is very nice and accommodative. He'll accept." However, Seema, the guardian was the guardian. She had a responsibility when her friend was suffering. She checked with Pramiladidi for medicine. But, whatever were found out, had expired the prescribed date for consumption.

"Nothing new!"

"No, no, Preeti! Why should we take risk? You know, we're now encircled by dreaded foes. And, although, I'm confident that Jenasir will be agreeable to our late submission, yet I don't want to put him in an avoidable embarrassing situation. People may gossip dirty words he being favourable to us. He is such a nice professor. Further, the medicine! And your Prince may think anything bad about me . . . . not taking care of his sweet-heart. Sorry, I can't take risk!" The statuesque stunner told flashing a bold wink from her lotus eye. She went out to check and on her return announced, "Both the Kumaris have just gone to temple. Ramuchacha is there. I'm going on his rickshaw to Mochisahi Chowk. Maximum by 8 O' clock, I'll be back. You take rest."

The guardian left the room in hurry, and confident, and despite Preeti's reminder, "Hey smarty, have you forgotten that oldie canteen Kumar's warning? Don't go alone." Yet, nothing worked. She had fully made up her mind to take full advantage of Kumaris absent; indeed without prejudice. As well as she wasn't ready to put her most favourite professor in an avoidable embarrassment and herself to be questioned for not taking care of her sick room-mate. She had sufficient good reasons. And so, she dared to venture. Even she didn't think to talk to their ever ready bodyguard next gate despite suggested.

This was as if the destiny had already fixed her future to recede to hell, comes what way. As she went on boarding on Ramuchacha's rickshaw, she saw, at the edge of the shadow of big banyan tree, the trembling of a black Ambassador car followed by blinking of its head light that reminded her the furious bulky Pandupur Balia bull shaking up from its crawling sleep at the sight of a cow released from a cattle den for an estrous mating.

Ramuchacha, it appeared to the girl, little tired. As they moved, she told, "Chacha, I am not in that hurry. You pedal with easy."

'This is the car which has been hanging around the hostel locality during the last few days. Usually the students from hostel don't hire car. Further, this car had followed them on one or two occasions during the past couple of days too.' As impulse dictated, she looked back and gazed as the car drew nearer, and was surprise to note—there's no number plate.

'This time, I'm alone!' She felt little intimidated. Still, she pushed, with the single most objective of—honestly—not to put Jenasir in trouble and medicine for her dear aunty's little girl. 'And, Ramuchacha is there. Should I not rely on an old faithful?'

As they moved on, she suspected of foul play. But, still, she was confident. 'What could happen at best?' Her memory cell recalled the newspaper reports about Puri city during last one and half years. 'Puri isn't like other city. Although crimes are there yet they haven't been so alarming like to that of other cities such as Bhubaneswar or Cuttack or . . . . even comparable with what are there in Rourkela. Relatively, Puri is a peaceful city with very little crimes. Thank to Lord of Universe's presence!' So she pushed on bothering not much, and chatting with Ramuchacha.

And she pushed on to be trapped in a tragedy, a girl so disadvantagely placed by nature, she wouldn't be able to get rid of in her entire life.

Taking benefit of municipality yellowish diffused street light; the black number plate less replica of Khandi Pandupur's bulky and furious Balia bull blocked the tri-cycle overtaking them by the side of the abandoned and feared old bungalow standing on woody sand heap. And two heavily built ruffians barged out of the car. And in no time, one caught hold of the old rickshaw puller Ramuchacha flashing an opened knife whereas other one grabbed her with a towel covering her head and lifted her to the car.

She screamed . . . . that's all. She could hear one offender advising and threatening the crying Ramuchacha, "If ever you're caught and questioned, say, you've dropped the girl at Mochisahi Chowk, and you don't know anything after that as you left the place with another passenger. Take this money. Or else, you'll be finished!"

She was bundle up to the car, her mouth sealed and hands tied behind. 'What's going on . . . . ?' She was helpless and she couldn't do anything when her life was sliding to hell. The statuesque stunner felt the run of monsters' lecherous evil hands un-zipping her dresses, one by one, and reaching her under garment brutally, she could ever think up to so happen as the car moved. And she was about to be exploited for her innocence and physical weakness. Her eyes started running with tear and she prayed which lost in the cloud of darkness and monsters' hunger for her flesh. Her kicking failed to save her. Nothing could save her as if she was destined to cursed-hood for life.

"Hey Dear Sambit! Please forgive me and forget me! I'm finished, please forgive . . . . ," cried her mind, her thought, her soul, her heart, her body; and that was all she, a crippled blossoming bud, crippled by her fate, could at best do.

At 9 O'clock dinner time, Preeti woke up to the dinner bell sweeping her still sleepy eyes and found the guardian was still not visible in the room. She went to dining hall, despite her confidence that Seema can't take dinner leaving her in the room with stomach

pain—such was the camaraderie—and she searched all around checking with boarders, visited common room, stairway hopping up to roof gate, lobby, and front road; all in vain. Ramuchacha wasn't in his position too. She was horribly struck up. 'What to do? The Warden and Caretaker have already been back in the hostel and they're in their evening round.' And she remembered their specific checking of Room No. 025 on the preceding days. She was scared of their imminent inquiries of the absence of Seema in the hostel. Again, she went on for a further deadly scanning of every nock and corner of Paharpur Ladies hostel and asking everybody at her sight hoping that funny girl might have been playing with her, she was very fond of. Again, she thought, 'No, she can't play when I'm laid down in pain.'

But, for how long? She was caught and asked sternly by Pramiladidi, "Where is Seema? She has not been seen?" The bichara gawari was in search of words, and the words were found evading her mercilessly. Till date, she hadn't encountered any hard questions alone in the hostel or in the campus. The guardian was always there by her side. She looked at Pramiladidi awful. She started dissolving . . . . dissolving from top to bottom like an ice cake thrown at the vicinity of vomiting volcano. With sight of furious Ms. Shantidevi, who was rushing towards her—might be instigated by any boarder—, her condition became further critical. She literally started shivering.

After a short awkward moment—experienced and exposed to such situations in the past—Ms. Shantidevi pretended to have cooled down, in her bid to extract the information—might she had sensed there was no alternative, and with Ms. Mili coming to know, the matter would be more complicated. More and more in-mates gathered around them. Some were critical and some were sympathetic.

Sarcastic buzzing—"Smarty must have gone to sea beach or casuarinas forest for a body message—she must have gone to temple with her boy friend for engagement—to any hotel for night pass with her boy friend Rabi fooling this proud-but-bichara Miss BCS"—started to have free pouring from the mouths of envious mates and seniors in the hostel passageway.

Slowly but steadily the situation stirred to blow up which was too much to put up with for Preeti. 'How can I bear all such non-sense and rubbish talks against my very dear Rabi and my respected aunty's good girl with whom I had spent so many days, weeks, and months together sharing so much good times, pleasantries as well as pains,' she thought.

"Idiots, stop this rubbish! You don't know my friends. Don't bark just out of envy," the usual shy and soft-spoken, and the branded ghungi gudia from the village Pandupur, furiously turning to the opportunistic buzzers, shouted at the top of her voice wrapped with pain and frustration, she was never seen in the past. And, she was about to slap the offender of her very dears' modesty and honour but prevented by Ms. Mili's roaring from the back, "Then tell, what do you know? And, where is that yours so good friend Seema?"

"Madam, please believe me! We are running short of practical note papers and stationeries. Besides, I was suffering from stomach pain and there was no medicine in the First-Aid box and you're not available. She had gone to Mochisahi Chowk to buy the stationeries and medicine on Ramuchacha's rickshaw . . . . she hadn't come back since," she replied breaking down.

Portly Ms. Mili floated to her office faster than the usual. All envious and anxious followed her. She dialed to Mr. Warden to check Rabi's whereabouts. With the call, the missing news of eye-stealer spread like a wild fire in the Gents Hostel. Both, the sympathetic and the envious boarders from Gents Hostel, gathered at the lobby of Ladies Hostel in no times along with Rabi.

"Matter is such! The stealer of boys' sleeps is missing," the boarders of ladies hostel started chirping.

"Where possibly she would have gone?" were in everybody's overflowing pair of lips.

"Have she developed relation, in the meanwhile, with any other chaps? But, not seen," the boarders from boys hostel gossiped.

"We are here. She could have got matching profile among us," buzzed a senior from the Gents Hostel.

"Modern city girl! Anything possible," whispered another; and gossiping, whispering and buzzing went on.

So also, the tormentor of their peace, Lalu Sarangi, sidelined in the recent past for his comment on Rabi— seemed hunting for an opportunity to recoup the lost ground among the boarders—arrived at the scene, running. As if this was a God-sent opportunity to corner and malign his competitor and cajole Preeti, he was trying hard since his school days, Lalu jumped to unsolicited advice to presiding Kumaries, unwittingly, "Madam, Rabi should be taken to task immediately as I've never seen these two girls without this Mr. Innocent accompanying them," and added, "The simple thought of Seema had gone alone in the dark evening is un-believable. Rabi must have played some mischief with her for monetary benefit. He is such a guy! Or else how could he, an urchin, manage his study without any known consistent source of financing?"

Rabi was terribly incapacitated with these unjust soul-biting assaults. He couldn't believe what he was hearing. He sat down, resigned to his fate, unable to bear the unfair accusation; bending his head-down, dearth of any way out; not pronouncing a single word, silently swallowing all the humiliations as destined; as if he had taken vow to forgive those creatures like the Great Jesus Christ.

The envious bears and monkeys—so far haven't been able to cosy up Preeti and Seema despite their desperate enticing efforts, present in the venue, nodded in agreement. But Rabi's room-mate Biju asked inquiring, "How did Lalu know that Rabi is accompanying these two girls wherever they're going? Does he chase them?" and demanded, "If this is the thing, why should he be not taken to task to gather lead about missing of Seema along with Rabi?" But, unfortunately, there was hardly any taker of this lonely valued voice and Biju left the venue in disgust.

"What a mockery of kismet? The college heart-throb found him under cloud of suspense," lamented a few with all sympathy.

Preeti, the vowed companion for life walked to the cornered Rabi swiftly. She looked at the tormentor of their peace, who was closely following her for her reaction after his provocative and deadly drop of dirt, and placed her hand tightly on her heart-throb's shoulder, displaying unreserved and unconditional devotion of camaraderie. She gestured visibly and clearly, 'You envious idiot Chabishpur kidda, bloody Kaaliram, whatever your stinking mouth may speak out about my Rabi, yet I'm not leaving him. Rabi is my LOVE! I know what my LOVE is . . . . better than you. Is it clear? You bloody, leeching bacteria of septic tank, get lost . . . . go to hell!' and shouted, "Stop speaking rubbishes about my Rabi and Seema. They're so good and so big! . . . . time will tell!"

Rabi wanted to request Ms. Warden not to telephone to girl's parents, and not to lodge missing person FIR with police, but restrained on his own. He examined, 'Both, not informing and informing, are dangerous. Again, who am I to advice such thing in this hostile situation?' He was in a tight spot. He looked at the crying girl by his side. He strongly felt: the simple unprejudiced Preeti's eyes asking him, 'You . . . . Rabi, go! Go to find out our dear ever funny jolly, smarty Seema. She is one among us. No, she can't be simple left to her fate or left to be taken care by the insensitive authority. Something is seriously wrong with her; rescue her before this is too late. She is in need of our help. This is testing time of our friendship.'

Rabi recalled the advice of Kesabkaka. He thoughtfully got up and without telling anything to anybody went to pick up the cycle from Biju and pedaling on potholed city street, lost in the darkness of night.

Lalu was frustrated; obviously, not being able to fish in the trouble water. Still, he didn't give up, in his effort to malign the under-privilege as always. He predicted looking at the ghungi gudia with a mocking smile, "Remain assured, whatever is there, Rabi is certainly involved! He'll be proved true to the son-of-his-single parent at the end!"

Rabi rushed to the city underbelly, the cluster of slums, searching for Ramuchacha. He found the residents of slum cluster were looking at him surprised as if he had just landed from a different world or he was a different creature—they saw for the first time. They, looking at him, found talking among them in an unfamiliar language, that Rabi couldn't get into.

This was quite natural because at this hour in the night they had experience of visit of either lathi wielding cock capped police to ferret out crime suspect or neatly cleaned white dhoti-punjabi clad political party agents to hire cheap slum dwellers for next day demonstration in front of DM Office or for political rally at Bhubaneswar's PMG square; but certainly none else from Rabi's type. Unfamiliar and suffocative county liquor smell invaded meek boy's inhaling organ. Also, he could hear heart rendering screaming of poor fair sexes—like the one he had heard occasionally coming out in the mid-night from the drunkard wife-beater Sada Tanti's house in Pandupur—from some of the thatched and polythene cover hut, dotting all around on the sand mound.

He found him in the midst of a strange world. And, he was also scar in this unfamiliar environment. Whatever, he had a task. He calculatedly selected an oldie to ask the whereabouts of Ramuchacha's hut but failed to extract any response. The oldie surveyed him from top to bottom. However, as Rabi went on asking, the oldie started slowly walking away—seemed to Rabi he was decisively avoiding. He turned to others in desperation and found they were too reluctant and in league, not to share . . . .

They were unanimous not to speak to an outsider. 'Here too, I'm a refuse!' Rabi told self.

'What a kind of camaraderie and solidarity?' he wondered. He found the doors were getting closed, one after another, on his face. And the men left behind were found heavily intoxicated and crawling on the sand; occasionally hissing, snoring, jeering and raving in their unconscious state.

'A hopeless situation!' Notwithstanding, he searched among those the persona of Ramuchacha, their unsolicited guardian and guide on the city streets. Unsuccessful . . . . he left crying, 'Where are you . . . . my dear mama's good girl? Where I will get you? What will I say to my Preeti? Neither I can say her—No, I haven't located Seema nor she has the strength to bear my reply of No. And what will I tell to mama? She'll certainly ask about her good girl.'

Non-availability of Ramuchacha aggravated Rabi's fear. He felt restless.

'Shall I go for asking help from Rekha's parents? . . . . No, it's too late! And they're Big People.'

"Shh, bloody! Who? . . . . Who's there knocking at the door at this hour. Get out, stupid, idiot!" Kesab seemed inebriated to his full, heard out-crying from the inner room as Rabi went on knocking on the door in the silence of the dead of the night with intermittent heart-shivering barking of stray dog and beat police whistle.

Rabi recalled what he had heard from some of his seniors in the hostel, "Kesabkaka regularly visit an adda where his friends from his college days congregate in the late evening and they drink hard stuff before leaving for their home." He had even heard that on some days he drunk so much that he couldn't drive his bike and carried home on rickshaw or he was dropped at his house by his friends. And he never entertained anybody at his home in night. "He drinks, eats and sleeps by the name of his girl-friend."

Despite this hard fact known to him, the humble Rabi went on knocking the door of Kesab as the last resort, and he had strong internal instinct that 'this is only Kesabkaka who can help him rescue his dear Seema who may be in trouble.' And he was ready for anything for the sake of the girl, 'and this is what Preeti wants too.'

"Kesabkaka, I'm Rabi," the frighten boy appealed. A blood-curdling silence descended on the site for a few minutes. But, he wasn't ready to give up. He had to rescue his friend, a reservation kept ringing in his mind, heart and soul. He kept on coughing and knocking letting insider felt his enduring presence at the door . . . .

Patience paid. Furious and thuggish Kesabkaka gave up. He opened the door, and started spitting out words as if he knew the whole story, "Your girl friend that Miss

Smarty, jean pantwali or that ghungi gudia Miss BCS, or both haven't returned to hostel. Isn't it?"

Rabi listened . . . . and listened without any tress of irritation bending his head—completely submissive—as he had a great stake in whatever Kesabkaka would say. After a pause, he again barged on talking and advising, "Let them go to hell! Why do you to bother? They're all kiddas from the privileges' septic tank . . . . shameless girls! After a few days, they'll be on their own as if nothing had happened . . . . completely cleaned up and washed. You, a humble boy, are getting exploited by these clever girls. Go back to your hostel, take rest and relax! Nothing will happen! If they still bother you, take a peg. What a relief? Ha . . . , ha . . . , ha . . . . !"

"Again, I warned you—they may implicate you to rescue them innocent! Hark, nothing is impossible! This is such a bloody world!"

He picked up a bottle of Rum hidden under the cot and shaking the bottle in front of the peasant, intoxicated Kesab Swain, the presumed HanumanGod continued, "This, an ex-student of our college, have offered me—very pure and original stuff, military canteen material—for my suggestion not to run after these kiddas—exactly like you—during his student's days. He listened to me and now a big officer, a Major General in Indian Army. This bottle is a good pain killer! God bless him, who has invented this for us—unfortunate lots!—for time-pass in this world of cheaters and turncoats."

However, Rabi listened to this entire unsolicited lecture with apt attention and maturity as he strongly felt any response in favour of the girl at this stage would annoy Kesabkaka. He had strong conviction that

'Kesabkaka isn't so bad and heartless. Yes, he has a feeling of resentment, and that isn't without reasons. He is right, and he has right to what he opines!'

His perseverance paid. Severely dozing Kesab slowly got stabilized and looked at disturbed and desperate peasant struggling with thought of the young girl's whereabouts. 'Who knows where she is and in what condition? She may be in life tearing distress in this inhuman world, full of wondering lecherous bears and monkeys.'

The inmates of Gents Hostels left to their respective address after the departure of the cursed Rabi. Lalu's smutty vomiting hushed as his' had no takers. He left the lobby, growling.

Kumaris were in full anguish. They zeroed in at Pramiladidi, who was at the receiving end of them—a convenient scapegoat. They shouted in league at the poor destitute, and a hire and fire employee, surviving at the job at the sole discretion of Ms. Warden. In such a situation, Kumaris used to forget that 'she's one-for-many assignments in a hundred plus inmate hostel and non-availability of medicine is none of her business.'

'Seema used to oppose the harassment with all sympathy to the poor scapegoat, and on occasions defended her,' Preeti recalled and cried, 'Where is that voice? And where is that good sense? Pramiladidi is looking after the lobby, office, students' attendance, sick students, and literally everything.' Kumaris let loosed all their anger over her for this irritant. After the privileged tuition session over the scapegoat, the presiding Kumari lodged a FIR in the VIP Road police station over phone and informed to the girl's parents.

"They did their duty. What more they could do to an indiscipline and over-smart gal," approved a senior as inmates were retreating to their respective addresses.

"So you want my help to rescue that or this girl. I've warned you in advance, haven't I? . . . . Despite that they didn't listen. Why . . . . do you know? For them, this is nothing. You know, you'll find in the end, the involvement of a Big People. Whereas this is very bad for you, and you struggle to rescue her. And you come to this branded ruffian for help." Kesab went on speaking hard lying on his bed closing and opening his eyes time and again sleepily.

Finally, he gave up to the patience of helpless peasant determined to rescue his friend—presumable in distress—in this dark night, and told dozily, "What is there in the life? Let's do something for the sake of the college heart-throb's sweetheart, haltingly . . . . But, Rabi, it will be a mad search, and full of risk!"

Rabi nodded confidently as he was determined to rescue his friend comes what way. 'This is what Preeti wants. And, I can't return to Preeti without her room-mate,' he had already finalised.

First, Kesabkaka made a call to his contact in police control room and got information about the FIR lodged. Later to Public Hospitals but in vain, and screamed in resignation, "I guess, this is a clear case of kidnapping organized by a Big Gun. Indication was there! He made telephone calls over a few numbers, and as he heard "Hellos!" from the other side, he got them disconnected, reacting, "This idiot is at home . . . . And this bastard is chewing his mistress breasts!"

The unfamiliar peasant couldn't understand anything in HanumanGod's gambling but he was desperate. As he had no credible one to help him in this hostile city, he hanged around with Kesab Swain, the only hope. Rabi noticed the last call wasn't picked up. Telephone went on ringing. And Kesabkaka went on making repeated calls over the number for once, twice, thrice and later reacted, "Bahanchode, it's Vikhu Bhoi and his gang. They must be at their adda on the Marine Drive with the girl, I'm damn sure, ... about ten kilometers from here. Shall we go Rabi in this night? And if we wait to morning, it may be too late! I've no problem but I can't do the job alone."

"What to do? I need one more helping hand for this operation . . . . Nope, my friends can't be trusted. They're bloody lechers . . . . mayn't miss the opportunity." And looking at Rabi he told, "No, you aren't fit!"

"Again, you've a bright future. If anything went wrong—there's every possibility—your future will be completely ruined. I don't like to be a party to this," Kesab Swain told.

Despite all these forecasting, Rabi looked at the HanumanGod with confidence and ready to go for anything if that even had remote possibility to rescue Seema—theirs best friend and mama's good girl—now in distress.

———◈———

Kesab went into the inner room and could be seen putting something looked like a revolver in his inner garment under his left armpit. This view got in peasant the glimpse of the gravity of their venture. Internally, he felt the collapsing of his life organs. Yet, he was rock solid in his determination—for sake up his friendship with Seema, for sake of Preeti's innocent appeal, and, yes, for sake of his very dear mama who too allowed the girl to sleep on her precious lap sharing that with her only chand-ke-tukkuda.

Carrying the touch-light in his hand, HanumanGod marched to Rabi. Locking the door, they rode the bike. On the way, they ignored frantic whistle blowing of lathi-wielding beat constables and home guards on night duty—always at the receiving end of departmental superiors, and the children from rich and privileged families found engaged in late-night luffadamis in drunken state, a regular feature. The occasional movement of two-wheelers disturbed their dozing and they lightened bidi yelling, "Madurchodes . . . . keep on disturbing! Bloody, can't yours bitches tempt you to the bed?"

The bike carried the two brave hearts to the outskirts of sleepy town to the deserted Marine Drive amidst heart-shivering chorus howling of she-jackals followed by wailing bark of stray dogs being disturbed by occasional bellowing of carrier whenever that was passing through the road side sleepy dingy shops cluster.

The peasant was getting frightened with each passing minute and passing mile, not only in the dead silence, fastening desert on the Marine Drive and howling and barking, but also by the unstable speedy driving of intoxicated Kesabkaka. Of course, the crescent moon light had little consolation to the single-mindedly determined Rabi to complete his mission of rescuing his friend wherever she was, and whatever be the consequence.

'He isn't a just ordinary friend and his friendship isn't just for the sake of any vested interest, and isn't fraudulent. It is pious—wrapped with sincerity, honesty and Godly sanctity. This is the testing time of our friendship,' Rabi valued in his dog-tired thinking machine.

After a long drive of a few kilometers, at a starting point of a sub-road on the right, Kesab directed Rabi to look at a blinking she-devil light at a distance inside the deep casuarinas forest. This reminded Rabi the heart-shuddering tales of witch and wizard, and their witchcraft and wizardry that his mother used to tell him during his childhood whenever he was wayward. However, the carrier didn't stop, leaving Rabi to wonder with many inevitable. Kesab drove for another one or two kilometer and stopped by the side of screw pine bush on a sharp road curve. He switched up the head-light and they stepped down from the bike. The commander explained, "That is the place where most probably the girl is kept under captivation. Now, we'll move there with the support of little moonlight. We've to remain prepared for any inevitable!" and warned with seriousness, "You've to stay put to full attention to my all instructions."

The foot-soldier nodded with agreement as the commander went on explaining modus operandi of the operation. HanumanGod drove the bike for probable another one kilometer that the gawar pre-occupied with warning of 'any inevitable' hadn't noted. Then they turned back with headlight off, and later at the point where they had seen the she-devil light they started walking on the sub-road full of pot-wholes resembling the road from Chabishpur to Pandupur. The manner HanumanGod was leading on the sub-road—Rabi guessed, 'He's certainly a frequent visitor to the site.'

'Anyway, how does it matter to him,' the peasant told self and followed his Commander-in-Chief like a sincere foot soldier. He noticed from the distance the dim she-devil light inside a room with window open. They walked on. As they got closer, he recalled his mama's story of 'the she-devil extorting the blood of her prey.' The thought frightened him further.

'Has the she-devil taken Seema to here? If so, what she would have done to her,' he cried and screamed, "Hey Pravu, please save my mama's good girl! She is inno . . . ." and felt a bold blockade of his face by a rough palm.

"Shh! No God will help! You be your own God here. Stop sobbing! Follow me," Kesab whispered.

The site of the black Ambassador car without number plate further confirmed HanumanGod's guess. He stopped. And Rabi whispered, "This is the car which was hanging around the hostel locality during the past couple of days." They parked the bike on the wayside besides the screw pine bush away from anybody's common site. They could see from the distance two crooks were guarding the dingy room while one was inside. They slowly walked closer to the site by the side of bushes and heard in the calmness of deep cool night Vikhu saying, "What a stuff we got after a long time? In our slum, all are milch buffaloes with suspended gourd breasts."

"Oo-er, yeah! What a body and pointed standing apple boobs like of film heroines? But, you have chewed so badly," expressed ecstatically the Vikhu's accomplice.

"Slimy . . . . mare waist! And, chunky thigh!" lecherous Vikhu concurred fisting at his accomplice who begged, "You've already got your quota. Now, this is my turn."

"Hey, she is bleeding," cried the third one from inside the dingy room with sign of fear. Vikhu entered the room and checking expertly expressed, "She was a pure virgin! It usually happens to a virgin."

"Next is my turn," appealed the insider.

"No, this is my turn," shouted the guard at the doorsill. "What is there in yours and mine? She is for all of us. We're brothers. Let us have the spirit of Pandabas. As soon as she got back her sense this time, we'll give her a foreign peg. U..ha! She'll enjoy yaar. This will make her active and co-operative," advised Vikhu with certainty.

Rabi heard the ear-biting lecherous praising, yelling and cheering of his friend's pious body. It seemed to him the offenders had fully exploited the hapless and innocent girl. They were seemed highly intoxicated— might be drunk with raw county liquor—the peasant thought which fastened the melting of confidence in him. He felt the sand beneath his legs sliding fast. And his memory went back and recalled the appealing eyes of mama's little girl. He heard the telepathy, 'Rabi, please bring back my jolly my bubbly my smarty and my statuesque stunner! Bring her, comes what way! You're my only hope. I can't live in this hostile hostel without her. I'm waiting.'

Here, he strongly felt, 'Kesabkaka is right with his warning. Rescuing the girl would be hard fought one! Still, I'm not returning without my mama's good girl.'

And, he found the solid determination in his HanumanGod.

"Kaka, I'm ready. We shouldn't waste time," whispered Rabi.

The Commander of the operation gave instruction to Rabi akin to what he had read in detective novel.

"Now, I'm sure, only three people are there. They're small time criminals used to commit petty crime, and for the first time, they're engaged, most probable by a Big Gun, for kidnapping and rape which may ended with killing of the girl and dumping the body in the deep sand mound. Now, I'm confident, we can overcome them! But, regarding the girl's condition, nothing can be said. She is bleeding. Let's hope for the best," whispered the agitated and frustrated Commander-in-Chief of the operation.

However, he was in full display of confidence to internally fainted Rabi.

"I can't wait any more. I'm slipping out of my pant," they heard one of the crooks shouting inside the room.

HanumanGod too couldn't bear. He covered his face with a napkin and picked out his revolver from the armpit and displaying the feared-weapon to the boy, he directed, "As soon as I fired at the direction of kitchen, you've to shout 'Cordon up! cordon up!' as loudly as possible. You've to do much of the talk as and when required leaving no scope to the crooks to identify me which would be most dangerous to all of us. As they'll start running towards the forest and sea beach scattered, I'll fire at the light and in the ensuing darkness with help of the torchlight we'll pick up the girl and move over to bike. The complete operation has to be done swiftly, within a few seconds only."

"Note: the girl would be either out of sense or intoxicated and barely could move on her own. Take this torchlight but 'ON' and 'OFF' it only when barely needed!" and warned, "Don't be emotional at any stage of this operation. Mind, no emotion! No cry!"

As one of the offender seen in the she-devil light pushing down his pant runner, HanumanGod whispered, "Madurchodes, I'll chop your penis," and fired.

Rabi shouted.

As expertly scripted, the rescuers rushed. Once inside the temple kitchen, they saw the girl was lying completely bared on the floor and seemed physically devastated; flooded with blood down waist and scars on body. The statuesque stunner's ever energetic body was completely motionless, and silenced.

"Ooh, my God! What these bastards have done to my sister," Rabi cried. Rabi couldn't keep the touch 'ON'. How could he see his mama's good girl's bare body lying uncared and devastated? The darkness of deep night rescued him from seeing that unfortunate sight. He, a simple peasant, was almost shocked and stock-still in the situation. He couldn't imagine that this could be one day the condition of a mentally strong and bold statuesque stunner who had on their first meeting fondled him. And, in the college campus, she could comfortable frowned lecherous bears and monkeys with daring words and physical poise.'

But, the HanumanGod was in his justified hurry. He murmured at the breaking up peasant, "Hush, stop crying! Open your shirt," and picking up the criminal's lungi, he ordered, "Bundle up the girl in your shirt and in this lungi and carry her on your shoulder to the bike before these bastards find out that we're only two—civilians, not police!"

The reluctant Rabi, shy of touching the bare body of mama's good girl, looked at Kesabkaka awful.

"Nothing doing! Call of the responsibility," the furious Commander-in-Chief screamed that forced the peasant to do the inevitable. As they walked towards the bike with motionless and silenced girl on Rabi's shoulder the HanumanGod busted the fuel tank firing from a little distance like Lord Rama's Hanuman did to Ravenna's golden Lanka. And later spitting he yelled, "Bloody carrier of criminals, get lost!"

As they were leaving, they could hear Vikhu shouting, "Sasura, they're only two! They've fooled us. Oops, what a stuff we lost! They'll enjoy her. Idiots, cowards, impotent, you rats, where're you hiding? I would have brought Mangu and Hira. Bahanchode, you bloody sister-sleepers . . . . come on! Let's catch."

The twosome heard the pausing run of criminals towards them in the sandy casuarinas forest as the faithful Hero Honda started carrying the cargo with victorious bellowing, driven by the victorious HanumanGod.

By the time the entire operation of rescuing the poor girl was over, it was early in the morning. She-jackals howling have been silenced. Flying black scavengers heard readying their wings in their nests, and crowed. Bit constables and Home Guards were found vacated their positions. And the stray dogs were in their sleep with sea bound cold morning wind.

The peasant, who found girl's condition beyond his comprehension, was in quandary and asked him, 'Where to take this girl? Now, the ravaged girl is on my shoulder. And I'm a suspect,' and again thought, 'Taking her to hospital or hostel will destroy her image. What'll happen to her future?' The poor peasant literally started crying in him. 'Whatever . . . . ; mama's good girl can't be abandoned to her fate.'

But, the bike passed the Medical Square, didn't stop; passed the hostel road, didn't take the turn. 'To where . . . . HanumanGod is taking? To Sadar police station . . . . ,' Rabi shivered. The sight of cock-hooded and baton wielding police forced him to cry, "Oh, my God!"

No, the bike moved towards the Commander's narrow lane . . . . and stopped in front of his house. He took them to his own house instead of hospital or hostel or police station. Rabi was abacked by the act of the once hostile Kesabkaka.

"Wherever on earth, we take this girl in this condition, is full of risk," told the HanumanGod, now fully stable and considerate, and opined, "I fear negative publicity. This could affect the moral of the girl at this teenage. Since we've rescued her from the certain jaw of death, let's take charge of her health and her rehabilitation, whatever be the consequence."

Both laid the devastated girl with all care and sensibility on the bed and covered her body with a clean chaddar. Rabi started cleaning her face, her hands and her legs guardedly and gently with cotton provided. But he failed to go further cleaning her body lifting the chaddar as directed by the savior.

In the meanwhile, Kesab consulted his doctor friend over phone and with confidence announced, "We'll treat the girl here!" "Clean her fast! This is required to prevent infection. Doctor is coming."

But, the peasant looked pity and crying.

"No, you can't do. We've to bring a nurse immediately." As if an after-thought dictated, he told, "This will further escalate the situation. Rabi, what's that your village girl's name? Yes, Preeti! She need to be called immediately."

He dialed to the proud custodian of Paharpur Ladies Hostel. Phone went on ringing once, twice, thrice . . . . Rabi could notice on the face of Kesabkaka, his frustration and despair. Fourth call was attended.

"Good morning Madam, I'm Kesab Swain, canteen contractor. I'm sorry to disturb you at this early hour," spoke apologetically before hearing broken—"Ha . . . . l . . . lo!"—from the other side. "Ooh, Kesabbabu? . . . . You're on the line! . . . . How are you? What a great chance? I was thinking of calling you yesterday night. But, you know that was too late for you. So, I prefer not to disturb you. Since the last evening, that Rourkela girl—'what's her name?'—Seema Pati is missing," and went on adding, "If you don't mind, I may request you for any tip if you have? This will remain completely confidential between you and me. The matter has already been intimated to police and her parents. Her father is out of station. They'll take little more time."

He looked very angry. 'Might be he was not happy with the seriousness the matter had been taken care by the authority,' thought Rabi. However, the snot-nosed but self-controlled Kesab replied, "Madam, she is now with me. You needn't bother. Rabi and I have taken care of her. I may request you to withdraw the FIR and tell to all that she is injured in an accident. Rest, we'll discuss in the college. If you don't mind you may give me her parents' phone number or inform them there's nothing to worry," and requested her, "Please inform Preeti about Rabi and Seema. You know at my home there are no ladies. Preeti's service is urgently required here. But, don't allow her come alone. Rabi is coming to pick up her."

There, in the hostel, Preeti couldn't have her dinner nor could she sleep. She collected the dinners and kept them to be eaten with her room-mate which she hadn't apprehended that that wasn't going to happen in that night. She couldn't eat breaking the practice of eating together; a practice that had been going on since their first day of boarding at Paharpur Ladies Hostel. Even on days of either/or's sickness they used to give company to each other; however, taking the minimum. Such was the bonding.

This was her first lonely night in the hostel since their first day of boarding. The room was silent. There were no routine funny talks concerning hostel Kumaris; Miss Femme and Supanakha's attempts to impress upon their Prince Charming; and bears and monkeys' lecherous comments thrown upon them. And recently added stories from Pandupur's Balia Bull and its wives; Gandua, Galu, Valu, Sarua, Hadu and their roving around the bushes; and Lilli's peasant comics and envious talks pointed at their village heart-throb and the 'alleged lazy girl!' Seema used to pursue those regularly on daily basis during their bed time, picking up from one angle one day and another angle on the other. And, Preeti in the meanwhile had been accustomed herself to Seema's bed-time talk. The bubbly girl had almost replaced her grandma.

She went on valuing her worthy friend in the silence of the deadly night when all the inmates and the proud custodians of hostel were asleep. The silence of the room was hunting and almost eating her.

She heard chipkali chirping, "Tik . . . . , tik . . . . !" "Seema has come!" She rushed to lobby and stared through the grill but the girl didn't turn up nor Rabi. She returned and heard chipkali's screaming again as she thought, 'Seema is in trouble!' These went on alternatively.

She was almost getting out of the room to all the sporadic noises and sounds, barking of stray dogs, whistle of police patrolling team and chattering of birds in the big banyan tree on the boundary of hostel in the silence of night. Door at the Room No. 025 was wide open and lonely inmate went on praying to her village tutelary Goddesses, and city's presiding deity with promises of special offering and diyas for safe return of her two friends.

Even over each barking of dogs outside the boundary, she was running to lobby, peered through the grill; only to return empty handed. This went on till she overheard the telephone ring in the room of Miss Mili Padhi, the proud custodian of their security and safety. The wired-machine ringed once, and went on ringing twice, thrice . . . . on fourth, Warden attended and she heard Warden was talking, but what, she didn't have chance to hear?

'Is there any information?' she asked her as talk went on.

And Warden opened the door to be stomped by a heartrending sight. She was shocked, the sight of . . . . she checked, she checked repeatedly—the girl was none other than college Miss BCS, sitting at her doorsill resting her head on the knees, replicating the look of an abandoned insane girl by the side of a city cesspool, ravaged of her body by the sex hungry ruffian in the passing night, motionless with swollen face and red eyes.

As Kesabkaka left for the bath room, Rabi thought, 'What an incredible person Kesabkaka is? A highly generous personality is living in the societal branding of ruffian!' Rabi now felt, 'Whatever he had heard about this man were one-sided fabricated malice, not worthy to be listened, wasting time.' He confirmed the notion of: If anybody is bad, this is the society that made him bad, and this is the society which is to be blamed!

With the responsibility at hand, Kesabkaka was found too busy. He boiled the water and got the cotton ready for cleaning ravaged girl. And returning back to phone, he talked, "May I speak to Mr. Pati?" He had hardly gone to the next sentence worn out and the ravaged girl was in front of them. Wrapped with a chaddar—she was unable to stand on her own and talk clearly—signaled them not to talk to her parents.

Kesab couldn't understand anything. Rabi was about to assist her. However, she fell down like an uprooted tree ravaged by a thunderstorm. Kesab dropped the receiver just saying, "She is all right. I'll call back to you shortly."

On gathering strength, she was unstoppable but couldn't finish. Rabi's revelation about the girl's parents were shocking. Further, she went on saying, "They've taken my naked photographs. They'll certainly misuse them. And I can't cheat my dear Sambit who loves me so much! Unfortunately, you, my well-wishers have rescued me—taking your life to risk—to be tortured by the societal vultures till my death like Bhagyabati aunty. I don't have her patience. For my parents, their careers and high society are more important than my life. I'm such an unfortunate daughter!" She spoke and broke down weeping and sobbing.

This was enough to melt the rock-strewn Kesab Swain—ever susceptive of modern educated girls. 'How could he remain unmoved with this stone-melting inhuman story,' thought the humble Rabi.

Kesabkaka had all sympathy to this innocent child, barely reached the age of understanding the complexity of this so-called civilized world, lying on his lap. He looked up appalling. His misgiving towards the modern city girl had started evaporating. He promised the unfortunate but good girl caressing her head with elderly care to collect the photographs comes what way before they were slipped to other's hands.

Soon, they heard their HanumanGod shouting at someone over phone, "Banhanchode, either you handover photo-reel along with the camera within a quarter of an hour or get ready to face this bachelor wrath! Mind, don't try to keep copy of photo reel."

But, the ill-fated girl was unconsoling and unstoppable. She jabbed Kesab's white haired chest and screamed, "Kaka, tell me, what's left in my life? I've lost everything that a girl feels proud of. I can't deceive my LOVE. I must die; I must die; I . . . . must . . . ." And she collapsed over her HanumanGod and her tone got silenced.

True to his command, the photo reel and camera reached their HanumanGod. And later the trio heard their HanumanGod threatening somebody over phone, "I forgive you for what you'd done last night. And now onwards, if any harm happens to my children mentally and physically in Puri or elsewhere under the sky, I'll kill you and your hirer. Tell this to that bastard Ghar Jamai; whatever he may be, he cannot escape this bachelor's wrath."

Moving counseling of Kesabkaka apart from lovely care along with round-the-clock vigilant attendance of the trio, and the special treatments by the specialist doctors, the ravaged girl physically recovered fast in the sanctum sanctorum of the HanumanGod. But, the scar, which had been planted in the psyche of the girl and the damage done to her body and its sanctity, however couldn't.

And, in the college, Miss Femme Fatale and her comrade-in-plotting, Kaaliram were found missing for a few days.

Keeping their promise to their revered HanumanGod, the trio concentrated in their study.

The Annual Examination was held and result was outstanding, further elevating the trio's status in the campus. The illustrious trio—Mr. Rabi Pratap, Miss Preeti Rath and Miss Seema Pati—were listed First, Second and Third in the college merit list leaving tormentor Lalu Sarangi at distance fiftieth, and Ruby and Rekha far behind in three digits difficult to remember. With publication of result Kesab Swain and the college top brass interest were further gravitated towards the trio.

GRADUATION ADMISSION

'Khandi Pandupur is to be liberated from the humiliating tag of Khandi. Its' people has to be liberated from cursed clutches of poverty, and manipulating grip of Choudhury elder.' Karan Mishra, the President of Pandupur Youth Club and the mentor had been advocating, "Khandi Pandupur can walk matching with other villages only through higher academic performance of its lads, followed by occupying the top administrative position in the government."

Pandua peasants agreed but weren't confident. This hard fact had been recognized by the villagers long ago; yet, except Choudhury elder's children, who studied in Cuttack and distance Delhi and were no use to village, none from the village could have been able to achieve any academic miracle. The consistent academic performances of Rabi in the school and college in the meanwhile were encouraging. They now felt that Rabi, who had been discarded 'a guttersnipe', had this distinct potential. 'He can secure high-ranking administrative services, which can help build the village image and can bring government grants for village development like it happened to other villages. Besides, he can inspire fellow village tots bereft of iconic leadership born and brought up in our own village.'

Khandi Pandua Rabi, as the true sonofthesoil, too was of the similar opinion. When the mentor proposed Rabi to get admission in Bachelor of Arts with Economics Honours and Political Science Pass instead of Preeti's suggested Bachelor of Sciences with Physics Honours and Chemistry and Mathematics Pass he was strong, the girl wasn't very enthusiast. Preeti protested and right away expressed her fear, "These Arts subjects aren't mark fetching. Rabi, the most scholarly student of the college, which has already been proved with Intermediate Science result, would certainly loose the scope of getting awarded the Best Graduate of the college and possible the Best Graduate of University, a morale booster for future career. And, we, the villagers, will be proud of," and asked boldly, "Are not the candidates with Physics, Chemistry and Mathematics subjects doing well in the Civil Services examinations?"

"Preeti is so obsessed with Rabi; God knows— What is there in their fate?" the mentor Karan Mishra murmured looking at the girl. And he jocularly jeered, "In fact, I believe you're scared of missing Rabi in the class rooms and academic block if he chooses Arts course. Am I right my little girl?"

"No, not that! Preeti is in fact scared of losing study supports which has so far helped her achieving academic excellence," Lilli yelled sarcastically.

"If truth be told, Lilli, this is nothing but an allergic comment . . . . bereft of any merit! And I'm confident, our little girl has merit and capacity to prove you wrong. Preeti, let's take this as a challenge and prove that you can achieve miracle without this—I quote: alleged umbilical cord," pumped up the mentor.

As soon as the envious and embarrassed Lilli hopped out of the cottage, the little girl cried with reason, "Kaka, you don't know and if truth be told, this will offer a free hand to the likes of Femmes and Supanakhas in our college not only to entice but also disturb our village's future hope and aspiration that I'm afraid of. This is what bothers me the most!"

"Well, don't you have faith on our Rabi, even after so many years of togetherness," the mentor counseled and advised with reason, "With Economics Honours and Political Science pass, he'll have the proper early grinding on social, political and economic subjects which, I strongly believe, would be a great help in appearing the top state and national level civil service examinations."

Back in the college, the famous teen murtis first piligrimed to their revered HanumanGod in the college unofficial assembly house. They touched the feet of their revered living deity like the Hindu pilgrims do to Lord Hanuman in Lord's abode with all piousness and reverence, going straight to cash counter from where Kesab Swaim used to preside over the canteen affairs, and allegedly directed many college affairs, perpetually munching wads of pan packed with smelly Gopal Zarda, and spiting red pan juice intermittently in the open spittoon kept under his high cushioned throne.

"Kaka, you've again started taking Gopal Zarda. I'm sorry: either you stop taking this poison or I'll stop coming to canteen. Decision is left in your durbar," threatened the statuesque stunner with furious Maa Durga's poise.

"Okay, okay Maa Mahisasura Murdini! I am sorry!"

"Old habit die hard!" Preeti buzzed.

The veneration of canteen contractor by the famous teen murtis was a big surprise to all present in the canteen as they had never seen such an act of any student before. 'Why they shouldn't when they knew the prayers background.' The brows rose and the eyes widened. They look at each other, and a few whispered, "Rare phenomena!" as they were stirred up with the thought of: 'How could a BCS College proud Intermediate Topper and another, the daughter of Director, RSP, Orissa's biggest PSU could touch the feet of a mere college canteen contractor, with a dubious character. And that too in full glare of public with so much of reverence and sanctity like one gentle and humble child offers to parents or the oldie devotee to reverend God in the temple! And, they weren't Kesab's relation as the caste and surname helped, reveals.'

Kesab too was surprised but reconciled with the fact that 'they perhaps are feeling indebted to me for my brave act of rescuing Seema from the cruel jaw of certain death, that too risking my life. And recalled, 'Before too, I had rescued one girl with similar problems in Badapanda beach,' and cried, 'but, she wasn't so obliged?'

He did help students even risking his life and money. Many had taken monetary benefit from him and promised to refund with interest but seemed forgotten with easy. Notwithstanding, the broad-minded Kesab didn't keep note of them. None had touched his feet and begged bowing head for blessing like these three.

However, Kesabkaka is Kesabkaka, although not a Mahatma but helped, as he felt proud of helping needy students in small and big way. He was kind-hearted and soft although looked rough and behaved pig-headed. He was heard saying on occasion, "Yes, I've nobody! What'll I do with so much of accumulation?" Many flatterers had taken advantage of his this personal attribute.

An overjoyed and proud Kesabkaka ordered in broken words, munching pan, "Get the Special fried pakadi with fried green chili and coffee for our Mr. Topper, Miss BCS and Miss Smarty."

"Kaka, please! This is . . . . ," cried Preeti, shied of flattering.

But, kaka wasn't dithering. And later looking at Seema, he continued, "Hot pakadi is my brave daughter's favourite! Is not it, Seema darling?"

"Kesabkaka, I'm really dying for your hot pakadi. I was missing them at Rourkela during the vacation," Seema confirmed running her watery tongue over the dry fleshy lips and a huge wink from lotus eyes. "There's difference between yours pakadi and others."

"Ooh my God! Seema, very naughty," Kesab jeered, and jumped off his pedestal, shaking. The honest flattering from the who's who of BCS further boosted his enthusiasms. He was ecstatic. He went to the store and picked up packed branded pulse meal and packed refined oil kept separately in a corner, and while handing over them to the chef he was seen instructing resembling his instructions when orders from Principal and 'Gang of Four' used to come, although fried pakadi in sufficient quantity were there in the display tray that everybody present could take note of.

Many eyebrows rose. And the murmurings started doing the round on hearing the offer of Special to the teen murtis.

In the past, whenever Kesabkaka was challenged for the discriminating offering of Special, that too, at the same cost, he openly acknowledged without any sign of remorse, and stomped them down with, "I agree, this is discrimination! Yet, what to do? Our system is such and we've to live with this. I'm a just human being, neither a prophet nor a mahatma!"

And, after the spat, he didn't fail to pass on consoling expression, "Please don't mind!"

And, on occasions, he returned the unrelenting challenger with his logic, "Are you not paying Special Homage with Special aarti and Special Offering to Lord Jagannath? In the temple complex, there are several deities but none get the offering of the kind Lord Jagannath gets from you, pilgrims . . . . Am I right?"

Some get silenced. Yet many settled down sarcastically mocking, "Why not say: this is nothing but a business trick!"

"Yes, this is! This is the truth that you must admit. And you must agree without any pretension too," Kesabkaka used to calm them down.

Whatever, the teen murtis weren't happy and weren't ready to concur with this VIP treatment. They talked among them, "What our fellow mates will think? They'll certainly have ill-feeling against us." They looked at each other remorsefully and pain in their eyes. Seema wanted to stop their kaka but hold back as Rabi ticked her hand.

"Drop this issue for time being! We'll talk later. Please don't spoil kaka's moment of joy. He's very emotional," Rabi passed the message clearly and the girls acknowledged.

As natural, Kesab's this expressed VIP treatment couldn't go down well with Ruby Dash, proud of her family status in the city. 'Wherever I go in Puri I get Special Treatment. The whole city salutes me! What this bloody, just a canteen contractor does here? I'm the daughter of city's richest person with our majestic building on the Grand Road rivaling Governor's House on the VIP road that the people use to stare with and wish to own such a one in their life time. Number of cars and a big army of servants!'

Certainly, the ignorance and avoidance of her by the ugly red-faced chimpanzee was suffocating and eye-souring. She was witnessing the unfolding events sitting along with Lalu Sarangi in one corner of the sprawling canteen—unnoticed of the trio—almost with fire in the eyes, munching the teeth.

'She was certainly scheming something,' Kesab Swain guessed. Since the day of kidnapping of Seema, Ruby had been very selective, reclusive and intriguing in her all kinds of interaction in the campus that the trio had been noticing. And, Lalu Sarangi had been her only accomplice.

She couldn't bear all these ego scoring flattering of Kesab Swain directed at the trio. She coughed to clear the throat with a full size singhdas gobbled unmindfully.

The trio turned to them.

"Hi, how do you do? You've done extremely well in the exam. Congratulation," jeered the stunning Seema and asked walking to her, "What's your future plan? Are you going abroad for higher study? . . . . Which university? Have you got visa?" and good-humoured, "These days you're mostly seen with Mister Lalu Sarangi? You're very close to each other! Has the matter settled down? You would be good pair! Both you're intelligent, beautiful, educated, and above all, rich and influential," and looking back at Rabi asked, "Rabi, how is my suggestion?"

Ruby looked at her overflowing eye-sore curtly and later moved to Kesab Swain with trademark pushing of the poor plastic chair back. She pulled out a hundred rupee note from her dazzling Gucci leather vanity and throwing the note on the table of kaka, she left screaming, "This is for your special pakadi and fried chili, and coffee!"

Kesab Swain was equally responsive and instantly responded jeering, "Wow! What a generosity from a stinking mouth? Thank you, thank you very much; but sorry babe, I can't digest this ill-gotten money," and handing over the note to his canteen boy, ordered him with teasing loud laugh, "Ha . . . . ha . . . . Chottu, take this note and drop it in Temple Hundi," and went on warning, "Again, I advise babe, don't repeat the crime. Don't force this bachelor to take law to his hand! I've forgiven you once. Mind, these are my children. I won't spare whoever he may be if the crime is repeated!"

This was like salting the blood spattered wound. She was fired. She looked back. But nothing she could say with an equally head strong thuggish with undeniable reasons. She was heard murmuring something halting for a while. Later, her accomplice in scheme followed her.

This was nothing new to Kesab as he'd had experiences of this type of incident and faced them in the past. This incident was just a flying dust for him and he assured the trio, "Nothing to bother about!" And, he laughed and simply brushed aside the privileged girl's display of immodesty joining his two palms over his head in the direction of city's presiding deity's abode and told, "Hay Mahaprabhu, please give some sense of modesty to this kidda of your septic tank," and concluded, "She is truly her mother's daughter!"

The incident left the trio nervous. They were down, and was melting which their HanumanGod made a note of.

Over the neatly cleaned china plate with Special hot pakadi and fried green chili the Special Customers' future academic plan were deliberated under the Chairmanship of Kesab Swain, their new guardian and the security cover. Kesab found appreciative of Topper's course choice. He proudly said naming a few IAS, IPS and OAS officers including Mr. Debasis Mohanty, the present DM of Puri, an ex-student of BCS College who had these course combinations in their graduation. He proudly revealed what he'd suggested to Mr. Mohanty. The trio believed him as they had seen Mr. Mohanty, while on a round of college campus after joining as DM, went to their Kesabkaka and was closet with him for a few minutes, which provoked envious eye blinking and gossiping among the students, the faculty members and the Principal.

427

"They're talking as if they're close-friends," the faculties buzzed and the Principal reacted, "Kesab Swain has good contacts."

It seemed to the trio, Kaka got a lot of satisfaction in his wise counseling. "I had these combination too in my graduation and also my . . . . ," he stopped abruptly as if he started something unwittingly.

"Kaka, you stopped half-way," asked the dim-wit gawari inquiring. A pensive silenced prevailed for a while. Topper pulled down his head with a sharp pity glance at the girl. She looked all. Everybody instead concentrated in engulfing the hot pakadi in their bid—'may be to avoid an unintentional guff,' Preeti concurred. And, later kaka curling the embarrassed girl's head told with a teasing smile, "Preeti, don't miss this opportunity. Grab it! You can steal the life time achievement of Best Graduate of the premier BCS College and possible the Utkal University with Topper choosing Economics Honours and Political Science pass combination and you Physics Honours, Chemistry and Mathematics pass."

Preeti wasn't happy with this selfish and narrow minded proposition. 'How could I when I've decided to accept Topper as my Gopinath,' she told to her. 'And I've decided to remain lifetime runner-up to him. I only deserve this much!' She kept quiet for sometimes. But, not for long. She checked, 'No response from me might be differently mean to all those present here.' She wanted to clear the air. She wanted to speak something but held up, as hot pakadi that she had already lifted to her mouth little large in quantity unmindfully, prevented her. Still, she couldn't hold up; and she was outpouring. Seema and Rabi turned to her as she turned red and paused. She looked at Kesabkaka grudgingly that experienced kaka could read in the fast changing face of rosy little Preeti. He kicked her leg under the table and winking his eyes, provoked her to outburst.

The ghungi reacted perfunctorily, "I'm not so mean to think on this line! But . . . ." She stopped abruptly as Kesabkaka looked back at her with a nervous smile. He poked and patting her head told apologetic, "I was just joking. You're such a nice little girl, I enjoy teasing you! Shall you not excuse yours this old kaka," and he cried, "Apart, I don't know why I feel so homely with you . . . . I've none to play with, children!"

Kesabkaka became emotional. Preeti felt humiliated with his apologetic response and rued, "Sorry kaka, I'm your stupid little girl. Please forgive me! You play with us as much you like. We're at your service. We've no elder here too!" She told embracing the oldie.

"You aren't stupid! You're a nice and beautiful girl," Kesabkaka told and nodded with a pleasant smile and all four enjoyed sipping special hot coffee just delivered.

Smarty's choice of Sociology Honours and Education Pass were rejected by kaka and he said, "These are easy subjects. For you lazy and knotty girl, this is okay! But, you shouldn't disturb others." Seema as expected wasn't that unhappy with kaka for such a trimming. She leisurely looked at him and cheered unfolding her hands wide, "Kaka, you spelled what's there in my heart," and musingly told, "But, what to do? I'm so tired. And, again, what's there in my life? I'm thinking up to be a social worker. So, the subject selection!"

Everybody turned to Seema with pain in their eyes. 'Seema hasn't forgotten the past!'

'Yes, how can she when the matter is so ravaging, beyond repair?'

She revealed, "I informed Sambit what had happened to 'my body' that night within week of the incident and left him to decide our future . . . . and, he hadn't called me back and even visited me at Rourkela and I hadn't searched him." She cried.

All caught her hand in disbelieve. They were stunned.

"Ooooh my God! Seema, what you did? You've spoiled your life," Kaka shouted. And with tear in his eyes and embracing the girl, he shouted, "What was the need of it, my child?"

"No kaka, I did what I believe is right and what my conscience dictated me. I don't like to live in pretence. If this is there in my fate, I've to live with this. And I hope, I'll get all the co-operations from my well-wishers," told the statuesque stunner with full conviction and went on, "It means he refused me. And he has every right for the same. What has happened to me was there in my fate. And this is the truth! I wanna live with the truth."

"I don't bother for the consequence!"

However, they assured they would be with her. Kesab played the elder guardian's role, "Seema, my sweet girl, for the sake of we all you've to forget the past and move on. There are many things one has to do in one's life. Time is the greatest healer . . . . promise to this oldie kaka here and now."

Devastated Seema got emotional and cleaning her teary eyes and hugging over her dear kaka, nodded.

As the curtain was drawn over the small party and the trio were about to leave with belly full of Special pakadi, Kesab looking at the trio told confidently and assuring, "Take my advice and forget all those that bacteria Ruby thrown at you. You remain faithful to your mates leaving all those kiddas to me. I know how to deal with and control them." The HanumanGod displayed his tight muscle pulling the sleeves up.

His guardian eyes run after them till they were shadowed by the Biology Block wall. A few drop of tears rolled down over wrinkled cheek and chin.

THE BIG BULL

As the trio entered the Arts Block on their way to college office, they heard a mild commotion in front of the Principal's office in the First Floor. They could guess from the passage in the ground floor, there was a big crowd.

"A Big Bull has trespass the campus," they heard one student running down to the ground floor, jeered.

'Yes, there's nothing new in this. The bulls used to trespass the campus as the two gates are wide-opened, and at some points, the long boundary wall had broken down paving free entry of all and sundry, but the most surprising was never a bull had gone up to First Floor,' Preeti thought. "Impossible, a bull can't go up," she told to her companions and later inquired, "but, why then there is commotion in the First Floor, and that too, in front of Principal's chamber?"

As usual, she was extra-curious, and so she looked at her escort flanking her on her right and left as always, and cautiously asked, "How a bull could reach the First Floor?" As no response came forthwith, she wondered and later settled down saying, "Nothing is impossible in this Lord Jagannath's temple city!"

But, Seema was found very enthusiast with the information and together with supportive Rabi speeded up and ran leaving behind the wondering and frightened gawari behind. She cried, warning, "Hey Smarty, hey Topper . . . . be careful!"

However, she followed them as she couldn't stay behind when her two companions could possibly be in trouble 'if there is certainly a bull!' but saw a bearded and heavily built man of their village Balia bull's colour, and in the attire of white churidar and ghee colour kurta, shaking hands with her heart-throb, and congratulated, "You're Rabi Pratap, this year Intermediate Topper. Well down! Congratulation friend! You're proud of our college. We'll talk."

'But no bull was visible at the sight,' Preeti checked all around for sure. 'And even to her utter surprise nobody was talking about the bull!'

'So, this man is the Big Bull that boy was commenting,' the pigeon-hearted took breath, assured of no trouble.

She went on thinking, 'The Big Bull told—our College?—is he a teacher or a staff in our college? Never seen before! None of our teacher or staff wears this type of costume. Is he a student? Nope, he can't be! He is looked so old! . . . . He looks like Chabishpur Gabbar Singh—Bishu Sarangi . . . . May be a goonda or politician? . . . . Why he will talk to Rabi? And what . . . what for?'

As they moved towards Swati Madam's chamber after the brief meeting with Big Bull, Preeti jeered, "The Big Bull, no doubt, is a perfect replica of our village Balia bull, isn't Seema?"

"Don't worry, he won't be the husbandGod of us like the Balia Bull of your village cows," Seema buzzed with her trademark funny style coming closed to gawari and at a safe distance of Rabi.

Rabi was surprised, and he found ghungi Preeti hiding her smile with her thin red dupatta competing for a look of an innocent ladybug. Alternatively, he turned to smarty and told, "You naughty girls have no other work. Mostly engaged in all such rotten talks. This is certainly Seema's invention. From this year onwards, you must not stay in one room; I'll suggest your hostel warden. This is since you're now from different streams of studies," and jocularly added, "If I be the President of College Students Union, I'll enact a rule to ban two students from different branches of study to stay together in one room."

"So, I'm spoiling your sweet-heart, you mean to say," Seema cried. "Well, I'm a bad girl!" She slowed down, distancing—'Certainly reluctantly!'

"Sorry, I was joking, yaar! This is all part of play. We're so inseparable."

"Hey Rabi, what you told? You'll contest election! You'll be a bloody politician," cried Preeti—appeared almost melting. "Don't you remember what Prafullasir said in school—now-a-days, this has been the vocation of cheaters, frauds, criminals, school and college drop-outs, and all kinds of social refugees like Bishu Sarangi? Don't you remember what the famous political thinker George Bernard Shaw had opined—the politics is the last resort of scoundrels," Preeti shouted and threatened, "I'll complain to aunty, Kesabkaka and Karankaka."

"Preeti, what you observe aren't true in all the cases. There're people who practice honest politics. Of course, they're unfortunately very small in number and had been marginalized these days," Rabi tried to explain.

<hr />

They heard faculties, staff and students in the campus, all having the issue of the Pratap Rathi aka Big Bull at their mouths and talking, "Was there Prof. Panda as Principal, this Pratap Rathi, who was during his student days had lost the election measurable, wouldn't have dared to enter the campus, forget about his standing in front of Principal's chamber and talking about contesting the Students Union election."

"He is about to join politics, so using the college election in a premier college as a stepping stone— he has taken admission in PG Dept. of English at Revenshaw College and now planning to transfer to our college as he is facing strong opposition to his candidature there, taking advantage of opening of this branch this year in our college—he isn't for academic but for politics—is the college for study or for politics?—he is looked so aged, a mismatch in our campus—he has already joined ruling party—no, no, he is in opposition."

Back in the hostel, the second year Bachelor students were found debating the invasion of Rathi, "This year, there'll be no study—he'll destroy academic environment—he is so powerful and he has lot of money—he won't allow any other candidate even to contest and, this Principal, only crying for blessing of Lord Jagannath, mightn't dare to take a strong stand on this issue."

"Still, ... there is hope if a scholarly student contests!"

"These days, they've been shying away from college students union elections leaving the ground to bloody scoundrels. If one such student contest we'll all vote to him."

Rabi heard all these cried talks but didn't participate. He understood he was one of the natural targets of most of the debaters. Later, he walked away silently; but, however, he was seriously pondering over the issue.

'Now, I'm one of the who's who of the college, being established in the campus with all round performances.' Also, it came to his mind, 'Of course, there's a large section among the boys who nurse feeling of resentment for my most of the time accompanying their most sought-after girls: Miss BCS and Miss Smarty. And, similarly, there are girls who resent these two girls flanking me all the time.'

'This is a fact to reckon with!'

'But, what to do—they're so close to me and we're so inseparable?' Again, he consoled himself, 'Now onwards, as we'll be in different branches of study, we'll have different time-tables and we'll hardly get opportunities to move together.'

And another, the most motivating thought that forced him to evaluate the option of contesting the college election with due seriousness was, 'Contesting and winning the election has tremendous potential to give an image makeover to our village Pandupur.'

'Yes, this is! And I can make up the academic loss of first year in the second year as the university examination is conducted in the second year of graduation and the subjects that I'm taking have no practical. Let's keep the option open for a discussion with due seriousness first with the two girls and then with Kesabkaka, Karankaka and mama,' and he retired for the day.

Next day, in the college canteen, the issue had a lively presence. Majority of the students present in the debate were found dead against Rathi. Some were jeering, "A tau is contesting the students union election. The most unfortunate thing to happen to any college!"

"To keep this Rathi and his money and muscle out of the campus, a highly credible candidate with distinct performance in academic and extra-curricular activities and personal honesty needs to contest," one opined, as Rabi flanked by Preeti and Seema entered the canteen.

The trio paid their obeisance to their revered kaka, which had been one of their daily pious ritual, straight going to his throne, touching his feet, and heard in chorus, "Aushman and Aushmati Bhab-ba-ha," from Biju and his entourage seating around a table, debating. Everybody laughed. And Rabi requested, "Kaka, no special please," and heard, Lalu jeering, "What a generosity . . . . to bichara fellow-mates! Perfect neta types! Is he contesting against Rathi?"

The debate stopped . . . . Then again commenced with a rued comment from Biju, "Whatever, Rabi is the most suitable candidate; but . . . . ," he stopped for a while and poking fun with beauties, added, "he won't be allowed by his beautiful escorts. They're enjoying the life. Why should they enter the muddy water?"

The statuesque stunner was all attentive to the debate and as she walked close to the debaters they stood up, astound, and looked at her as if they were praying for grace from an arch angel, denied to them since long. A stunning silence rained over the venue with the stunning walking out of the girl from the who's who of the college to commoners, for the first time. None took their seat. As Rabi and Preeti followed Seema, the bears and monkeys were found fighting among them to offer their chairs. With the occupancy of the trio on the chairs, everybody took their seats albeit stunned, and hesitantly, debate started san Rabi and Preeti's active participations, who were found lost in buddhic musing—each having their own issue to cook.

'What's cooking in their mind? Are they not comfortable with we small people,' the debaters asked to themselves intermittently looking at Rabi and Preeti while Seema melted with boys passing pleasantly on the advent of tau in college politics.

Later, the topper went to Kesabkaka and both were found engaged in a close parley.

Kaka, a veteran of college politics having contested the students' union during his student days and later being in the back ground in every year election, opined, "Not a bad idea! Let's wait! Don't open the mouth on the issue till a consensus has emerged among the students on the gravity of the situation and types of candidate should contest."

But, the ghungi Preeti was found dead against the proposal as they gathered for parley along with their mentor later in the afternoon and she went on pulling, "We've come here to study . . . . not for dirty politics! All types of people will come close to Rabi, and try to 'charm' him. He'll be drifted away from the main purpose and from us," and with display of rejection, cried, "No, baba, no! I'm sorry, kaka. I'm dead against this proposal."

'For an unprejudiced lover, this is natural,' agreed the participants in them. Kaka smiled and caressing the cascading hair of the girl told, "She has a reason . . . . yes, this can't be simple ignored," and winking at the girl assured, "Again, I can say confidently that who's such a fool to lose such beautiful girl in favour of a roaming Femme Fatale or Supanakha?"

Seema, pushing a green fried mirchi into her nostril, sneezed in order to catch the attention of all. She teased Preeti with a huge show of displeasure directed at Rabi, and cuffing at kaka, told, "Am I not so beautiful? You've all praise for Miss Khandi Pandupur; Ooh sorry! Miss Pandupur; completely ignoring Miss Smarty from modern city Rourkela. Kaka, this isn't fair!"

Serious Rabi, in his effort to placate Preeti's apprehension, told, "Preeti isn't wrong in her observation," and confirmed looking at the deer eyes, "but, still I can assure her in the presence of revered kaka, there is no force in this world which could drift me away from my dear Preeti!"

"Wow! It is so! Let us make a Bhishma Pratigya!" Seema shouted and Rabi vowed keeping his hand on trio's on the sweet plate.

"And, together, I could plead to Preeti to see the reason in this opportunity for building a positive image for our village and inspiration for Pandupur tots. This is what our village needs, for an image make-over. Can we not do this much for our village?" Rabi appealed.

With the arrival of the "Gang of Four", Kesabkaka got back to his throne and the trio concentrated at the tea while watching the foursome talking something to kaka occasionally glancing at them.

"A large number of students and equal percentage of faculties were found dead against Rathi; yet, none was vociferous to oppose," observed the trio. Kaka was also having the same observation.

The debates on the invasion of the Big Bull in the campus went on and on for days ahead of notification for filing of nomination for the election.

"None is telling the truth! Why not tell the truth?" Preeti strongly resented and shouted, "Everybody is scared of Big Bull and his money and muscle power. And, he has political backing. Can Rabi be fit to fight him? Where is money and where is the muscle power?"

To her utter surprise, kaka, Seema and Rabi kept quite—'as if they had no fitting answers, and they were pretending her so far,' Preeti thought.

Meanwhile, Rekha reached the venue searching for Rabi.

She told, "Last night, daddy and SP were discussing, as per the police intelligence report if a scholarly student contests the election he can give a fitting challenge to Rathi, and to his money and muscle powers. My Rabi is a Topper and a good cricket player and has a good fan followings. So far as the muscle power is concerned, I assure my daddy and SP will take care. He is so happy with my Rabi. We all will donate whatever little fund will be required. And, we all will campaign for him. What more he needs?"

GHAR JAMAI

One fine afternoon, as Rabi was waiting to the girls standing at the entrance of Arts Block in the college on their way to hostel, a car jammed in front of him. He could recognize the car. The driver handed over an envelope and left to pick up the daughter of the First Family of city's Grand Road at the campus gate. The girl waved her hand.

'Should I destroy the letter,' he thought of as he recalled the occasion when a similar envelop from this girl had landed at his hand via the dim-wit Preeti, and the consequence of opening of that letter. And, in between, all that had happened . . . . He was in an impasse, yet holding the letter amid passing envious comments from the witnesses of the present delivery, "May be a party invitation! Open yaar . . . . read! Alas, what a good fortune? None is thinking about us. So unfortunate lot!"

While another applauded, "Topper yaar! He deserves. But keep it secure from . . . . !"

Seema coming from back snatched the envelope and Rabi heard yet another witness's forecasting, "Eeesh, buddu is cut red-handed!"

The message read:

Dear Rabi,

Hearty Congratulations!

Indeed, I'm sorry for this belated one. I was out of the station for a long time, on a business trip. And, your class mate, my daughter Ruby hadn't informed me. Anyway, our business is planning to felicitate the Topper of the our city college in a big way. I thought what could be the best occasion other than your class mate's birthday which is being celebrated tomorrow.

We've booked the Banquet Hall in Tosali Sand on the Marine Drive. You're cordially invited. Our car will pick up you at 7.30PM at the hostel gate. If so desire, you can bring your friends to give a company to my daughter.

Wish to see you tomorrow!

Mr. Naresh Panda

MD, M/s. Dash Transport

They read and handed over the letter to their mentor for his opinion.

He thought for sometimes before telling, "Well, let me think over this further . . . . We'll talk tomorrow."

"Felicitations, what's wrong in attending? Don't inform Rekha. You three together go. For your information, I've a friend working in the Tosali Sand. I've already informed him. And, I'm thinking of visiting the resort at that time," advised Kesabkaka and alongside warned the two girls, "Ruby may fume at the sight of you two girls flanking Mr. Topper to the venue, and so, this is left to Topper to manage the situation, a great responsibility and I'm sure he has the guts to take care of you with all sincerity during that testing time of your friendship. On the occasion, you three need each other. A calculated gambling!"

But, Preeti wasn't so happy and enthusiast. She wasn't convinced as the happening on Reshmi's birthday in DM's bungalow was still fresh in her memory and that she quoted. Kesab, caressing the little beauty, assured, "Preeti, my little girl, don't worry! You three are my dearest children; my soul! I won't allow my soul to suffer. My point is—know the world where you live in and know its people and manage them! There lay your future."

As expected, as soon as Rabi flanked by two elegantly costumed chic houris got down from the car at the resort gate, girlie Ruby along with her parents rushed to receive him. He was in no time skyjacked from his escorts.

The dewed-deer-eyes of Preeti stared at Seema in despair and Seema directed her to their HanumanGod, entering the restaurant in the resort. Seema told, "Kaka keeps his words. So caring! We're so lucky to get such a nice man in this hostile city."

"Thank God! We are saved," buzzed the dying Preeti.

There was a stunning, lavish arrangement with fairly medium gathering of city's who's who.

'For just a birth day, such a costly arrangement!' The gawari was abacked. Yet, she hadn't reacted like she did on past occasion, remembering the hard kicks of the uncompromising Seema walking within striking distance.

In fact, in the gathering, they two were the star attractions; in short, the stealers of the programme. They heard the invitees buzzing among them, "Who are these two girls? . . . . Are they from our city? From . . . . which sahi? Which lane? Which colony? We've never seen before? May be new arrivals to BCS!"

And there were no dearth of lecherous element as elsewhere. Of course, they weren't sneezing, growling and chattering; however, they are competing among them surreptitiously to catch the attention of beauties. They hanged around the houris in guiding them for cold-drink, juice, soup, and even some offering their own chairs to seat.

Seema whispered to Preeti, "Let's enjoy the hospitalities of high society's bears and monkeys. It seems here these creatures are civilized, isn't it Miss BCS?"

"Ooh yes, Miss Smarty!"

But, Preeti eyes' were running after her abducted heart-throb and his new escorts. And, to their utter discomfort they heard one guest jeering with another, "Is it Birthday Party or Ghar Jamai booking party?"

"Ooooh my God! Is it not Felicitations or Birth Day Party," gawari jumped crying. "What I'm hearing? Hey smarty . . . . act! Or else, Aunty will fire both of us. Don't forget—you've promised aunty, you won't allow her chand-ke-tukkuda to be a Ghar Jamai," Preeti murmured at the ear of Seema looking at the entrance of the hall their dependable guardian last seen. She prayed, "Where are you, our HanumanGod? Please rescue my aunty's chand-ke-tukkuda!"

They rushed closer to the captured Rabi. And as forecasted by their HanumanGod, Ruby fumed. Despite that, they were reluctant to vacate their position—the aunty's dewy eyes still fresh in their mind although they had full confidence on Rabi and his Bhishma Pratigya— by the side of Rabi.

Rabi with all sympathy to the girls rescued them with pretending oops, "They're uncomfortable in this gathering of mostly unknown people. I shouldn't have brought them. Anyway, since they've come as requested, it is better, they should be with us."

"Rabi, I propose you to contest for the President in the College Students Union election. I think you're the most suitable candidate against that goonda Rathi. And, Ruby is keen to contest as your running partner for Vice-President or General Secretary," Mrs. Dash advised.

But, Rabi kept quite, surprising all. His eyes were fixed at the entrance. Other's followed. They saw Rekha with DM entering the hall. Eyes caught eyes. Walking, ... running . . . . jumping portly replica of Supanakha landed at the epicenter in no time. She was burning.

And, she heard Mrs. Dash saying, "What do we not have? We would employ money and muscle power quite fitting to Rathi to fight the election."

The daughter of the VIP Road First Family's busted loosing no time, "Shhh . . . . what's the need of all these useless things? Rabi can win the election on his own; so much the goodwill he enjoys among the students. Besides, the district administration and college authority will certainly take care of the law and order."

Ruby couldn't hold her. She broke down and kicking the floor in disgust, shouted, "Ooh mummy! What's going on? Daddy has cocked up everything! Such a foolishness!"

The intelligent Seema thought further late might result in further complication of the situation and the possible collision between the two privileged kiddas embarrassing their dear and elegant DM uncle, and so she appealed tickling elephant tummy of Ruby, "Hello birthday girl! It seemed almost all the guests have come. Let's go for celebration!"

Ruby wanted Mr. Topper to be by her side but dismayed being deprived as Rekha pulled the boy to introduce him with the top honchos of city and district administration. And, here, Seema was insisting to go for celebration.

Mrs. Dash and Chairwoman, M/s. Dash Transport picked up the microphone and announced displaying a cheque book, "Dash Transport as part of its CSR programme announced a scholarship of Rs.500/— per month to this year Intermediate Topper of our city's premier BCS College and this will continue till he completes his Master Degree. And, I'm privileged to request Mr. Topper to collect the post-dated cheques for his Bachelor Degree and join the cake cutting with the birthday girl."

A big applause reverberated the gala hall and DM acclaimed shaking the hand with Mr. Panda, "Indeed, a good initiative! But Sir, I've a suggestion. Instead of donating this way, which may be considered a sympathetic gesture having bad moral implication on receivers, and so his or her self-esteem; if we, the generous alma mater of BCS, constitute an endowment for scholarship to bright and needy students of the college, it would do a far better service to our gurubhais, and ultimately, to the society."

"You're very right Sir! This is certainly a very good and innovative idea and we must propose to the college Principal to take the initiative," seconded the ADM while Mr. Panda was wordless. The members of Dash-Panda family were nervous, and worried lot as if their scheme frankensteined on them. They were plunged into a Catch-22 situation . . . . not found ways to get rid of it.

The two uninvited but still star attraction in the party were overwhelmed but not displaying. 'DM did the talking they wished to do!'

Still, the party had to move on. A nervous Mr. Panda perhaps felt further continuance of the parley mightn't do any good for his family's cause and he invited Ruby and her mates to cake cutting. The sulking

Ruby, surrounded by her eye-soring competitors, amidst their itching chorus—'Happy birthday to you!'—did the cutting, lifted the cake and searched—"Certainly, she was looking for the Topper," Seema buzzed at the ear of Preeti.

She took the piece of cake to her own mouth and left the venue to the surprise of the guests saying, "I'm sorry! Not feeling well!"

Mrs. Dash frowning at her consort, followed the birthday girl. And as Mr. Panda followed Mrs. Dash up to the car to see off, a guest lamented, "What a pathetic condition of bichara Ghar Jamai? A cursed life!"

"Ya-a-r, she has run away with the CSR cheques," shouted yet another, jeering.

After a good and satisfactory dinner in the absence of the irritating star host, the trio touched the feet of DM and boarded a taxi arranged by their HanumanGod instead of bothering the already disturbed bichara Ghar Jamai for the lift supposed to be provided to star guest, by the host.

On the way, the bubbly Seema opened her fun basket, puckering brow, "Mr. Topper would be a perfect bichara Ghar Jamai. Is not it, kaka? What a pity look of Rabi's would-be father-in-law?" She went on bubbling till she was elbowed by the overwhelmed and trumptic Preeti with all sympathy to her heart-throb.

"So, how is the party, children?" asked kaka sarcastically.

"No matter what, I had taken gup-chups, chicken soup, a full plate of mutton biryani, salad, kupta and prawn curry . . . . besides sweet rabbidi and ice-cream to conclude with. Nice and lavish arrangement! But, the bichara Preeti wasted her time hanging after her heart-throb, scared of overflowing Miss Femme and Supanakha," Seema commented.

However, Rabi had something else in his mind. He asked, "Kaka, I found Dash-Panda were completely bowled out in their own backyard. How all that happened?"

"I had glimpse of their game plan in advance, and accordingly, had discussion on the matter with DM," Kesabkaka told to the surprise of the trio and added, "Henceforth keep me informed every step that Ruby, Lalu and that Pratap Rathi take. Of course, I've my own networks. Further, we're now seriously thinking about your candidature to contest for the President in the College Students Union. But, the decision will be taken if you children are comfortable. But, I'm confident if Rabi contests he would certainly maul Pratap Rathi like he mauled the batsmen and bowlers on the crease. This is what the majority of professors of our college strongly believe, and also the district administration. Regarding yours security, you leave that to this bachelor. I may suggest the girls, why not you think to be running mate/s of Rabi for Vice-President and General Secretary Posts? Again, this decision is left to you. But one thing that I love to propagate that you three can be a formidable combination and can help build my dear college's image and the moral of the students—majority of them are very unhappy in the presence of Rathi—if you contest the election."

"If ghungi Miss BCS will contest I'm sure this beautiful jodi will constitute a formidable winning combination," cheered Seema and in no time heard, "No baba, no! I . . . . no way! Why do you Miss Smarty not join as running 'partner' of Rabi," and added with no loss of time as if she was dictated by an after-thought as always, "Mind, only to contest the election; nothing beyond that!"

Tipping kaka at his back, the boisterous Seema yelled, "Kaka, see yours this envious girl! With so much of condition; sorry, I'm not contesting."

GUINEA PIG

"**P**uri DM transferred to Kalahandi" and "Students will get concession for traveling in buses: State Government Cabinet ordered," read the headlines in the morning newspapers.

"Blessing in disguise!" the guardian announced unfurling the newspapers in front of Preeti who jumped up at the top of her ecstasy as she could see the scope of the end of Rekha's contemptuous overflowing over Rabi. The guardian concurred with her and told, "Patience pays! Has been proved!"

As they joined Rabi on their way to college, the overwhelmed Preeti wanted to celebrate over the news with him but to her surprise she found her heart-throb was silent and upset as if he wasn't in league with her. Yet, she curled with him, poked him, and told exploding, "Supanakha is finished! A great news for all of us."

Still Rabi was silent. No response. Suspense was all around. They were walking. Preeti as the last resort looked at her eveready guardian for her guardianly intervention.

"Well, we understand this will affect yours a secured source of earning. And, we'll be losing one of our major strength in this hostile city. At the same time, you shouldn't forget the unbearable posturing of the DM's privileged daughter towards your beloved— innocent and lovely Preeti. After all, you two have accepted to each other and it has become necessary on your part to consider the mental state of Preeti in front of overbearing, aggressive and hostile Rekha," the guardian told with judgment and added, "We may look for another source of income. There are plenty of such." And, she bubbled amusing, "If no sources is found out, we've the generous CSR Scholarship from Dash Transport. You've to just apply and accept their condition." And, the bubble in no time was hit with a heavy elbow from the frowning ghungi Preeti.

The two startling news were also found their lively presence in the campus as they were at the mouths of almost everybody.

"What happened? Mr. Mohanty is an able and efficient administrator—this year Rath Jatra passed on without any accident and the gruesome flood had been prevented due to timely and proper up-keep of river embankments and round-the-clock vigil—he has almost impacted his presence on the district administration within a few months of taking charge as DM and bureaucratic red-tapism has been minimized—he hasn't completed even one year of his tenure . . . . and transfer from Puri to Kalahandi?—Certainly, this is a punishment transfer; may be due to he is so strict in administration or not obeying politicians' or businessmen's unjust dictate. Or the government found it difficult to implement some of its dubious policies in the presence of an upright officer as head of district administration," the trio found the faculties, staff and students were discussing among them and were found highly disturbed too.

As the trio proceed further, they saw cheerful Ruby, who had almost eclipsed from the campus since that eventful night of her birthday party, getting down from the car along with Lalu.

"What a combination?" Seema murmured. However, the sight had a clipping impact on Rabi and Preeti. They were scarred.

In the meanwhile, they had reached the canteen and saw the 'Gang of Fours' deeply engaged in a parley with their admired Kesabkaka. As they got closer to the assembly, they heard, "There is certainly a hidden-hand working." The trio could notice, there was hardly any enthusiasm on the face of any member in the parley, and they were appeared as if they were clueless on raging issue and they were completely out-maneuvered.

"Hidden-hand! . . . . What's this, Rabi . . . . Seema?" Preeti asked in her characteristic style of suspense.

Kaka got up and told with heavy breath, appeared highly disturbed, "Children, now you go and attend the class. We'll seat in the evening or tomorrow morning."

They also didn't find Dr. Swati in her chamber and Rekha was missing in the campus.

Back in the hostel, Rabi noticed Biju was discussing with fellow mates in the hostel common room, "The government has announced the concession just on the eve of the colleges' Students Union elections which is nothing but an attempt to meddle in the college affairs.

The ruling party wants to plant its students' leaders in colleges' Students Union. And, the concession order has been made without clarifying many pertinent questions such as: modalities and services besides provisioning compensation to private transporters who are now running maximum services. This may lead to confusions, and unfortunate incidents necessiting politicians entering into campus politics so far has been very minimal in our state in compared to other states. I think, the future is going to be messy. Again, it seemed to me, this is a calculated move to cripple the powerful college Teachers Associations' grip over the students, campus, and educational administration in the state."

True to the prognostication of Biju, the next day's newspapers had headline news of students demanding concession clashed with bus staff and owners refusing to give concession at different places spread all over the state. At Puri too, there were reports of clashes between students and staff of buses running by the transporters including Dash Transport. Some students, who were travelling by bus and demanded concession, were roughed up by Dash Transport staff at Puri bus-stand.

Pratap Rathi, who was till yesterday struggling to get the students' attention and had managed a minuscule followings, was found by the trio surrounded by a large number of students, and he was arguing with faculties to stop classes as a protest over attacks on students.

However, Rabi and Seema entered the Arts Block and Preeti walked to Science Block ignoring the gathering.

"They're Toppers. Let them go! After all, they are the signatures of college," they heard from their back Rathi's followers jeering.

"Why? Will they not get the benefit of concession," asked another.

As the classes were found abandoned, Preeti walked to canteen, their common meeting point these days.

"The students had almost boycotted the classes. Even Dr. Jena's class," shouted Preeti in front of their revered Kesabkaka and lamented with pain and frustration, "This is for the first time during the last two years, I find Dr. Jena's class is boycotted, such a rahu has invaded the campus." And, she stopped . . . . as her eyes were found fixed at the sweet rack.

"Kesabkaka, have you started selling Salepur Rasogolla," asked Sasanka, who was following Miss BCS's of all her footfalls since her entry into the canteen, finding her eyes fixed at the rack and her greedy tongue running over her plump lips.

"No, no! This I've got for Preeti," Kesabkaka replied and added looking at the girl, "Preeti, I have forgotten to tell you. I would have given you yesterday. But, I was highly disturbed. Today, I've kept it on the display rack so that you won't miss. Rabi was saying, this is your favourite. I requested to one of my Salepur friend to send," Kesab told handing over the packet.

"See kaka, how caring is my Rabi? Thank you, kaka," and while receiving the packet told, "Kaka, will you not take? Let's share together before the two haughty have come. You know, Rabi won't allow me to eat comfortable although he told you my choice. He is always teasing and jeering me saying fasto. Am I fat? Tell me, kaka; am I really fat," Preeti pleaded unfolding her hand wide open—like flower opening its petals in front of honey bee—in front of her elderly kaka while bears and monkeys lecherously staring at her and coughing, sneezing and buzzing followed.

Kaka was disturbed and told self, 'So beautiful! Who won't stare at her? But, ... very childish!' And, he couldn't escape without consoling the little girl, "No, Preeti! Indeed, you're so lean and thin. Rabi is saying so because he loves you so much," Kaka attended with low voice.

"This is especially for you, three. I won't take. Recently, I'm detected little high with diabetes."

"Ooh my God! You've diabetes? So, kaka, you shouldn't take any root vegetables . . . . potato, yam, arum, etc. and sweets too," cautioned the girl and refused to open the packet, "If you won't take, I won't. Let's wait," and pleaded, "But, kaka, you'll take a small piece, at least to give us company."

In no time, the other two reached the venue and seeing the packet in Preeti's hand, Rabi shouted, "I know the fasto must have emptied the packet. We were searching her in Science Block, but she is here emptying kaka's canteen."

Soon the goal table confab started. The issues were such: DM's transfer, class boycott, students concession, students union election, students clashes with bus staff, Pratap Rathi gaining support, etc. Three along with their mentor seated around a table with rasogolla.

But, Rabi had something in his mind and buzzed, "Let's share the sweet with others. Preeti, you do the job. We are talking."

Kaka seemed not happy; however, he kept quite. Preeti was appeared shy and reluctant to perform the assignment that Rabi could guess, and, so he advised, "After all, we're friends. We're now in our graduation. We must . . . . you go!"

As Miss BCS went on distributing, there was a lot of enthusiasm among the boys. All the eyes were running after the beauty that the guardian eyes of Seema and Kesabkaka could notice.

'The sight was like an apsaraa distributing nectar to asuras.'

"Really great!" one acclaimed and put forward, "Preeti, why don't you contest the election? We swear, even if you so desire we'll swear by the name of Lord Jagannath to vote you. You're the most suitable candidate to fight against this Big Bull. Is not it, my friends?"

"Mahisasura Vs Durgatinasini Maa Durga! Hip hip hurray," cheered another.

"You're talking about me to contest? No baba, no! I can't be among you boys! Horrible," Preeti cried while offering the sweet.

"Why? If you can move around with Rabi, what's wrong with us?" growled a bear. And, this was too much to be acceptable to the guardians whose eyes were on track with Preeti's every footfall and ears at the every word pronounced by the boys. Seema instantly walked to Preeti's add, and that was enough to stop growling, chattering, jeering, humming, ... 'Her move understood!' A satisfied kaka applauded, "Perhaps, they're by mistake born to two different parents. So caring of each other!"

"Children, do you know, DM has been transferred because Ruby had insisted for it. She had made it a condition for her resuming the college. Rekha's frenzied behavior in the birthday party had messed up our plan. DM was very unhappy, and his family may shift to Cuttack. This is a big loss," Kesabkaka revealed in sorrow. And, he cautioned to remain highly vigilant.

"And, further, there is information that Rathi had forged his graduation mark to get P.G. admission in Revenshaw College before getting transferred to BCS. We are ascertaining this fact. If this is found correct, then Rathi is ruled out in the election."

"Kaka, we've heard that Rathi is organizing a students' march to Private Bus Owners Association Office tomorrow. Shall we join?" Rabi asked.

"Right, this is an important point. But, I want you to meet me tomorrow morning regarding this. From tomorrow till the class boycott is withdrawn, you two girls needn't come to college," advised Kesab.

"What??? Only Rabi will come? What are you talking, kaka?" Preeti cried and appealed, "No, no, not at all! If he comes, I'll come."

"And, I too," appealed Seema competing, and cajoling mentor for permission.

"But, let's wait and see to Ruby's next step," the confab was rounded up with Kesabkaka's advice.

Next day's newspapers were packed with news of students clashes with bus staff at different places all over the state. As the trio were entering the campus, they saw Pratap Rathi standing on the step of Arts

Block in front of a progressively larger gathering, and was rabble-rousing, "When our Government has made it a policy, who are these bloody transporters not to implement? Are they above the Government? The Central Government had got the concession policy implemented in the Railways. This is a welfare minded State Government's policy, which none of the previous Governments thought of for the welfare of the students under the pressure of profit-minded transporter. If the transporters won't follow the dictate of Government, we'll force them to fall in line. Let's go to bus-stand and board the bus without tickets. Let's see what they can do? We're in thousands and when put together for the whole of state, our strength is in lakhs. We're a big force! They're how much: hundreds, thousands . . . . not lakhs," and they heard, "Students Unity Zindabad! Students Unity Long Lives! Pratap Rathi Zindabad!........................!"

Rabi and Seema were appeared mobilized with eloquence of Pratap Rathi. They discussed among them, "Rathi, whatever he may be, is right! Since the Government has a taken a decision, it should have some good points for the students. Of course, there are scope of loopholes which can be dictated and rectified in due course of time of implementation of the policy."

Preeti trailing behind Rabi and Seema—on the first sight of her revered teacher, Dr. Jena talking to HOD Economics at the bike stand on the right side at the entrance—walked to them leaving her companions walking with fast-steps towards the gathering after paying their sincere obeisance to professors. She heard Dr. Jena jeering to HOD Economics, "So you've stolen my discovery. Intermediate Science Topper is now in your department," and heard from Economic professor, "Trend is such these days. Perhaps, Rabi is eyeing for Civil Services."

Later returning to the rabble-rousing, Dr. Jena yelled, "Here is a point. The Railway Concession Policy has been made and implemented by the Central Government. Why then this bus concession policy made by State Government has to be implemented by the students? And, unfortunately, the poor students are beaten up on the road by the hired goons of private transporters."

"Why do the students march to Bus Stand if at all the students are required to implement this policy? Instead, they should march to DM Office to petition demanding the implementation of government policy decision."

All of a sudden, for surprise of his audience, Pratap Rathi's rhetoric stopped and his reddish Gabbar Singh eyes were found jumped to the extreme back of the gathering. He descended from the step and walking to the Topper, as if he was waiting to him, and holding his hand, told with pouring sympathy, "Look at our friend, Rabi Pratap . . . . !"

Lalu Sarangi, forever searching for opportunity to bang on Rabi, jeered, "Title, Rabi himself even doesn't know! How could others? Ha . . . , ha . . . , ha . . . !"

"What's there in the title, friend? Let the small people talks the small things," Rathi shouted, as Rabi down his head with pain and frustration.

And, Pratap Rathi continued adorning the robe of mahatma, "He is a fatherless, and so poor. With the implementation of concession, he can manage his study travelling from his village on daily basis instead of staying in expensive hostel," and exhorted Rabi to join the march to bus-stand, raising his hand with display of camaraderie—the nation's politicians were well-versed in.

In no time, the rabble rouser mobilized the students to go for the kill.

Dr. Jena lamented, "I'm sorry to say, we're shortly going to hear a big fight between hapless students and the goons of private operators, and later students with police," that Preeti was attending seriously. "And this is exactly what Rathi wants to happen so that the students would be forced to look for a messiah— powerful with muscle power and money to provide lip-service—to lead them and he had gotten a golden opportunity to solidly entrench himself in the college campus prior to Students Union election, and later, in state politics contesting for state assembly membership from Puri. Now, who will stop the students? Even he is deviously made the Toppers part of this bloody hungama. And he must have planted some goondas among the marchers to throw stone on police barrack on their way to bus-stand." And, he advised looking at Prof. Das, "Let's prepare for long a vacation."

This had a shivering impact in Preeti. 'Frightened!' Her two buddies were in certain trouble. She looked at Dr. Jena appealing who could only advise, "Go and stop Rabi and Seema! That foolish girl has also gone."

'Yes, what could Dr. Jena at best do when such a Big Bull is in the prowl,' Preeti confined and told to her, 'Only Kesabkaka could save her friends. Bull to bull!'

She rushed to the canteen and saw their HanumanGod was busy over phone. On seeing her, he moved his face away from her, it seemed to Preeti. Whatever she wanted him to attend to her but found him not obliging. 'Is kaka avoiding? No, it can't be . . . . He is angry . . . . Yes, he should be! We haven't taken seriously his advice,' Preeti told to her. She pleaded like a grandchild to grab the attention of grandpa and tried to pull the telephone receiver in vain as kaka again moved his face away from her along with the receiver.

She stopped as she heard her kaka started blasting someone, "Sir, we've information that Rathi's admission in your college prior to transfer to BCS is based on a forged mark sheet. Ergo, either you declared Rathi's admission null and void or get ready to face legal action under IPC. Prior to this, I advise you to stop Rathi leading a morcha of innocent students against PBOA immediately. There is possibility of clash between students and PBOA goons. And I have sure-short information that he has pre-planned this. If this happens you know who will be in trouble first. I won't spare you for your collaboration in getting a criminal admitted in BCS. Now, I believe, you understand my pain to call you from this distance. You can only stop Rathi. Act or get lost! The decision is in your court."

"Note: if anything happens to my college students, this bachelor won't spare you, whoever and whatever you may be!"

He banged the receiver and shouted looking at the girl, "Where are your friends? Have you people forgotten what I've suggested just yesterday?"

Preeti wanted to request kaka to rescue her friends but couldn't speak a single word being on the line of fire. She pulled back . . . . and back till she hit a chair and dropped down sobbing, crying and murmuring.

"Hey Bhagaban, Didi is crying!" Chottu screamed. The oldie snot-nosed melted and walking to the little girl and caressing her frizzy-free hair, informed, "Just wait! They'll be back here very soon, unharmed. But don't repeat this kind of foolishness."

Preeti lifted her head as if she got her life back; she got up, looked at her kaka and embracing him requested, "We should go, kaka! We shouldn't waste time, to rescue them!"

"Don't worry! Rest assure; nothing will happen! I had prior information on the morcha format, and I've planted my people to guard these two fools. Now that bloody Rathi will hide like a rat. He must be searching for a hole," Kaka cheered.

Chottu, hanging around with a very few eaters in once highly busy canteen, murmured, "Idiots Big Bull has spoiled the business of the day, and probable, for the week." He sat down by the side of the girl as soon as Kesab vacated the position and whispered, "Didi, you get into the store room and hide there, and see how I'm pulling Rabibhai and Seemadidi to crying."

"Ooh yes, why not? Good idea! Let's fool Mr. Topper and Miss Smarty—they're always branding me dim-wit," the excited gawari exulted and clapping her hand with Chottu eclipsed inside the store room and switched off the light.

That was matter of a few minutes. She heard kaka firing at Rabi and Seema, "I like to slap you. You're so foolish," and heard a slow duplicate voice from inner room, "Slap! Slap!" All eyes moved towards the dark room, and later to two girls' gossiping and laughing by the side of inner room—searching . . . . and Seema asked looking at Chottu, "Who prompted? She must be Preeti."

"Where is Preetididi? She hasn't come here since morning? Hey Bhagaban, you have left her to Big Bull and Kaaliram. They must be breaking her bones. Or, the mosquitoes may be socking her blood! What kind of friends you are? How could you come, leaving her behind," Chottu chided while Kesabkaka—keen to be part of the child's game—substantiated the twosome's worst fear by walking fast to the parked bike displaying unhappiness, and gesturing to go for search.

Rabi and Seema landed at each other's piercing eyes, and Rabi cried, "Oh shit! Where she would have probable gone? She is such a big burden on us!"

Still, Seema had doubt, she walked towards the store room; but stopped short of further pushing and screamed, "No, no . . . . this room is so dark! The pigeon-hearted can't hide here! Rabi, let's go and check where is your mama's little girl?"

"No, no! I've seen her following the rally," Chottu told.

And, in the meantime, they heard mosquito thrashing slaps. Seema looked at Chottu, who announced turning to store room, "Maa Durga Durgatinashini badharrahia!"

Preeti emerged from her hiding, crying, "Ooh Jhansika Rani! If I'm pigeon-hearted, if I'm a big burden, what you are? Thank kaka! It is for him, you're rescued today! Or else, that PBOA's goons would have grinded your bones by now."

As the teased Preeti tried to attack Seema, she shouted, "Rabi, see how many red spots on the face of your sundari. Mosquitoes had feasted upon her beauty."

"Really," cried the girl running to the basin mirror. "This is all because of this Chottu."

"No, no! This is because of you dim-wit. Why blame other?" Rabi told checking the face of Preeti. "God knows, when will you be matured?"

"She has been matured since the start of her once-in-a-month problem," whispered Seema at the ears of Rabi, and instantly got thrashed. "Always playing!"

The tuition session started on the round table with revelation by Kesabkaka, "Pratap Rathi, by the time you reached PBOA office, would have vanished. Isn't it?"

"Courtesy my dear kaka," prompted Preeti to the surprise of Rabi and Seema.

"On the way to bus-stand, some elements from your morcha might have thrown stone at the Reserve Police barrack's guard," Kesab continued and added, "before you reached your destination, somebody must have whispered on Rathi's ear something that had frightened him and after that he must have told you, 'the loyal foot-soldiers marching to usher an epoch making revolution'—there's an urgent call and I'm just coming—and that's all. He didn't come back leaving you orphaned. Am I right? And you abandoned your morcha out of fear being informed by an unknown person that the goons are waiting to feast on your bone, blood and flesh with sticks and rods."

"This is how our nation's leadership works. And you people follow such elements without applying your minds. This is happening every now and then, and everywhere; still nobody learn anything; and history is going on repeating. This is nothing but momentary euphoria of masses. And, our leaders are very competent to exploit this."

Rabi and Seema downed their heads like two kindergarten tots under fire whereas Preeti was euphoric and was pushing kaka to act. A punishing silence descended on the venue for a while. None of the two offenders of mentor's advice had guts to open their mouths.

"Kaka, you're only saying, not doing anything. Slap these buddus!" The little girl took the right hand of kaka to heat at Seema saying, "How this is Maa Jhansika Rani?" And she twisting her Rabi's ear, screamed, "Say sorry to kaka and to me. Mind, or else, I'll write to aunty!"

And little later kaka opened the pages of BCS College Madalapanji:

"A couple of years ago, such a candidate had contested unsuccessfully for the President of the College Students Union and defeated measurable. Do you know the reason? Previous to that he was General Secretary and during his that tenure he tried to hoodwink the students of college but was exposed. He had organized a students' movement to occupy the adjoining Bhoot Kothi land, an eyesore to all the stakeholders of our college which is running short of space for expansion. As you know a legal case is pending on the ownership title of the land; and since long nobody is staying there. He harangued the students against the state government, district administration and college Principal for showing no interest to occupy the land and kothi. He persuaded a group of students and lead them akin to what Rathi did today for a forceful takeover of the land and the building on behalf of the college so that he could comfortable win the next year election for President beating the anti-incumbency effect. But before the students reached the Bhoot Kothi, he got the information that there were goondas with lethal weapons planted by the disputed owners to thrash the students. And he withdrew him exactly the way Rathi did today leaving the already emotionally charged students to face the challenge who got thrashed. This time this man has the blessing of a big political party and its top leader in the state. But, still, he is caught on the wrong foot."

"He must have engaged his man among you to throw stone on Reserve Police barrack while passing through that on the way to PBOA office with objective of irritating them so that in a skirmish between the students and bus operators' staff and their hired goons, the police force, which subsequently be called for restoring law and order that might necessitate use of force, would be by the side of bus owners inflicting maximum injuries on students paving ways to politicians to interfere, and subsequently, hijack the students leadership. This was exactly what happened sometimes back at an engineering college in Western Orissa where about eleven innocent students lost their lives. This is nothing but a political game our political class merrily plays. Therefore, you educated are expected to apply your mind."

"Don't be a 'Guinea Pig' in the hands of feudal minded politicians."

"And, you two Guinea Pigs are rescued due to my kaka's timely action. Am I right kaka," Preeti acclaimed elbowing Rabi at his waist.

"Hey gawari, when you become so intelligent? Stop puffing up! You fasto will burst. Don't forget that you dim-wit would had been with us but for your fear," Seema shouted down Preeti, and later turning to kaka requested, "Kaka, let's go for a matinee show at Laxmi Talkies. Film 'Love Story,' kaka very interesting film."

"And, a very interesting escapes! Am I right, Miss Smarty? Kaka, see, how she's trying to divert your attention," Preeti jeered.

"Very smart!" Kesab laughed poking the chin of Seema and added, "This is a film for you . . . kids; you go and enjoy. I'm an old man . . . . an odd man among you," Kesab tried to recede pushing a pan pack into his mouth, and ordered handing over a hundred rupee note to Chottu, "Chottu, go to book three balcony tickets for my children. Tell that counter boy my name, he will get tickets at a good place for comfortable viewing."

But, he had to surrender as Preeti demanded, "No three, four tickets! Mind, if kaka isn't going, I won't go," and added, "kaka, you know whenever we're going to see movies in your city, loafers are almost after us passing very lewd comments. We wanna see this film but . . . ."

"Is it? You should have told me before! Today, I'll set those sasuras right. How could they dare to disturb my children?"

In the intermission, kaka was found engrossed in a deep thought.

'Very interesting film, but kaka is silent,' the children asked to them looking at their kaka.

Preeti shaking kaka and dropping his head on his chest told cajoling, "Kaka, you aren't looked happy . . . . ?"

Kesab couldn't resist, and breaking his silence, bombed, "Where is the commitment? Where is the sacrifice? People drops tears while reading novels, and viewing dramas, theatres and films. Now-a-days, LOVE has been restricted in writers' fictions and in these film scripts. Beyond these, there is no LOVE . . . . 'only crocodiles tears!' And, the sacred institution of LOVE has become the convenient time-pass! Making LOVE and refusing that at easy has become a fashion."

"However, I've full confidence on our 'Romeo and Juliet'. They'll be classic example of successful LOVE," Seema proclaimed poking at Juliet's lion waist.

"But, there is no LOVE without tragedy! Tragedy gives opportunity to test the sanctity of LOVE between two hearts, souls, establishing their relation. To overcome the tragedy, there is the need of commitment and sacrifice," Kesab told triggering pain in the heart of the self-assumed traitor of LOVE and she asked to her, 'Am I doing right by hiding my papa's hidden agenda from Rabi, aunty and my well-wishers? Certainly not! I must reveal whatever be the consequence.'

"May I request you all to spare sometimes? I've some points to tell—I'm sorry—I have hidden from you for so long," and she cried with tear in her deer eyes. Seema—who could guess what was gonna be told?—caught hold of the self-assumed traitor, giving her strength.

"Okay, my little daughter! Don't worry, I'm there. If you're committed and ready to sacrifice there's always a way out, may be a tricky one," consoled Kesab.

As they gathered at a sea-side eatery after the matinee show, Preeti tried to speak but couldn't proceed as her throat got choked. She was found highly disturbed. Seema took over and revealed, "She is extremely sorry to Rabi, aunty and all her well-wishers, and beg pardon for not revealing till date them what's there—she knows—in the mind of her parents. Her parent are dead against Preeti's future relation with Rabi, who doesn't have social recognition, although they've taken the lead role in getting Rabi and aunty social space in the village. They did that with the selfish purpose of using the mother-son for Preeti and her siblings' education. But, one aspect is very clear that they trust Rabi for his personal integrity, and this is the reason why they allowed their daughter to mingle with Rabi and accompanied to Puri for college education."

And the love-struck girl cried resting her head on the chest of her dear kaka and added, "But, that doesn't matter to me as I know what my Rabi is; and my aunty is. Whatever, I don't see my existence without Rabi! I'll die; I'll die if he's denied to me!"

Kaka looked at Rabi and Rabi went on saying, "I know our union won't be so easy. This is the reason why I had tried to convince Preeti—we would rather remain good friend if not partner in life but she's so immured . . . . Yet, I'm committed! I'm ready to go to any extent. And I believe my mama would be with my decision."

"That's a good boy and a good girl," cheered the lovelorn but bubbly Seema and putting Kesabkaka's right hand on Romeo's head and left on Juliet's requested overflowing, "Kaka tell, 'God bless the jodi! Aushman and Aushmati Bha..ba..ha!' Whoop, what an auspicious moment?"

"Children, I'm very happy! I enjoy your company. You're so playing and interesting," ecstatic Kesab revealed and taking breath with pause added, "Let's hope for the best!"

The provident had such a design that a few minutes hadn't gone, two intoxicated rahus descended at the venue from nowhere with their filthy tongues, "Wow, Kesab! You've got two apsaraas flanking you like that 'old Gandhi!' Being in the college campus, you've a big advantage. Book these girls for your birthday. Only the drinks, you have been offering, are boring. Let there be something special. Let's celebrate with beauties this year!"

"What yaar! At this age, you decided to break your Hanumanhood," jeered with a knuckle one of the two, following.

Children downed their heads and Kesab couldn't look at the children. He was munching his teeth like the Pandu's son pahalman Bhim when Draupadi was losing her costumes to the evil hand. He stood up as he was later fired with verbatim, "Sorry yaar! We've caught you at the wrong time. We're leaving but request you to spare these girls to us for at least one night," and each one was hit with one each fisticuff strong enough to knock them down and bleeding profusely and were loaded in a cab to hospital.

He took the children in a cab to drop them in hostels in the heart tearing silence that they never had in the past when they were together. There were no cracking of jokes, no body-poking and frowning. Children could notice their kaka was completely demoralized and broken.

"My past won't allow me to live in peace," they heard their so strong and so bold kaka was murmuring and crying like a child.

As the cab turned to VIP Road, Seema directed, "No, please! . . . . Drive straight to kaka's house."

"Children, please leave me to live my cursed-life! . . . . I'm a gone case," he screamed with dewy-eyes.

As soon as the cab reached the kaka's address, two girls guided their kaka when Rabi paid the fare and asked the driver to leave despite the throat chocked protest, "Children, how you will go?" and he got the answer when Seema requested over phone to Miss Warden, "Madam, we are staying in Kesabkaka's house tonight. He isn't well. We may kindly be allowed."

The cursed kaka tried to persuade the trio, "Bacchoo, this is a very complicated world. People are so cruel; they can't see the good but can notice . . . . They enjoy gossiping bad thing. They will bad-mouth which may affect you and your social status. You've a future!"

"Kaka, don't tell these sermons which we know. We'll stay with you so long as we wish. We don't bother for what other say. We bother for our kaka and that's all," the statuesque stunner told uncompromising and two girls soon found engaged in house-keeping and Rabi went for marketing.

Kaka laughed for the first time since the evening incident breaking his crying silence as the two pretty girls burned their hands trying to cook, and cried, "We're so unfortunate, we can't cook something for our dear kaka."

He joined and all four found cooking their dinner with the tuning of music from tape-recorder fitted with one after another of Seema's choice modern disco songs, Preeti's choice bhajjans and Rabi's choice "Zindagi ka safar . . . ." competing.

"You'll certainly be in trouble in your in-laws house," Kesab forecasted. "You haven't yet learned even how to fire the gas chulla and placing utensils over that, forget about cooking on cow-dung cake fired oven."

"I am sure, I won't have any problem. My aunty is so caring," the overwhelmed Preeti sung but couldn't complete as she was kicked at her feet by her aunty's son and heard, "Apply your mind! Don't puff up at least in the presence of . . . ."

"Kaka, when is your birth day," Seema asked. A pin-drop silence rained for the moment. Children were searching answer from kaka looking at his face while he was trying his best to avoid pretending as if he heard nothing with jingling noise of utensils. Whenever any one of them asked repeatedly, he crashed the utensils with one another making noise. But for how long? Sweet, sweet mouths were so bolshie. As they seated around the dining table with ringleting aroma of fried rice, dal, chicken curry and chutney, the question was repeated by Preeti who was known for initiating eating whenever they had gathered in the past.

But, to the surprise of all, Kesab initiated, "I'm hungry. It's too late. I can't wait." He was in an artificial hurry—felt the trio, sure of fact. He didn't look at others and about to lift a handful of fried rice mixed with dal. Yet, he failed and told, "I'm a good cook. Enjoy the foods when they're hot. My little girl's chutney is 'The Best'. Hey smarty, taste your favourite fried rice. Yaar topper, your favourite chicken curry? Chicken is full of bones! Shall I remove them for you; your mama must be doing for you. Take in small size or else it will chock your throat." And, instead, he got his throat chocked, and he dewy-eyed.

"Kaka, we're sorry, if we have hurt you," Preeti appealed and kaka found the trio were equally crying. He announced, "Sorry children, from this year onwards, I've decided not to celebrate that cursed day!"

"You mayn't celebrate but you can't prevent us to celebrate our kaka's pious birth day," spoke the trio in chorus. While picking out stick bones from chicken pieces to feed the little mouths, he repeated, "Children, just see, I'm a gone case, a spoiled one! Why should you spoil your image being with me? What has happened today may keep on repeating. Ergo, I request you . . . ."

But, he found his appeal had no takers.

FEUDOCRACY

"Goddamnit! I can't believe, he could be so self-seeking! Even, before he asked we proposed him to campaign for him and for his running partners. But, he and his two proud beautiful escorts—'so sure of their win now!'—have declared their candidatures even without informing us," next day morning, as Rabi was entering the hostel room, heard his room-mate Biju talking to a small gathering of class-mates.

"Why not? They're now toppers, beautiful and charismatic. They're now who's who of the college," Biju feeling cheated and hurt lamented and after a short pause told, "I know, our country has no dearth of politicians who simple forget their vote-banks after the election. But, here is a guy who surpassed them even before being elected!"

"Well, why he shouldn't when the deck is cleared with Pratap Rathi's apparent withdrawal? Politics is such, the profession of scoundrels! How could he be an exception," tick-tacked Sasanka aka tickle boy.

And, Lalu Sarangi passing-by the room doorsill taunted, "What one can expect from a gutter? Ha . . . ha . . . ha . . . . ! This just a beginning; the worst is yet to come! You people will be proved a Big Fool one day."

The cool, calm and humble Rabi walked to Biju and announced with all sympathy, "If what you alleged is found true, take for granted that I'm not contesting.

Now, are you happy? Please don't disturb me. I haven't touched the books since yesterday with this bloody Big Bull issue. You know that HOD (Economics), Prof. Das is very top and uncompromising." In one stroke, the topper calmed down all and got the room vacated.

But, hardly he had settled down for his study, he heard a mild buzz in the veranda. Still, he ignored.

"What's a surprise, ya-a-r? Miss BCS and Miss Smarty have been so please to grace this bachelors' castle so early in the morning," lecherous tickle boy keeping his left hand inside his left trousers pocket—and never shy of acknowledging whenever questioned by friends—tickling and tick-tacking, jeered.

Biju peering at Rabi drawing aside the door curtail, jeered, "Bichara Lalu, why are you going? You've already been rejected . . . . However, keep on trying! What's wrong in trying? Godblessyou!"

And, they heard from inside the room, "Biju, what were you talking? That declaring candidature? Withdrawal of Big Bull? What are these?"

"Yaar Sasanka, hark here . . . . this gentle man! What he is talking? As if he knows nothing! Rabi, have you not yet understood? Or simple fooling us? This morning, I had been to college ground for jogging and I found the entire campus is flooded with posters and banners with your photographs, flanked by yours ever accompanying two beauties, announcing yours candidatures for President, Vice-President and General Secretary," Biju screamed.

"What? Who has done this?" Rabi shouted jumping up of the study chair and asked, "Ooh, may be for this the two girls have come?"

"My good friend, please tell—where you three were yesterday night? You must have done it yesterday along with that veteran Kesabkaka. These days you've become so shrewd. You're now no more that yesteryear's shy gawar. You've very cleverly got a veteran to work for you," Biju taunted.

The tickle boy tick-tacking told. "Whatever, first you go and rescue your sundari escorts from luring tongue of Jambuban."

And, the trio walked to the visitors' room near the hostel gate.

"Preeti and Seema, why don't you contest in the election for President and Vice-President independently? You've such personality! Is not it a shame to be a running partner of an urchin, an unrecognized boy," Lalu was found advising to the girls, the trio heard as they're approaching the visitors' room. "What you are? And, he is? He is using you girls to get social recognition. Don't be the stepping stones for a social outcast palling your image. This I may suggest."

"Thank you, thank you very much Mr. Lalu . . . . Sarangi for your voluntary goddamnit solicitation," Preeti snapped and subsequently advised, "You can be a good 'whatisthatcalled?' a Solicitor-General without a black coat."

"Besides, you'll be a fitting running partner of Miss Gem-Ruby. Why don't you contest? Am I right friends," jeered Preeti.

Everybody laughed but Rabi. And Lalu, being isolated, left the room murmuring something that deserved to be ignored.

"I'm sorry Preeti, I'm not at all that happy with your this type of coarse talks," the humble Rabi not so happy with the comment of Preeti, advised her in despair.

"If you aren't happy, why don't you stop your good friend Jambu . . . . sorry Lalu, not sparing any opportunity to abuse you," the aggressive Preeti, known for her celebrated shyness, instantly got him back. They entered into an argument.

"Do you think that Lalu deserve Rabi's attention?" Seema shouted turning to Preeti.

"How many times shall I tell you, this is my problem? Why you're so disturb? Why you girls poking your noses in this non-issue and unnecessarily buying enemies for you in this 'not so girl's friendly society?' Nothing but privileges' arrogant indulgences! Again, how long he'll do? Despite all his bad-mouthing how many class-mates are with him and how many are with me? And, are you not with me?" the humble boy shouted, and directed, "You go and concentrate in your study. Whatever is there we'll talk on the way to college. Heaven won't fall in just few hours," and reminded, "Have you forgotten our resolve that during morning and evening study hours there will be no non-academic discussion?"

"Besides, mind, at least in my presence don't use coarse words to anybody. Now, get lost!"

And, turning to Seema, he requested, "Seema, you too, can go now. Let's concentrate in study, yaar! You know yesterday was completely lost. We shouldn't drift away from the prime objectives for which we're here. Other things will follow! The economics subject is very top, yaar! Besides, Prof. Das . . . . not-sparing!"

And, Biju reasoned, "Preeti, you're a learned girl. You know what has happened to Panchali in epic

'The Mahabharata'. Had she not been arrogant and overarching for her beauty and high family lining, the destructive disaster wouldn't have been visited the great and illustrated Kuru family. Rabi is right when he says our is not a girl's friendly society, you must co-operate him. Don't be crazy and emotional, I may suggest."

"I'm sorry; I'm sorry! But what I can do? I can't stomach all those abuses directed at Rabi," Preeti cried while flushing self out of the room like an obedient Hindu house-wife to the command of her husbandGod scripting a scene to be envied by the beholders and Biju murmured, "Rabi is so lucky. What a beautiful jodi? Heaven will envy!"

"Whoop, how could bichara Lalu resist?" the tickle boy yelled.

"This is just a prelude. He'll leave you high and dry. One day, you'll be nowhere," Lalu soothsaid to the departing girl at the entrance.

Preeti hissed, "Shut up, bloody, stinking mouth! This is between me and m . . . Rabi, who are you?"

"Tell, 'My Rabi', yaar, ... clearly! Why you're so shy of telling the truth? We all know and recognize," the tickle boy tick-tacked.

Again, returning back to the visitors room, she reluctantly begged running her eyes from her heart-throb to Seema to Biju to tickle boy, "Shall I go?"

"No, no, don't go; stay here and munch our heads," screamed the disturbed Rabi and asked to Seema considering, "Since you've come, tell, what for you have come to here? . . . . is it for that posters and banners issue?"

"Sorry, I'm not contesting," Preeti snatched from Rabi and told, "I'm going. I won't go to college till the date for nomination papers filing has gone. If my mama will come to know that my photos are postured and bannered on the college wall along with Rabi she would straight call off my study and luck me in the house barn."

She ran to her address amid the jingling song of her nupurs on the envious ankles along with tick-tacking from tickle boy's pocket.

"Let's see Miss BCS, ... who . . . . is . . . . not going? I know Baba Shiva and Maa Parbati can't be separated," Biju jeered. "Hark, I warn, Femme will have her field day in your absence."

"If neither Preeti nor Seema is contesting along with you, you'll be a big flop," Sasanka forecasted tick-tacking.

Rabi turned to the forecaster and smiled, rejecting. Still, the forecaster wasn't relenting.

"Dear Sasanka, what do you mean? Do you think I'm so mean to use my girl-friends like politicians using their wives and sisters besides hired beauties from film industry for voters attentions and electoral benefit? Do you think my relationship with Preeti and Seema is for so mean end? How could this come to your mind? Is it because I'm born to a widow? I am branded by privileged society 'an urchin, a guttersnipe and whatnots!' I'm sorry to say, this is one of the most unfortunate thinking of you people," fired back Rabi in no time and further added, "I would rather enjoy defeat if at all I contest, which hasn't been decided yet, without my two dear friends as running partners. And, regarding their participations in the election, the choice would be their only," and added, "I vow before you, if I alone contest I won't use my two dear companions to campaign for me. I assure . . . . still, I can win; I'm confident! I am saying so because I trust my friends and my well-wishers."

"Rabi, first of all, we have to identify who are the people involved in posturing and bannering? And what's their intention," Biju suggested and Seema wanted, "Let's lodge complain in Principal's office."

As they entered the campus, they were astonished to see their photos so beautifully designed, postured and bannered all around the campus. The boys and the girls were all found celebrating. Some of them found carrying the individual photo posters of their choice dreamboat or dream girl and talking, "Great relief! The Big Bull, tau ran away like a rat."

While another acclaimed, "Thank God, we could now say our friends in other colleges: not tau but 'Topper and Beauties' as our Students Union's President, Vice-President and General Secretary. These days, this is very rare. We can proudly say so. This will improve our college image."

And, they heard the students were declaring as they passed them, "We'll certainly vote to these teen murti!"

Also, the morning lamenting of Biju in the hostel was found re-run by his friends' and well-wishers necessitating them to give numerous clarifications. Some satisfied and some refused to buy, saying, "Politics *may essay hi hota hay!*"

But, the question of Dr. Jena hurt the trio hard.

"Yes, for this you Rabi and Seema have left Science stream. You know very well that I wouldn't have allowed you any relaxation. I had a great career expectation from you trio. Extra-curricular activities—sports, cricket, song, debates, quiz, events management, etc. are okay but not the bloody politics." And, he declared, "You're finished! Very soon you will be hawked by the political vultures."

And, later turning to Preeti, he directed, "You follow me. Leave these two gone cases!"

They appealed to their revered teacher to listen but got refused. Despite trimming and rejection, the humble students followed their affectionate teacher and closest with him in his chamber.

And they heard at their back a few senior murmuring, "Dr. Jena thinks all the good students should study Science, as if Arts and Commerce courses are meant for rejected of the society and have no significance in the human society."

"He is so proud of his faculty of study. This is nothing but intellectual bankruptcy!"

"No, this is all because Science and Technology have overtaken the maximum developments these days."

In the launch break, along with Biju as the trio gathered in the canteen, their dear mentor explained, "This is the beginning . . . . certainly the handiwork of any political party's 'so-called!' students wing. Other will follow with their offers. Soon, we'll know—'it's just matter of time!'—who are involved? They're now sure of you trio could be good winning combination.

Rathi's emergence from nowhere was a blessing in disguise which had created a favourable pitch polarizing students in favour of quality candidates to contest and his eclipse so sudden from the scene would ensure their win."

"If you'll lodge a complaint against the yesterday's posturing and bannering, those idiots will lay low for a while and re-surface with fabulous offers just two days or three days before the election or if they find you're still not co-operating then after the election . . . . certainly. And if you won't lodge complain, they would approach you or invite you for discussion with this or that support within one or two days. Funding would follow. And the most important is: their agents will run after you for their commissions. Even they can go to the extent of threatening and using force which needs a lot of mental strength on the part of you to fight them. They can hire hooliganic elements from among the students to stand against you in case of your non-cooperation as per their wish."

"You might ask why so? Reasons are: you're good orators. You're talented. And above all, you're glamorous. And, you've personalities and physical characteristics, which matters much in our country these day. You could be tomorrow's cult figures and be utilized in general politics in future. Today's voters have become increasing fade up of these old Gandhi capped politicians and now looking for new personality, traits and characteristics in their leadership. The clever oldies in politics are well-aware of this latest development, and so devised a new political maneuver that would help them retain the control over the political affairs in the country remaining in the background. And, they might not hesitate to harass your parents and near and dear if you don't yield to their pressure! The time will come when you, moralistic and ambitious and wish to do something for the society and nation would neither leave them nor live with them, and one day you'll be one of them."

"Ours' is a 'so-called Democracy!' Or rather I would say a 'Feudocracy!' in which our colonial era desi Feudal Lords retained their grip over the nation's governance through a cleverly designed electoral mechanism in which they've got them elected ligitimising their ruling in the increasingly democratized world. They were the people who were the backbone of British Raj. As soon as they became sure of feringhees were leaving the Indian shore, these people adorned the Gandhi Cap and overnight became ardent 'so-called' Gandhians."

On the way to hostels, there was no usual gossiping, joking and mocking. They were completely immured with the thought provoking 'master talks' of their mentor—recalling, evaluating and analyzing his opinion word by word, sentence by sentence, thought by thought.

Next day, the overjoyed Preeti, adorning new clothing, had just reached their hostel gate followed by Seema to join her heart-throb on their way to college, she was ambushed with a strange site. She found a white sari clad lady, sitting in a hooded rickshaw, was jeering with a familiar tone to her gent's co-passenger, "Is this girl our laadlee—little girl?"

"Appeared so! . . . . Ye-e-s, she looks like her. Let's get down and check," the gent's co-passenger again with a familiar tone jeered.

Preeti was now sure of her aunty and Karankaka's eminent presence—uninformed and sudden—, started shuddering as she was in the Seema's advised and her heart-throb's appreciated boyish costume—that she knew her aunty disliked and even aunty had let know her dislike to Seema during her last visit to Pandupur. And, she checked as she suddenly felt her boobs not cooperative and seemed overflowing naughtily although she wore a tight bra under the T-shirt. She quickly checked her bra hooks pulling herself to back of the pillar and found they were intact.

'Shall I get back to room quickly and change the dress,' she thought. Yet, she couldn't move, the after-thought prevented, 'What the so-dear aunty and Karankaka shall feel if I run away for whatever reason without attending them?' She was stunned and standstill till Seema interrupted her shouting, "Arre, our dear aunty and Karankaka! What a blessing? Preeti, ooh my God—you're still standing? Come on; welcome . . . . !"

But stop short of pushing Preeti as she could too understand the dilemma of the most obedient and humble girl.

"Aunty, you know, there was heavy rain while we were returning to hostel yesterday. And, her other two pair of dress were so dirty and stinking as she wasn't able to clean them because of class load. I suggested her why not wear for a day my dress. This is better than missing the class for the day. Frankly speaking, she wasn't interested. She is your so obedient little girl,"

Seema clarified unasked as the aunty and Karankaka walked close to them and they were paying their pious obeisance touching their elders' feet.

Aunty moved her eyes all around and running a quick stare at the smiling Karan told, "I don't think Lord Indra had graced this town during the last one month. If he had graced my two laadlees yesterday exclusively, they're certainly blessed. I should give a Special Offering to the Lord on my return to village. Am I right, Karan?"

Karan Mishra laughed and told, "This is okay!"

Caught on the wrong foot, the aunty's little girl and good girl cajoled their aunty leaning their heads against her chest.

"I wasn't interested. This is this Seema, your good girl's doing. She's always forcing me to wear this jean pant and T-shirt saying I'm looked smart in this dress. And you know, she has bought this new pair especially for me from Rourkela. And, 'whattosay!' your chand-ke-tukkuda is also supporting her."

"Tell me, am I really looked smart? Tell tell me aunty," the little girl asked standing straight in front of her affectionate aunty and pulling and pushing her.

Aunty, who rushed to them with so much of pain and despair, lost her own self in this environment of ecstasy. Warm tear started flooding her cheek and chin and she couldn't hold back and pronounced pulling the little girl to her and caressing her cascading frizzy free hair, "Yes, my little girl, you look so beautiful in this dress! You wear this."

"Whoopee! Whoopee! My aunty is so good, so understanding, so great! I'm proud of you," the little girl planting a huge kiss on the aunty's cheek, acclaimed—tip-toeing.

"So, aunty's little girl got a convenient scapegoat in me! Okay, okey! Go go on blaming me. I'm now going to inform aunty's piece-of-moon," Seema told and as she walked out aunty stopped her shrieking, "Is Rabi not accompanying you to college? Are you going separately?"

"No, not that so, aunty! Our bodyguard is always around us, escorting, protecting, shadowing and guarding whenever wherever we're going. Especially, your little girl! But, today, your little girl was little early. She wanted to show her new . . . . ," she explained smiling but stopped abruptly being fired by pierced eyes of Preeti. "Sorry! Sorry, ... to buy stationeries from nearby shop before going to college."

"Sorry Seema, I've checked, there are no stationary shops nearby . . . . This is alright. Stop searching excuses," told Karan. "Go and call Rabi! We've some important points to discuss. We're in hurry! By the evening, we should be back at Pandupur. Or you know this inhuman society and our village busybody . . . . wouldn't hesitate to blabbermouth anything."

Two girls were nervous. 'What could be? Is it that posturing and bannering in the campus? Ooh my God! Who would have possible told them? This may be bloody Lalu's doing. He must have licked,' they thought. The two beauties in a flash turned red, out of fear. They were immobilized and looked at each other.

"Bhabi, let's go to Gents' Hostel. Rabi mayn't be allowed to Ladies Hostel," Karan told and as he was getting up, Seema requested, "Just wait! I'm calling him. He's allowed up to lobby in our hostel," and quickly walked out.

"Karan, look at these little deer eyes! I'm a mother, I'm a mother," aunty cried and expressed her determination, "Shh, whatever be the consequence, I can't be party to injustice done to my little kids. I'm sorry!"

"Yesterday, the owner of Dash Transport, a distance relation of Choudhury family 'as they say', had visited your grandpa and us and proposed . . . . ," but stopped as Rabi requested almost crying, "Kaka, please 'for God's sake!' don't say to mean 'my grandpa.' I don't have anybody as such. My mama is everything for me. If I accept them as my 'so and so!' this would be a great injustice to my mama, who has been struggling so hard, you all know, against all the odds; and to all my well-wishers including you, Kesabkaka, school and college teachers, dear Seema and dear Preeti. For me, that old man is nothing but Choudhury elder, a symbol of exploitation!"

"Rabi," Bhagyabati embracing him on her chest and consoling with tears in her eyes, told, "my dear child, after all, he is your father's father which I and you can't deny. He certainly deserves respect on that count. Any disregard in view of his treatment to us however isn't expected from a noble birth! Let's maintain dignity in talks and dealings, leaving all that he is doing to be judged by Lord of Universe."

In the meanwhile, the little girl had understood what for her aunty and Karankaka had come. She looked at her aunty . . . . her eyes praying, 'I can't live without your chand-ke-tukkuda. Please don't deny me your Rabi, aunty . . . . please!'

"No, no Preeti, don't cry. I too can't leave without you," the little girl obsessed aunty told embracing the little girl to her and cleaning her eyes with sari veil.

"They wanted you to contest college election as running partner of their daughter and later join their family business and get back the Choudhury title," Karan added.

"So, this is the issue! Ha . . . . ha . . . . ha . . . . , great! And, you my dear kaka and my dear mama come here to persuade me." Rabi embracing his mother asked, "You, tell me if I accept this proposal, will you be happy? What's there in Choudhury title? Of course, a social status. The Choudhury is—I repeat—a symbol of exploitation, a relic of bloody colonial past. Although I'm born to that blood, yet I hate that blood which could pushed to street their own daughter-in-law and gene, and can bear the branding of them 'bitch' and 'guttersnipe.' I'm proud of being brought up, 'even though a painful one!' outside that. I'm proud of my poor and deprived mama."

"And, I've given words to Preeti—I'm sorry, I haven't consulted—and I hope my mama and my well-wishers will certainly co-operate me and they'll feel proud of my decision. And, she is such a humble personality! But, at one fell swoop, I know our road isn't that so smooth."

With this, Rabi had silenced everybody.

"Now, Choudhury elder fears if I win the election, I'll be a figure to reckon with for him. He has found in Dash-Panda Family's scheme a convenient opportunity to exile his eye-sore from our village. As we aren't going to be trapped in his scheme of thing, he may join hand with Raghu uncle, Bishu Sarangi and Dash-Panda family. A big fight may be expected in days to come. I'm prepared for! Ergo, I've decided not to contest the college election," Rabi told.

"So, you won't contest," shook off the little girl and told, "I know my (biting the tongue) sorry our Rabi will listen to me!"

"Let's concentrate in study and further consolidate our position. We've to lift our village from Khandi Pandupur to Pandupur and rescue our villagers from the evil clutches of Choudhury elder, our ultimate objective," the aunty's little girl—now getting a new lease of life with her Mr. Dependant's bravado—announced. And, she requested, "But, kaka you just co-operate us taking care of my aunty in our absence in the village. She is our inspiration. If anything happen to her, we cannot manage our self. And, all our plan will be soiled."

"She may be targeted. And, the time will come when Choudhury title will be snatched from Choudhury," Seema soothsaid.

Two elders were surprised to see the maturity, determination, commitment and characteristics in their children. They had no words to appreciate, completely bowled out by their 'once so little' offsprings. Later, the trio along with their two elders met their Kesabkaka in the college canteen and got assured that their lovely birds were secured under his tutelage.

The elders visited Lord Jagannath temple before leaving to Pandupur but not before Seema's bubbling articulation, "Aunty, you rest assure, I wouldn't allow (ringleting her statuesque structure with lean and thin lovely body of Bhagyabati frightened of an attack from the ghungi Preeti or humble Rabi or both) my Rabi, ... sorry, ye-s sorry, ... Preeti's Rabi to be a Ghar Jamai ever," and heard from smiling aunty saying, "You're my knotty city girl . . . . (looking at Preeti) but certainly a good girl." All had a hearty laugh.

As the elders boarded the bus, the trio heard aunty advising Rabi, "Don't leave my little girl and good girl alone. They're so beautiful and so good, could be envy of any!"

With the notification of nomination filling date, all eyes were at the trio who were instead found more concentrated in their study attending classes too regularly, and surprisingly found paying scant interest to Students Union election and avoiding, although their names were much talked about among the most suitable candidates.

"Were they threatened by any political party? Or have their parents refused them? Or are they feeling insecure? . . . . Or is it the Miss Femme Fatale-Kaaliram's combined luffadami? None of the facts could be ruled out," started doing the round in the mouth of their fans in the campus. Also, some were of the view, "The trio may have something surprise." With the nomination filling last day draw nearer, the silent fans of the trio started openly pleading before the famous teen murti.

So also, the minority opponents weren't left behind. A rumour by them was doing the round: the trio may have been paid handsomely not to contest the election by any political party or candidate.

"I've the proof," the tormentor found telling a group of die-hard supporters of the trio on the last day of nomination filling.

This was too much that Rabi could bear any more. Humble peasant, for the first time found lost control over his temperament and coming face to face of the tormentor asked, "Show me the proof!" and instantly Lalu gave a bank account number and told, "From where you got thousands of rupees to deposit in your account?"

"Shut up! I've no account number. Even if, as you say, it is there, how did you know the number?" countered Rabi.

"It's done certainly to defame Rabi," shouted Seema.

"Let's file a FIR against Lalu in the police station. He certainly knows who has opened the account in the name of you and who has deposited money in that," Biju shouted.

ECLIPSING SUN

To Rabi, Preeti and their mentor, the graduation result was as par expected line. Rabi, the village's golden boy, topped his branch of study, but he wasn't at the top of the Best Graduate list of the premier college. Preeti was at the top. To the semi-literate Pandua fans of Rabi, this meant something else. "Is their 'hope and aspiration' distracted from his study? Certainly, his friendship with girls is to be blamed! These days girls are very shrewed. They are using gullible boys for their benefit." The villagers found analyzing and gossiping among them.

For the hawkish Raghu Rath, the proud father of the Best Graduate, this was a blessing in disguise. As if he was hunting for this opportunity, he didn't lost time to host the list before the grudging villagers unasked, who had been in the past enviously criticising whenever they were getting the opportunities saying, "Preeti's success so far is due to her umbilical connection with Rabi since their early school days." And Rahgu, who used to silence his critics on any other issue mercilessly, was lying low over this.

But, to the surprise of Panduas, now he had a logic, and propagated, "Preeti is the best. This has been proved after Rabi and Preeti took different courses of study. So far my daughter was a victim of the mother-son's conspiracies," and declared, "they have a vested-interest in doing so. Sorry, I will not allow. Enough is enough!"

'Preeti and Rabi love to each other,' Panduas had glimpse of this long ago. This assumption of villagers had been further ascertained after they played the role of a 'LOVE pair' in a popular dance-drama 'Kedar-Gouri'—the local version of 'Romeo and Juliet'—held in the annual village fair before the result publication. "The performance was awe-inspiring," the villagers acclaimed.

Bulinani was highly impressed. Lately, she had become a fan of the pair, surprising the peasants. Once, she told in front of a few peasants who wanted to know the reason of her change of mind, "Sorry, I had a misgiving. They're jewels, inspiring true lovers!" "Hey Maa Garachandi, help the jodi," she, a kumari and now of above half-century in age, and as many used to say a victim of mysterious LOVE and rebuffed the marriage, prayed even without any hesitation in the very presence of village ladies, elders and children.

Pandupur like any other villages or to say any human habitations around, in general, was no dearth's of such love relation which culminated to marriage in a society which predominantly believed and practiced the age-old tradition of 'arrange marriage' and that too, within the same caste and creed, and social strata. And whenever and wherever, there was violation of this practice due to LOVE, there was social strife and flow of bad bloods, and even in some case, punishing exiles from village, and suicide and murders.

"Human history is full of such incidents," the BCS College English lecturer, Ranjit Mohanty, as rumoured, a victim of such an indulgence and had been banned for entry to his native town for his fault of falling in LOVE with one of his student from the family of an influential politician, used to lecture and elatedly illustrate, "In the mythology and history a large number of bloody wars were fought to settle or avenge the sacred LOVE affairs."

He had plenty of examples, and it seemed to his audience in classes, the stories were in his finger tips. He used to tell quoting instances from the epics Ramayana and Mahabharata to historical Kalinga War, to Pruthiraj-Jayachandra and Zahangir-Anarkalli, and Dillip Kumar-Madhuballa-Kishore Kumar from ever-interesting gossips packed Bollywood. Whenever he dwelled over this issue, he was very elaborate and detail with students showing so much of interest, occasionally deviating from the course core curriculum.

"He's a specialist on the subject," the back benchers used to whisper. Of course, this provoked mild buzz on several occasions; but that had very little impact on Ranjitsir and his enthusiasm. He blamed Jayachandra for his intolerance to his daughter's LOVE which provided opportunity to Jabans to invade Indian territory, settled down and ruled for maximum period in the medieval India and primarily responsible for unfortunate partition of India. While he was elaborating the affairs of Zahangir-Anarkalli and of Dillip Kumar-Madhuballa-Kishore Kumar, he was rather very emotional.

The back-benchers comments, "Unless one is a victim of 'Intense LOVE' he can't be so illustrative and details." And, their search revealed Ranjitsir's reason of exile from his native town.

And, he rationalized quoting the instance of Odia kabi-samrat Upendra Bhanja. "He was so elaborative and detail in his literature because he himself was victim of LOVE." The students were in fact very sympathetic to the teacher which could easily be learnt from the attention they used to pay in his class.

Preeti was very fond of Ranjitsir and very attentive to his teaching always seating in the front row. This had been reflected in her result in literature subject. She was the top scorer in literature papers among all the Intermediate students, a rare achievement for Intermediate Science faculty. On occasion, she used to recite the lecture of Ranjitsir before her heart-throb and Seema—on their way from hostel to college and back and while they were whiling away their time in Puri sprawling golden sea beach.

"In a nutshell, Ranjitsir seemed favour the institution of 'LOVE marriage' irrespective of caste, creed, sect, religion, region, language, and whatnot's which as per him could contribute in building rich and quality society, and happy and healthy family life. He furthered his advocacy for the cause with examples such as LOVE marriage between Indira and Feroze which the father of the nation, Mahatma Gandhi himself patronized and Utkal Gana Kabi Baishanb Pani, the greatest dramatist of Orissa who married to a lower caste washerwoman despite himself being a upper caste Brahmin," Preeti revealed after long research on the subject.

In the recent past in Pandupur itself, there took place a tragic incident concerning the magical 'LOVE affairs' that led to marriage between Rati and Braja which divided Pandupur village into two warring camp. And the social strife that followed hadn't yet settled down. This type of incident used to visit the Pandupur very often these days.

"This had been a new phenomenon," the fading generation of the village rued for these linking to modern co-education and invasion of film culture, agreeing with Choudhury elder.

"Thank God, our village doesn't have a High School, otherwise it would have been wide-spread and inter-caste," exhorted the camp followers of Choudhury elder. But, Karan Mishra didn't concur with them, and he had words of decent, and on occasions gone up to the extent of quoting the verses from the poems of Upendra Bhanja that the popular folk dancers sung elevating the beauty of LOVE between prince and princess for the literature and cultural ecstasy of the village elders. He silenced them saying, "LOVE between two opposite sex is a natural phenomena and a natural instinct that must be respected." However, he advocated caution, "Yes, one shouldn't be vulgar." He even had gone to the extent of shouting down powerful few fans of Choudhury elder's who vandalized, and contributed to the closer of Pandupur High School with the screwed propaganda.

The now known 'LOVE affair' between Rabi and Preeti had special significance for Pandupur's silence majorities and Karan Mishra. For them, the pair were very special and significant. Rabi was a genius and a big performer in academy (although trailed behind Preeti in the Best Graduate list), sports, culture, and above all, personality and character. He was an inspiration and icon to the village tots. And the Panduas had started seeing in him scope for social and economic emancipation of their village, and above all, hoped to lead them against ridiculers of their village. Preeti was his companion. 'And, she is Rabi's LOVE!'

"Both if get married and stay back in village," Bulinani agreed with Karan Mishra, "they can do a lot for the village." The majority of the villagers were in league with the pair's love, of course in silence; obviously, with solid reasons.

Rabi had already been discarded by rich and influential Choudhury elder. "And, now by the clever and other influential village strongman, Raghu Rath!" Pandua peasants cried.

"Rabi is an outcaste, son-of-a-widow. Who knows—who's his father? How can we give our daughter to a sonofabitch," Prema, the reverend mother of the girl was heard saying fellow village ladies on the stage of Pandupur presiding deities one evening at the hearing distance of Bhagyabati.

"How could he even allow a trailer to hang around the Best Graduate of the district Premier College," Raghu Rath forcefully propagated unlike in the past, as and when Pandua elders asked him pairing Rabi with Preeti. He was found irritated, displaying.

The ever envious Lilli wasn't far behind. "Preeti, you're a perfect match to Rabi? But, who is his father nobody knows!" Lilli jeered with an envious ascent. And, with a pause, thought-provokingly continued, "Sorry, regarding matching of you two, this isn't what I am only saying. This is the opinion of all who have viewed your role with Rabi in the dance-drama 'Kedar-Gouri'. Nobody could play so perfectly unless they're in 'intense LOVE' with each other. What were the poise, the look, the body movement and the body language? And what were the reflections of feelings? Even your friend, that city girl smarty Seema, was astounded and I heard her whispering at Bhagyabati aunty's ear to complete the engagement process between you two before anybody played any luffadami."

"And, now, you've a great dedicated fan in our busybody Bulinani."

Preeti hadn't reacted with words. No, this wasn't that she was running short of words. But, she stood up—seemed immersed in her thought—and after a short while of intense glance at the distance fading cricket ground under fast approaching dusk where her heart-throb was displaying magic with bat and ball to his fellow village lads and passers-by, she walked towards village temple for evening aarti, and to pray to Lord Gopinath, a replica of Gopapura's Kanha to give her strength to fight all the vagaries opposed to her immersion with her own Gopinath, in cute, humble, generous and talented princely Rabi.

Since the day following the result publication, Rabi and Preeti hadn't been allowed to come closer to each other, not to have even eye contact. Even Preeti wasn't allowed to talk to her revered aunty at water pool, bathing ghat and temple platform, forget about being allowed to visit aunty's cottage, being overshadowed by either mama or Lilli.

"Raghu Rath is an opportunist! As soon as he found his daughter is grown up and can stand on her own and awarded Best Graduate of the college leaving behind Rabi, Rabi is kicked out from her life," viewed Bulinani in front of Karan and the village lads.

"What a treachery? Karan Mishra too should be blamed for his foolhardy suggestion to Rabi to take up Arts Course in his graduation," questioned some die-hard fans of Rabi. Many suspected Karan Mishra's intention questioning, "Has Karan joined hand with Raghu?" But, Rabi was silent when this matter was taken up. And, his mother was incommunicado, restricting her inside the tiny hovel, 'seemed surrendered to the mighty of her fate which is blinking at her with passing of time, refusing to settle down!'

'What they would be thinking? What they would be planning?' Preeti thought. 'They must be thinking I've cheated them. Karankaka has spoiled everything. No, I shouldn't have taken Science Course. Sorry Rabi, sorry aunty, please forgive me. I'm innocent. But, I'll die for you!'

A blanket ban had been imposed on Preeti by her father Raghu Rath with strict instruction not to be closed to Rabi. Even, she wasn't allowed to visit her aunty, her revered living deity. 'She is the lady who had laid my academic foundation and guided me in my matriculation. And, she is the mother of my murjada purush—my LOVE—my Rabi,' Preeti was crying.

The cousin sister Lilli, father Raghu, mother Prema and cousin brother Ramesh were seemed shadowing her whenever she was out of Rath abode. Every letter came to her was read and checked before being handed over. And, anything she wrote, was checked. Even pen and paper were lucked and only given with permission from papa or mama. Priya wasn't trusted. She was in a virtual house arrest. Sometimes Lilli was found working like a spy trying to extract latest development, if any, between the love-struck pair. For Preeti, Lilli's every move and dealing was seemed intriguing.

Another thought that hunted the girl time and again was: Lilli might be a competitor of her for Rabi as their village girl Rati was competitor of her cousin sister for Braja which culminated Rati marrying Braja. So, Preeti whenever provoked by Lilli avoid her, and when it was absolutely necessary responded with care as she, the Best Graduate from district's premier college, feared the village little-literate and school dropout more than their city counterparts for their mental toughness and manipulation skills. To Preeti, Lilli seemed tougher than city grown up smart and educated Rekha, Ruby, and her other class-mates. She had witnessed how Rati, a just seventh standard could manipulate the LOVE of her own cousin sister, educated with matriculation study, and eloped and married Braja through the court registration.

The stories in the Hindi films started hanging in her thought. She was scared of repeat of those in their case. At times, she thought of different plans. Option of leaving the village along with Rabi surreptitiously and getting their marriage solemnized through court registration as done by Braja and Rati, did too come to her mind.

'Whether Rabi accepts such an option? No, he won't! He is my Hero. My chosen hero, he can't be so cheap. And, so also, my revered aunty, mayn't accept such a proposition, she is so moralistic. Besides, this act would reinforce parent's accusation of Rabi—that he's a son-of-a-widow, a guttersnipe, and a man with low-morale. No, this isn't acceptable! I can't accept my murjada purush to be branded as a guttersnipe or loafer. Again, what the village youngsters to whom Rabi is now an icon to emulate, and beacon of 'hope' for raising village image and to emancipate Khandi Pandupur, would think, and what would happen to the village youngsters' aspirations? And, what would happen to the village causes which have started shining despite all huddles raised by formidable Choudhury elder and his camp followers? No, I can't be found accused of sacrificing village causes for my own selfish end. I'm also to be blamed for taking mark fetching subjects in graduation. What a bloody foolish mistake I'd committed!'

"Rabi is yours and he'll remain yours for forever," Bulinani told as and when she found Preeti seating alone. "Preeti, my little girl, don't lose heart! Have confidence on Rabi! He is committed."

Lately, the impact of separation started reflecting in the performance of Rabi in playground, in interaction with the village lads, mates and elders; at evening temple platform melody, card game, and where not's. In one melody to the surprise of all, he, a great fan of funny Kishore Kumar, sang the heart-breaking song '*Jane kahan gaye woh din*' of immortal Mukesh from Hindi film '*Mera Nam Joker.*' The entire village was stunned with the melancholic tone. The character was understood. The gathering swelled, out to enjoy the sweetness of the enchant leaving aside the literary meaning. Yet, he couldn't complete, and he disappeared in the darkness—to his tiny cottage—to his poor mother's lap pretending throat congestion.

"Yes, the throat congestion is there," all present were felt in grieve, and were sympathetic but helpless.

'These days, he is mostly found thinking and reserve, and spending time alone, unseen before. This is like a bloody cyclonic black cloud over-shadowing the promising moon on the full-moon night: appeared— might be out of envy,' the Panduas thought.

The issue was the talk of the village. Everybody was concerned. And most particularly, young lads, who'd seen in flourishing Rabi an inspiration, were found highly disturbed. Even this was found mention in the whiling away session among them. Debates started doing the round among the Pandupur lads and youths, whether to help Rabi to get ride up his malady or left him to fend for himself. They were scared of influential and powerful Choudhury elder. And, the clever Raghu Rath and his family's sudden change of bonhomie with Rabi and his mother, was telling impact on them too.

In one of such debate in an evening gathering at temple platform, Ramesh, sitting behind by the back column shouted, "Rabi, a guttersnipe," and opined tersely, "let the urchin live his own life!" This was beyond the limit of toleration. This swift and abusive remark reduced the serene and sacred temple environment tense and unbearable. Many found angry and red-faced but couldn't immediately venture to rescue the deprived from the filthy titling in his absentia—clearly scared of jackal-clever Raghu Rath, lately found hobnobbing with powerful Choudhury elder, seemed with suspicious intent.

However, the pig-headed and outspoken Karan Mishra just arrived didn't. He asked tautly, "Given a chance, would you Ramesh have chosen the fate of Rabi," and shouted, "What's his fault and what's his mother's? So far cheated, who doesn't know? What have they not done for the village, helped building its image; and to your cousin sister, now you're proud of her achievement? And, you, to pass the matriculation, you were struggling for years together, that enabled you to get a job in Panchayat Office, to earn your livelihood? Have you forgotten your late night visit of their cottage stealthily to clear your mathematics doubt? Everybody know how Preeti has been benefited because up the selfless support of Rabi and his mother in her school study, and till, she reached her graduation?"

Ramesh was in denial and hummed. As he sensed situation might lead him to further embarrassment that he couldn't face like his uncle, looked for an opportunity to skid away. The omni-present frequent power-cuts in the rural Orissa in the meanwhile came to rescue him as a blessing in disguise, and he stealthily decamp the venue unnoticed to escape further outburst.

"And, in return, what did he get except filthy rubbish? Should I ask you Ramesh, how all of sudden Rabi becomes an urchin and guttersnipe for you and your extended family," an unstoppable and agitated mentor roared.

There was no response and reaction. A studied silence rained over the venue for a while.

"Opportunist to the core! Khandi Pandupur will remain a 'khandi' for ever," he concluded with resignation and walked towards club house folding his dhoti above the knee and shuffling towel between the left and right shoulders with anger and resentment.

The most disturbing for Khandi Pandupurias and the well-wishers of mother-son was: the frequent meeting of Choudhury elder and Raghu Rath these days. They found them in intense parleys on several occasions, unseen before as they were known for their perpetual enmity till the recent past. Bulinani narrated, "They are aahi(snake) and nakulla(mangoose) destined by nature not to keep eyeball to eyeball. But, now . . . . ! Hey maa, what they're now cooking?"

In a late black out evening, Bulinani noticed a man of Raghu Rath features entering Choudhury abode. She informed Karan who got into verification and confirmed the same figure came out when the entire village had gone asleep in the mid-night. "A rare view!"

"And alarming!" Now, they were sure of something intriguing was going on. And, they were afraid, "This could be against the mother-son. Going by the present situation, there are sufficient reasons for the bonhomie of two arch-rivals."

"They're such opportunists, they can go to any extent," Karan confirmed to Bulinani.

THE GREAT ESCAPE

That was at the dead of the mid-night. The entire village was in its usual slumber. A hullabaloo on the village street woke up Preeti and her siblings. Through the street window, they noticed some villagers were running towards the eastern edge of the village while a few walking laid-back. She wanted to go. But, she wasn't allowed although the village girls including cousin Lilli were on the street and talking something occasionally staring at her—'intriguing!'

At home, it appeared to her, her parents hadn't slept so far and were looked restive.

She heard the sound of bamboo knots' burst and saw reflection of blazing light. 'Certainly, somebody's house is on fire,' she guessed. "When Lilli and other girls were out on the street," she demanded her parents, "Why I'm not allowed?"

'In the similar situation in the past, she was allowed,' she recalled and analysed, 'Why not today?' This aggravated her suspense. 'Is it concerning my aunty's cottage,' she cried as the thought invaded her and begged mama to let her go. But her appeal went in vain as the reverend mother was reluctant to attend her. She seemed resolute and told, "Grown up girl from good family shouldn't go out in the mid-night! You aren't like other."

As a last resort, she stood by the window staring at the street in panic and saw Choudhury elder—it seemed to her, he was highly elated as if he won a long fought battle—coming from his house but knew everything and told to her papa, who on sight of him went out, "Thank God, the shame of the village is removed. They are perished by their own omission and commission!"

The villagers heard without any response. 'Certainly, the villagers aren't in league with him. They were looked unhappy and disturbed—distancing,' Preeti felt. "What's the shame . . . . what's removed? What has actually happened? Is he talking about my Rabi and aunty, his bête noire?" she asked to Priya. Both almost started crying with apprehension.

She searched for Karankaka and Bulinani, who used to be in the forefront whenever there was any disaster in the village. She tried to recall, 'Yes, Karankaka was there in the village. I've seen him in the afternoon talking to Rabi in field-padia—seemed he along with village lads was persuading Rabi to play as he was found distancing him from participating in any village activities lately.'

And, later, she heard Choudhury elder was telling her papa, "Let bygones be bygones! Get ready for tomorrow's programme. Guests will arrive at exactly 10 AM. I'm sending my cart to Chabishpur bus-stand. Bridegroom is from a big family. Our lovely and scholarly Preeti will certainly match their requirement. Tell our lovely little girl to agree to their proposal of going for higher study after marriage. Don't worry for any other things. I'll take care. She'll marry like a princess. Now, there is no more huddle!"

"My Rabi, my aunty! Hey Bhagaban, they've killed my Rabi . . . . my aunty!" Preeti shouted and collapsed on her sister.

These were the words and verbatim that her family members, her villagers, her friends and those who came with marriage proposal, heard from her for days, for months and for years together. She was found sneaking to the site from the round-the-clock virtual house arrest, which was progressively loosened with passing of months and years, where once stood her dear aunty's cottage and where she was playing with her heart-throb and her heart-throb used to mock her, jeer her, cheer her and also slap her; and where her aunty taught her lessons and laughed at her for her excess indulgence of fixing her eyes at Rabi and aunty was preparing her favourite coconut cake and fried fish; and the city girl had one morning cheered them saying, "Tathastu!"

She was also found lost her sense lying senseless on several occasions and lifted to Rath abode on the shoulder of Bulinani who almost was shadowing her whenever she was out of her house. Nobody had any word. The entire village, with very little exception, was crying with her. 'A rare diva has reduced to skeletal piece for laboratory exhibition.' Tears were there in every eye on sight of her.

The villagers heard her crying, sulking and at times, found her cleaning her tears, and appealing, "Aunty, see how Rabi slaps me. He is telling me motti, chandi, jinn! . . . . Aunty, am I fat? Am I chandi?"

"Sorry, sorry Rabi! I'll do what you will say. Please, excuse me today. Now onwards, I'll start dieting. Aunty, don't give me any fish, meat, cheese and coconut stuffed cakes. They're full of fat. Don't know, Rabi doesn't like me look fat," she touching her ears and kneeing-down, begged.

She, raising her hand above, shrieked, "My Rabi will be a big officer, a big gun, an OAS Officer, an IAS Officer like motti Rekha's father or my friend Seema's father— one day he'll be Puri DM. And, I, as his wife, should look like a wife of IAS, slim and smart like Swati aunty."

And on occasion, coming to Karan Mishra's doorsill, she requested, "Kaka, please tell where should I and Rabi take admission. Where he has gone?"

"He has gone to get Forms for yours admission. Tomorrow, he is coming," Karan assured and Bulinani added adjusting her wears and tarnished ponytail, "My little girl will study much more. You're so talented. You'll be best in the university too."

"She's a mad girl. She'll beat. She'll bite," the small children foul-played with her, shouting, mocking, joking and jeering. And some threw dust, sand, pebble and spit as and when Bulinani and any village elder were found out of sight.

"Am I mad? Idiot, what non-sense you're saying?" And pulling a plank, she ran after them shouting, "I'm the Topper and I'm the Best Graduate of BCS College. I'm Miss BCS," and calling village girls, she told, "Do you know, my friend—smarty Seema, what she was suggesting me—to contest for Miss India title and Miss World title. And to be advertisement model and film heroine! I've the body features and personality of Reita

Faria. You know—who's she? She is the first and only Miss World from India so far."

"But, sorry, no . . . . I'll be a teacher. I'll teach our village children. Rabi and Karankaka will set up a High School in our village. They have promised me. Choudhury elder's people have burnt our village High School."

And, this way first year had gone, so also second and third about to . . . . There was no information on where about of Rabi and his mother, and the villagers were not ready to accept Choudhury elder's clarification to police. And, Karan Mishra wasn't revealing and intriguing in his response. Although the villagers were crying for the sudden eclipse of their village's 'hope' and 'aspiration', yet nobody had the necessary means to explore. They were in such a setting.

As police investigation didn't get the tress of human body particles in burnt remain in the cottage although Choudhury elder and his camp followers gave eye-witness, "All of a sudden in the mid-night cottage was found burning from inside, a clear-cut case of self-immolation. The circumstance was such! They were frustrated after Rabi lost to Preeti in the college Best Graduate list, and subsequently, Preeti rebuffed his demand for continuance of the relationship with him."

"This was quite natural—how could a District's Premier College Best Graduate move around with a trailer, disgracing her degree?"

"It might so happened that after the burning of cottage, the burnt remain of mother-son's bodies might have been taken away by wolves before the day break," Choudhury elder explained. "Our village backyard has plenty of them."

"So, Preeti and Rabi were in LOVE. And, Preeti betrayed him," Police Officer jeered.

"Not exactly! How this is betrayal as it seemed from outside—one-sided one? This is social reality," Choudhury elder replied. "This is rampant these days. In fact, a fall out of modern co-education! Thank God, we don't have High School in our village. Or else every family in our village would have such incident destroying the established social foundation of our humble village."

"But sir, you ought not to forget that the development of the village and society, and above all, the nation won't take place without higher education," opined the Police Officer.

"Who care for the village, society and nation's development so long as the own family interest is the major obsession? These days, who are opposing the higher modern education on the pretext of retaining the age-old 'so-called!' culture and social integrity, are sending their children to cities and abroad for the same betraying what they preach in their own village. This is the tragedy," the snot-nosed Karan Mishra roared.

"Sorry, I'm no way concern on this issue. I'm an Investigating Officer . . . . your village internal matter," banged the officer and told, "I must talk to the girl's parents and the girl. There's an angle! Before closing the case, this is necessary."

"Who are they? Please call them," Police Officer shouted but couldn't proceed immediately as Choudhury elder invited him for the launch in his house, and to the villagers' surprise, Raghu Rath was also called but not Preeti and her mother.

But, Karan's questions to Police Officer baffled Panduas. "Incident took place in the mid-night. Usually, the villagers used to sleep in the night. How could so many witnesses assemble there to celebrate this 'sudden' bonfire?"

"But who will talk to Investigating Officer on this angle after he had taken launch in Choudhury's House along with Raghu Rath," the villagers rued among them and settled down in hush.

Subsequent to the closure of Police Investigation, the hawkish Raghu Rath, once famous for his presence of mind and acumen ship and playing lead role in almost all of the village affairs was found silenced. "What happened? He has been restricted in his house, rarely moving around in the village as he was earlier," the villagers were found gossiping with passing of days and months.

"Choudhury elder has taken out the best of Raghu Rath," screamed Bulinani.

And, he stopped leading his camp-followers. "Bichara Raghu Rath . . . finished!" celebrated his opponents.

"Finally, the wily Choudhury elder got rid of his two eye-sores in one stone. Let's see!" reacted Karan before his camp followers, leaving them bewilder.

And the most worried were the parents of children who were once improving in their study under the guidance of tutor Bhagyabati at a nominal cost in their village itself and had started dreaming for their children, a bright future.

The domination of Pandua lads in Chabishpur High School, which was nightmarish to Bishu Sarangi, waned. So also, their performance in the sports and in the cultural programmes. And some were started openly saying, "Bishu Sarangi might have a hand!"

"Khandi Pandupur is back to square-one," Karan jeered. Karan Mishra was found withdrawn from the village affairs. And whenever he was approached by the youngsters he rebuffed them saying, "Ours is an insipid village. It is a curse to born in this village. Nothing can be done here!"

But, Karan, who was once upon a time seeing a bright future for his village in the energetic presence of Rabi along with Preeti, couldn't bear his eyes to see Preeti's deteriorating condition who had almost reduced to a skeleton physically, and crying dancing mocking staring musing talking sulking teasing laughing abusing insistently progressively with passing of days, months and years. And in recent days, the girl was falling sick very often. And her parents were silenced, and occasionally, crying whenever Panduas were asking anything to them concerning their little sweetie golden girl.

"Preeti, my little sweetie girl, I can't see you any more in this condition. Believe me, your Rabi and your aunty are very much alive. Very soon, they'll come to take you from this hell," Karan tried to convey the girl, when she was at his doorstep running after his children who teased her, believing with this news the girl might change.

"My Rabi is coming. My aunty is coming," shouted the little girl as loudly as she could and started dancing, singing and clapping, "My Rabi is coming. My aunty is coming. Bulinani, Saruabhai, Galubhai, Dalli, Malli . . . . do you hear, what Karankaka has told? My Rabi is coming and my aunty is coming. Must be coming with Forms for admission in PG course in Vani Vihar. We'll together study there. This time, I won't take mark fetching subject. Sorry Karankaka!"

Soon the disgruntled banner sena along with Bulinani gathered in numbers and demanded the explanation from Karan Mishra so far regarded as the other villain by some of the die-hard fans of Rabi as he had suggested their hero—they knew—to take the course which was—as per them—primarily responsible for Rabi's falling from grace of Rath family and possibly could be the main reason of joining together of two Big Guns of their village to conspire for the eclipse of their iconic hero and lovely aunty. As the demand heightened, Karan collected an old newspaper he'd preserved in his house and told hoisting, "Last year, our Rabi has been selected for IAS. Now, he's in probation. Time isn't far when he'll visit us as DM of Puri District. And he'll beg for our little girl sweetie Preeti's hand," and continued when he was pressed by some suspecting peasants to tell how all these happened, "I had shifted the mother-son to a safer place before some people, who were earlier successful in sending

Biswanath Mohapatra in-exile and burnt our village High School, threw the ball of fire on the cottage."

Taking breath, he cried dewy-eyed, "But, I'm sorry, I couldn't keep their little girl normal. I don't know what they will feel when they find their little girl in this state; so far I have been informing them that their Preeti is quite normal. Now, I'm afraid," and looking all around he asked crying, "Hey, where is our little girl? Preeti, where are you? Please for my sake, for sake of our village, for sake of our golden boy, be normal. What I'll say to your Rabi and to your aunty?"

"Good Heaven! Rabi is saved," the peasant exhibited their sign of relief. "Old Choudhury, let our hero and aunty come, we'll fix you once and for all!"

All looked for Preeti as if they felt it was their responsibility to keep their hero's sweet-heart safe and secure. They looked around searching the little girl. Youngsters cried, "Preetididi, Preetididi, where are you?" and elders including Bulinani, Karan, Sarua, Dukhi, Gallu, Dalli, Malli . . . . begged, "Preeti, our lovely aunty's little girl, where are you? Please come out!"

"My laadlee must be hiding somewhere," Bulinani cheered.

"Search, search! Ha . . . . , ha . . . . ! You won't get me. I'm here . . . . on the tree," Preeti, shaking the champak tree at a distance, cheered. "Don't tell Rabi. Let he search me. Aunty will certainly beat him. I'll complain her, he's always slapping me, saying me motti. Kaka, Bulinani tell, am I fat? I'm lean and thin like Saruabhai."

Everybody's attention in no time shifted to the tree.

"Hey Bhagaban! Preeti, you'll fell down," Bulinani cried.

"Please come down slowly. What that bloody Choudhury has done to my lovely little girl," the mentor cried.

"Who says you're fat? I'll tell Rabi. And I'll beat Rabi if he'll ever say our little girl—motti. You please get down, ... get down please!"

Sarua and Gallu climbed the tree to bring her down while other quickly joined their hands beneath the tree to save if she fell down.

"No, no Kaka, you shouldn't beat him. Gent's hand is very hard. Only aunty will beat," she shouted and jumped to Bulinani and got fainted.

All present found nursing their village archangel. And the mother Prema was found weeping at her doorsill as the villagers were taking care of her laadlee.

The mentor was heard shrieking as the little girl got back her sense, "I promise," touching his gullet, "I won't beat your Rabi. But, I'll certainly beat you if you climb the tree again like a monkey."

"Ha . . . . ha . . . . ha . . . . ," the girl jeered, "My God! Karankaka is saying I'm a monkey. Am I? Tell Dalli, tell Reena . . . . Bulinani!"

"Sorry, sorry! You're not a monkey. You're our sweetie little girl—Preeti," begged the mentor. "Preeti, I've one more good news for you. Shall I tell? No, I won't tell if you don't seat in front of us silently," the mentor demanded.

She sat down keeping her forefinger on her mouth but was blinking her eyes like a chained dancing monkey in front of her master.

"Your friend Seema Pati, that Miss Smarty has been selected for IPS this year."

"Hadn't Raghu uncle joined hand with Choudhury elder, our Preeti would have been by now an IAS or an IPS," Dalli soothsaid.

"Kaka, shall I talk?" the girl begged shaking mentor like a normal child surprising everybody present.

"Yes, our little girl, tell whatever you like. We're here to listen you," the mentor, Bulinani and all present told. "We're ready! No chit-chat! Our sweetie sweetie Preeti will speak."

"I'll be a teacher. I will be a teacher in our village school. I'll teach A for Apple—this is mostly produced in which state? Do you know? . . . . Himachal Pradesh and this is my Rabi's favourite fruit; B for Ball, cricket ball, who is the best bowler in India? . . . . Kapil Dev and my Rabi is a good bowler; C for cake, aunty's stuffed cake, my Rabi's favourite. Nani, do you know," combing Bulinani's head by her thin fingers and picking a white hair, told, "one day . . . . my aunty," flicking her eyes, "had kept freshly made stuffed cake under their cot. You know, this is also my favourite. I crawled under the cot and was eating. Rabi came and shouted at her mama, 'Where is my cake? Where is my cake?' I told 'mau . . . . , mau . . . . , cat is eating.' You know, the snot-nosed came with a turned blade and shouted at me, 'Either you give me my cake or I'll dig out it from your belly. Ha . . . . ha . . . .' When I show my belly, he shouted, 'You mad-girl! Shut up! You motti, dholli!' and run away. Ha..a . . . . ha . . . . ha . . . . !" She went on pulling up her tattered kurti to show her belly and Sarua, Gallu, Dukhi, Gandua, Vallu, ... and Karankaka around made a quick U-turn shouting, "Preeti stop!" while Dalli, Reena and other girls encircled her sitting on the Bulinani's lap, shadowing. And the mother Prema ran into house crying, "Hey Bhagaban, save my laadlee!"

"Kaka, you remember, you and Rabi had promised me, you would open a High School in our village. One day Lalu Sarangi teased Rabi for studying in their village school. Do you know my Rabi had cried that day? I couldn't control him. Were there a High School in our village, it wouldn't have happened," Preeti cried till Bulinani embraced her cleaning her eyes with her sari veil.

"You're a good teacher. From today, to start with, you teach my children," the mentor told the girl. "How beautifully she teaches us A, B, C? Such a talented teacher like our dear Bhagyabatibhabi!"

"No kaka, they're saying me mad. I won't teach them," she cried.

"They're small children. Forgive them!" requested the mentor.

"Now, you'll teach us. We want to write the matriculation examination privately," Sarua, Gallu, Dukhi, Vallu, Gandua, Hadu and all other school drop-outs requested in unison. "Karanbhai, let's open tuition class in the Club House."

As Karan remained non-committal and intriguingly silent, they told, "If you suspect our intention, you may seat along with us. For sake of our lovely teacher, we'll study. We'll appear the examination if it helps our little girl get engaged and remain happy till Rabi returns. Without Rabi, our village is lifeless. Sorry, we can't bear our sweetie Preeti in this condition anymore. We're ready to do whatever is required to keep our Preeti happy and jolly!"

"Karan, don't worry. I'll be with our sweetie Preeti in the Club House. This will be a good initiative," Bulinani told confidently.

"Preeti madam, please you won't punish me if I fail to write or answer the questions correctly. I'm three year elder to you," Sarua requested. "I'm very dull, you know."

"I'm taller to Preeti by one and half foot. Preeti madam can't touch my ears," jeered Hadu.

Still, Karan wasn't that enthusiast with the proposal. And, he maintained studied silence disturbing the proposers who intermittently stared at him.

"But, this may irritate some people and they may burnt the Club House like they did in case of High School and bhabi's cottage," Karan Mishra told in hopelessness.

"We'll guard the Club House in rotation. In the night, we'll be all there. Enough is enough! Now, we won't spare whoever comes on our ways."

"Preeti Madam, you'll give us task to remember in the night so that we won't sleep and so guard the Club House."

The tuition classes started and ran with the right earnest. The elderly students got into the study with their young tutor. So also, the young stars were busy clearing their doubt. From morning to late in the evening tutor was busy. Students were taking all care of their lovely little teacher.

"We'll grab the top position in Bishu Sarangi's backyard this year for sake of our teacher . . . . comes what way," vowed the regular students.

But, in spare time, Preeti was found walking to the site where once stood her aunty's cottage. She slept there as she was sleeping in the lap of her aunty and crying madly. Once she was there she had to be lifted on the shoulder of her elderly students or Bulinani.

As per the suggestion of the doctor that Preeti might further normalize, Karan Mishra suggested her students to rebuilt the cottage. And, within a month the enthusiast Panduas built the cottage and demanded Karan, "Where are our golden boy and aunty? As you suggested, we've done our job. Now, this is your responsibility to fill it up."

SONOFTHESOIL

To the surprise of Panduas', during the last few months Choudhury elder was found progressively lying-low in the village affairs. The proud and majestic sessions with his camp followers at his sprawling veranda were found restricted to a few minutes and had reduced even to once or twice in a week. His movements in the village too had considerable fallen. And, he was found these days absent in the village for long time. On inquiries, the curious villagers gathered from his camp followers that he was under-treatment in Cuttack.

In one fine early morning, the villagers were woke up to a strange hullabaloo in front of majestic Choudhury House. And, within a minute the entire majestic Choudhury House was found cordoned off by the lathi and rifle wielding forces on the very eyes of Panduas of all intents and substances who were once scarred of a mere splitting look at the majestic house. The Police Officials, who were in the past paying dutiful obeisance to the house patriarch, were found by the anxious Panduas very adamant and aggressive, and talked calling the Choudhury elder's name— unceremoniously! For the Panduas, the sight was first of its kind in their living memory.

"Choudhury, your house has been cordoned off. There is hardly any scope to escape. You better accept the order of the High Court and give your DNA sample. We've doctor with us."

"He is not here. He has gone to Cuttack," they heard the elder Choudhury lady pronouncing from inside.

"No, no, he's there in the house. I had seen him yesterday night," shouted Preeti and Bulinani seconded.

"The Commanding Officer isn't from local Delang Police station, most probable he's from SP Office," Karan whispered to the peasants. "Local police station officer wouldn't be so harsh," told another villager.

"Choudhury is hiding like a rat," Bulinani jeered. "Wow! What a fate?"

"What's the matter? Has the Choudhury elder committed any crime," Panduas asked to each other. "There was nothing as such?" But, his die-hard camp followers were not seen which heightened the suspense of the Panduas' further.

"Choudhury, we've search warrant from the Court. Either you open the door or we'll break it open. Choice is yours. We've concrete information that you're at home," shouted the Commanding Officer. "Now, my boy will count ten to one. We expect you to co-operate!"

"Start—ten, nine, eight . . . . three, two, one," Preeti counted jeering.

The force break-opened the door and within minutes Choudhury elder was flushed out—"Like a thief from his hide-out. Ha . . . Ha . . . Ha . . . ," shouted Sarua to the jubilation of the surprised peasants.

"No . . . no . . . . captured like an otter fishing in calm water," cheered the little girl clapping and dancing. In the very presence of Panduas, the doctor collected the DNA sample.

But to the surprise of the Panduas present, the Commanding Officer came close to the little girl and told, "What a brilliant comparison?"

"She's the Best Graduate of the BCS College," Bulinani told to the Commanding Officer.

"What for this is done?" Panduas were found talking among them. They looked at Karan Mishra.

"Rabi have filed a case against Choudhury for his birth recognisation, he was denied so far. The DNA test will confirm his birth to Dibakar Choudhury and so also his claim that he's the sonofthesoil."

"Karan, you've done all these all-of-alone and know everything keeping 'even me' in dark. Not fair!" Bulinani cried.

"Because, you are a loudmouth!"

Baia demanded, "What do you mean by 'even me' Bulinani?".

As Bulinani evaded, Karan revealed, "She is the person who had informed me in advance 'the conspiracy'."

"So you two have joined hands in-between, keeping us in the dark!"

"Too many cooks spoil the broth!"

As the police personnel's got back to their vehicles, the little girl cried, "Arrest this Choudhury! He has burnt our village High School. He has burnt my aunty's house . . . . my Rabi's house."

"Raghu, stop your daughter! I've sufficient proof of your hand in burning of the cottage," shouted Choudhury elder and warned, "Mind everybody! I'm down, not dead!"

Despite all the earnest effort of the villagers under the guidance of Karan Mishra, the little girl didn't return to complete normalcy. And, her health was deteriorating. The mentor was highly disturbed; so also, the Panduas.

"What Rabi will say when he finds his LOVE in this state? And, bhabi find her little girl...................." the mentor told the peasants in the club house. "So far, I've been informing them that Preeti is okay but under complete surveillance of her parents and siblings. I was afraid if he was informed of our little girl's this condition he'd have been distracted."

"Let's inform Rabi and bhabi the present condition of our little girl. Further delay of their arrival may have very bad impact on girl's health. Our little girl only can be rescued by them, her major obsession," opined Bulinani. The peasants agreed.

THE UNION

As per the plan, in one early morning, Preeti was woke up and was guided to her aunty's cottage. She found Seema's favourite Reebok full shoe and Rabi's Bata boot at the street doorsill of one-room-cottage. And, aunty's slipper was missing.

'A ham-fisted setting!'

"Ooh my God! They're in one room," cried Bulinani, provoking.

"And, even aunty isn't in the room!" yelled Dalli.

Preeti frantically knocked the door and heard from inside the city girl requesting, "Rabi, please don't open. Motti will disturb us!"

"Okay, let the mosquitoes bleed dry the motti's blood," Rabi jeered.

"Preeti shout! Don't stop! Knock the door! This smart city girl is very clever. She may elope your Rabi," Dalli, Reena, Gallu, Hadu and Sarua shouted.

"If you tell, we'll break open the door. How can the city girl elope our village boy, that too from our lovely sweetie sweetie little girl? We're with you—Preeti," Sarua, Baia, Hadu and Dukhi told.

"Ten, nine, eight, ... three, two, one!"

"You're very harassing. No, I'll open the door. I want to see my little girl, not seen her for so long! How she is now," cried aunty inside the room.

The trio heard from inside somebody failed down and knocking stopped.

"Hey Bhagaban, Preeti failed down! Bulinani, her head is bleeding," the peasants screamed.

"Rabi, please open the door," shouted Bulinani. "Preeti has failed down. She can't hold her, so weak; her head is bleeding."

"Is this girl my little daughter?" aunty cried lifting the lean and thin serpentine body—crying for her care—to her lap and the villagers were found nursing the Best Graduate of the district's premier collage and would-be life partner of insipid Khandi Pandupur's first ever IAS.

Aunty cleaned the girl's head with her sari and bandaged the wound tearing her sari veil. She ordered Rabi and Seema, "Take my little daughter to hospital and return with her only after she is healed."

"Mama, don't be crazy. It's a minor injury. Biswanathdada along with Puri DM is coming. The foundation stone of our village High School will be laid. So many works are there to do, Karankaka is alone. This is very important," Rabi pleaded. "Seema, you along with Bulinani take this mad girl to hospital," ordered Rabi and jeered. "This WHP is a big stumbling block for all the good work! Isn't Seema?"

"Aunty, you hear! Again, he's saying me WHP," Preeti cried looking at her aunty.

"Don't worry, the train has already arrived. You've to just board," aunty assured the girl caressing her and ordered, "Nothing doing! Can't you see my little girl's condition? How could you be so unmindful of her? All boys are like this," the little girl's aunty shouted. "Health is wealth!"

"What an IAS yaar! You don't know—Health is wealth! Bhabi has to teach you," jeered Bulinani stroking at the boy.

In no time, the banara sena arranged a cart. Rabi and Seema along with Bulinani carried the patient to the cart and the banara sena followed them on foot and bicycle to the nearby Chabishpur health centre. A beeline was soon formed to the hospital surprising the neighbouring villagers.

The Panduas were found to their surprise their once upon a time maligned 'guttersnipe', 'urchin', 'sonofabitch' had been bestowed with VIP treatment on the very eyes of Bishu Sarangi at the health centre. Nobody was uttering Khandi Pandua or Khandi Pandupur. The attendant recorded in the register and the doctor wrote in the prescription—"Preeti Rath from Pandupur, brought by Mr. Rabi Pratap Choudhury"— even without being prompted. And, the sepoys from local police outpost saluted Rabi Pratap Choudhuty, and almost escorting him unasked on his every move. Bulinani and Panduas were astound.

In the evening, there was almost a small fair in front of the Rabi's non-descriptive cottage. The entire village was in celebration mode. After their hero's declaration that his share of huge Choudhury clan property be donated to Pandupur High School, the villagers were enthusiastically demanded a Grand Feast. They wanted this along with Rabi's engagement with their sweetie sweetie little girl. Everybody wanted 'Choudhury daughter-in-law' to make a declaration on the issue.

"How will I take the decision unless bride's parents consented? Again, I'm the mother of the bridegroom. As the tradition demand, the proposal should come from bride's family and they've to arrange matchmaker to match the horoscopes," Bhagyabati demanded messaging the head of the little girl resting on her chest. "Sorry, I can't break the tradition. People will blame!"

"Aunty, suppose the horoscopes won't match, what we've to do?" Seema asked and winking at Rabi, jeered, "Hello Mr. IAS—50-50 chance—get ready for a life of a Sisupal . . . . possibility can't be ruled out. You had promised to bachelorkaka if not Preeti you would remain a life-time bachelor like him."

The deer eyes turned to aunty in despair.

"This city girl is always a knotkhatti! However, Preeti don't worry, if the horoscopes won't match, we'll modify that," Bulinani assured pulling Preeti to her lap and aunty laughed. "The matchmaker will take care."

"Why? This isn't fair! Tampering the horoscope is cheating. I was thinking if the horoscopes won't match I would have got an excuse," pleaded Mr. IAS. "Also, mama just think, what my colleagues will say me? Um, marrying just a gawari, and that too, a school teacher; teaching A for Apple, B for Ball and C for Cat. Not, at all! They're marrying smart IAS and IPS Officers or the daughter of Chief Secretary and Cabinet Secretary or Ministers and Ambassadors or NRIs and Chairman of big corporate. Mama, please once think, marrying a Big Gun's daughter will help me in my future career. Is it not

Seema? This is a life-time decision. We're supposed to be very judicious in this regard."

"Hay Bhagaban, who will guide this muffasali mama? She has almost been stolen by this fasto!"

"So what? Our Preeti is Miss BCS and the Best Graduate from BCS College and you're a trailer. You're lucky to get the hand of such a beautiful and talented girl without much effort. It's shame to marry a trailer on the part of our laadlee Preeti. Still, she is doing a favour," peached on Bulinani.

"You may be an IAS but my Preeti will produce IASs," acclaimed the mama-aunty.

"Alas, what mistake I've done! Had I not vowed in front of the snot-nosed Kesabkaka, I would have been saved," Rabi cried and frowned mimicking at Preeti and winking at Miss IPS.

The little girl pulling her face towards her aunty cried, "Aunty, see! Rabi frown me again and winked at Miss IPS."

"I'm too old to take care of 'your Rabi' any more. Always quarreling and fighting like the small child! Now, you take charge of him," the aunty handing over her a lath laughed.

"O my God, the proposal hasn't come, the horoscopes haven't been matched, aunty is saying the girl 'your Rabi'. This is nothing but broad day-light cheating of tradition and custom, and that too, in front of a Police Officer," Seema jeered.

Preeti ran to Rabi with the lath but failed to reach him and kneel down.

"She was so feeble," cried her aunty and all viewers with sympathy.

Her students soon came to her rescue grabbing Rabi and shouted, "We won't allow you to puckered brow at our little teacher-madam. Today, our result has published. We've all passed our matriculation. Rabi, do you know your Preeti has taught us? She is so good a teacher. Preeti Madam, we've brought for you your favourite coconut sweet."

"Ooh, this is great! But, I'll take a small piece since you've brought. I shouldn't disappoint you. You know the coconut sweet has high percentage of calorie. It'll make me motti. And, you know Mr. Rabi Pratap Choudhury, IAS doesn't like motti lady. I'm sorry, Saruabhai!"

"The tradition demands 'you shouldn't call Rabi by his name.' You can instead say, "ha..i..e..a; hey; um; oye; while addressing," cheered Seema winking and Bulinani seconded, "Yes! Yes! You should adhere to age-old practice, part of our village culture. Mind or else, your grand father-in-law will scheme something!"

"Our Preeti in these days found too modern," laughed the aunty-mama.

"Whoop! I'm sorry! I was very low, he hasn't heard me," the little girl apologized biting her tongue and with a reflection of after-thought, told, "So what? We haven't engaged so far. We're still friends."

"Preeti, my little girl. Follow what is told," aunty directed guardianly.

"Tathastu, aunty-mama!"